"Lucas," she breathed....

His mouth covered hers, and a piercing joy flooded her body. She leaned into his embrace, her mouth returning the kiss with reckless abandon.

"Consuelo..." Her name was a caress when he spoke it softly against her ear.

His passion brought a shock of sudden realization to her. Desperately, she twisted away from him, shoving him so hard that he stumbled backward.

"Leave me alone, Anglo," she gasped, her breathing ragged. "My father would kill you if he knew."

"Consuelo, listen—" Lucas reached for her.

Backing away from him, she reached down among the fallen eucalyptus leaves and picked up the gold-filled oilskin packet. "Here!" She flung it wildly at him. "Take it! Take it and go as far away as you can!" She turned and ran, her fist against her mouth to hold back the sobs.

Dear Reader,

For your summer reading pleasure, we present our Harlequin Historicals titles for August, four adventuresome tales that bring the past to life.

In Mary Daheim's *Improbable Eden,* an unsophisticated young woman discovers love when she is swept up into the dangerous world of intrigue at the English court of William and Mary.

With *Golden Prospect,* her second Harlequin historical, Shirley Parenteau takes the reader to the Yukon and Alaska as she weaves a delightful story of fame and fortune during the Klondike gold rush.

Surrounded by madness and deceit, the lovers in Catherine Blair's *Devil Wind,* must put to rest the past before they can build their future, while the characters in award-winning author Elisabeth Macdonald's *Estero Bay,* are swept into the age-old fight between the old ways and the new, set against the backdrop of California's wild central coast.

We hope you will join us for some summer reading fun.

Yours,

Tracy Farrell
Senior Editor

Estero Bay

Elisabeth Macdonald

Harlequin Books

TORONTO • NEW YORK • LONDON
AMSTERDAM • PARIS • SYDNEY • HAMBURG
STOCKHOLM • ATHENS • TOKYO • MILAN

Harlequin Historicals first edition August 1991

ISBN 0-373-28690-2

ESTERO BAY

ELISABETH MACDONALD

spent the first ten years of her life in the wild and lonely country of northeastern Utah, where Butch Cassidy once had his hideout. The vivid impressions of those years left her with an abiding interest in the history of the American West. Elisabeth is well-known for her historical sagas, which often have a Western setting. Now she turns to the very edge of the West, her adopted state of California, for a romance of the fateful passing of the great ranchos.

For my dear friend, Avis, and her house by the sea, where this story began.

Prologue

"T' starboard, Mr. Morgan! She's stove in!"

First mate Lucas Morgan grasped the line taut in his hands as he struggled across a slanting deck awash in the cold night sea. His eyes followed the seaman's pointing finger and he groaned at the sight. The coastal steamer *Golden Gate* was mortally wounded. She listed against the rocks, her bow shattering as the violent surf battered her relentlessly. Terrified shouts from struggling sailors were lost in the roar of the ocean. A towering wave slammed Lucas against the deck. He cried out and thought he heard the ship itself scream in pain.

"God damn it!" he shouted, struggling to his feet with the aid of the line. Damn the deceitful California coast. And damn the captain, drunk in his cabin as he had been every night of the voyage from San Francisco to San Diego and back again up the coast.

"She's a-breakin' up, Mr. Morgan!" The young seaman's face was stark white through the drifting fog, his eyes wide with fear. An explosion of sound drowned his words. A rent in the bow split the length of the ship. Water poured into the hold.

"All hands!" Lucas bellowed. "Boats away! All hands to the boats!" Wet rope tore his palms as he fought his way back up the slanting deck. In twenty years at sea, he had never seen higher seas or a thicker fog. The ship groaned and shrieked in its dying agony.

Working desperately, the crew strained to lower away
from a ship breaking up beneath their feet. Lucas watched
a lifeboat fall into the waves and capsize at once.

"Jump for it, boys!" he shouted, wondering as the words
left his mouth how many men would survive. Thank God
there were no passengers on board. "Abandon ship! Abandon ship!"

Watching the crew plunge over the side into the foaming
ocean, Lucas cursed the captain again. This wasn't the first
time Lucas had been first mate to a drunkard, but it would
be the last. He'd had enough of the devil sea. "Damn Captain Wyatt," he muttered. Cursing, he ripped off the hatch
cover and lowered himself into knee-deep water surging
through the passage to the captain's quarters. He couldn't
leave a drunkard to drown.

Shoving aside a floating sea chest, he braced open the
captain's door and stared inside. Flickering light from a
lantern gleamed eerily on Captain Wyatt, lying facedown in
the murky water. Dead or drunk, Lucas wondered, as he
seized the captain's head and lifted his eyelids. Even in the
gloom, he could see the pupils were fixed. Drowned in his
own cabin, the old bastard! An empty rum bottle floated
among the remains of the captain's last meal. Lucas staggered as the ship shuddered from bow to stern. Damn! If she
didn't break up and he stayed aboard, the Pacific Steamship Company could avoid salvage.

"No! Dammit, I've had enough!" he said aloud into the
roaring darkness. It seemed a lifetime since 1850 when he'd
first shipped at age twelve, as a cabin boy, around Cape
Horn with ice in the rigging, cuffed about by the crew and
grown to manhood in one voyage. Last month he'd been
passed over for a captaincy in favor of the owner's brother-
in-law, who would no doubt prove as incompetent as the
captain of the *Golden Gate*.

On the desk the ship's log lay open. The ink of the captain's last entry, dated August 15, 1870, bled across the wet
page. The *Golden Gate*'s strongbox stood open; beside it lay
an oilskin packet with straps attached. Before the captain
had fallen into the water and drowned he must have been

preparing to abandon ship. They were homeward bound to San Francisco, and the *Golden Gate*'s strongbox was filled with coins and gold nuggets from trading up the coast. The captain plainly had meant to take it overboard with him. It was the duty of Lucas, as second in command, to save it.

Quickly, he stuffed the gold into the oilskin packet. The water rose to his hips as he worked. The captain's limp form nudged eerily against him. Shoving aside the floating dead man, breathing heavily in his haste, Lucas tied the packet about his waist beneath his canvas jacket. A rush of water turned the captain's body and the dead face stared up at him. Something sour clogged his throat as Lucas fought his way through surging water toward the doorway.

As he climbed back onto the deck, he knew there wasn't a chance in hell the ship would stay whole through the night. Waves crashed over her as she settled deeper into the rocks gutting her. Slipping and falling he fought his way across the slanted, wave-lashed deck, and gained the larboard rail.

The crew was gone. He could hear faint shouts from the fogbound darkness. Far away on the shore a light gleamed, and Lucas allowed himself a small hope. Along this coast it was the custom for the inhabitants to light fires when they knew a ship was in trouble. And to loot her in the morning, he thought, hoisting himself over the rail. To hell with that! To hell with Pacific Steamship! Take a care for Lucas Morgan! He stared for an instant into the churning ocean below, the oilskin packet weighing about his waist. Then he plunged into the foaming water. Heavy surf caught him as he began to swim strongly for the light on shore.

Chapter One

Fog grayed the night air, a thick curtain muting the sound of breakers pounding the shore cliffs. On the beach, a fire glowed through the mist like a dying red sun lost beside the sea.

Consuelo Estrada stood in the main doorway of the adobe ranch house, peering anxiously into the darkness. The faint voices of the vaqueros and her father drifted up from the beach. When one of the Indians brought word that there was a ship in trouble, Don Augustino had ordered the fire built. It was the custom of the Californios to answer a ship's distress signal in this way, on such a night as this.

Papá should not have gone to help, she thought, her cold hands laced tightly together. He was not a young man and since her brother, Felipe, had been killed in a tavern brawl the don had grown frail in a way she could not quite define. Sometimes he even seemed unaware of his whereabouts. In the past year she'd learned to check all his decisions about rancho business, and had set their old retainer, Rafael, to the duty of being with her father always.

Behind her, in the great room where a warm fire glowed against the night chill, Consuelo heard her aunt mutter annoyance at the open door. Without a glance at Tía Isabel, who was embroidering beside the whale oil lamp, Consuelo picked up a wool rebozo from the back of a cowhide chair and threw it about her shoulders. In the shaft of light pouring from the doorway, she crossed the courtyard to the adobe wall.

Cold wind caught a tendril of the black hair Consuelo wore drawn back from her slender high-cheekboned face. Impatiently, she smoothed it into the elaborate knot, her luminous dark eyes frowning into the foggy distance. Perhaps she should go to the beach and persuade Papá to leave the saving of those cursed shipwrecked Anglos to his vaqueros and Indians.

"Consuelo!" Tía Isabel's voice broke through her thoughts. "Come inside. You'll catch a chill in that wet night air."

"*Sí,*" she called back. It was an automatic, placating response. Instead of obeying, Consuelo hugged the rebozo about her and shivered as the mist thickened, certain to turn to rain. Old resentment toward her aunt, always concealed, surfaced now. Why did Isabel acquiesce in everything the don wished to do? Why hadn't she tried to persuade him to leave this work to stronger, younger men? As always, Consuelo shrugged away the feeling. Isabel kept her own counsel as befitted a poor relation in her brother's house. She ran the rancho household efficiently, and she was never unkind, but always aloof.

Suddenly Consuelo's throat tightened with fear. Papá and Tía Isabel were all the family she had left.... Papá should not be risking his health to save the cursed Anglo sailors. It was the Anglos' fault her mother and her only brother were dead. Familiar anger flooded along her veins, and she moved impatiently, deciding what she must do.

The sound of *carreta* wheels rumbling along the damp road from the beach reached her ears, and she hurried out toward it. Pray the Holy Mother her father was not lying in that cart, felled by a heart attack while helping Anglo seamen.

Damn the Anglos anyway! The anger simmered inside her. If only the Americans had never come to California after their War between the States... if only the great drought of '65 hadn't killed most of her father's cattle... if only the Anglo lawyers he'd hired to prove title to Rancho Estrada hadn't bled him mercilessly for money.

Consuelo had been six years old when her mother died, but memories of the old life were still vivid in her mind. Once her mother, Amparo, had worn Chinese silk gowns made in Paris, gold necklaces set with pearls. In those days, her father had dressed in velvet breeches and jackets embroidered with gold. Since the coming of the Anglos, the gold necklaces and silver-studded saddles from Spain had all been sold, to pay the lawyers and the title fees and to buy supplies for a rancho that was no longer self-supporting. And Amparo was dead of the terrible Anglo disease called smallpox.

Consuelo bit her lip, eyes burning with unshed tears. They had kept her from her mother in fear she, too, would catch the smallpox. At six, she hadn't understood the reason. That child's rage and fear still haunted her. An Anglo had died at Bain's Settlement, they said, unaware of childish ears listening. The Indians who lived there were dying. Amparo had gone to nurse the poor Indians displaced by the closing of the missions. Then she, too, died of the disease.

So long ago, Consuelo thought, and still so painful a loss. Father Amateo told her it was unchristian to blame and damn the Anglos. In spite of his admonitions, she couldn't stop hating those who had destroyed the gracious way of life of the old Californios, who had killed her beloved mother and her only brother.

The creaking of *carreta* wheels grew louder as oxen and cart took shape out of the darkness. With growing apprehension, Consuelo saw it was not her father who rode beside the *carreta,* but Pablo, the head vaquero. He shouted at the housekeeper, who was watching from the kitchen veranda. "Rosa! Bring the women to help take care of the injured."

"What is it?" The noisy arrival brought Tía Isabel from the house to the courtyard wall.

"My prayers weren't answered," Consuelo replied in a harsh tone. "The Anglos survived." She pretended to ignore the reproving look her aunt gave her, searching the darkness for the shape of her father's tall stallion.

Anxiety clutched at her heart, for no other horseman rode up from the beach. Consuelo ran to Pablo's side. "My father," she demanded, "where is he?"

"At the beach." Impatiently, Pablo shook her hand off his wet and sandy serape. A tall, stout man, he easily lifted an unconscious sailor to carry him into the vaqueros' bunkhouse.

"Is Papá all right?" she called anxiously after him. When Pablo did not reply, she glared at his retreating back. Papá shouldn't be down there in the cold and damp, helping drag those worthless Anglo sailors out of the water. Impulsively she ran to Pablo's waiting horse, mounted and whipped it toward the beach.

Reining up the horse within the circle of firelight, Consuelo looked frantically for her father. He was not among the men loading another *carreta* with retching, groaning, half-drowned sailors.

When a vaquero turned from the waiting *carreta* and laid a man back down upon the sand, something cold touched Consuelo's heart. Despite her harsh feeling toward the Anglos, death was never pleasant to look upon. Sadness coursed through her.

At the sound of her father's shouting somewhere farther on, she spurred the horse forward. The fog had turned to rain now. Her rebozo had been lost somewhere in her haste, and cold wind chilled her through her wet blouse.

"Papá! Papá!"

In response to the panicked cry, Don Augustino galloped toward her. Consuelo drew in her breath in relief. Mounted on his favorite horse, directing the rescuers, he looked almost like his old self—strong and in command—not the vague, indecisive old man he'd become since Felipe's death.

A vaquero rode out of the wet night to intercept him. "We've been up and down the beach. That must be all of them."

"*Sí.*" The don nodded. Caught up in his old pattern of command, he scarcely acknowledged Consuelo's presence. He signaled the driver of the *carreta* to move on. Then he turned to Consuelo, his face tight with disapproval. With a sharp gesture, he indicated she should return to the house. Instead, she held the nervous horse in check, staring defiantly at her father, even as she trembled.

"Wait! Here's another!" someone cried. Two Indians held the unconscious man by the shoulders, dragging him along the wet sand. When they lifted him into the crowded *carreta* of groaning men, Consuelo saw by his sodden clothes that he was an officer. She recognized the stripes on his sleeve from her trips to and from school at Monterey aboard the packet boats. Her heart constricted as her eyes turned to her father and a flash of memory filled her mind.

The rancho was no place for a motherless little girl, Papá had told her as they stood on the pier at Monterey. Sea gulls wheeled and cried above them and harbor seals barked in the distance. There had been tears in Papá's eyes. Consuelo hadn't wept. She'd felt frozen inside, utterly lost and abandoned. Her beautiful mother was dead, and her father was sending her away. Her small world had no center.

Her child's heart must have realized, even then, that nothing would ever be the same again. In the lonely years at the convent school, she had come to the certainty it was all because of the Anglos: Rancho Estrada was impoverished, and her mother and brother both dead.

Papá jerked his head once more in the direction of the house, a silent order, and again she refused to go. Wheels creaking, the *carreta* began to move. Consuelo urged her horse alongside.

She looked down at the officer lying slack on the floor of the cart. Old pain clutched at her heart. "You should let him die!" she cried out angrily, her throat aching.

"Consuelo!" Her father's voice was harsh and reproving.

Struggling for composure, she refused to look at him. Somehow, she could not tear her eyes from the officer. Rain pelted on a face battered by the offshore rocks, water diluting the blood from his wounds. That pale still face, streaked with blood, was at once strong and vulnerable. Unable to look away, she found a familiar dream sliding into her mind for no apparent reason.

Once, when she was very young, with a ripening girl's dreams of love, she had dreamed of a lover who would come to her from the sea. Like the heroes in the books she read at the convent school in Monterey, he would be tall, darkly handsome and dashing. But now, she chided, amazed at herself, you're a woman of eighteen, nearly a spinster, and you know dreams don't come true.

Papá rode up beside her. "A bad night's work," he said. "We'll come back for the dead when we've taken care of the injured."

"Take care of yourself, Papá," she begged, studying him for any sign of the weakness the doctor had warned her about. She couldn't bear to lose Papá . . . he was all she had left. Papá, Tía Isabel . . . and Rancho Estrada.

Again she glanced down at the officer's oddly appealing face. Annoyed at herself for feeling drawn to him, she jerked her horse's reins and urged it ahead. Anger sharpened her tone as she called to Papá, "We'll have to watch them when they get well. After all, they are Anglos."

Pity for the injured men warred with Consuelo's dislike of Anglos as she watched them carried in to be placed in the vaqueros' bunks. Rosa and the Indian women were busy washing and binding wounds. The injured would be cared for, of course; it was the Christian thing to do.

Shivering now in her wet clothes, Consuelo hurried into the house to change. She had returned to the great room to warm herself before the fire when Tía Isabel appeared, carrying her bag of medicines, herbs and bandages. With a fierce look at Consuelo, Isabel spoke in a stern voice. "We need help with the injured, Consuelo."

Two years ago, when Consuelo turned sixteen, her aunt had reminded her that one day she would be the doña, and that meant she must be prepared to care for the sick and hurt of the rancho. She had been pleased then, with her aunt's rare attention and with the gratitude of the people she helped. And it had been fascinating to learn how to set a vaquero's broken arm, how to deliver a baby. But it would not please her to do anything for these Anglo sailors, Consuelo thought rebelliously. She turned away from Isabel without answering. After a moment, Isabel shook her head and left the room.

Consuelo ignored the twinge of guilt and reached out her hands to the warm fire. She had only feared for her father. Now that she was certain he was safe, she would simply ignore their uninvited guests—except to urge Papá to send them away as quickly as possible. Let Rosa and the Indian women care for the seamen. Resolutely, she shut her ears to the shouts and the noise of frantic activity outside.

A man cried out in pain. Consuelo pretended not to hear, determined to shut out the sounds of suffering men. But that agonized cry echoed over and over in her head. Guilt gathered in her heart. They weren't just Anglos out there, they were suffering human beings. Isabel needed her. Catching up a shawl, Consuelo stepped out onto the veranda.

Torches had been lighted around the courtyard. Their flickering light cast a mysterious aura through the silver drizzle of rain.

Before she could cross the courtyard, two vaqueros appeared, carrying an unconscious man between them. Her father guided their way with a torch, passing her without a glance as he led them toward Felipe's old room at the end of the veranda.

No! He couldn't mean to take the man there! Staring after him in disbelief, Consuelo felt hot anger clog her throat. Since Felipe's violent and senseless death at the hands of an Anglo, no one had used that room . . . no one except Father Amateo when he came on his monthly rounds of the ranchos.

Furious, she grabbed her father's arm and whirled him to face her. "No Anglo sleeps in Felipe's room," she cried. "Please, Papá!" Her chest ached with uncomforted sorrow for her adored older brother, dead of an Anglo bullet, and she fought against threatening tears.

"The man is an officer of the ship," Papá replied, frowning at her. "I can't put him with the vaqueros and common seamen."

It was the man she had seen at the beach. That she had felt drawn to him then only increased her pain and anger now. The vaqueros laid the man on Felipe's bed and she cried out in anguished protest, "He's an Anglo pig. One of those who killed my brother...your only son."

As always, Don Augustino's eyes filled with tears at the mention of his son. He slumped, as though the strength drained from him. In a low strangled voice, he answered, "It was the drunkards in the tavern where Felipe gambled. You can't blame this man."

Trembling, Consuelo fought back tears. "You're a fool to do anything for them, Papá, after all they've done to you."

Don Augustino's lined, aristocratic face hardened as he regarded her with stern eyes. Arrogance transformed his visage once more, and his voice was filled with pride. "The hospitality of Rancho Estrada will never be questioned, even by my daughter."

The scent of burning pine filled the great room. Light from the flames in the wide adobe fireplace flickered on the white plaster walls. In a cowhide-covered Spanish chair drawn up to the long trestle dining table, Consuelo stared, unseeing, at the rancho books spread before her. She had meant to work on them this evening since Papá no longer paid attention to the rancho finances, had meant to try to find some way to pay the vaqueros' wages. Most of the young ones had already moved on to more secure jobs. The old ones and their families stayed out of loyalty.

Since Mamá died, Papá had always been loving in his awkward, masculine way. Seldom had he spoken to her so harshly as he had a few minutes ago. She wasn't sure whether to weep or cry out in anger. But his words had sent her back into the house determined once more to do nothing for the sailors.

He was wrong, her heart cried in silent protest. Why should he still honor the proud tradition of the old Californios, the gracious, even lavish, hospitality to all? It was a way of life gone forever with the coming of the Americans.

Since Felipe's death, Papá had been a broken man. Tentatively at first, but later more confidently, Consuelo made decisions and gave orders to keep the rancho running. It was she who had set the prices when the horse traders came last month to buy from the last of the renowned Spanish-blooded Estrada horses. And it was she who paid the tradesmen in the town of Cambria and ordered supplies. Now, against her wishes, Papá had opened his house to Anglos as though these were the old days of easy living. Living was no longer easy for the Californios. The Anglos had stolen—taken legally, they said—many acres of the rancho. Because of the Americans, she had grown up with no mother to love her, and now her father was growing old with no son to follow him.

Without looking at the books, she knew the negative balance. The money from the horse traders had gone already to pay the merchants. She had used it before Papá could ask for it. In his hands, money melted away like mist in the morning sun. Papá had never thought about income and expenditure in the old days. Before the drought and all the cattle dying there had always been hides and horses to sell. Now there weren't enough cattle left to bother with a rodeo.

The bill for taxes on the rancho had come. She closed her eyes tight, trying not to think of the impossibility of paying it. Whatever happened, she must hang on to the rancho. It was her center now...the rolling hills sweeping down to the sea, green velvet in spring, golden with mustard blooms in summer, ripe with wild grains now in August. This land was the Estradas' only defense against the Americans.

"Consuelo, I need you." Isabel's voice, tinged with a note of pleading, interrupted Consuelo's unhappy thoughts. Consuelo sighed, knowing her aunt would persist until she gave in. Standing there in the doorway, Isabel seemed a commanding figure, tall for a woman. She had an aquiline Spanish face, and her graying hair was arranged in the same severe style she had taught Consuelo.

"All the women are helping Rosa tend the seamen. You must help me with the officer." Isabel turned away as though certain of compliance. Looking back, she added,

"You do understand the Californio customs of succor and hospitality."

Protests rose in Consuelo's throat until her aunt fixed her with piercing black eyes. Those eyes had commanded obedience from her ever since Isabel came from the Convent of the Sacred Heart at Monterey to act as dueña. Surely she had mistaken the pleading undertone in her aunt's voice. Without a word, she followed Isabel down the veranda.

Pausing reluctantly in the doorway of Felipe's room, Consuelo was instantly unnerved by the startling blue eyes of the man lying on the bed. Bloodshot from saltwater, those eyes were alert and wary, compelling her to stillness. She could not look away.

"Help me with his clothes," Isabel ordered and began pulling off his canvas jacket.

Consuelo looked down into his watchful eyes as they worked. Blue eyes, not the dark and flashing eyes of her dreams. Wet brown hair clung to his forehead in salty curls. His face was torn and swollen from his battering in the rough sea. Slowly, his mouth twisted into a painful grin.

"Bella señorita," he said hoarsely, "beautiful angel."

Surprised by the unexpected words, Consuelo stepped back, dropping his sodden jacket on the floor. Coughing racked him until he spit bloody seawater into the basin Isabel held.

"Who are you, *señor?*" Isabel asked when he again lay still on the pillow.

"First Mate Lucas Morgan," he croaked through swollen and cracked lips, wincing as he spoke.

"You're a fortunate man, Señor Morgan," Isabel told him briskly. "And you're safe now at Rancho Estrada." She reached to unbutton his wet shirt.

"Doña Isabel!" Rosa, her voice frantic, interrupted. She peered into the room, her plump face pale with fear. "Come quickly. One of them—he's dying!"

"Take care of Señor Morgan," Isabel said with a stern look at Consuelo as she picked up her bag and hurried after Rosa.

Lucas Morgan watched Consuelo, adding to her discomfort at being left alone with a despised Anglo. Between his racking spasms of coughing up seawater, his blue eyes never left her face except when he closed them in a grimace of pain.

At last, the unwelcome thought came to her that he was not simply Anglo, he was a hurt and suffering human being. So she told herself, as with uncertain fingers she began to unbutton his shirt. Yet when he once more whispered *"Bella"* and reached up to touch her face, his blue eyes soft with admiration, Consuelo felt her heart turn over in her chest.

Lucas was drifting, a curious warmth enfolding him despite the icy tremors shaking his body. A soft-eyed angel moved in and out of his clouded vision. Her hands were unbelievably gentle as they spread ointment on his aching face. He gasped as she touched a deep wound. Pain shot through the center of his being, and darkness swallowed him.

He groaned, a rattling sound deep in his chest. The hand fell slack at his side, and the blue eyes closed. Was he dead? For a moment, panic gripped Consuelo. Instinctively, she placed her hand over his heart. When she felt the beat against her fingers, she let out her breath in a long sigh of relief.

A pulse in his brown throat throbbed steadily just above the shirt Isabel had left half-unbuttoned. All that wet clothing must be removed before she could check for broken bones and body wounds. Consuelo began to undo the remaining buttons. The damp hair on his chest was rough beneath her suddenly trembling fingers. Then she felt something cold and slick around his waist. For a moment, she could only stare at the lumpy oilskin belt.

The wet knots of oilskin were more than her fingers could manage to untie. From the pocket of her bright calico skirt, Consuelo took a small sharp knife and cut the straps. She gasped in disbelief at the sight of the coins inside the packet.

Why was this Anglo carrying so much gold? she wondered. Whatever the reason, he was an Anglo, one of those who had impoverished her family. She should keep the gold. It would be only a small repayment for all the Anglos had stolen from her father. The thought was bravado, she knew, for dishonesty was not in her nature. But it was pleasant to think of getting even.

For now, she decided, she would hide the gold for safe-keeping. It would not do for her father to lay his hands on so much money at once. Nor would it be wise to leave it where it might fall into the hands of the feckless vaqueros. Repressing a twinge of guilt, she quickly concealed the belt in the deep pocket of her skirt, glancing out the doorway to make certain she had not been seen.

Hurrying now, Consuelo finished removing the unconscious Señor Morgan's wet clothing. His skin, though cold and damp beneath her fingers, sent an unexpected flush through her. As she bound his broken ribs, she forced herself to pretend she did not see the strength and maleness of his nude body.

Pain poured through Lucas Morgan as he awakened and tried to sit up in the unfamiliar bed. Groaning, he lay back against the pillow. Light from a candle on the bedside table flickered softly on the whitewashed adobe walls and the low, rough-timbered ceiling of the small room. A faint scent of wet eucalyptus blew through the open window.

Memory flooded back. His hand flew to his waist in panic, seeking the belt filled with gold. Except for the tight linen binding around his ribs, he was naked beneath a heavy wool blanket. Despair filled his heart. Had the oilskin packet been lost in the violent sea? Or had his saviors helped themselves, maybe even the girl whose beauty had haunted this night's feverish dreams? Either way it was lost, and he reminded himself grimly that Pacific Steamship would likely hold him accountable.

Sleep would not return to his pain-racked body. Scenes from the past rose hazily in his anguished mind. Gloucester, the town of his childhood, where only merchants and shipbuilders did not follow the sea. His own father had been a sailor—a wanderer who slept with the pretty barmaid who became Lucas's mother, and sailed away never to return.

Lucas had grown up in the tavern, learning to run errands or sing chanteys for the drunken sailors, accepting their coins in payment. The most poignant memory of his mother was the false bright smile she wore while serving those same sailors, and he knew now she must have accommodated them in her room behind the tavern while he was sent on errands. That brilliant smile had seemed hideous to him, for it did not belong to the loving woman who held him and told him stories of the magnificent future awaiting her wonderful son. He'd loved her fiercely and hated the men who pawed her. But she knew no other way of life, found no escape, and the poverty eventually killed her. When Lucas was twelve she died of consumption in her cold, barren room. After that, he lived on the wharfs, and he fought the other wharf rats for his berth as cabin boy aboard the *Marybelle*.

Since then, there had been years of fighting to get ahead, to leave behind memories of deadening poverty. Fighting and sometimes cheating. He had learned the sailor's life well. And in the past few months, he had come to hate it and the sea. He was tired of danger and bad food, and always being wet and cold. The wreck of the *Golden Gate* was an omen. He would never go back to the sea, not even for a captaincy. Perhaps he could find a way to start a new life here on this beautiful coast among the kindly Californios.

Was it a dream, or was the lovely *señorita* there, lifting his head to help him drink a potion that smelled faintly of poppies? Her touch was like an angel wing soothing the burning wounds on his face. In the flickering candlelight, he met her warm dark eyes, tried to reach out to her and could not lift his hand. His own eyes intent on her face, he saw her glance at his waist, naked now, the oilskin belt gone.

"The gold?" he muttered, his battered lips forming the words painfully.

For a moment, she hesitated. "Safe," she whispered, the word so low it seemed a part of the wind in the trees. Then she placed cool fingers against his swollen mouth to silence him. "Sleep, *señor*," she urged softly.

Reassured, he touched the fingers still lying against his face, his eyes clinging to hers. Lucas let out a long sigh as the poppy brew stole his senses. Drowning in the warmth of the dark eyes watching him, he slid into a healing sleep.

Chapter Two

Lucas turned restlessly on his pillow, shoving away the blanket in a futile effort to cool his burning body. He muttered to himself, feverish, unintelligible words.

His only relief seemed to come when Consuelo carefully sponged his heated skin with a cool wet cloth. He quieted now as she laid a cloth across his forehead, and his breathing eased.

The infection must be internal, Isabel said, perhaps from the broken ribs, for he coughed up bloody mucus. Of all the surviving sailors, only Lucas Morgan still lay incapacitated. It had been three days, and the men, even the one with a broken arm, had grown restless. Through the open door, Consuelo could hear their raucous laughter from where they lounged in front of the bunkhouse.

Turning to dip the cloth in the basin of cool water and wring it out, Consuelo threw a hostile glance toward the distant men. Their presence was a burden on the food supplies of the rancho, and now, Rosa had confided, they were trying to seduce the Indian women. Papá must send them away. She sighed, knowing he would do no such thing. It would be left to her.

It was her turn to stay with Señor Morgan, to cool his skin with wet cloths and try to bring down the fever that Isabel said should break soon. Her turn and her duty, she thought, still annoyed with Isabel for having insisted upon it. Yet now, as she laid the cloth against his sensitive inner elbow, she found she couldn't think of this man as an enemy.

He drew a deep, rattling breath as she lifted his big calloused hand and gently sponged the length of his tanned muscular arm. Studying his flushed face, she noticed for the first time the hint of a cleft in his strong chin, a faint crescent-shaped scar on one stubbled cheek. His shoulders were smooth and tanned, except for faint white scars that ran like stripes across them. Dark chest hair showed above the linen binding his ribs. An unfamiliar warmth rose from the center of Consuelo's being, crowding her heart until her breath quickened.

Suddenly she was looking into two brilliant blue eyes. Embarrassed that he had caught her staring, Consuelo felt a flush mount her face.

"Señorita," he whispered through dry lips, and his eyes turned toward the pitcher of water on the bedside table.

Quickly, she filled a tumbler. Easing her arm behind him, she carefully lifted his head to drink. He winced and drew in a sharp breath, but drank thirstily. The bare skin of his back, the softness of his hair against her arm created a sensation both infinitely pleasurable and terrifying. It was much like touching the hot tiles of the kitchen stove, and her throat tightened painfully.

When she quickly removed her arm, he fell back against the pillow with a sigh. *"Bueno,"* he whispered.

"You may speak English, *señor,*" she said, more sharply than she intended because her reaction to touching him had surprised her so. "We have all learned the Anglo tongue here at Rancho Estrada."

The blue eyes regarded her steadily. Suddenly, Consuelo was breathless and uneasy. She wished Isabel would come to relieve her, and knew she would not. With commanding black eyes, Isabel had set her to this task, and those stern eyes had kept her in line for many years. Consuelo had always wished she felt easier with her aunt. Perhaps it was the years in the convent that had made Isabel so unbending.

"You are kind," he muttered hoarsely, attempting a smile with dry, cracked lips.

"It is the custom," she replied quickly, denying to him and to herself that she would care for him for any other reason. She looked away, unable to meet his stare.

Only when he moaned softly did she see that those eyes were growing dull and glazed. At once she wet the cloths in the basin and began sponging his hot face, carefully closing his eyelids as he seemed to sleep. Perhaps the fever would break tonight as Isabel hoped. If it did not, this Anglo would die.

From the clay-tile stove in the kitchen, Rosa removed a huge kettle of frijoles, muttering imprecations on the Anglo sailors who ate so heartily.

Isabel took a pottery bowl from a shelf and filled it with some of the cooked frijoles. She tasted them judiciously, then crossed to the long table where Consuelo was grinding red pepper. After sprinkling a bit of the pepper on the beans, she handed the bowl to Consuelo. "Take this in to Señor Morgan. Now that he's better, he must eat more to regain his strength."

Words of refusal rose to Consuelo's lips. Isabel had taken the night watch when Lucas Morgan's fever had broken at last. By morning, he slept deeply and comfortably. That was three days ago, and Isabel had been plying him with food ever since.

Isabel's eyes sharpened. With a resigned sigh, Consuelo took the bowl and walked down the long, adobe-paved veranda to Lucas Morgan's bedroom.

He was sitting on the edge of his bed, smoking one of her father's cigarillos. The day was warm and he wore only his canvas pants, washed and pressed for him by Rosa's Indian helpers. In the moment before he became aware of her presence she studied the way his brown hair curled at the nape of his neck, the proud set of his well-shaped head, the wide tanned shoulders with the odd white scars. Something warm and pleasant grew and expanded inside her. When he turned toward her, the breath caught in her throat painfully.

Color mounted his face and he reached quickly for his shirt, which was lying on the bed. He winced as the movement caught at his injured ribs.

"Isabel says you must eat more." Consuelo held out the bowl to him, trying to still the pounding of her heart as his eyes met hers.

"Your aunt is likely to kill me with kindness," he said, chuckling as he eased into his shirt. But he took the bowl from her and began eating. She turned to leave and he called, "Please stay."

Consuelo wanted to get away from this Anglo, from his blue, blue eyes and his gracious way of speaking. When those eyes, dark with admiration, met hers, her pulse leaped and raced. The feelings this man aroused in her were not those she wished to feel for any Anglo. With inbred courtesy, however, she remained there in the open doorway, watching him eat.

"I walked around my room all morning," he confided, setting the empty bowl aside. "If you wouldn't mind walking with me, *señorita*, I'd like to try the courtyard for a bit."

"Are you sure you're strong enough?" she asked, hoping he didn't guess that her objection was less from concern for him than from her reluctance to touch him.

"It's the only way to regain strength," he told her, buttoning his shirt.

She waited unwillingly for him to rise and reach out to her. Careful of his tightly bound ribs, Lucas slipped his arm through hers for support.

Consuelo drew in a sharp breath at the feel of his hard calloused hand covering hers, the rough dark hair of his forearms against her sensitive wrist. Setting her mouth tight in denial of such sensations, she led him slowly along the veranda.

Halfway through their circuit of the courtyard, Lucas paused, his face suddenly pale. When they reached the adobe fence, he let out a long sigh and leaned gratefully against the wall.

Across the dusty yard, in front of the long low adobe bunkhouse, the sailors lounged in the morning sun, talking, laughing, playing cards. Lucas watched them for a moment. "Have they been much trouble to you?" he asked, turning to look down at her.

"I think they should go to San Simeon," she announced crisply, "where there are taverns. They bother the Indian women."

Lucas's face darkened. "If your father can provide transportation, I'll send them into town."

"Early tomorrow morning," she assured him, determined to arrange for the sailors' departure herself.

"Good." He smiled at her, and her heart quickened. His concern for the well-being of the people of the rancho surprised her. It didn't fit into her preconceived notions about Anglos. They were greedy and heedless and cared for no one but themselves.

"Why are you frowning, *señorita?*" Lucas Morgan's eyes were warm as he studied her face.

Consuelo started, flushed with guilt at her errant thoughts. To her surprise, she heard herself saying, "You mustn't leave yet."

His grin widened, eyes intent on her face. "I hoped you'd say that."

Their eyes held. A burst of wind from the ocean rattled the grapevines along the veranda, blowing Lucas's unbuttoned shirt so that she could see the white scars against his brown skin.

"Señorita?"

Only at his question, was Consuelo aware she was staring. "The scars on your shoulders..." she began.

Lucas's face colored, and he quickly buttoned the shirt. "A heavy-handed captain who meant to make a man of me with a cat-o'-nine tails."

She drew in her breath in horror, imagining those scars as open wounds, red with blood.

"I was sixteen," he said, his voice curiously flat, "sixteen and rebellious." He looked away. "I learned."

Learned at sixteen, she thought, watching his stiff, averted face. Scarcely more than a boy... to be beaten and hurt so terribly. Why had she assumed this man's life had been an easy one?

Don Augustino had come from the house to sit in the shade of the grapevines. He smoked a cigarillo, watching them without comment.

She saw that Lucas's face had grown pale again, and she pulled at his arm. "Come sit here by Papá. Rest for a bit. I'll come back shortly," she assured him.

Alone once again in the great room, Consuelo found her heart was beating so hard she could feel the pulse throb in her aching throat. Her whole body seemed to tremble with unexpected emotions from her unwanted and surprising response to Lucas Morgan.

Grateful for the shade of the veranda and its overhanging grapevines, Lucas carefully eased himself down on the wooden bench beside Don Augustino. His broken ribs had begun to heal in the ten days he'd been at Rancho Estrada, but were still painful. The whitewashed adobe wall was warm against his back and immensely comforting. The don gave him a polite nod. *"Buenos dias"* he said and offered Lucas a cigarillo before closing his eyes, and leaning back to blow smoke into the still, warm air.

Lucas turned his eyes to the dark blue ocean beyond the cliffs, glistening like silver in the sunlight. The *Golden Gate* and its drunkard captain lay in the depths out there.

Five drowned sailors had been buried in the rancho graveyard. In the morning the survivors would go to San Simeon, where there were taverns and women and perhaps a ship to San Francisco. As for himself, he found he was reluctant to leave this peaceful place and the beautiful girl who had begun to haunt his dreams.

Idly, he surveyed the rancho around him, a scene grown familiar in the short time he had been here. From the courtyard of the Estrada adobe the land sloped away, rolling through golden summer hills along the willow-shrouded banks of Villa Creek down to the cliffs above the sea.

Two Indian women knelt in the shade of the veranda, grinding corn in stone metates. The cornmeal would be patted into tortillas to be baked in the clay ovens behind the kitchen. Through the open kitchen door, he could see the women moving in the constant bustle that seemed to take place there. The storeroom door was open, revealing barrels of corn and beans, and dried beef hanging from the rafters.

Beside him, the don puffed sleepily on the cigarillo. Glancing at his host from the corner of his eye, Lucas smoked his own cigarillo, wondering what the man was thinking.

In front of them, the low-walled courtyard squared off the dwelling. Two cats slept in the sunshine on the worn adobe paving, and several scraggly chickens scratched the dirt. An ancient Mexican sunned himself, smoking his pipe, occasionally reaching to pat the shaggy multicolored dog sleeping beside him.

From down by the creek Lucas could hear the voices and laughter of women as they did the household washing. Children's cries blended with the melodious rise and fall of their mothers' chatter. Two worn-looking Indian men hoed between the rows of corn and beans in the garden. A hundred yards beyond them were the corrals and fenced pasture where a few fine-blooded Spanish horses grazed.

Once more Lucas glanced at his silent host. Time had blurred the aristocratic features with jowls at the chin and folds beneath the dark eyes. Don Augustino's cotton shirt was thin from many washings, his fringed leather vest worn and soiled. The thick black hair was heavily streaked with gray. A big man once, Lucas thought, shrunken now by time and adversity.

As though suddenly aware of Lucas's scrutiny, the don turned those dark deep-set eyes full on him. *"Señor?"*

Lucas started, for it seemed the don had overheard his curious thoughts. For a moment he searched for words. "Your cattle," he asked, "do they summer in the mountains?" With a wave of his hand, he indicated the foothills clad in late summer's golden grass, the Santa Lucia Mountains a deep hazy green beyond.

"Si." Don Augustino shrugged, his dark face settling into bitter lines as he spoke in heavily accented English. "They fend for themselves in the hills. The few that are left..." His voice trailed off. A sigh lifted his broad chest, and there was a defeated expression in his eyes.

"For years, Rancho Estrada was one of the biggest suppliers of hides on the coast. The schooners vied for our trade. Then came the great drought five years ago. No rain fell all through the long winter. The grass did not grow. By spring the pastures were dust, the cattle starving. We tried to skin the cows as fast as they died, but it was of no use. Others were doing the same, and the hide trade was dying, too."

Don Augustino blew smoke explosively into the still air. "The horses I saved...but the cattle...it was impossible. They breed now. Perhaps someday I will have many cattle again. The Americanos—" He paused to spit venomously into the courtyard. "When California became part of the United States, it was demanded that the old Californios prove their right to their land." His voice rose, impassioned by remembered injustice. "This land was granted to my father by Governor Figueroa himself. But the Americanos with their lawyers and surveyors said I must pay for it. Now the land is *encogida*—how you say—shrunken. Only the debts increase."

"How much land?" Lucas asked, for there seemed to be no other dwelling within miles of Rancho Estrada.

"Nothing compared with the original grant." The don sighed heavily and stared down at the glowing tip of his cigarillo. "The good days are gone. Americanos steal everything. Señor Hearst tries to buy the whole coast."

Last night at the supper table, Don Augustino had told how Domingo Pujol had quietly bought most of Rancho Santa Rosa from the impoverished owners, and how those Californios, whether unwittingly or not, had sold the same land to George Hearst. Pujol had won the subsequent lawsuit, and the don chuckled heartily as he told the outcome. A Californio had for once got the best of the Anglos. But Hearst had endless resources and was still buying. Lucas had glimpsed anger in Consuelo's eyes, even though the story ended happily for the Californio.

So the world of the rancho was not as easy and pleasant as it seemed. With a sense of melancholy, Lucas knew this carefree, indolent life was passing. It could never survive the influx of ambitious Americans who would inevitably come here. Ever since the end of the Civil War, Americans had been moving west, searching for gold, for free land, for easy fortunes to be made. This beautiful coast would draw them, already was drawing them. Cattlemen and dairymen came for the free grass and miners to the quicksilver boom in the mountains nearby. Fortunes could be made here, too. If only he hadn't lost Pacific Steamship's gold, there might have been a reward, something to begin to make the fortune he had vowed on his mother's grave would be his revenge against her poverty-stricken life.

The surprising thought came that he could simply have kept the gold. Who would have known? With the gold at the bottom of the sea now, such an idea was of little consequence. Strangely, somewhere in the back of his mind the thought persisted that the gold was safe. Impossible, he told himself, and sighed for the loss of what might have been.

Chapter Three

"All this," Consuelo said with an expansive wave of her hand that took in the land from the mountains to the sea, "is part of Rancho Estrada." Pride filled her dark eyes as she turned on her horse to face Lucas Morgan.

Lucas let out a sigh of relief as he watched her dismount from the trim black mare. Consuelo couldn't have guessed that after years spent on a ship's deck he would find this sudden transition to horseback difficult. Not once had she slowed her pace since they left the rancho. He had ridden a mule across the Isthmus of Panama, but that was something quite different from galloping the California hills on a Spanish thoroughbred.

Dismounting, he watched his companion. Wind from the sea blew Consuelo's black calico skirt around her slender figure as she stroked the mare's silky head and fed her a sugar lump. It molded the white linen blouse to her rounded breasts. Lucas felt his pulse leap and pound. The same gentle fingers now caressing the mare had stroked his feverish flesh, bringing him surcease.

This morning at breakfast, Don Augustino had announced that Lucas was well enough to ride, and could tour the rancho. Still unsure of his strength, Lucas had agreed reluctantly. He wanted to see the country, and time had begun to hang heavy. The sailors had been gone for several days now, and he had let those days slip away, caught in a pleasant limbo.

But just before they were to leave, a messenger from a neighboring rancho rode in and spoke with the don. With no explanation, Don Augustino declared that the obviously reluctant Consuelo would take on the duty of guiding their guest around Rancho Estrada.

He wasn't sorry for the substitution, Lucas thought, watching her lovely olive-skinned face as she walked past him to the edge of the hill and stared into the blue distance. The sea wind tugged at her hair, sending wisps curling about her slender neck, and Lucas was filled with a yearning unlike anything he had ever experienced. No other woman in all the lonely wandering years had touched his heart like this girl.

"This—" her graceful gesture took in the scene before them "—this is my favorite place in the world."

Lucas's gaze followed that expansive gesture. Rolling hills, dry and golden with wild oats of late summer, shimmered in the bright haze. To his right, Estero Point reached out into the sea, and Estero Bay curved inward, a necklace of white breakers at its throat. Southward, Morro Rock jutted from the ocean, and beyond it, Point Buchon formed the southern arm of the bay. Lucas knew the landmarks well. He had been sailing up and down the coast of California for two years.

He stood beside her, intensely aware of the sweet scent of her hair, the golden curve of her neck. "It's very beautiful here," he said after a moment. "I think I could stay forever."

Like all the greedy Anglos, Consuelo thought, with a sudden flash of resentment. She glanced at him from the corner of her eye, then quickly away. Papá shouldn't have insisted she ride with this man, but then Papá couldn't know that this big American she had been so determined to hate sent her heart skipping erratically every time their eyes met across the dining table.

Never had she felt this breathless ache in the presence of any other man. Ramón, her brother's friend, had often looked at her with more than admiration, but she felt nothing for him. Why an Anglo? She wished he had gone away with the other sailors.

"You must have seen many beautiful places in your travels," she said, and saw that he didn't catch her inhospitable meaning.

"Yes," he replied. Slowly at first, then caught by her obvious fascination with his words, Lucas told of the places he had seen: Hong Kong and its Fragrant Harbor, the lovely Sandwich Islands and San Francisco, where green hills rimmed a vast blue bay.

As he spoke, they walked slowly across the hillside, the horses following. At the edge of the hill a small cairn of rocks had been built atop some larger rocks. Immediately, Consuelo scattered it.

"Quicksilver prospectors," she said, her tone harsh. "Ramón, our neighbor, has armed his men to drive them off, but still they come onto private property."

Dusting her hands, she sat down on a flat rock. Despite her annoyance at the cairn, her mind was still filled with the pictures Lucas Morgan had created with his words. "It would be wonderful to see those places," she mused as Lucas eased himself down beside her. "I've never been farther than San Luis Obispo, or Monterey where I went to school."

"Monterey is as beautiful as any of those places," he said, smiling at her, the cleft in his chin deepening. "Were you at school long?"

"I was at the Convent of the Sacred Heart until I was ten and my father had too little money to pay for my schooling there. That's when Isabel left the convent and brought me home to stay. My mother had died long before...." The last words faded away, for the sadness was with her still. And she remembered that it was an Anglo disease that robbed her of her mother. "I was six when the smallpox—" she added in a shaky voice and could say no more.

To her surprise, Lucas took her hand, cradling it between his big, rough sailor hands. The blue eyes looked down at her, soft with compassion. "Ah, poor little girl," he said. "It must have been very sad and lonely for you."

She managed to nod, not looking at him. "Everything changed then. I was sent away to school until there was no more money—after the Anglos came and the great drought, no fiestas, no happy times."

She turned her face away, fighting back tears. As though he guessed her pain, Lucas began to talk quietly. "My own mother died when I was twelve. That's when I went to sea."

"Went to sea at twelve?" She stared at him in astonishment, her own sorrow forgotten. On his own as a boy of twelve, she thought, beaten by a vicious captain at sixteen. Why had she thought life easy for all Anglos? Behind that calm, rugged face Lucas Morgan concealed more suffering than she could have guessed.

"I was a cabin boy." With one hand he made a deprecating gesture. "I became a sailor because there was no other choice. But I was a good sailor. I made my own living without asking quarter of any man."

The tears suddenly stinging her eyes might have been for her dead mother and the lost carefree life. Or they might have been for a twelve-year-old boy cast into the hard world alone. "Your father," she protested. "Surely he..."

Lucas's face hardened. He withdrew his hand from hers and began to fumble in his jacket for a cigarillo. "I never knew my father." The words were freighted with bitterness. Consuelo's heart constricted with pain for him.

Lucas turned to shelter his flint from the wind as he lit the cigarillo. She watched the hard lines around his tight mouth, wondering at words yet unsaid. Had his father deserted the family? Or did he mean he was a bastard child? Even as she ached for the unhappiness in that set face, she dared not ask.

Lucas sat beside her, staring out toward the sea, smoking his cigarillo. The silence grew and grew. At last he cleared his throat. With a sidewise glance at her, he began, "The don told me about your brother's death."

Abruptly, Consuelo stood and moved away from him. She mustn't weep in front of this man. He was an Anglo, one of those who had killed her beloved brother.

Lucas followed her, his hand touching her shoulder briefly as though to offer comfort. She didn't want his sympathy, she thought, as anger flushed through her.

"An American killed him." Consuelo fought the tremor in her voice. "Over a woman, they said."

"It happens." He spoke quietly.

"It shouldn't have happened!" she cried out. "He was a foolish boy—" The words choked in her throat and she could say no more.

"I'm sorry." Lucas's voice was gentle.

Consuelo moved away, avoiding his nearness. She mustn't succumb to this Anglo's kindness, she told herself fiercely.

Silent, Lucas watched her struggle. The wounds Consuelo suffered were too fresh. Though he longed to hold and comfort her, he sensed that it was too soon for that kind of closeness between them. She would not welcome his touch.

Sighing, he smoked his cigarillo, staring out toward the restless ocean. The beauty of the scene filled his eyes, but his practical nature saw something more there. "There's still no decent anchorage along this coast," he mused thoughtfully. "And no decent land transportation, either."

"*Sí.*" Consuelo frowned in surprise. She had fully regained control of her emotions. "The roads along the central coast are still trails, knee-deep in dust in summer and mud in winter. It's easier to meet the steamer at the nearest beach and row goods out in lighter boats."

"And impossible to do even that when the seas are high," Lucas replied. There was a wharf at the whaling station at San Simeon, but the swells in that small bay made it too dangerous for the coasters to tie up there. The bar at Morro could be crossed only at high tide and was chancy even then. At Port Harford to the south, they sometimes used chutes or bosun's chairs from cliff top to steamship—wasteful and dangerous methods.

With another sidelong glance at his companion, Lucas wondered if he might have just now stumbled upon a way to make a new life here. He could fill a need, and in the process perhaps help his kindly hosts. For in spite of their fa-

cade of pride and bounteous hospitality, he knew the
Estradas had fallen on hard times.

Lucas let out an unconscious sigh, half-sorry that their
old carefree Californio way of life had to pass. But California was American now, he told himself, and a man with a
packet of gold could make his fortune here. He remembered the dull shine of it in the captain's flooded cabin. Was
it only because the gold was gone that his conscience played
with the possibility of keeping it for himself? No matter. It
was gone and he would not have that choice to make. But if
only he had that packet of gold!

Just below where they had stopped, a creek ran through
the hills, down to the beach. Fresh water, Lucas thought,
and a thrill of excitement ran through him.

"Does the bay have a solid bottom?" he asked.

Consuelo looked at him in astonishment. Only a sailor
would have an interest in such things. "This land has been
in my family for a hundred years," she said softly. "It came
to my mother, and will one day be mine...." Her voice
trailed off for she saw he wasn't listening.

Of course it had a solid bottom, Lucas told himself,
scarcely aware that Consuelo had spoken. The rocks indicated that much. Suddenly he could envision a wharf here,
reaching out into the sea. A busy wharf for the coasters. The
need was here. Already Italian and Swiss dairymen were
moving in, buying cheap acreage from the subdivided ranchos, establishing themselves on this coast as their relatives
had done in Marin County across the bay from San Francisco. They would have butter and cheese and eggs to ship
to market. Quicksilver mining had created a boom in the
nearby town of Cambria. There had been much talk at the
rancho about the influx of prospectors and of the fortunes
to be made in mining cinnabar ore for quicksilver. Farmers, ranchers, miners. They all needed a safe and efficient
way of shipping to the markets in San Francisco.

A wharf. Lucas Morgan's wharf! Morgan's Landing! He
could build it without that gold. Surely the bankers in the
town of Cambria would see the value of his plan and back
him. Until he convinced Captain King to sign him on as

cabin boy he had worked the Gloucester wharfs. Since then, he'd studied wharfs in most of the ports around the world. He knew them inside out, knew how they were put together. At once his quick mind began to calculate the timbers needed. It was perfect. Even the lumber was close by. Only a wagon was needed to haul it from the mills near Cambria. He could buy a boat from the whalers at San Simeon to run a lightering business while the wharf was being built.

He was certain Don Augustino would be glad to sell this worthless tract by the sea. Then he could stay on here. His heart quickened as he watched Consuelo catch up the black mare's reins. He remembered vividly her gentle hands, her warm eyes as she soothed his miserable feverish nights after the wreck. And it filled his heart that just now she had shared with him her deeper heartaches. The need to touch her, to hold her, ached in him, but he could wait. He would not be going away. If there were no other reason to stay here, this dark-eyed angel was reason enough.

Chapter Four

Lucas let out a long sigh of relief when they rode into the rancho yard. The dull ache in his ribs had grown more and more insistent, until the ride home seemed interminable. He winced as he dismounted.

A small Indian boy took the reins of both horses and led them away to the saddle shed. It seemed to Lucas there was an extraordinary amount of activity around the corrals. Small children clung to the wooden fence poles, yelling and staring at the huge, ugly long-horned bull penned up there. Vaqueros were rounding up horses and turning them into the horse corral nearby. Dust filled the air, gilded by the lowering sun.

Tight-lipped, Lucas struggled to conceal his pain as he walked slowly beside Consuelo toward the house. If she knew he hurt, she gave no indication of it. Her lovely face was calm and distant, and had been so all during the ride home. It was as though those moments on the hilltop above the sea, sharing past dreams and old pain, had never been.

"You should rest now," she told him as she opened the gate in the adobe fence.

So she had noticed. The concern in her dark eyes touched him. He wanted to reach out to her, but she moved away.

"I think I'll sit here on the veranda and watch the sunset," he told her. He glanced at the Indian women scurrying about the kitchen veranda and the storeroom. "Everyone seems excited about something," he observed.

Frown lines appeared on her smooth brow. Her mouth tightened and her voice was low and angry. "There will be a bull and bear fight when Ramón arrives in a few days."

With no further explanation, she went into the kitchen. Lucas was left alone to ease himself carefully down on the veranda bench.

A swath of shimmering golden light lay on the ocean where the sun stood just above the horizon. A beautiful land, Lucas thought once more. He wondered when he could speak to Don Augustino about his idea to build a wharf. The pain in his ribs eased slowly. He leaned his head against the adobe wall and closed his eyes.

A low grunt, the bench sagged, and Lucas opened his eyes to see Don Augustino beside him.

"You liked my rancho?" he asked, offering a cigarillo.

Lucas leaned to take a light from the don's flint. Blowing out the warm smoke, he smiled and nodded. "Beautiful country, Don Augustino. I'm thinking, if I can arrange a loan, I'd like to buy some of it from you."

An acquisitive light gleamed in the old man's dark eyes. "Yes?"

"Near the ocean," Lucas began, "for a wharf I want to build."

Before he could continue, the don suddenly leaped to his feet. Lucas saw a pillar of dust rising along the coastal trail.

"Look! Who's coming, Rafael?" the don called to the old man stretched out in the sun beside the veranda.

Groaning, Rafael got to his feet and ambled to the adobe fence surrounding the courtyard. Peering into the distance, he cried, "*Quizás* Tomás from San Simeon!"

Don picked up his ancient sombrero and crossed the courtyard. The rider drew his dun-colored horse to a halt, scattering squawking chickens in all directions. The barking dog fell silent at a command from old Rafael.

Pleasantries were exchanged. The rider delivered his message in rapid-fire Spanish, indicating Lucas at one point. Lucas thought wryly that if he meant to stay in this country, he'd have to learn more Spanish than the few words and phrases he'd picked up in his travels.

If he stayed here—the thought halted as Consuelo and her
aunt came from the kitchen to greet the horseman. He
watched Consuelo move gracefully across the courtyard and
lift her dark head toward the rider, a smile lighting her
golden face. Her musky fragrance, mingled with the scent
of the eucalyptus outside his window, was imprinted forever in his mind. Had this woman affected him so pro-
foundly simply because of her tender nursing? The sweetly
reluctant way she'd shared her past heartaches with him today on the hilltop had deepened his feelings to much more
than mere attraction to her beauty. She was the reason he
felt so at home here—and the reason he wanted to stay.

Consuelo knew he was watching her. Even as she exchanged pleasantries with Tomás, she felt Lucas's gaze as
deeply as though he'd touched her. Only with an effort did
she restrain herself from turning to look into those blue
eyes... blue as the azure sky arching above the sea. Lucas
Morgan. The Anglo. She hated Anglos. Then why was it
when Ramón Salazar, the man her father wished her to
marry, looked at her with desire she felt unclean, and yet
when she met Lucas Morgan's longing eyes something inside her sparked and burned?

Her face grew warm with her thoughts, and it was a moment before she could compose herself. Leaving her father
and Isabel exchanging gossip with Tomás, Consuelo walked
toward Lucas, carefully avoiding his eyes. It didn't matter
now, how this Anglo made her feel. Tomorrow he would be
going away.

"Tomás says a Pacific Steamship coaster will call here
tomorrow, with an agent come to investigate the wreck of
the *Golden Gate.* He'll be taking the crew to San Francisco."

"Tomorrow?" Lucas sat up straight and winced with
pain. He seemed surprised, as though he'd forgotten the
world beyond Rancho Estrada.

Consuelo nodded and waited expectantly. Lucas Morgan
was silent, his mouth tight as he stared out toward the
ocean. Quickly, she turned away, her full skirt brushing his
knees. Why did her throat ache like this? Why should she

care if this Anglo went away forever? After all it meant one less Americano plundering this coast.

Those moments of sharing on the hilltop this afternoon had touched her more deeply than she dared admit. He had told her of his past, and now she found it difficult to see him simply as one of the hated Anglos.

That first glimpse of him, when she'd thought him her dream lover from the sea, flashed into her mind. A trick of the night, she told herself, for although Lucas Morgan was tall, he had blue eyes and light brown hair that curled close to his well-shaped head. He was not dark and dashing.

She was certain now that he was less than honest, for he had never spoken to anyone of the oilskin packet of gold, concealed at present beneath her mattress. Perhaps he had stolen it. Every rule she'd been taught about proper conduct told her she should have returned it by now, but when she thought of the debts it would pay, temptation ate at her heart. It was salvage, she told herself, and salvage had always been a Californio custom. The battle raged inside her head as she hurried into the kitchen to set out food and wine for Tomás.

"No salvage at all?" The agent's voice barely concealed his suspicion. His sharp ferret eyes looked around the dining table in the great room, where Rosa, plump and sweating, and the dark, silent Indian women were serving a noon meal for their guest. "No sea chests or strongbox?"

Lucas's fists tightened with annoyance at the insinuations in the man's voice. He saw that the agent's attitude had insulted his host. The man was a boor and a fool, and certainly a stranger to the mores of shipping along the California coast. Salvage was legal to the Californios, whatever the shipping companies' objections.

Eventually, the agent would get to the subject of the gold. In his mind, Lucas saw again the rich gleam of it inside the oilskin packet. All the hard years of sailing the seas for little pay rushed back to his mind . . . all the ugliness of his childhood poverty. Desire for that gold surged through him, as compelling as desire for a woman. It represented escape from poverty. It would buy a new kind of life. But even had he the courage to steal, or to borrow it, the fact was it was gone. His new life would have to be earned the hard way, as everything in his life had been hard.

With his habitual politeness, Don Augustino shrugged and sighed. "Some lumber and ship fittings. A few sugar barrels came ashore, but they were broken and the sugar dissolved in the sea." He leaned back in his cowhide-covered armchair, one of two that usually flanked the wide adobe fireplace.

"Brandy kegs?" the agent asked. His hostility had not affected his appetite, Lucas thought wryly. The man's plate was loaded with beef and beans and tortillas.

"None," the don answered quickly, looking straight into the agent's eyes.

Consuelo and her aunt were silent, speaking only to command the serving women.

"Must have been a poor cargo," Don Augustino continued in a soft musing tone. "Nothing to salvage."

The agent gave him a sharp look. "There was gold on board."

Lucas caught a flicker of interest in the don's dark eyes before he answered the agent.

"Too bad." He glanced with elaborate unconcern out the open door toward the sea. "Gold I could have used. Sugar and brandy—well, perhaps."

Did he have the gold? Lucas wondered, staring at his host's bland face. Lost. His heart sank. Lost, whether to this Californio, or to the ocean. Carefully controlling his voice, he said, "The gold is no doubt out there in the rocks at the bottom of the sea."

Obviously frustrated, the agent turned accusing eyes on Lucas. "If the captain was dead, the gold was your responsibility." His pale eyes narrowed. "It would be easy enough for you to pretend it was lost."

Furious, Lucas jumped to his feet. "I didn't steal the blasted gold." He glared at the agent. The fact that temptation had entered his mind made the accusation sting all the more. Yet he couldn't tell all the truth, for then Don

Augustino would become a suspect. The Estradas had saved him, cared for him. Even if they had taken the gold, Lucas couldn't betray them.

The agent's eyes flashed and his voice was low and vindictive. "Still, it was your responsibility, Mr. Morgan. You failed the company. You're fired, Mister. And I'll see that you're embargoed in every port on this coast."

"You can go to hell!" Lucas growled. He paused, then announced in a voice unnecessarily loud, "I won't be going to San Francisco with you." The sudden silence at the table made him wonder if he'd made a wrong choice. Don Augustino stared at him in surprise, as did Doña Isabel. Although Lucas's eyes sought Consuelo's, she refused to look at him.

The agent's face was a curious mixture of anger and disbelief. "You? A seaman?" he snapped. "What will you do here?"

"What would I do in San Francisco if I'm denied a ship?" Lucas retorted. He managed a self-confident smile. "I'll think of something."

A blue-gray haze lay in the distance where the Pacific Steamship coaster waited for the ship's gig carrying the agent. Leaning on the courtyard fence, Lucas watched him go, the boat rising and dipping in the waves. Dust raised by the horses of Don Augustino and his vaqueros drifted in the slight breeze.

He felt her presence, smelled her fragrance and was stirred to his depths even before he turned to meet Consuelo's dark eyes.

Quickly, she looked away toward the distant ship. "Good riddance to the Americanos!"

Lucas grinned. "But I'm an Americano."

Something in her glance as it crossed his sent a wave of hot blood surging through him. With a toss of her head, she turned away as her father rode in. "I think perhaps my father will open some brandy tonight."

Watching the don dismount and walk jauntily toward him, leading his horse, Lucas wondered if the serving of the salvaged brandy tonight would be to celebrate the acquisition of an oilskin belt filled with gold.

The sea-tainted brandy had given Lucas a headache. Restless and depressed, he sat up in his bed and pulled on his trousers. A cool wind from the sea swept through the window, heavy with the pungent scent of eucalyptus. Perhaps if he walked a bit it would ease this disquiet.

There had been no mention of the gold by Don Augustino all evening, no inkling that he had it or knew of its whereabouts. Perhaps, as Lucas himself had told the agent, it was at the bottom of the sea.

He had tried to sleep, but his mind whirled in circles. Would the don be willing to form a partnership in a wharf built on his land? Would the banker in Cambria listen to this scheme proposed by a stranger? And why had Consuelo so studiously avoided him all evening?

He saw her now, as he came around the corner of the house, the white of her shift gleaming in the moonlight beneath the eucalyptus trees. When he realized she had been watching his window, his heart surged and seemed to catch fire, sending hot blood coursing through his body.

"Consuelo," he whispered, loving the sound of her beautiful name on his tongue.

She started and turned to look at him, her dark eyes wide and brilliant in the moonlight. "Lucas," she breathed and he was filled with joy at her first use of his Christian name.

He was so close to her now he could smell her fragrance, see the outline of her nipples against the thin muslin of her shift.

"What—" he began, and she interrupted.

"I've been trying to decide," she began nervously.

Decide? he wondered. What did she mean? Surely not that she meant to come to his room? It would be unthinkable for the daughter of a don, and yet... desire flooded Lucas's heart.

He was standing so close and yet Consuelo could not move. Her feet seemed rooted to the spot as she gazed into his shadowed face. The breeze from the sea blew the eucalyptus branches aside, and she saw the moonlight glinting on his eyes. The passion in those eyes held her as surely as his hands gently clasping her shoulders, drawing her inexorably toward him.

It was wrong! He was a hated Anglo and a thief. Watching the agent leave, she had been torn by guilt. She should have returned the gold to him; it belonged to Pacific Steamship. But then, he could have accused her of stealing it.

Ever since supper, she had struggled with her decision. She had no proof Lucas meant to steal the gold, but the way he'd denied knowledge of it to the agent proved his dishonesty. Had he denied it because he guessed one of the Estradas had it? No. Why would he bother to protect them?

The gold coins inside the packet had gleamed seductively in the light of her bedside candle. Impulsively, she had decided she must return them at once, before the temptation to keep them became too strong to resist. Perhaps when Lucas Morgan slept she could steal into his room and hide the packet in his bed. Never expecting to be discovered, she had watched from the shelter of the eucalyptus, waiting for his light to be extinguished.

Now it was obvious he had misinterpreted her presence. She should cry out, strike his hands from her. But her protests seemed stuck in her aching throat, and she was unable to pull away.

He drew her close against him, his arms holding her entrapped...so close she could feel the hair on his chest through her thin shift. Her nipples hardened, her breasts ached in a new, strange way.

When his mouth covered hers, a piercing joy flooded her body. Without thought, she leaned into his embrace, her mouth returning the kiss with reckless abandon.

"Consuelo..." Her name was a caress when he spoke it softly against her ear. "Beautiful. Beautiful..." His mouth spread fire at the base of her pulsing throat. Gently his hands moved down her back, cupping her hips to press her fiercely to him.

The hardness of his arousal pressing against her thighs brought a shock of realization. Desperately, she twisted away from him, shoving him so hard that Lucas stumbled backward.

"Leave me alone," she gasped, her breathing ragged. "My father would kill you if he knew."

"Consuelo, listen—" Lucas reached for her, his big, rough seaman's hands lifting in supplication.

Backing away from him, she reached down among the fallen eucalyptus leaves and picked up the oilskin packet. "Here!" She flung it wildly at him. "Take it! Take it and go as far away as you can!" She turned and ran, her fist against her mouth to hold back the sobs.

Chapter Five

The kitchen was redolent with the odor of spices and cooking beans. Indian women rushed to and from the clay ovens in the yard. Near the ovens a small Indian boy turned the carcass of a young calf on a spit over a bed of glowing coals.

Grinding hot red peppers in a mortar, Consuelo stood at the long kitchen table. As she gave the pestle a vicious turn, she glared resentfully at the bustle of activity. Before dawn, a rider had come from Rancho Santa Lucia. Don Ramón and his party would be here today with the bear they'd captured. Isabel had set the household in action to prepare for their guests.

Consuelo had heard the horsemen ride in, but she refused to go out to greet them. Ever since Felipe was killed, she'd felt uneasy with Ramón. It was unreasonable, she knew. An Anglo had shot her brother, but if he hadn't been drinking and wenching with Ramón, it would not have happened.

Although Ramón was older than Felipe, they had been fast friends. Felipe unaccountably admired Ramón's swaggering ways, his easy camaraderie. Just nineteen years old, Felipe seemed to think it an honor to be included in Ramón's escapades: the horse-racing meets, the rodeos at Rancho Santa Lucia, the nights of gambling and drinking in Cambria's taverns.

Sadly, Consuelo recalled how pleased Felipe had been at the gift of a gun and holster from Ramón. Had he not drawn that gun the night in the tavern...

The old pain poured through Consuelo once more as the picture filled her mind: Felipe's pale dead face when they brought his body home, his treasured embroidered vest soaked with blood. Ramón had wept and sworn vengeance on the murderer. But the killer had fled the coast, and the American sheriff had made no attempt to find him. Felipe's senseless death had gone unavenged. Consuelo caught back a sob, knowing that in a way, the murderer of her brother had killed her father, too.

Suddenly an arm wrapped itself familiarly around her waist. "Ah! Consuelo, my girl." The husky voice was accompanied by the odor of brandy and tobacco as Ramón pressed his cheek against hers.

"Do not presume, Don Ramón!" she replied in a furious voice, stepping away from him.

She turned to meet Ramón's black eyes, arrogant and possessive even as they were admiring. He was a good-looking man, of medium height, strongly built, with a great barrel of a chest. His smile revealed strong white teeth, and lit his swarthy features with a certain charm.

"I've brought a treat for you, little one," Ramón said. "One of my vaqueros captured a grizzly bear. We'll have a bull and bear fight for your pleasure. A rare treat, too, since the bears are growing scarce."

"Blood and death are no treat, Ramón," she said in a shaky voice, wishing he didn't feel the need to prove his manhood in this way. She had seen one such fight, long ago, and had had to run away into the bushes to vomit up her disgust and horror.

Tía Isabel came into the kitchen, giving Ramón a searching look. She disliked him in an almost unreasonable way, and never hesitated to chastise him for ungentlemanly behavior.

Glancing at Tía Isabel, Ramón muttered under his breath. The dislike was mutual.

"Perhaps you should be supervising this horror you plan to provide as entertainment." Isabel's voice was cold, the words were not a suggestion.

Ramón gave her a condescending smile. "Pablo tells me you have an American guest. No doubt he'll enjoy our show."

Surely Lucas Morgan was not a man to enjoy the spectacle of violence and ugly death, Consuelo thought. An image flashed into her mind of his intent face as he bent to cover her mouth with his. The sudden heat pouring through her body had nothing to do with the peppers she was grinding. She'd behaved like a fool, and her face flushed at the memory. At least he had his gold now; perhaps he would go away. This morning he'd ridden into Cambria with her father on some unexplained errand. She hoped he wouldn't return, but was astonished at the pain that possibility brought.

Remembering his mouth gentle against hers, she felt an ache grow in her chest. She had wanted his kiss, wanted the hated Anglo's arms about her. Embarrassment at the memory of her wantonness flooded through her. She could not bear to think of it.

"We have much to do preparing to feed all our guests." Isabel glared at Ramón. "You will leave us to our work, please."

Ramón laughed. His eyes moved slowly, boldly over Consuelo's slender form. Capturing her hand in his, he kissed it lingeringly. "Until later, my girl." With a burning look at her, he sauntered from the room.

Isabel glared after him. "Ramón presumes too much," she said in a cold voice. "You're not betrothed to him yet."

So Papá and Isabel had discussed such a betrothal. Apprehension grew in Consuelo's heart. Perhaps Ramón had even spoken to Papá already. Protest rose to her lips, but she bit them to silence. She felt nothing for Ramón. He was her brother's friend. Now that Felipe was gone, he seemed to be trying to take the place of a son to Don Augustino. But to marry him was unthinkable.

* * *

The hilly little town of Cambria had grown haphazardly along the banks of Santa Rosa Creek. It nestled deep among golden summer hills thick with stands of dark green Monterey pine trees. Riding down busy Main Street, Lucas and Don Augustino passed a drove of hogs being driven to the butcher. Some of them broke loose and ran into the yard of a neat clapboard house, rooting at a vegetable garden at the side until a screaming housewife ran at them with her broom. The don broke into hearty laughter at the sight.

The town had a New England air to it, Lucas thought, even the small white clapboard Catholic church on a small rise above the town. But it was similar to New England only in the style of the buildings, not in the frantic traffic on its streets. Freight wagons hauling furnace wood and supplies to the cinnabar mines in the hills; ranch wagons, buggies and mounted horsemen churned up a continuous cloud of dust. Board sidewalks fronted the business establishments. Some of the stores had raised platforms in front to facilitate loading and unloading the many wagons parked along the street. The sidewalks were crowded with shoppers, miners with boots red from cinnabar ore, in for a spree, and a few drunkards lolling in front of the many saloons.

In the long wakeful hours after Lucas's encounter with Consuelo last night, his mind had explored a thousand different avenues. He'd built his wharf inside his head, calculating the lumber needed, longing to see its reality with an intensity that made his head ache. The bastard son of Rose Morgan would be a man of property; her faith in him would be vindicated at last. He fantasized about returning to Gloucester a wealthy man, raising a marble shaft above his mother's grave.

He seldom thought of the man who'd fathered him, but he did now, wishing that shadowy person might know when the son he'd never acknowledged became a success.

The packet of gold lay beneath his pillow, returned to him by a girl whose presence left him weak with longing. He hoped what he could build would prove to her his worth.

Perhaps then she would acknowledge the bond that had grown between them.

Tossing in the bed, he had told himself that now the agent had him embargoed, he had no trade. Pacific Steamship owed him something, and the rationalization became perfectly logical. He would borrow the gold to build his wharf and pay it back once it was operating.

When he'd approached Don Augustino early this morning with a proposition to buy the land at Estero Bay, the Don's enthusiasm had been overwhelming. It gave, Lucas thought, some indication of how badly he needed money, for he'd insisted they ride to Cambria at once and make the deal.

They arrived at their destination and left the horses at a hitching rack on the street. After climbing the dusty stairs to the offices above the Coast Bank, they learned that Don Augustino's lawyer, Vicente Rios, was in San Luis Obispo, the county seat.

"He'll be gone a couple of days," the elderly clerk told them.

"Tell him we'll be back then," Lucas said, and puzzled, he followed the hasty retreat of Don Augustino down the stairs.

"No need to wait for Vicente," the old man insisted, clutching Lucas's arm. His dark eyes, often vague and distant, were gleaming now with what Lucas recognized as greed. Don Augustino had caught the scent of gold and was not to be deterred. "We'll go to the bank, and my friend, Señor Lathrop will transfer the property."

Lucas frowned. "Are you certain he knows what must be done?"

"*Sí, sí.*" Don Augustino pushed open the glass doors into the musty-smelling bank. "He often takes care of such things."

Bert Lathrop was a porcine gentleman with thinning gray hair. Seated behind a wide mahogany desk, he listened with a bland face as the don explained the proposition.

"This country is growing and prospering," he told Lucas pompously. "A new wharf at Estero Bay will speed that growth. We're always glad to welcome a progressive businessman like you, Mr. Morgan."

From a small cabinet at the side of his office, Lathrop took a bottle of whiskey and three glasses. They drank to the success of Lucas's proposed wharf, then Lathrop left them in order to oversee the preparation of the necessary papers.

They had another drink when Lathrop returned and carefully laid out the papers for their signatures. Lucas counted out the gold coins from his pocket and became a property owner.

As the horses slouched downhill toward the distant buildings of the rancho, Lucas let himself dream a bit. Tomorrow he would go to Estero Bay and lay out his plans, order lumber in Cambria and inquire about renting a pile driver and hiring workers.

What would Consuelo think of it? he wondered. This morning she hadn't come to the table, for she and Isabel were busy in the kitchen. He'd longed to see her, yet had dared not press his luck. If only he could look into her beautiful eyes, he was certain he would know which was true—the sweet passion of her kiss or the bitter anger with which she'd flung the gold at him.

"*Dios!* Look!" Don Augustino shouted, startling Lucas from his thoughts. He pointed to the commotion around the corrals. Horses galloped back and forth, their riders shouting; a great cloud of dust rose from the pounding hooves. An angry bear, tied fast to a pole litter, was being dragged by a stout horse.

"My friend Ramón Salazar has arrived with the grizzly bear he promised," the don said with pleasure. "His rancho borders mine on the east in the Santa Lucia Mountains. He runs cattle wild as mountain goats." He paused, grinning. "Are you a gambling man?"

"No." Lucas smiled. The old New England carefulness had never left him.

"Ramón will bet on anything," the don continued, "especially his horses." He chuckled and gave Lucas an arch look. "Too bad they aren't as good as mine."

Lucas shot him a searching glance. Beneath Don Augustino's voluminous serape was a leather bag containing a good share of the salvage gold he'd refused to deposit at the bank. He hadn't guessed the old man was a gambler, and hoped he'd hang onto the gold, if only for Consuelo's sake.

"We'll have a bull and bear fight now, like a real fiesta." Unable to contain his excitement any longer, Don Augustino spurred his horse to a gallop and rode toward the corrals.

"Señor Lucas Morgan," Don Augustino shouted as Lucas walked into the courtyard after siesta. The don and another man sat in the shade of the veranda, smoking cigarillos, drinking glasses in hand. Don Augustino's flushed face indicated the wine had been flowing freely. After calling for Rosa to bring more wine, the don turned to Lucas. "This is my amigo, Don Ramón Salazar. You're in for a treat today, a bull and bear fight, thanks to Ramón."

The man seated beside the don straightened languidly to stare at Lucas. "The Americano?" he asked Don Augustino, and the word had the inflection of an insult.

Both men laughed and Lucas felt the heat rise in his face. It was the wine, he told himself, and the companion, for Don Augustino was a man who set great store by polite behavior.

"Come join us," Ramón invited with a mocking look, as Rosa waddled up with a jug of wine and a glass for Lucas. Speaking rapidly in Spanish, Ramón turned to Don Augustino.

The wine was raw and harsh. Lucas drank slowly, studying Ramón. The man had an easy charm, underlaid by the arrogance he had just displayed. Not a man to trust, Lucas decided quickly. He wondered why the patrician Don Augustino would call such a man his friend.

To his disappointment there was no sign of Consuelo. She and her aunt were probably still busy, judging by the number of Indian women bustling around the kitchen area.

Glancing toward the corrals, he saw several vaqueros leading the enormous bull he had seen earlier. The massive-horned creature snorted and pawed the earth as the vaqueros' horses forced him to follow. They disappeared over a small rise leading down to the creek. The bear on his litter was dragged behind them.

A vaquero dashed up on his horse, sending a cloud of dust into the courtyard. "Ya! Ya! It is ready!" he shouted and whirled away.

Ramón emptied his glass of wine and stood up. Don Augustino was weaving a little as he walked. "A small wager, *señor,*" Ramón said to Lucas. "The bull or the bear?"

"I'm not a gambling man," Lucas replied coldly, and when Ramón smiled knowingly, he added, "It's a fool's pastime."

Ramón's eyes flashed, and Lucas knew he had made an enemy. The moment passed as Don Augustino grasped Ramón's arm and began to speak in Spanish. From the little he knew of the language, Lucas guessed they were deciding on a wager between them. It seemed to him the younger man played on the don's emotions, laughing and raising the bet.

"Come, Señor Morgan." Don Augustino beckoned to Lucas. "Americanos never see a spectacle like this."

He was mistaken in that, for Lucas had seen such fights advertised as entertainment in San Francisco, although not for a year or so. San Francisco was more civilized now, no longer a roaring frontier city. From what he had heard he would have preferred to forgo the spectacle. But it seemed he had no choice but to follow the two men to a clearing beyond the corrals.

The noisy crowd stood in a loose circle around a shallow pit the size of a horse corral. Vaqueros were tying one of the bull's legs to the bear's leg with a long rope. At a signal from Ramón the riatas holding the two animals were shaken loose. Men and horses scrambled quickly to the safety of high ground above the pit.

Silence fell. The two beasts surveyed each other. Then the spectators began shouting, a wild and unintelligible roar of sound.

Lowering his huge head, the bull rushed his adversary. Too quick for him, the bear grasped the bull's horns in its powerful front paws and sank its teeth into its opponent's nose.

The sight of first blood excited the onlookers to greater heights. They rushed back and forth, shouting, adding to the enveloping cloud of dust rising from the struggle of the two animals.

Suddenly the bull, with a desperate effort, wrenched his head from the bear's grasp and retreated a few steps. The bear stood on hind legs, waiting. Now the bull seemed to gather all his energies. He charged. Despite the blows with its paws, the bear rolled over in the dust, struggling to defend itself against the lunges and thrusts of its opponent.

Sickened, Lucas watched the spectators shouting with a savagery that matched that of the animals. He was no innocent. He had seen murder and death in the dark alleys of the world's waterfronts, seen a man's back made bloody jelly by a cat-o'-nine-tails, felt the leather slice open his own shoulders. The scar on his cheek was from a knife meant to kill him. But to bring two animals into an unsought battle to the death seemed to him unnecessary and inhumane. Aware of Ramón's amused glances, he kept his face still and grim. The don's intense interest in the battle disgusted him.

The animals drew apart, and charged each other again. They rolled over and over in a terrible death struggle. Suddenly, the bear rolled from the body of its prostrate foe and dragged itself feebly a few yards away. With a tremendous effort, the bull pulled himself erect, then lowered his head for the charge. With a roar the dying bear made a frantic effort to escape, scrambling futilely in the dust. One last thrust of the bull's horns and the grizzly lay dying on the bloody ground. Its body twitched once and was still.

The wounded bull raised his head, uttered a triumphant bellow and slowly walked away. The crowd's screams echoed his victory. But he took only a few steps before the death chill seized him. For a moment he braced himself, his head gradually drooping, then dropped to his knees. A last convulsion shook the huge body and the bull rolled over on the bloody battlefield, the dead victor.

To Lucas, the sight was pitiful in its savagery. Keeping a calm face, he swallowed the bile rising in his throat. All about him, men pounded one another in furious excitement. Interrupting one another, they recounted the battle, demanding payment for bets.

Don Augustino, that most gracious and hospitable of men, stood transfixed. He stared at the bloody battleground and the dead combatants, his eyes glittering with a kind of savage joy.

Sickened, Lucas turned and walked back toward the house.

From the shadows of the veranda, Consuelo could see Lucas leaning on the adobe wall, smoking, staring out toward the sea lying silver in the moonlight. She clenched her fists, trying to drive from her mind the sweet wonder of his kiss. All day she had avoided him, fearful of the strange force that seemed to draw her to him.

In the flickering light of the torches placed around the courtyard, she could see old Rafael passed out against the wall, his dog lying beside him. Rosa would be furious with her husband. One of Ramón's vaqueros, who had played fandango for dancing earlier, was slumped nearby, idly strumming his guitar. The barbecued calf was nothing more than bare bones now, the bean pots empty, the wine jugs drained.

A long sigh escaped her, and Lucas turned at once, holding out a hand toward her. "Consuelo, I must talk to you."

Oh God! she dared not allow herself another chance to succumb to this Anglo. His blue eyes and gentle mouth were too tempting. Turning on her heel, she swept into the house, ignoring him.

Within, a lamp still burned over the table where Don Augustino and Ramón played at monte. Tears of anger pooled in Consuelo's eyes as she paused in the open doorway. Her father was in the grip of his terrible addiction: gambling. His eyes gleamed. Sweat poured down his face although the night was cool. As she watched, Ramón laughed and laid down his cards. Don Augustino shrugged and shoved some gold coins across the table.

Gold! Where had her father come by gold to gamble with? Oh Lord, had Lucas given it to him? He didn't know Don Augustino's fatal weakness, or he wouldn't have done anything so foolish.

Ramón rose as though to quit the game, and Don Augustino reached out to draw him down again. "One more." With a shrug, Ramón sat down again and gathered up the cards.

Shaking with anger, Consuelo burst into the room. "No, Papá! Enough!" she said harshly. "Enough gambling for today."

Ramón laughed, his eyes moving over her figure in a familiar manner. "One more, Consuelo. Just one more, your papá asks."

Turning furiously on him, she cried, "You know Papá, Ramón. Don't indulge his weakness."

Ramón merely smiled, leaning back in his chair.

Taking her father's shoulders in her hands, she tried to urge him to his feet. "Papá, you will go to bed now," Consuelo commanded.

He looked up at her, frowning. "Leave me alone, daughter. I have money and soon I will win all of Ramón's, too."

Lucas Morgan came into the room, watching them curiously.

Consuelo turned in fury on Lucas. "Did you give him money to gamble?"

Lucas stared at her in surprise. "Of course not. I paid the money for the land I bought from your father today."

"What land?" she cried, shaking with anger and fear. Surely her father hadn't been so foolish as to sell the rancho.

Don Augustino stared up at her with dull eyes. His chair pushed back from the table, Ramón watched them with a puzzled half smile.

"Estero Bay." It was Lucas who answered. "I'm going to build a wharf there."

"Estero Bay!" she exclaimed, hearing nothing after those words. "My mother's dowry. My dowry! Papá would never sell that. He couldn't."

"Why not? His name was on the deed," Lucas replied, obviously astonished by this information.

Consuelo fought back the sobs gathering in her throat. "The American judge changed everything to Papá's name, but it was understood Estero Bay was to be mine!" She turned on her father. "You promised," she cried. "Papá, how could you?"

Elbows on the table, Don Augustino sat slumped in silence, staring down at his hands and the scattered playing cards.

"And you!" Consuelo whirled on the startled Lucas. "You Anglo pig! You're no better than George Hearst. Both of you are destroying the Californios as fast as you can!" She had told him how much that piece of land meant to her. He obviously hadn't cared.

He'd proved he was just like any other grasping and dishonest Anglo. He'd kept Pacific Steamship's gold and planned to make his fortune using it and her land.

Ramón chuckled softly. Consuelo glared at him. But he was not the one guilty of deceit and thievery.

"Consuelo—" Lucas began, reaching out to touch her shoulder.

Violently, she thrust his hand away, and faced him, trembling. "I made a terrible mistake. I should never have given the gold back to you. I want you out of this house by morning." Consuelo drew a deep breath and met Lucas's shocked eyes. Cold fury shook her voice as she cried, "Señor Morgan, you're no longer welcome at Rancho Estrada."

Chapter Six

"It is the old custom," Don Augustino assured Lucas, handing him the horse's reins. "Californios provide their guests and friends with horse and saddle, to be used as long as needed."

"I do need a horse," Lucas agreed, "but let me pay you for it."

"No! No!" The don was vehement, adding in a harsh voice, "My daughter shamed me with the words she said to you last night. The hospitality of Rancho Estrada must never be in doubt. *Por favor,* take the horse."

Isabel watched with a grim face from her post before the closed kitchen door. The morning was cool, the sun a blurred disk behind a thin vein of clouds. Lucas could hear the chatter of the women working at the ovens behind the kitchen. Down by the corrals, Ramón and his vaqueros were mounting for their homeward journey, waiting for the don to join them.

Consuelo had not appeared this morning. Lucas had a faint, uneasy feeling that Isabel was guarding the kitchen door because Consuelo was there behind it.

His spirits were low as he finally took the reins from Don Augustino's urging hand. Yesterday he had been filled with excitement over his plans for the future. He had had hope for a new life, a life he longed to share with the girl who had stolen his heart so quickly. But Consuelo wanted no part of a future with him; she had made that abundantly clear. He had no desire to take sides or to be part of this battle—Anglo against Californio—but it seemed Consuelo had taken up against him.

"*Bueno.*" Don Augustino gave him an expansive grin. "Everyone on the coast will be watching the progress on your wharf, Señor Morgan."

"Thank you again for your hospitality, Don Augustino." Lucas held out a hand and the don shook it heartily. "Perhaps I can repay you some day."

The don merely smiled vaguely as he turned away to mount his own horse. "*Vaya con Dios,*" he called over his shoulder.

"*Gracias,*" Lucas replied, but the don had already wheeled the horse and ridden away in a cloud of dust, joining the vaqueros and Ramón, who were whooping as they spurred their mounts toward the hills.

"You can pay *me* for the horse and saddle," came a harsh voice behind him. When he turned, Isabel's dark, hostile eyes met his. "I don't live in the past as my brother does. And I won't gamble the money away."

Without a word, Lucas dug into his pocket and laid the gold coins in her outstretched hand. "I would like to say goodbye to Consuelo," he told her as she turned away.

Isabel whirled on him, her face cold. "No, *señor.* Consuelo said farewell to you last night. My brother has failed her, as he has failed all the women in his life, and he did it with your help. She has no more to say to you." Quickly, she crossed the courtyard and slammed the kitchen door behind her.

Disconsolate, Lucas mounted his horse, directing it down the trail toward Cambria. He had nothing to take away with him except the clean sailor's clothes and the gold in the packet strapped around his waist. If he had hoped to take the promise of a beautiful girl, that hope was faded now. Yet he could not quite make himself believe her harsh words when he remembered how she had given herself to him in her kiss. The warmth of her. He angrily thrust away the thought, knowing it could bring only pain.

* * *

Hidden among the eucalyptus trees, Consuelo watched the horse and rider move along the coast road southward until they disappeared beyond the golden hills. The distant muffled roar of the ocean sounded a dirge beneath gray skies. Why did his leaving make her feel so bereft? Consuelo asked herself angrily. Why was she watching him like this, secretly filling her eyes with his tall form?

When he was gone from sight, she turned away, berating herself for this weakness. Lucas Morgan was a hated Anglo, not to be trusted. Like all the Anglos, he was dishonest, bent only on taking or destroying everything the Californios had left.

From her weak and irresponsible father, Lucas had bought the land that was to have been her dowry. She'd known of the promise since childhood. She'd roamed the hills and the beaches with a proprietary interest in every tree and every blade of grass. It was *her* place . . . lost now to the Anglo, who would despoil its pristine beauty with a wharf.

Consuelo's face grew warm, and she trembled with the memory of how she had enthusiastically returned his kiss, shamelessly, wantonly. She said a quick prayer for the Holy Mother's forgiveness. The baffling urges that filled her at his touch were part of the mystery. She didn't know what she longed for, hadn't guessed at the powerful forces that drew men and women together.

For so long she had dreamed of a lover. Yet she'd snubbed the rough young men who came from the local ranchos and from Cambria town to pay court. She was well aware it was whispered that she thought herself above them because of her education at the convent in Monterey. But after Felipe was killed, Consuelo had been her father's only child and solace. She could not think of leaving him alone. And, of course, Isabel had been a fiercely protective dueña.

Just now, before Don Augustino rode away to journey halfway with Ramón, he had been angry at her refusal to come from her room to bid Ramón goodbye. She wanted to see Ramón even less than she wanted to face Lucas Morgan.

"You have become a disobedient daughter," Don Augustino muttered, an expression of confusion in his eyes in spite of his harsh words. "And an impolite one," he added. "You know Ramón is much attached to you."

She gave a look of defiance. "Ramón takes advantage of you, Papá. Would you let him take advantage of your daughter?"

Shock and disbelief filled the don's flushed face. "Stay in this room!" he commanded. "When I return from escorting Ramón, we will talk."

"The Anglo paid me for the horse he took," Isabel told Consuelo. They stood together at the long kitchen table, assembling enchiladas for the evening meal. Dried peppers and garlic and dill hung from the low rafters. An old clay stove filled one side of the long room, its tiles smoky and discolored. Pine cupboards filled the other walls. "And I made your father give me some of the gold, too."

Consuelo stared at her aunt in surprise. "Papá gave you some of the gold?"

Isabel nodded. "For the birthday fiesta he's planning for you. He's going to invite the Cambria Jockey Club to bring their horses to race, and hire musicians so we can have a fandango."

Dismayed, Consuelo stared at her aunt's grim face. "He knows we can't afford such a party. It's not like the old days."

When she was a child, before the great drought and before her mother died, it seemed there had always been fiestas and excitement. Either here or at the other ranchos: Santa Rosa, Piedra Blanca or San Simeon. Horse races. Bull and bear fights. Roping contests. Fandangos.

Nostalgia overwhelmed Consuelo. She sighed, carefully rolling a tortilla around the filling of meat and salsa.

"Do you remember, *tía,* how it used to be?" she asked in a low, sad voice. "Mamá dancing in her ruffled silk dress and her Paris lace mantilla and Papá, young and handsome, sitting in his silver-studded saddle, in charge of it all."

Painful tears pooled in her eyes. Isabel stared straight ahead, grim-faced, almost as though she had not heard.

"It seems as though all the good times died with mamá. The Anglos came, and the great drought, and everything changed." She drew in a deep shuddering breath. "One day, I fear, it will all be gone, and we'll have to sell to George Hearst like the other Californios."

Isabel's harsh voice cut her off. "No one can see the future. And the past is past. Your father has said we'll have a fiesta for your eighteenth birthday, and so we shall."

"Eighteen. I'm an old maid," Consuelo replied ruefully.

"By choice," Isabel reminded her, leaning across to arrange the enchiladas in the long baking pan.

"You never married, *tía*. Why must I?"

A closed look came over Isabel's face, a look familiar to Consuelo. Her aunt refused to speak of any past other than the years she'd spent in the Convent of the Sacred Heart in Monterey. When Consuelo returned from convent school Isabel had left as well and come to Rancho Estrada to care for the two motherless children, Consuelo and Felipe. Watching now as Isabel passed the long earthenware baking dish to Rosa to be placed in the clay ovens outside, Consuelo wondered if there had been anything in her aunt's life except the convent and Rancho Estrada.

"Enchiladas, good!" Don Augustino cried in high spirits as he passed Rosa at the kitchen door. "Too bad Ramón didn't stay to eat with us."

"There's scarcely enough for ourselves," Isabel rebuked him. "And certainly not enough for all those *bandidos*."

Don Augustino merely shrugged and gave her a bland smile, passing off her sharp remarks as he always did.

"Come, daughter." He took Consuelo's arm and urged her along. "We must talk."

Consuelo drew in her breath sharply, meeting Isabel's narrow-eyed look. Her father was angry that she had behaved so harshly toward Lucas Morgan last night, and that she had been so cold to Ramón. He set great store by his reputation for hospitality and polite behavior. But she'd been certain he would forget, as he did so often lately.

Tightening her mouth, she followed him into the great room where a low fire burned against the chill day. She would listen and not argue, but nothing he could say would make her take back a word, or lessen her anger at the loss of her dowry land.

"Did Isabel tell you about the fiesta for your birthday?" He sat down on the settee, then abruptly stood and began to pace, strangely excited.

Having steeled herself to be chastised for impolite behavior, she could only stare at him in surprise. "We can't afford it, Papá..." she began.

He waved off her protest impatiently. "You'll be eighteen years old," he said. "More than old enough to marry. Ramón spoke to me again this morning. I wish to announce your betrothal at the fiesta next week."

Shock coursed through Consuelo, and she felt a creeping fear that her father might actually force her into this marriage. "How could you, Papá?" she cried, facing him squarely. "How could you even consider marrying me to a man I don't love?"

Don Augustino seemed genuinely amazed by her reaction. "Ramón is my friend, almost a son," he protested mildly. "He's a wealthy man, with many cattle and horses. He'll provide well for you, and he doesn't even ask a dowry."

"You sell me cheap, Papá." Consuelo's voice shook. "Mamá would die of shame at such a thing, and I'm sick with shame that I mean so little to my own father."

"It's for your welfare, daughter." Augustino's eyes unexpectedly filled with tears. "I wish to see you settled where you'll be cared for, and Ramón has long wished to wed you. It was just that I couldn't bear to let you go after Felipe..." His voice trailed off.

Sympathetic tears filled her eyes, for she was all too aware how he had clung to her in the months after Felipe was killed. Why this sudden change of heart, she wondered, and what had Ramón said to persuade him?

In a carefully controlled voice Consuelo replied, "As you say, Papá, Ramón is like a brother. I can't marry him."

Unexpectedly, Augustino's face hardened and he seized her arm painfully. "You will obey your father." When she struggled to escape his clutching hand, it only infuriated him. "You will obey!" he shouted.

"Papá!" she cried in anguish, seeing that he was out of control. At last she succeeded in freeing herself, and she ran from the room, wondering frantically how she could save herself, her sadly ailing father and Rancho Estrada.

Lucas passed Lull's Merchandise, Cambria's largest store, and Camozzi's Saloon, where he had shared a drink with Don Augustino after buying the land from him. Now he felt a twinge, recalling how Consuelo had accused him of stealing the land from her irresponsible father, the land that was to have been her dowry. Perhaps he should find the lawyer, Rios, and discuss the purchase with him, as well as his future plans. There was something too slick about the banker who had handled the land transaction. It hadn't seemed important when Don Augustino told him Rios was in San Luis Obispo, and that Mr. Lathrop would handle the transaction. But he hadn't liked the banker much, and besides, he would need a lawyer for his business.

Leaving his horse at the Phoenix Livery Stable, Lucas paid for a room at the Davis Hotel, then walked on down the busy street. He was sharply aware of his surroundings, for this would be his home now. He watched sea gulls circle under the low gray sky, alighting to peck at the animal droppings littering the street. The women he passed glanced at him curiously, clutching shawls over their calico and linsey gowns. In the near distance the screech of sawmills added to the din of horses, wagons and pigs.

Rios's office above the Coast Bank was at the corner of Main and Bridge streets. Once more, Lucas climbed the dusty stairs to the second floor. Opening the frosted-glass door, he stared in astonishment at the diminutive man behind the massive oak desk.

"Sir?" Vicente Rios stood, a questioning look on his swarthy face. A good foot shorter than Lucas, he had brilliant dark eyes and a neat black mustache, and his dark hair was combed slickly back from his broad, intelligent forehead. He was dressed in an immaculate gray-striped suit, and a heavy gold watch chain was looped across his black vest.

"Lucas Morgan," Lucas introduced himself. He held out his hand and received a firm handshake from the lawyer. "I'd like to discuss some business with you."

"Ah, yes," Rios said, indicating a chair for Lucas. "The news is around town already that you intend to build a wharf at Estero Bay."

"That's right. I understand I'll need a franchise from the county." Lucas removed the wide-brimmed hat he had bought on his previous visit to Cambria.

"The city of Cambria once tried to build a pier," Rios said. He leaned back in his chair and studied Lucas with sharp black eyes. "It washed out in heavy seas before it was finished."

"Mine won't." Lucas took the cigar Rios offered and leaned forward for a light.

"Leffingwell has a pier north of here," Rios began.

Lucas interrupted. "It's too short for anything but small boats."

Rios puffed his cigar and waited in silence, studying Lucas shrewdly.

"Don Augustino Estrada speaks highly of you, sir," Lucas said. "I'd like to retain your services. I hope you can steer me to honest merchants and lumbermen, and tell me about the labor market here."

"Just now, the cinnabar mines are booming," Rios replied. "Most of the men who aren't working in the mines are out prospecting on their own." He paused thoughtfully. "There's an Indian village south of here called Bain's Settlement. See a fellow called Soledad. He's a good worker and dependable."

For the next hour, Lucas sat across from Rios, sketching out plans for the wharf as he had worked them out in his head. Then he made lists of lumber, timber for pilings, hardware and the lighter boat he planned to purchase in San Simeon to carry on a lightering business while building the wharf. Rios grew more enthusiastic as Lucas's careful planning and expertise became apparent. By the time the two men shook hands in farewell, Lucas was certain he'd found a friend in this new country.

Beneath a sky of thin clouds gilded by the afternoon sun, Lucas shouldered his way down the crowded board sidewalks to Lull's store. There he would order the bolts, nails and steel he needed for the wharf. And he'd buy clothes and boots and bedding for himself.

Inside Lull's, where a fire in the round cast-iron heater took the chill off the day, Lucas found himself more than welcome when stout, bearded Mr. Lull saw his gold.

As he gathered up the clothes he'd bought, wrapped in brown paper, Lucas's eye fell on a silk shawl displayed inside the glass-fronted counter. The brilliant roses in its pattern were as red as Consuelo Estrada's lips; the knotted red silk fringe gleamed in the dark store. Suddenly, Lucas could imagine Consuelo wearing that shawl around her soft shoulders, imagine the way her dark eyes would light up at the sight of such a lovely thing. A pang shook him when he recalled their angry parting, and her furious declaration that she wished never to see him again.

"The shawl," he said to Mr. Lull, "I'll take that, too." In spite of the knowing look he received, Lucas's heart thudded wildly.

He was imagining Consuelo wrapped in the silken folds, her dark hair loose as it had been the night he held her, her shoulders bare beneath the shawl, her dark eyes gleaming with welcome for him and his embrace.

Chapter Seven

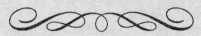

"Papá must always show off," Consuelo said to her aunt. "It's that, more than celebrating my birthday." She knew they couldn't afford this fandango her willful and increasingly irresponsible father had insisted upon. So much money had been spent for food and for *aguardiente,* the locally made brandy—more, she was certain, than was available to pay for it. She watched Isabel give the pestle a vicious turn on the mortar, where she was grinding basil leaves.

"He wanted to announce your betrothal," Isabel said. "That's the real reason." Her voice trembled, and her eyes darkened in distress. "Ramón charms him as he does so many others, but I..." She emptied the mortar of herbs into a huge pot of beans simmering on the clay stove, and didn't finish her sentence.

"I told Papá I have no wish to marry Ramón. I don't love him." Almost wistfully, she added, "Sometimes I wish I did. It would make everything so much easier." With unnecessary force, she brushed the peelings and debris from the scarred kitchen table into the scraps pot. "Papá was very angry when I wouldn't give in."

Isabel sighed. "You were always stubborn and willful, even as a child, my dear. But it's the men, not you and I, who have the power here." Bitterness filled her voice as she added, "They always win."

Consuelo stared at her aunt in surprise. "But *I* won. Papá told Ramón he would have to court me, that I think of him as a brother and that he must win my consent himself." She didn't add that she was certain her heart would never consent.

Isabel did not reply, and Consuelo studied her tight-lipped aunt. The sharp comments about men surprised her. Isabel often won, though only in the management of the house. In all other matters, her aunt deferred to Don Augustino's whims. She recalled how carefully Isabel kept out of any quarrels between the don and his children.

For the first time, she clearly saw her aunt's position as a poor relation—and how she hated it. Impulsively, she hugged Isabel, who stared at her in surprise.

"I'm going for a ride before our guests arrive," she announced.

"Consuelo!" Isabel cried out in objection.

"There's nothing to do except change my clothes." Consuelo gestured decisively around the warm kitchen, the stove crowded with pots giving off wonderful spicy odors. Rosa and the other women were already filling platters with the abundance of food.

As she urged Mirlo, the little black mare who was her special pet, into a gallop, Consuelo thought sadly of the days when her brother, Felipe, rode beside her. That was long ago, before he grew up with a wildness in him that had resulted in his death in a tavern brawl. That he had been with the reckless companions Ramón led only reinforced her decision to refuse Ramón's offer of marriage. The quarrel with Papá had been painful, especially when she saw how unsure and confused he became when she stood adamantly against his wishes.

At the top of a hill, Consuelo pulled the mare up to let her blow, for her sides were heaving from their headlong ride. Below, the hills, tinted golden by autumn, rolled away toward the ocean; dark green stands of eucalyptus and pine were tucked in pockets among them. In the distance, the ocean gleamed silver-blue in the midday sun. At China Point on the north shore, the tumbled remains of an old rock house lay silent beneath the trees. An offshore breeze was blowing, bringing warm air from inland.

Estero Bay lay before her, white breakers on golden sand. The land her mother, Amparo, had been given as dowry by Don José Carrillo, Amparo's father. Now it belonged to the Anglo, Lucas Morgan. Fierce resentment seared Consuelo's heart. Even from this far away she could see a building going up on the shore. Men, small as ants in the distance, were working at raising the walls. Already, Estero Bay was Anglo. No longer Californio. No longer hers.

Yet there was something admirable in the fact that Lucas Morgan did what he said he would do. With her father it was always tomorrow, which often meant never. And the wharf would even be an advantage to Rancho Estrada if they ever had cattle to ship again.

Some of her anger drained away as she watched the workmen below. Despite the unethical source of his funds, Lucas Morgan was doing a kind of service. But still she jerked the horse around, annoyed at herself for peering at the workmen, for trying to find Lucas Morgan's figure among them.

"Damn the Anglo!" she cried into the wind as the mare raced homeward. "Damn him!" But her words did not erase the haunting memory of his kiss, or still the longings that troubled her heart.

Guests were already arriving when she rode into the rancho and gave her horse to the Indian boy, Sancho, whose sole duty was to care for the horses of the family.

"Look at you!" Tía Isabel scolded as Consuelo came into the kitchen, where the table was already crowded with bowls of food. "Your hair all blown, and guests arriving. Hurry now, and get ready." She made a shooing motion with her hands. As Consuelo hastened away, Isabel called after her. "Sancho says he saw the Rios's carriage on the coast road."

Smiling as she quickly brushed her hair, Consuelo thought how one always knew of Vicente's arrival. The flamboyant little man drove a carriage with his personal banners flying on each side, visible for miles. With him would be his plump, sweet wife, Angela, the only friend near her age that Consuelo could claim. Suddenly, the whole fandango appeared in a new light. She would have a visit with Angela, and in spite of his occasionally pompous behavior, Vicente was always fun.

She had known Vicente forever. His family had been her parents' friends, as well as relatives.

When they were children, she had sometimes protected Vicente from the cruel teasing of Felipe and the other boys who made fun of his size. Consuelo was proud of his achievements; he was a lawyer and a prominent citizen in spite of his size and race. He was a doer, like Lucas Morgan. Quickly, she brushed away the unwelcome thought of Lucas.

Having rearranged her hair, she dressed in her best skirt of bright calico with three tiers of ruffles around the hem. After donning an embroidered white linen blouse, Consuelo ran out to greet the Rios.

At the courtyard wall, she felt the blood drain from her face, then her cheeks flushed hot. Vicente's Indian driver sat at the front of the shiny black landau carriage, the bright red banners on tall staffs fluttering in the breeze. Standing beside the two-seated carriage was Lucas Morgan, dressed in obviously new clothes, a smart gray felt hat on his head. He was courteously helping Angela alight from the carriage as Vicente and Father Amateo stood by.

Fury mounted in Consuelo's breast as she watched him behaving as though he were welcome. Quite forgetting that a short time ago she'd felt a grudging admiration for him, she wished she dared remind him that she'd told him never to come here again. How dared he show up like this . . . and with the Rios!

"Consuelo!" Angela cried and seized her in a smothering hug. Angela's pregnancy was far advanced and she wore a loose, flowing gown of pastel-flowered silk. Despite the enveloping embrace, Consuelo managed a telling frown at Lucas Morgan over Angela's head.

"Your father asked that we invite Lucas to come with us," Vicente said, watching the two young women with indulgent affection. "He has a franchise to build a wharf at Estero Bay. I thought it would be good for him to meet his neighbors, soon to be customers."

''Señorita Estrada.'' Lucas removed the wide-brimmed hat, an enigmatic expression in his blue eyes.

She nodded politely, not meeting those searching eyes, and turned to embrace the aging Father Amateo, stooped and thin in his long brown robe.

In Consuelo's room, Angela shed her rebozo and her hat, and loosened her corset stays. She was small and round, with a perfectly oval porcelain-smooth face. And she was a bit vain, choosing to dress in Anglo style, with all the discomfort such clothing brought.

From her chatter, Consuelo was at once aware that the Rios had accepted Lucas Morgan as a friend. Vicente had obtained the franchise for him, helped him find material and workmen, had even decided to invest in the wharf.

''And my father told you to invite him to my birthday fiesta?'' Consuelo inquired when Angela finally ran down.

''*Sí.*'' Busy smoothing her elaborate coiffure, Angela eyed her curiously in the mirror. ''Do you object?''

Consuelo's mouth tightened. ''I told him never to set foot on the rancho again.''

Angela's dark eyes widened. She laid down her brush and stared at Consuelo. ''But you didn't!'' she cried. ''The hospitality of Rancho Estrada is legend.'' She smiled brightly. ''Don Augustino was surely trying to mend your words.''

Frowning, Consuelo looked away. She wouldn't discuss Lucas Morgan with Angela or anyone. She turned the conversation easily to the coming baby, a joy to Angela and Vicente after nearly three years of marriage.

The two girls strolled out onto the veranda, the vivacious Angela repeating all the latest gossip along the coast. Isabel was in deep conversation with Father Amateo. While he was here, marriages would be performed and babies baptized among the people of the rancho.

Inside, the dining table was already heaped with gifts brought for Consuelo's birthday. Outside, horse races arranged by Ramón had begun on a track the vaqueros had laid out on a level area toward the hills. Dust rose along with the shouts and cheers of the spectators. Consuelo bit her lip, hoping against experience that her father wasn't gambling on the races. He'd spent an exorbitant amount for this fiesta, even hiring the band from Cambria that had just arrived.

Because the weather was so fine, they were serving the food outdoors. Rosa's husband, the elderly Rafael, was supervising the setting up of tables in the courtyard. Consuelo frowned at the old man. Isabel demanded that the house servants keep themselves neat and clean at all times. "Rafael," Consuelo said sharply, "is that blood on your pants? You must go change before it begins to smell."

He started, then screwed up his wizened face in a grin. "No, no, *señorita,* no blood." He bent to brush at the red stain on his dark pants. "Dirt. I fell from my horse when I was catching the calf." He pointed to the calf carcass rotating over glowing oakwood coals. "See…" He brushed off part of the red dust.

Consuelo nodded and smiled, sorry for having chastised the faithful fellow.

Angela led the way into the kitchen, where she insisted on tasting everything. "I've been eating like a horse since the baby started," she confided happily.

Indian women hurried from the kitchen, carrying the food just as the horsemen rode in from the racetrack. Rafael and another man were carving the roast calf onto the huge platters Rosa brought. On the courtyard table appeared platters piled high with food. A keg of *aguardiente* was tapped, and there was tea for the ladies.

The crowd descended on the table. Consuelo and Isabel had to keep the Indian women running back and forth to replenish the quickly emptied platters. Stylishly dressed Anglo ladies from Cambria ate as heartily as their dark-suited husbands. Californios, both men and women, were dressed more casually and more colorfully: the men in dark trousers trimmed with embroidery and wide-sleeved white shirts, the women in bright calico skirts and loose ruffled blouses.

Why had her father invited all these ill-bred, ill-mannered Anglos? Consuelo wondered, watching the women with their high-pitched laughter, and the men devouring everything in sight, including Papá's brandy. Papá was showing off, of course, as she had told Isabel. It would hurt his overweening pride to have these Anglos know that Rancho Estrada was insolvent, and that this year's taxes would likely go unpaid.

If Ramón was unhappy that no betrothal would be announced today, he failed to show it. Consuelo watched him move among the crowd, smiling, charming the silly Anglo women with extravagant compliments, discussing business with the men. He was good-looking, she thought, and carried himself with confidence. If only she could feel something for him, how much easier it would all be. If only the thought of kissing him left her as weak as did the memory of Lucas Morgan's kiss.

Vicente had taken Lucas in tow, introducing him to the important dairy farmers, the mine owners, the bankers—all the people Lucas would do business with one day. Whenever Lucas's blue glance crossed hers, Consuelo looked quickly away. Her resentment at his appearance here had not lessened, and yet she found herself repeatedly looking for his tall figure among the crowd, admiring the easy confidence with which he met one and all. And she kept fighting the memory of his kiss each time she saw him.

With siesta, a quiet fell over the rancho, broken at last by the horsemen riding back to the racetrack. The ladies were driven in their carriages to watch the racing, parasols open to protect them from the afternoon sun. Consuelo and Isabel stayed at the house, for there would be supper to serve, and the courtyard had to be cleared for dancing.

A golden glow filled the western skies. The band—two guitars and a fiddle—was playing for a few dancers, while other guests finished the supper set out on the long kitchen table.

"You must open your gifts now, Consuelo," Angela urged, as everyone began drifting away from the depleted supper table. She ate the last bite of custard cake, her eyes sparkling.

Consuelo laughed, knowing Angela was even more eager than she to see what lay in the pile of gifts on the dining table. She watched as Angela went into the courtyard to announce that Consuelo would open her gifts now. The band went on playing and the dancing continued, while a small crowd made its way into the great room.

Most of the gifts were practical: a sack of dried garbanzos, a braided horsehair hackamore, leather slippers from Angela and Vicente. Some of the Anglo ladies had brought linen doilies and runners edged with hand-crocheted lace. Consuelo barely managed to smile and thank them for the useless Anglo fripperies.

She saw that Vicente and Lucas Morgan had come into the room, and her heartbeat quickened. All afternoon she had scarcely seen Lucas, for he must have been watching the racing. Now she gave him a sideways glance, not daring to meet those intense blue eyes. Damn him, she thought, struggling to keep the smile on her face. Why had Papá invited him? And why had he accepted after she'd ordered him never to come here again? She hated him, she told herself, for cheating her father and herself, for stealing the gold, for being so admirably ambitious. But more than anything, she hated him for the feelings his presence aroused in her.

"Open this," Angela demanded, handing her a package wrapped in the brown paper the stores in Cambria used. Angela's dancing glance met her husband's, and Vicente winked. Lucas Morgan, standing in the doorway, one broad shoulder propped against the doorjamb, looked down at his feet, his strong face faintly flushed.

Puzzled by the exchange between Vicente and Angela, Consuelo tore open the package and stared at the heavy China silk rebozo, certain that it was from Lucas Morgan. Against an ivory background, embroidered roses in all shades from pink to scarlet gleamed in the candlelight. The knotted silk fringe was an odd shade of red. There were gasps of admiration from the ladies, and Angela squealed with delight. Consuelo's hand moved sensuously over the silken beauty of the shawl, loving its beauty, yet knowing it was given by a man she had declared her enemy.

"Put it on." Angela took the rebozo and draped it around Consuelo's shoulders.

Its touch was as warm and comforting as Lucas Morgan's had been that night beneath the eucalyptus trees. At that unexpected thought, Consuelo's face flamed, and she quickly removed it from her shoulders.

"Cinnabar red," Vicente announced, taking the shawl and holding the long bright fringe in his hands. "It becomes you, Consuelo."

"Gracias," she said, making the word do for both Vicente and Lucas. The latter smiled and bent his head as her glance quickly crossed his.

Unexpectedly, Lucas stepped toward her, taking the rebozo from Vicente's hands. Draping it around her shoulders again, he said in a husky tone, "You may thank me, *señorita,* by honoring me with a dance."

Before she could object, he had led her into the courtyard where the band was playing a waltz. His arm was around her waist, his warm, strong hand holding hers as she followed him to the swaying, sensuous music. She was scarcely aware of Ramón frowning from the sidelines.

Shaken by Lucas's touch, she dared not meet the blue eyes she felt intent on her face. The rebozo slipped from her shoulders where he had placed it, and his arm tightened to hold it against her.

"Do you like the shawl?" he asked.

Consuelo nodded, still not meeting his eyes, for she was desperately afraid he would read there the extraordinary feelings he aroused in her. This man was her enemy, she told herself sharply, and there was an edge to her voice when she spoke. "It's much too expensive a gift, Señor Morgan, for mere acquaintances." And much too intimate, was her thought as the soft silk caressed her bare arms.

"But we are more than mere acquaintances," he replied, his mouth so close to her ear she could feel his warm breath.

Her throat tightened and she couldn't answer. His body touched hers, moved away, touched again in the flowing rhythm of the dance. This Anglo aroused aching longings in her body that no other man ever had, not the dashing boys from the neighboring ranchos, certainly not Ramón.

Despite the old dislike for Anglos, she admired Lucas's decisiveness. Lucas Morgan was not a man to waste time or opportunity. If only Papá were more like that. If only she could be.

For a moment she gave herself completely to the movement of their bodies together, the music filling her mind, her body instinctively following his lead. When the music ended and he pulled away, she felt bereft.

"I must go back to my guests, *señor*." She spoke hastily, running the words together, knowing she mustn't touch him again or she would forget her anger and be completely undone.

"Another dance later?" he asked, his blue eyes soft, importuning, turning her limbs to water.

"Perhaps," she replied, almost brusque in her need to hide the feelings his nearness aroused. Without meeting his eyes, she hurried inside, laying the silk rebozo across the china chest that had been her mother's. Inside lay the last of her mother's treasures—the black lace mantilla, the tall tortoiseshell comb set with brilliants and the gold silk wedding gown. Now, Consuelo thought sadly, she would place the silk rebozo there, too, and try not to think of it again.

Lucas watched Consuelo's slender figure disappear into the house, his arms still warm from the touch of her, his chest burning where her firm young breasts had pressed against him. So beautiful, and so proud, he thought, fighting down the ache of longing in his loins. And still so angry at him and all Anglos. He glanced toward the bunkhouse, where he knew Ramón and Don Augustino were playing at monte with some of their visitors. The don had bet heavily on the races today, and Lucas was sure he had seldom won. It was a sickness with him, Lucas knew now. And he was certain all the gold he'd paid the don for Estero Bay would soon be in other pockets.

No man could gamble so wildly without losing everything. What would become of Rancho Estrada then? And what of Consuelo? In the short time he'd known her, this need to care for her had grown in him. He'd come to admire the way she tried to seem so strong, struggling against her poverty and her father's whims. But even he had nothing to give her yet. Only the shack he had built on the bank of Coyote Creek, sheltered from the sea winds of Estero Bay, and away from the babble of the Indian families Soledad had brought with him and his laborers from Bain's Settlement.

All he had to give her was a dream, much less than her father, or Ramón, who Angela had confided was courting Consuelo, could offer. Tomorrow he would ride to San Simeon and hire help to row the lighter boat he would buy and bring back to Estero Bay. Until the wharf was finished, he would run a lightering business. But he had no place for a beautiful woman.

A curtain of dust hung above the coast road as the departing guests drove homeward from the fiesta. It was mid-morning. The Indian women were still cleaning up from breakfast; the sky was a pale glazed blue with a bank of fog lying offshore.

Don Augustino waved farewell to the last carriage and walked back toward the house. No one had slept last night; the dancing and eating and games had continued until the sun rose above the Santa Lucia Mountains. Watching her father, Consuelo saw his face was gray with fatigue, and a twinge of apprehension went through her. She was weary, too, and glad the celebration was at an end.

"Papá," she called. For a moment he seemed disoriented, then he turned toward where she stood on the veranda with the three glum musicians beside her. "We must pay the band, Papá," she said. Her heart sank when she saw the look of dismay and guilt cross his tired face.

Grabbing his arm, she drew him aside and asked in a low, urgent voice, "Surely, Papá, you have some of the gold left, or some silver coins? These men were promised payment, and they came all the way from Cambria to play."

Don Augustino's face sagged, his eyes moving wildly about as though he were seeking an escape. "Papá?" she demanded.

A long silence... the only sound beyond the women's kitchen chatter was a faint twang of strings as one of the musicians picked up his guitar.

"I have no money." Don Augustino's voice was low and strangled, the words spoken reluctantly.

Fear clutched Consuelo's heart, then anger at her father's fecklessness boiled hot in her chest and she glared at him. "You gambled it all away?" She knew with dread certainty the answer to that question. Papá's compulsive gambling had already brought them to the brink of ruin.

"All gone," he croaked and turned his face away from her.

"Everything?" she asked, incredulous.

Shamefaced, he nodded.

Stunned, Consuelo stared at her father, who stood immobile as though his confession had drained him of all power to move or speak.

"Señorita?" one of the musicians called.

Fighting down the angry accusations and recriminations rising in her throat, Consuelo turned away from her father. She crossed the veranda to the musicians, and said in as cool a voice as she could muster, "Perhaps you would take a horse in payment?"

"You shouldn't have done that," Don Augustino said, his voice almost toneless as they watched the musicians drive away in their *carreta,* a fine Estrada horse tied behind it. "All the horses belong to Ramón now."

"Holy Mother of God!" Isabel muttered, for she had joined them on the veranda.

"Papá, how could you?" Consuelo cried, staring at his slumped figure. Anger at Ramón flashed through her. He knew Papá's weakness, and he alone of the Californios would take advantage of it. In the old days, when Papá gambled with Felipe and Ramón, it had all been in fun. But this was different, for they stood to lose everything.

"It doesn't matter." The don shrugged, then straightening, he turned to look at her sternly, his face resuming the old prideful expression. "It doesn't matter," he repeated. "When you and Ramón are wed, it will all be the same family."

Chapter Eight

From the veranda, Consuelo watched in helpless frustration as Ramón's vaqueros gathered the finest of the Estrada horses to trail back to Rancho Santa Lucia. She couldn't blame Pablo, who had announced he was going with the horses to work for Ramón. But it would be difficult to forgive her father, whose reckless gambling had brought this upon them.

Beside her, as helpless as she, the tight-lipped Isabel muttered imprecations upon Ramón between evocations of the Holy Mother. When Ramón rode up to the house to say goodbye, Isabel turned and walked inside.

Tears stung Consuelo's eyes, for she saw Ramón was leading Mirlo. It was almost more than she could bear to lose this little pet. She blinked back the tears and stared defiantly at Ramón and her weary, cowed father.

"The mare is yours, Consuelo," Ramón declared expansively, his dark eyes gleaming, his smile self-satisfied. "My birthday gift to you."

"Your generosity is beyond belief, *señor*," Consuelo replied sarcastically, then felt ashamed, for it wasn't Ramón's fault her father had gambled away the horses. She was filled with relief that she wouldn't lose her Mirlo.

Disregarding her tone, Ramón gazed fondly down at her. "I know how much Mirlo means to you, my girl." In that look, she saw the charm that had intrigued so many women.

"*Gracias,* Ramón," Consuelo murmured, reaching out to stroke the mare's silky head, wishing she felt more grateful for what Ramón obviously saw as a generous gesture.

Consuelo reminded herself that Ramón had been a child of poverty. He grew up on the outskirts of San Luis Obispo, where it was whispered his mother serviced the soldiers for money to feed her numerous children. He never knew his father, and he had left home early. When the coming of the Americans made it easier for him to acquire land, he chose the less desirable land in the mountains. There were rumors about the origin of his money…about the *bandidos* who hid out at Rancho Santa Lucia. Yet she was certain he'd never forgotten his desperate childhood, for beneath the veneer of charm there was a blustering arrogance, as though he meant to get even for that childhood.

"Ah, Consuelo," he said now in a cajoling tone. "You know I'm a generous man. You'll know the extent of my generosity when you are my wife."

Consuelo turned her furious gaze on Don Augustino, who seemed to have absented himself from the scene except in body. He would not look at her. Dear God, she thought, had he gambled her away, too? Was she, like the Estrada horses, mortgaged to Ramón in payment for her father's gambling debts?

"Goodbye, *señor,*" she said coolly to Ramón. "Sancho will take my mare to the pasture now." Her mind in turmoil, she turned and walked into the house.

Don Augustino refused dinner, saying he would go at once to his siesta. At sunset, he rose for a bowl of the soup Rosa had made from leftovers, then retired once more. He did not want to talk.

Consuelo and Isabel talked half the night, distractedly trying to figure a way out of the dilemma Don Augustino had brought upon them. The Estrada horses, famous for their speed and endurance, were gone, except for the few culls left for the use of the vaqueros and the don. Her father had control of the property, and Consuelo was certain he would now have to begin to sell it off to raise money to live on. Neither of the women had any idea how many, or how few of the don's cattle still roamed the hills.

"The crops were good this year," Isabel said wearily as the hour grew late. "With the beef we can slaughter, and our beans and corn, at least we won't go hungry."

"But the land taxes will soon be due," Consuelo said, her anger rising at the thought of paying the hated Anglo tax.

"And must be paid in gold or American money." Isabel sounded utterly defeated. "I can't think what we will do, Consuelo. I'm too tired to think, I'll go to bed and pray to our Holy Mother to help us."

Consuelo had little hope for help from that quarter, but she said nothing, for her aunt was deeply religious. After a moment, as Isabel rose wearily and drew her rebozo about her shoulders, Consuelo said, with far more confidence than she felt, "Tomorrow I'll ride to Cambria and talk to Vicente."

The morning sky was a brilliant, cloudless blue. The off-shore wind still blew seaward bringing the warmth of the inland valleys with it. Consuelo stood on the veranda waiting for Sancho to bring her mare. She was dressed for her ride in dark cotton pantaloons beneath her best calico skirt, a loose linen blouse and tan cotton jacket. The sidesaddles used by the Anglo ladies were awkward to her, and the pantaloons allowed her ride astride, even in town.

She had little hope that Vicente could offer a solution, beyond a loan to keep the rancho going temporarily. And Vicente was careful; he wouldn't loan money with no guarantees, not even to old friends.

It was Rafael, not Sancho, who led the mare up to the hitching rack in front of the adobe fence of the courtyard. Consuelo was annoyed to see that he hadn't changed the dirty pants she'd noticed yesterday. The red stains where he had fallen from his horse still clung to his dark cotton trousers.

Cinnabar red. Vicente's words about the rebozo Lucas Morgan had given her came back like a thunderclap. The

mountains were full of prospectors looking for cinnabar red
ore. Quicksilver!

"Rafael!" she cried, so sharply the old fellow jumped.
"Where did you fall? Where did you get the red dirt on your
pants?"

He looked embarrassed. "*Señorita,* I'm so sorry. I had no
others to change to."

"Never mind," she said, excitement mounting inside her
now. "Get a horse and take me to the place at once." As
Rafael ran to do her bidding, she wondered whether the
Holy Mother had answered Isabel's petitions.

Rafael took her to an arroyo among low hills thick with
oak and manzanita. A spring seeped from the earth so that
the area was much overgrown with weeds and grass. Perhaps, Consuelo thought, it was because of this growth that
the cinnabar-red earth had escaped prospectors' eyes. The
place was on Estrada land, of that she was certain.

Rafael hacked at the hillside with a hatchet he had
brought. Sunlight gleamed on the red ore. As its warmth
penetrated, tiny droplets of quicksilver seeped to the surface, glittering rich and unexpected in the dirt.

Quickly, Consuelo filled her kerchief with the red earth.
Then she sent Rafael home and whipped Mirlo in the direction of Cambria.

Vicente was nearly as excited as she when Consuelo un-
tied her kerchief and laid it on his desk. The boomtown aura
in Cambria was infectious. He'd filed claims for enough
clients to be certain that this was, indeed, cinnabar.

"And on rancho land?" he inquired, his eyes gleaming.
"We'll file a claim at once. I'll advance the money to prove
the ore, and then, my dear, you can sell to a mining syndi-
cate and Rancho Estrada will be solvent again."

He had listened, serious-faced, to her tale of financial
woe, and now seemed genuinely pleased that here was a way
out.

"How much?" she demanded, and he laughed.

"A moment ago you were broke, and now you start dickering." Vicente sobered. "It depends on how rich the ore assays are, and how big the vein seems to be." He looked thoughtful. "My cousin Henry worked at the New Idria mines. I'll ask him to look it over after the claim is filed."

"We'll have to give you a share in payment, Vicente," she said. "As I told you, there's no money to pay anything or anyone."

"Of course." Vicente said with a knowing smile. "But now, my lovely wife would never forgive me if I didn't bring you home to take dinner with us."

Consuelo rode slowly out of Cambria to the coast road, where pines shadowed the dusty track. Angela had urged her to stay and visit longer, but this offshore wind had made her restless. Perhaps it was the unfamiliar heat, pouring out from the interior valleys. She had relaxed and laughed and talked at the Rios's little house, relieved that there seemed a way out of the financial dilemma her father had created. Now she wondered at the sudden tension that seized her.

Reluctantly she admitted to herself that her friends' talk of Lucas Morgan had left her filled with a vague yearning. He had brought home his lighter boat, they said. His workers were putting up a warehouse, as well as hauling rock for the foundation of the pier.

So he was back from San Simeon already. Glancing up at the sun, she decided there was plenty of time to ride to Estero Bay and see what Lucas Morgan had accomplished. She allowed herself the reckless hope that one day an Estrada cinnabar mine would ship flasks of quicksilver from Lucas's wharf.

The autumn sun was brilliant in a cloudless sky, the hot wind stirring the willows as she rode down the hills to Coyote Creek. Sea gulls cried out, wheeling above her, then planing back toward the beach out of sight beyond the willows.

Beavers had dammed the creek, making a little pond beneath the overhanging willows. It looked enticing on this hot day, she thought, then jerked Mirlo to a halt, stunned by the sight of a man splashing in the water.

Lucas turned at the sound of her arrival. They stared at each other in silence. The moment seemed suspended in time there in the warm autumn air with only the distant cry of seabirds to break the spell.

A hot, inexorable flame spread through her. She could not look away from that pale, strong body, the chest downed with dark wet hair, nor could she speak. Her throat, her chest, her heart, all seemed strangled by a need that grew and grew, drawing her to this man she had sworn to hate. She forced her gaze away as Lucas waded to shore, seized the pants he had hung on a willow limb and quickly pulled them on.

Breathing hard, he walked barefoot across the grass to stand beside her horse. Dear Lord, he thought, she is so beautiful, so proud, and I want her as I've never wanted another woman.

"The workers are taking their siesta," he said, well aware how lame his words sounded. "I'd thought to cool off before I went back to work."

Her face was scarlet and she was looking everywhere except at him. Finally, she seemed to regain her composure and spoke crisply. "Vicente was bragging how much you've accomplished. I thought I'd see for myself."

Lucas smiled up at her, his heart pounding at her fragrant nearness. "If you'll ride to the beach with me, I'll show you what I've done."

After pulling on his boots and donning his cotton shirt, Lucas quickly mounted his waiting horse and led the way down the willow-lined creek to the beach.

"This is Morgan's Landing," he said with a wave of his hand, and Consuelo stared in disbelief at all he had built in this short time. The warehouse, on a rock foundation, was roofed and the siding nearly finished. Huge timber pilings lay stacked above high-tide level. In the Indian camp farther down the beach, the quiet of siesta prevailed, except for the distant wail of a baby.

Consuelo studied the scene in silence, determined not to think of the moments at the creek, of Lucas's virile body and the primitive, almost overwhelming longing that had surged through her as she stared at him. She shoved the thought away, half-listening as he told, with pardonable pride, of his plans for Morgan's Landing.

The lighter boat was tied up at a temporary dock built on the beach. He must find a pile driver soon, he said, to set the great supporting timbers firmly in place. Without it, he wouldn't be able to complete the wharf before the winter storms.

He had accomplished more than she could ever have imagined. She told herself vehemently that he was only another Anglo taking over Californio land, enriching himself at the expense of the old settlers. "All done with stolen gold," she said in a cutting tone, and wished instantly to recall the words.

Lucas's blue eyes widened in surprise, and his face twisted in an expression of chagrin. "I intend to repay it all," he protested quickly. "Once the wharf is operating."

For a moment their eyes warred, and it was Consuelo who looked away. When Lucas spoke, his voice was even and polite. "May I offer you a cup of coffee before you ride back to the rancho?"

Why didn't she just say no and be gone? Consuelo berated herself as she followed Lucas up the dim trail along the grassy creek bank. Why had she come here in the first place, except for idle curiosity?

At Lucas's tiny lumber shanty, scarcely big enough to hold his bedding, bundles of clothing, tools and food, he reined up and dismounted. Consuelo watched him walk toward her, something fierce and hot growing in her inner self, some need beyond denying. When he paused beside her horse, reaching up to encircle her waist with his big hands, his eyes warm as the blue skies above them, she knew the outcome was inevitable.

Her heart beat so wildly, she was certain it would burst from her chest as Lucas lifted her down. They touched—her breasts against his shoulder, then sliding down his chest, igniting a flame that filled her veins with fire.

Lucas's strong arms were around her, holding her against his body. He bent his head toward hers, and Consuelo was consumed by the desire burning in his hot blue eyes.

His mouth covered hers, gently at first, then more demanding, his tongue teasing at her lips. A shudder of desire shook her body, and Consuelo strained against him, her arms around his neck, her whole being given up to a longing that had been building since the first moment she looked into his eyes.

Yet, when he bent to kiss her pulsing throat, she managed to murmur a hoarse "No, Lucas," before all the years of training and tradition, all the old hatreds, fled and she was once more lost in his kiss.

"Consuelo...beautiful love." Lucas kissed the cleft of her breasts where she had unbuttoned her blouse on this hot day. Her fingers threaded through his crisp brown hair, holding him against her, wanting the burning moistness of his mouth against her breast.

Their mouths locked once more. Lucas's hands moved down her back, cupping her hips against him so she could feel the fierceness of his desire, that same urgency throbbing through her own body.

Still raining kisses on her face, Lucas lifted her easily in his strong arms. Blind with longing, she did not object, not even when he laid her on the grass beneath the willows. He was beside her, holding her, kissing her mouth, her throat, pushing away her blouse to tease her taut nipples with his tongue.

"Lucas," she whispered, taking his face in her two hands and lifting her lips to his. His eyes blazed with a longing that found an answer in her aching body.

His hand moved along her thigh, lifting her skirt. His touch was gentle, yet it set her afire. Rising need poured through her, until she wanted only the feel of his skin against hers. With careful hands, he removed her pantaloons.

Exquisite sensations followed the trail his gentle fingers made along her thighs. They found the throbbing center of her, and she gasped with unexpected pleasure. Again and again, those fingers stroked and teased until tension lifted her hips to meet his touch. She moaned softly against his mouth, then cried out as the bubble of pleasure expanded and burst, leaving her trembling.

Lucas's breath was hoarse and hot against her throat. Pushing himself away, he pulled off his shirt, his boots, his trousers with frantic haste. Then he gathered her again into his arms. Those warm hands were everywhere on her skin, arousing the nerves to fever pitch.

She let him take her hand and guide her to caress his hot, silken manhood. A fierce, undeniable need poured through her. "Lucas, please," she cried.

"I don't want to hurt you, sweet Consuelo," he whispered, looking lovingly into her face.

The need pounding within her could not be denied. Of its own volition, her body lifted, straining against him. "Please..." she sighed.

With exquisite care, his fingers probed, opening the way. At his touch inside her, her thighs tightened convulsively. "Please, Lucas. Please."

Slowly he pressed against her, taking his time, his warm eyes watching her face.

Consuelo could bear it no longer. Grasping his hips in her hands, she flung her body against his and took him into the hot, aching depths of her. The pain surprised her, and she cried out.

"Sweet love," he whispered. "Lie still, only a minute, and the hurt will pass."

The sensation of Lucas inside her swept away all memory of the fleeting pain. Instinctively, Consuelo lifted herself to him, wanting all of him.

"My love," he whispered, holding her, thrusting against her, gently at first, then with mounting urgency. Her body answered his in a wildly increasing tempo.

The green willows hanging above them were lost in a hazy vortex. Sensation built and built until her whole being seemed to explode in such utter rapture her heart stopped beating. A primitive cry of release broke from her throat.

She heard Lucas cry out and felt him burst within her. Then he was kissing away the tears of joy on her face, his heart pounding wildly against her own.

Lucas lay beside her, cradling her against him, his eyes closed as his breathing slowly eased. Only the hot wind rustling the willows broke their sated silence.

Passion ebbed away, like a receding tide. Reality brought a sudden, cold stab of regret, and Consuelo drew in a sharp, painful breath. She had committed a grievous sin with a man she had declared her enemy.

At the sound, Lucas's arms tightened around her and his mouth, gentle and sweet, sought hers. Instinctively, she clung to him, knowing it was wrong, knowing now she should never have come here, but still seeking comfort in his embrace. The night he first kissed her should have been warning enough of the fires that would blaze between them.

How could it be a sin? she thought, as he turned his head to kiss her throat. It was so natural, so perfectly inevitable, and, God forgive her, so wonderful.

Stroking his hair as he lay with his face against her breast, Consuelo pictured again the boy she had heard about on that day of sharing on the hilltop above Estero Bay. A boy who had suffered, yet grown into a gentle and loving man. What she felt for him was more than desire, more than passion.

"Querido mío," she whispered, flooded with joy at the truth of the words.

Lucas lifted his head, a questioning look on his face.

"My love," she translated and felt her heart leap and pound at the adoration in his eyes.

"Querida mía," Lucas answered, and kissed her softly.

He lay beside her and pillowed her head on his broad shoulder. Carefully rearranging her clothing, he smoothed back her hair and looked into her face. "I knew you were my love, Consuelo, from the moment I opened my eyes and saw you standing over my bed."

She smiled at him, curling close against his body, certain now that Lucas Morgan was her fated lover. That he was Anglo meant nothing. She had fought him and tried to hate him, only to end up loving him. If only this hot, golden afternoon could last forever, here beneath the willows, in Lucas's arms, the rest of the world lost and forgotten, no sins to confess, no family to consider.

Sea gulls circled, screaming, in the hot blue sky. From the beach came the babble of voices as the Indian workmen returned from their siesta. The sound of hammers followed.

Reluctantly Lucas released her, sat up and reached for his trousers. "We have to go," he said, looking tenderly down at her.

Tears stung her eyes. "I wish—" she began, and he drew her up into his arms, his mouth warm and sweet against hers.

"I wish it never had to end," she whispered against his shoulder. She could never have guessed at the perfect, blinding joy she had found in his arms. It didn't matter who or what either of them might be. The past faded, and there was only the passion they had shared, that she longed to share again.

Lucas cupped her cheek in one hand and looked at her with eyes of love. "Someday, my darling Consuelo, it will be forever."

He helped her with her clothes, his strong fingers trembling as he buttoned her blouse. And his touch once more ignited the flames his loving had damped down.

"I don't want to leave you," she cried, pressing against him, wanting him as urgently as she had just a short time ago.

Lucas smiled. "Soon, I promise. I'll build a place where we can be together." He searched her face, his eyes reflecting the longing aching through her. "Tomorrow," he promised, "I'll come to Rancho Estrada and ask your father for your hand."

Chapter Nine

The offshore wind had died in the night, and a high thin fog hung over the coast. Lucas rose stiffly from his cold bed, hurrying to start a fire and set his blackened coffeepot to boil. This shack was little protection from the weather, and would be useless when the winter rains began. He planned to have moved into the warehouse by then. From there, he could oversee the Indians and the building of the wharf.

Yesterday had changed everything. Now it seemed more urgent to build a house where he could bring Consuelo—almost as urgent as building the wharf itself. He had spent a restless night, filled with dreams that left him aching with longing for her. It had been madness to lose all self-control that way and make love to her. But she had wanted it as much as he, and her pleasure had brought him a wondrous joy.

Over the years he'd been with many women, as sailors do, but not one of them had engraved her image on his heart as Consuelo had done from the very beginning. Now he couldn't imagine a life without her.

For weeks he'd watched for some sign that she returned his feelings. Her resentment of the troubles other Anglos had caused had stood between them. Yesterday, at last, she'd let herself trust him. He meant to ask Don Augustino for her hand in marriage, and he'd promised this would be the day. He'd made love to her, might even have given her a child. All his plans had to be speeded up. Even the wharf had to somehow be built faster.

As he drank the scalding coffee from a tin cup, Lucas thought with faint apprehension of confronting Don Augustino. There would be difficulties with the church, too. The old Catholic priest, Father Amateo, was very fond of Consuelo, and would be protective. There would be banns to be read. It didn't matter, he told himself. Whatever he needed to do to make Consuelo Estrada his wife, he would do it.

"Señor Morgan!" someone called in a breathless voice, and Lucas heard a runner crashing through the brush along the creek bank. "Señor Morgan!" Soledad appeared around a clump of willows and stood panting before Lucas. "There is a ship signaling in the bay, *Señor.*"

Lucas seized the signal flags propped in a corner of his shack, and followed Soledad back to the beach.

Soledad ran easily, on broad bare feet. He was taller than the other Indians, and lighter-skinned. His black eyes were bright and intelligent, and he was obviously a natural leader. Lucas had quickly come to trust him, and to rely on him for communication with the workers who didn't speak English.

Lucas signaled from the beach, the red flags snapping in the suddenly brisk breeze. Then he read the return signal through his glass. The *Electra* was not off-loading. Her captain would be coming ashore. Lucas had known Captain Roberts from his days in San Francisco. He was an upstanding fellow, but Lucas was puzzled that he would come ashore simply for a visit.

He sat on a rock beside the driftwood fire the workers made each morning, and watched the ship's dinghy plow through the waves toward him.

George Roberts, a heavy-set, muscular man with a bushy red mustache, waded ashore and shook Lucas's hand heartily. "I heard about your franchise, Lucas," he said, looking around at the pile of timbers, at the Indians nailing the sidewalls of the warehouse. "Wanted to see it. I've always wondered why somebody didn't build a pier in this cove. No high surf or swells like those that plague San Simeon."

"I'll be glad to have your business," Lucas said, offering him a mug of coffee Soledad's wife had brought. "Once the pier is under way, I'll send out fliers. In the meantime, I'll be doing a lightering business here."

Roberts gazed dubiously at the huge timbers to be used for pilings. "Looks to me like you need a pile driver."

"Can't build a wharf without one," Lucas agreed. "Pick me up on your way back to San Francisco. I figure on renting one there and towing it back here."

"Why not come with me now?" Roberts asked, sipping the scalding coffee carefully. "They've just finished the pilings for a new wharf at Santa Barbara. The pile driver they used will have to be towed back to San Francisco. I'd wager you can get a better price because you'll be towing it halfway back for them."

Lucas stared at him, his mind whirling with possibilities. There were few pile drivers on the northern coast, and the chance of finding one so close hadn't even occurred to him. He'd accepted the idea of waiting the weeks for a ship to San Francisco and the time it would take to tow the pile driver south. Excitement filled him at the thought of beginning that essential work within so short a time. He could lock the warehouse, send Soledad and the Indians back to Bain's Settlement to await his return. It meant that he could build a place for Consuelo much sooner.

And yet, he'd promised her that today he would speak to her father and make the marriage arrangements. How could he break that promise when she had given herself to him so beautifully and completely? The thought of her turned his body hot with longing. He walked away from Captain Roberts, pacing the sand as he struggled with a decision.

It would be another month before he could even get to San Francisco to look for a pile driver. Everything depended on the progress of this wharf—the home he would build for Consuelo and the income from wharfage fees that would be their livelihood.

Captain Roberts was waiting, watching Lucas's hesitancy with a quizzical expression. "We sail before the tide changes," he said.

Everything depended on finishing the wharf. Everything! "Give me an hour," Lucas told him, "to secure things. I'll sail to Santa Barbara with you."

While Captain Roberts and the sailors who had rowed him ashore drank coffee and wolfed down the enchiladas Soledad's young wife brought them, Lucas carried his goods from the shanty to be locked in the warehouse. He put the horse into Soledad's care, with instructions to take the Indians back to their homes until Lucas sent for them.

"One more thing you must do for me," Lucas told the young man. "Carry a message to Rancho Estrada for Señorita Consuelo."

"Beloved," he wrote on a page torn from the ledger he had purchased to keep track of expenses. Then he stared, almost unbelievingly, at a word he had never written or used before.

"I must break my promise to come to you today. Our entire future together depends on the wharf I am building, and I know you will understand that is the reason I must go to Santa Barbara within the hour, while transportation is available."

He explained briefly about the pile driver, and promised he would come to her immediately on his return.

"I love you, my dearest Consuelo," he finished the note. "With all my heart I yearn for the day when you are my wife, and we can be together always."

Folding the note, he gave it to Soledad. "Take my horse and go at once," he commanded. "This must be delivered today."

Consuelo awakened early, her body aching with longing. She had been dreaming of Lucas Morgan, and the incredible magic of their coming together. She wanted him inside her, thrusting against her until her body soared and trembled and she was lost in a wild, blind joy.

Sighing, she turned on her pillow to look across the bedroom. Isabel's bed on the opposite side of the room was empty. She was up and gone, her day's work already begun.

Lucas would be here today! The thought brought Consuelo upright in the bed, her heart thundering with anticipation. The unfamiliar soreness between her thighs was a vivid reminder that she had sinned. Deliberately, she fought down the qualms that knowledge brought. After all, Lucas was coming to ask her father's permission to marry her, and she would insist it be given. There were obstacles, but she would not think of them now.

She was helping clear up from breakfast when she heard the sound of horses, and Rafael calling a greeting. Quickly setting down the platter of tortillas, she ran out to the courtyard. Her heart fell in disappointment when she saw Vicente and his cousin Henry walking toward her.

Over coffee and hot tortillas filled with melted cheese, which Isabel served them at the dining table, Vicente told Consuelo of Henry's work at the New Idria quicksilver mines. He'd been discharged and blacklisted by a dictatorial superintendent for a minor infraction. Unable to find work in other mines, he had been prospecting in the Cambria area.

"The ore you brought assayed very high," Vicente told Consuelo. "I've filed your claim, but Henry should see the place, to know how deep the vein might be and whether it would be worthwhile to work it."

Consuelo tried to concentrate on what Vicente was saying, all of it important to the future of Rancho Estrada. But a part of her strained for the sound of another horseman—Lucas Morgan come to claim her as his betrothed.

"We'll need you to ride with us, Consuelo."

Startled from her thoughts, she stared at him, then stammered, "I'm expecting a visitor. Rafael found the place. He can guide you."

Vicente's eyes narrowed, his lips pursed as he studied her flushed face. "Rafael is old, and he is a servant. You are the owner. It is your responsibility to help us." He frowned. "I thought this was of utmost importance to you?"

"Of course it is," she muttered reluctantly.

"Then there's no question," Vicente said decisively. "We'll leave at once."

Consuelo sighed, knowing she couldn't refuse to do something Vicente thought so important. Lucas had work of his own this morning. Undoubtedly he wouldn't arrive until afternoon, and she could manage to be back by then. If he came earlier, Isabel could ask him to wait for her. Yet she hated to be away when he came seeking her hand. And she wanted to touch him, feel the warmth of his arms around her and bask in the closeness she had needed for so many lonely years.

Vicente paid his respects to Don Augustino. Since Consuelo's birthday, the don had languished in his bed, with no particular symptoms beyond an overpowering fatigue. To Consuelo's relief, Vicente did not trouble the don by telling him the nature of his errand.

"He's not himself," Vicente told her with a frown, as they waited for Rafael to bring up the horses.

"No," Consuelo agreed, "he's not."

At first, she'd thought her father was pretending illness, trying to coerce her into marrying Ramón. But today he looked truly ill. Stung with guilt that she had neglected him, she asked Vicente to send the doctor and Father Amateo out to see her father.

Consuelo sat on a rock at the edge of the arroyo and watched Henry Rios, with his shovel and hatchet, explore the red outcrops of cinnabar. Vicente followed him, his dark eyes bright with excitement. Rafael carried the heavy tools.

Would Lucas be hurt that she wasn't there to greet him? she wondered. Would he wait for her? She hoped he wouldn't approach her father without her. But he had so much to do at the wharf.... She paced restlessly, watching the men, impatient to be finished and back at the rancho, so she could meet Lucas.

"What is it worth?" she asked when Henry told her the prospects for developing a mine here seemed excellent.

Vicente and Henry exchanged dubious glances.

"The Keystone Mine is for sale for twenty thousand dollars," Vicente replied.

He paused significantly. Twenty thousand dollars, Consuelo thought—to take care of her father, and Isabel, and Rosa and Rafael, and the vaqueros and their families, and the Indians. So many people. The amount seemed to shrink.

"That's for an operating mine," Henry said, "with furnace in place, roads built. This place—" he made a sweeping gesture "—needs everything. That requires a lot of money."

Consuelo's heart sank at his words. "Will we be able to sell it, Vicente?" she asked, fearful of another disappointment.

"Of course." He smiled at her. "We shall most certainly try."

Soledad tied his horse at the hitching rack, and walked slowly across the courtyard to the veranda. He had lived here as a small boy, and remembered the cool vastness of the adobe with a child's pleasure. It was unfortunate to arrive in the middle of siesta, but he couldn't wait, and Lucas had said to deliver the message immediately. He must hurry back to Estero Bay, where the other men were making ready for the move back to Bain's Settlement. His wife and his baby son were waiting for him.

He walked into the great room, still and silent, then back to the veranda lined with doors. A voice, muttering restlessly, sounded nearby, and Soledad peered inside to see the don tossing in his rumpled bed.

"What do you want?" Don Augustino's voice was harsh, reflecting his physical discomfort. "Come in here!"

Hesitantly, Soledad approached the vast bed where the don lay. "A message, Don Augustino, for the *señorita* from Señor Morgan. Is she here?"

"No," Don Augustino growled, glowering at him. "Señor Morgan, eh? Give me the message." He held out his hand peremptorily.

Soledad trembled, at a loss as to what to do. Señor Morgan had said the message was for Señorita Consuelo. Would it be wise to trust it to her father for delivery?

"Here, you!" The don's voice rose, harsh with impatience.

All his life, Soledad had been commanded by the Californios. Not until the coming of Lucas Morgan had he commanded anyone except his wife. Almost automatically, he surrendered the note to Don Augustino's grasp. He could only stare in helpless silence as the old man crumpled the note in his hand without even looking at it.

Consuelo waved one last time as Vicente and Henry rode away. They had returned from the hills to a bountiful dinner, provided by Isabel, but no sign of Lucas Morgan.

Shading her eyes against the afternoon sun, Consuelo stared down the coast road. Sunlight reflected off an ocean like burnished silver. No dust rose from the road other than that of Vicente and Henry's horses. Lucas Morgan had not come. The fire he'd kindled burned in her loins. He would be here, she told herself. He had promised.

"*Señorita?*" Rafael stood beside her, sombrero in his brown, wrinkled hands, a different expression on his ancient face. "Will we have our own mine to make quicksilver?"

Consuelo sighed and turned to the old man. The day was not yet gone; something must have delayed Lucas. Shaking her head, she said, "It takes much money to develop a mine. I think Vicente will sell the claim for us."

"We could work it ourselves," he insisted stubbornly, and she stared at him in surprise.

"I suppose we could if we had the money," she answered slowly. "We have enough vaqueros and Indians with nothing to do now that we have no horses or cattle."

"But Rancho Estrada has cattle," Rafael protested. "Every spring at rodeo we brand cattle."

"Why doesn't my father sell them?" she demanded, amazed at this bit of information. Why hadn't she paid attention and known of this? she chided herself. A twinge of self-pity caught at her and she thought how incredibly difficult it was to set aside the passive, unquestioning woman's role she had been brought up to assume. She had just begun to try to take up the reins of the rancho her father had let slip away from him. Now she realized she was ignorant of far too many things about rancho business. She knew only of the bills to be paid.

Even when she married Lucas she would have to take charge here. Papá could no longer be trusted. She must learn the business thoroughly.

Rafael shrugged in reply to her question. "The don thinks only of selling hides like in the old days. But no one buys hides now." His old eyes sharpened. "Don Ramón sells his cattle for beef in San Francisco, and he is rich."

And my father would have me wed to him, Consuelo thought. But now there was Lucas, a different and exciting life ahead. Later she would think about selling cattle and the mining claim. Once more she turned to strain her eyes toward the coast road, longing for the sight of Lucas Morgan.

Twilight lay over Rancho Estrada. In the distance, the glimmering sea faded into darkness. Consuelo stood at the courtyard fence. Her eyes ached so from watching, they felt burned and dry as though they might shrivel in upon themselves. Behind her the night sounds of the rancho faded— the women patting tortillas for breakfast, a child wailing from the married vaqueros' quarters, laughter beside the camp fire at the Indians' *ranchería*.

Her heart felt like cold lead inside her chest. Unshed tears gathered painfully behind her eyes. Lucas Morgan had said he loved her and he had promised to marry her. But perhaps such promises came easily to an Anglo eager to take a girl's maidenhead. She had given herself to him and had committed a mortal sin in his arms gladly, even willingly. Even now, the memory of that rapture set her blood afire.

Surely he would come tomorrow. Suddenly she grew apprehensive that something dreadful might have happened to him.

She trusted him, she reassured herself, well aware how difficult it was for her to trust. Growing up, she had learned not to trust others—not her feckless, gambling father, not the mother who died, not her careless brother, not even Isabel, who always took the don's side. And certainly not the hated Anglos. Caught up in passion, she had allowed herself to trust Lucas Morgan. With a whole heart, she had accepted his declarations of love, and his promise to marry her. She would not believe that, like the others, he had deceived and failed her. He would come tomorrow.

But fear clutched at her heart. Perhaps this was retribution. She had sinned grievously, and had believed the sin would still lead to happiness. Consuelo bent her head on her arms folded upon the adobe wall, and wept.

Chapter Ten

The perfect crescent of Santa Barbara Bay lay smooth and quiet in the windless day. Lucas stood beside Captain Roberts in the wheelhouse as the *Electra* dropped anchor and the sailors rushed to lower the dinghy.

Offshore, the Channel Islands lay in a glowing haze: Santa Cruz, Santa Rosa, Anacapa. The village of Santa Barbara nestled within its amphitheater of high hills and distant mountains. Autumn colors were already fading on those hills. Above the town the old mission gleamed white in the sunshine, its belfry a landmark for miles at sea. In the town below, closer to the golden curve of beach, the red tile roofs of the houses surrounded the old presidio amid ancient oak trees.

"We'll go ashore on the first boat," Captain Roberts said, and called the mate to take over. He grinned at Lucas as he indicated the new wharf projecting out into the bay, still not long enough for the *Electra* to anchor beside it. "There's your pile driver."

From this distance, Lucas studied the pile driver mounted on a barge tied to the new wharf. Its heavy hammer rested on the barge deck, held in place by the steel hoist and cables, and attached to the steam boiler that powered it. He must make arrangements with the owner at once, even before he took up Captain Roberts's invitation to visit at the house of Don Carlos Silva. The *Electra* had brought Don Carlos's young son, Antonio, back from San Francisco along with his tutor, a supercilious Englishman. They joined Lucas and Roberts in the dinghy.

A long ground swell lifted the boat and laid it on the beach. It grated against sand as the sailors leaped out to seize the gunwales and run it up on the land.

Before he set off with Antonio and the haughty tutor, Captain Roberts pointed out the large adobe house that belonged to Don Carlos. "Join us when you've finished your business," he said.

Lucas watched them walk uphill into the town. Antonio was little older than Lucas had been when he first went to sea. Quite a different life, he told himself as he turned down the beach toward the wharf. Antonio had been raised in the kind of luxury this country afforded, sent to school in San Francisco. He had confided to Lucas that he would be going to Spain in the spring to complete his education. He was an arrogant young fellow, as he obviously felt befitted his station in life. It crossed Lucas's mind that perhaps Consuelo's brother had been like that. Even she, a girl, had more than a bit of the arrogance that seemed part of the blood.

The thought of her struck him with an intense need to be done here and on his way back to her. He hurried toward the pile driver barge, where the owner, one Patrick Murphy, greeted him heartily.

"A wharf at Estero Bay!" he exclaimed when Lucas had explained his errand. "About time." In a slight Irish brogue, he told Lucas he had been waiting for a tow back to San Francisco. Could Lucas arrange it?

"Captain Roberts of the *Electra* has agreed to the tow," Lucas said, relieved at the man's willingness to come to the isolated Estero Bay. "After the job is finished, I'll arrange a tow to San Francisco."

They settled on the price and the arrangements over whiskey at a nearby waterfront bar. Promising to contact him tomorrow, Lucas told Patrick goodbye and made his way along the dusty streets to the house of Don Carlos Silva.

The vast adobe house was built in a square, with passageways on all four sides leading into a central courtyard paved with tiles. Brilliant flowers tumbled from hanging pots attached to the roof of the veranda. A small colorfully tiled fountain tinkled softly in the center of the courtyard.

Lucas found Captain Roberts and Don Carlos drinking wine in the shade of the veranda. The don, a middle-aged man with thick black hair and a heavy black mustache, wore immaculate white trousers and a white shirt with a brightly embroidered yoke.

He called one of the servants to bring Lucas a glass for wine, then sent her to rebuke a group of children playing loudly on the patio.

"The captain tells me you're building a wharf at Estero Bay," he said politely, and listened with interest as Lucas told of his plans.

The bottle of wine, from his own vineyards the don said, was nearly empty when the doña appeared. When he saw her crossing the courtyard, the don winked at them. "She's come to tell us it's time to stop drinking and begin eating," he said with an affectionate laugh.

Doña Ramona was a plump, sweet-faced woman with a brilliant smile. As she stood beside her husband, asking them in to supper, her hand sought his.

An ache grew inside Lucas's chest as he watched the tender interchange of glances between the don and his wife. Two small children hurtled across the courtyard and threw their arms about the doña's waist. Laughing, she bent to hug both at once.

This was what he longed for, Lucas thought, watching the scene with a smile. A home, a place of his own, a love of his own. All the things he'd never known, only observed as an envious spectator.

Happiness erased the old ache, for now with Consuelo all this would be his. He would build a home for her, and his heart leaped at the thought of the nights of love they would share. The laughing children ran to do some bidding of their mother's, and Lucas let himself dream of his own children, his and Consuelo's. Tears stung his eyes, and he blinked them away, knowing how foolish he would seem if his companions could guess his thoughts.

* * *

"We must leave you this evening," Don Carlos said as the Indian women were clearing away the remains of their supper. The dining room of the Silva house was centered by a long, elaborately carved table. Sideboards on two walls held an array of fine china and silver serving pieces. Handwoven draperies in muted colors hung at the floor-to-ceiling windows.

"The aged grandmother of an old friend has died and we must attend the rosary. You will excuse us, *por favor.*"

Both Lucas and Captain Roberts stood, bowing politely to the doña as they thanked her for the meal.

Don Carlos instructed the serving woman to bring brandy to his guests beside the fire in the sitting room, and with a polite nod departed.

"The don's own brandy," Captain Roberts said, rolling the liquid about in his mouth with a look of pleasure on his grizzled face. He smoothed his thinning red hair and leaned back comfortably in the cushioned chair.

"He lives well, doesn't he?" Lucas looked around the well-furnished room. There were Chinese rugs on the wooden floors, comfortable cowhide armchairs, and cushioned settees covered with bright homespun materials.

Roberts bent to light his cigar, then looked at Lucas, his face serious. "Don Carlos is an old Californio, from the days before the gold rush and the Mexican war that made California a part of the United States." He smiled wryly at Lucas. "Those who came later are known simply as Mexicans—the gold rushers and those who fled the repression in Mexico."

"How is it," Lucas asked, puffing at his own cigar, "that Don Carlos lives well when so many other of the Californios have been reduced to poverty?"

"If you speak of men such as Don Augustino Estrada," Roberts answered, "unfortunately, Augustino is a gambling man. Other than that, he's no different from the rest. The Americans came here after the hide trade ended, happy to lend money to the Californios at ruinous rates. The Californios had always lived by barter, and didn't understand

what was happening to them until they began to lose everything—silver, jewelry, horses, land—to repay the loans."

"Don Carlos owes for all this?" Lucas indicated the lavish furnishings of the room.

Roberts nodded glumly. "And for the education of his
son, who will never have the means to live in the style he's
accustomed to."

Lucas stared into the crackling fire in the wide adobe
fireplace. Back at Rancho Estrada, it had struck him how
sad it was to see the passing of an old way of life. Don Carlos lived on a far more lavish scale than the Estradas; his
descent into poverty would certainly be more painful.

At least Consuelo wouldn't suffer anymore, he vowed to
himself, warmth spreading through his body at the thought
of her. Long ago, he'd vowed to escape the poverty his
mother had always known. The ugliness of it, and the
knowledge of his illegitimacy, had haunted his childhood.
Now he'd nearly succeeded in that escape. He was a man of
property. He'd see that the woman who would be his beloved wife would never experience the pain he and his
mother had known.

Smiling, he leaned back in his chair, letting his mind drift
in contemplation of the happy future.

Next morning, Captain Roberts departed to oversee the
loading of cargo on the *Electra*. He went with Lucas to
speak again to Patrick Murphy and make arrangements for
the tow back to Estero Bay.

"I'll take shares in the wharf for the towage fee," he told
Lucas as they walked back down the beach to where the
Electra's boats waited.

Concealing his relief, Lucas heartily agreed. Pacific
Steamship's gold would not last forever. Once the wharf itself was underway, Vicente had assured him the bank would
loan him money. Roberts's offer simply eased possible financial problems that might arise later.

The *Electra* had to go to San Pedro before returning to
San Francisco. That morning Doña Ramona had kindly in-

vited Lucas to stay with them until the ship returned to Santa Barbara. He quickly agreed, thinking this would give him time to work with Murphy and learn about pile drivers.

Chapter Eleven

The first heavy rains of autumn fell, day after day, making the time seem endless. Dr. Frame and Father Amateo could not come to see Don Augustino, for the roads between the rancho and Cambria were a sea of mud. Confined to the house by the weather, Consuelo stood in the doorway and stared unhappily at the falling rain and the gray, heaving ocean. She couldn't have ridden to Estero Bay in such weather even if pride hadn't held her back.

Lucas Morgan had promised. The sound of his voice still echoed in her mind. *I'll come to the rancho tomorrow and ask your father for your hand.* If only there was some way to plug that inner ear against those words.

She'd believed his words of love, given herself to him with all her heart. She hadn't asked for his promise—her pride would never have allowed that—she had given herself freely. She would never humiliate herself by going to him to ask if his promise was sincere. Dear God, if only there was some way to know why he hadn't come to her.

A sigh escaped her as she leaned her head against the doorjamb. She felt rather than saw, Isabel's curious gaze across the room.

"You should rest, Consuelo," Isabel said, misinterpreting that sigh. "Rest while your father's sleeping." When Consuelo made no reply, she added, "Perhaps the rain will stop tomorrow and Dr. Frame will come."

"Perhaps," Consuelo answered absently, for her thoughts were not of her father although his illness worried her. He still spent most of his time in bed, arising only for the noon meal. He had lost a great deal of weight and seemed very weak.

Where was Lucas? The question played over and over in her mind, as she struggled to believe he had not deceived her. She had trusted him as completely as a woman can trust a man, giving herself to him with wanton joy, going against everything her careful upbringing had taught her.

Pain struck through her with the thought that everyone she had ever trusted had failed her. Papá was a man lost in time and unable to cope with his changing world. Isabel was a poor relation with no power to help and surely no empathy for a young girl in love. Even her mother had failed her by dying when a small child needed her most.

Then there was Felipe. Consuelo could admit now that while she had loved her brother, she had never really trusted him. He loved to tease, and was a bit of a bully, more ready to carouse in the taverns than to take on the responsibility of the rancho.

In the four years after their mother died, Consuelo had spent the winters in Monterey at the school of the Convent of the Sacred Heart. A tutor had come to the rancho to teach Felipe, whom Papá hoped one day to send to Spain to obtain a gentleman's education. After the great drought, when the don's money was gone, so was the tutor. Felipe hadn't cared. Learning hadn't been something he set great store by. It was horse racing, cockfights, bullfights and the monte games and loose women at the taverns that had interested him. She wasn't supposed to know, but she had overheard the gossips saying Felipe had been killed by a jealous lover who fled abroad with the woman in question.

Am I a loose woman now? The idea stunned Consuelo. She had been relieved at the evidence that she hadn't conceived a child in that one passionate encounter. Her guilty secret could remain hers alone.

"But I loved him," she whispered to herself without thinking. And he had called her his love, promising they would be married. The memory of his big hands caressing her sent her heart pounding. It had been too wonderful, too perfect. Surely something urgent had kept him from her. He would come, she promised herself, needing desperately to believe it. She would be in his arms again, uncaring for her sins, only wishing to share his love for all her life.

The next day the rain eased off. A cold wind sent clouds scudding eastward over the mountain, and the ocean rolled in great, heaving swells. Dr. Frame and Father Amateo arrived, riding astride, for no vehicle could negotiate the muddy roads.

They brought a note from Vicente. Consuelo took it from Father Amateo with unconcealed eagerness. Perhaps he would write some news of Lucas. Hurriedly, she ushered the two men into her father's bedroom, then rushed back to the great room where she sat by the fire and tore open the envelope.

Her heart fell as she quickly scanned the paper and saw there was no mention of Lucas. Vicente was trying to sell the mining claim, he wrote, adding that the property taxes would be due next month. Consuelo's spirits sank further. She had hoped for a quick sale of the mining claim to ease their immediate financial situation. They had no money to pay the taxes, and she was certain Vicente knew that. She could ask him for a loan, but the possibility of repayment was dim. George Hearst would be waiting to buy, either at a tax sale, or at whatever price her father would accept.

"The winter grass will start now," Isabel said unexpectedly, startling Consuelo from her unhappy thoughts. She stood in the kitchen doorway, her questioning eyes on Vicente's letter.

Consuelo sighed and waved the letter. "The taxes are due and Vicente hasn't yet sold the cinnabar claim."

Isabel's mouth tightened. "With new grass," she said, "Rafael says the cattle will come down from the hills."

Rafael continued to insist there were many Estrada cattle, and he'd promised to ride with Consuelo to show them once the weather cleared.

"He says he could lead the rodeo," Isabel continued mildly, eyeing Consuelo as though not quite sure she should push this.

"He was once our head vaquero," Consuelo replied. "I'm certain he could." She smoothed out Vicente's note and studied it, frowning. The words *property taxes* stood out as though in bold print.

"The vaqueros have grown lazy and quarrelsome with nothing to do," Isabel added.

Consuelo allowed herself a rueful smile, knowing her aunt would never come right out and suggest the rodeo, merely hint at it. "Property taxes due." She read the words again and knew there was no choice. The mining claim would sell, but perhaps too late. The cattle must be gathered and sold. She decided she would not consult Papá on the subject.

With a decisive nod to Isabel, Consuelo said, "I'll tell Rafael to begin the rodeo at once."

Just then, a grim-faced, Dr. Frame came from Don Augustino's bedroom, stroking his curly brown beard thoughtfully. "Your father has suffered a heart attack," he told Consuelo.

Stricken by the terrifying words, she reached out to clasp Isabel's hand as her aunt came quickly to her side.

Words stuck in Consuelo's throat, but Isabel demanded, "Will he be all right?"

The doctor studied the two women, as though assessing their strength. Finally, he spoke. "I'll be quite frank. His heart is badly damaged, but with rest and care he should survive."

When Consuelo and Isabel turned to each other with relieved smiles, the doctor held up his hand. "But wait. There must be no more brandy or cigars and no more horse racing or gambling. He must be quiet always, with no emotional upsets. Do you understand?"

Consuelo nodded soberly. She loved her father in spite of his many faults, and she knew he loved her in his own off-hand, masculine way. The possibility of losing him was more than she could bear to contemplate. But the doctor's attitude was encouraging, and she must cling to that.

"Consuelo, your papá wishes to see you." Father Amateo came from the bedroom where he had been hearing

Augustino's confession. His ancient dark eyes met hers, but she could read nothing there.

Consuelo hurried to her father's side, leaving Isabel to invite the doctor and Father Amateo to partake of the dinner Rosa was already setting on the table.

"Dr. Frame is very concerned, Papá," Consuelo said. She sat on a low stool beside the bed and clasped her father's hand, determined that he mustn't guess how the doctor's diagnosis had alarmed her.

Guilt clutched her heart with icy fingers as she looked into his gray, haggard face. Had she been so wrapped up in dreams of Lucas Morgan she hadn't noticed how terribly ill her father had become?

"No more brandy, no excitement of any kind. What a life!" Don Augustino was trying to make a joke of it, but there was fear in his dark, sunken eyes.

"You will obey him, won't you, Papá?" she asked, stroking his cold hand.

Don Augustino nodded somberly, then sighed deeply. "Even that is no guarantee, my daughter." Tears welled in his eyes. "I can't bear to think that I might leave you alone, uncared for."

"You mustn't think of it," she protested, her throat tight.

"You must marry soon, Consuelo. And it would please me if you'd consent to wed my good friend, Ramón."

"Ramón!" she cried, unable to control her quick anger. "I've told you, Papá, I don't love Ramón." Her voice fell as she deliberately curbed the anger for fear of provoking him.

"My heart." Papá held her hand in both of his. His wavering voice was pleading, as were his sunken eyes. "You do Ramón ill. He's a wealthy man and he adores you. Anything you desired would be yours." He drew a deep sigh. "You'll learn to love him, and I—I will be at peace."

Hot tears spilled down her face. If Papá loved her, how could he think only of his own feelings in deciding her future? Yet she recalled the doctor's words and feared to cross him.

"Lucas Morgan," she managed to say in a low, shaky voice, "wishes to ask for my hand."

Don Augustino's eyes widened, and he stared at her in disbelief. "That Anglo! A dreamer with nothing. He's spent all his gold. The winter storms will finish off his wharf and he'll have to go back to the sea."

"Please, Papá," she begged, stroking his shoulder in an attempt to soothe his agitation. "Please wait until you speak with Lucas."

He would come, she told herself, desperate to believe it in her longing. Her certainty faded with each day, but she could use him as an excuse to evade promising to wed Ramón.

"What will you do, my daughter?" Father Amateo asked as the two of them strolled the veranda together after siesta. Sunshine came and went as clouds drifted across the sun and were blown away. Dried leaves from the grapevines scraped across the tiled courtyard, where a gray cat slept on top of the adobe wall.

Through tear-blurred eyes, she looked at the kindly old man, stooped in his long priest's robe. He had been her confidant for many years, and the affection between them was that of a kindly uncle and a beloved niece. Today she was glad he'd grown forgetful, and hadn't asked to hear her confession. How could she ever confess to him that she had sinned with Lucas Morgan? Only on the day she and Lucas asked the priest to marry them could she tell the truth.

He sighed and patted her shoulder. "If Felipe were alive, all would be well."

Consuelo stared at his serene face, and resentment boiled in her soul. It wasn't true. She had loved Felipe, but he was always unreliable and untrustworthy, thinking only of a good time. Perhaps he would have settled down and taken charge now that their father was ill, but it did no good to speculate on that. Felipe was dead, and there was only she to save Rancho Estrada.

"You must marry, Consuelo," Father Amateo said. She wondered whether he had spoken with her father, and was certain of it when he added, "Ramón Salazar has long wished to wed you. For your father's sake, I urge you to consent."

Everyone was against her, Consuelo thought in despair. Father Amateo, Papá. And Lucas Morgan had deserted her.

A certainty grew in her that she must go to Estero Bay, for only then could she know the truth. Even if it meant the bitter swallowing of her wounded pride, she had to know.

Isabel disliked Ramón, and Rafael did, too, although it was not Rafael's place to reveal such feelings. Rafael and Rosa had been at Rancho Estrada forever. It was Rafael who had taught her to ride a horse, and had indulgently let a small girl follow him when he rounded up cattle. Perhaps with the help of these people who loved her, she could find a way out of all this trouble without Ramón.

"I'll think about it," she told Father Amateo, and he looked displeased. She knew he had been certain she would meekly consent.

"Not for too long," he said sternly. "Your father wishes to see you safely wed, so that he can die in peace."

"He will not die!" she cried in anguished protest. To her dismay, she began to weep. Father Amateo looked chagrined. He embraced her comfortingly, and spoke no more of marriage.

It began to rain again after Father Amateo and the doctor left. To Consuelo, it seemed the sky was weeping with her for her father's mortality, and for the dreadful future being forced upon her.

The weather cleared the next day, the sky a washed and polished blue above a dark restless ocean. Consuelo had hoped to ride to Estero Bay, but Ramón and his vaqueros arrived just as she and Isabel were eating dinner. They all wore new clothes and bragged loudly of the cattle drive to San Francisco from which they had just returned. Pablo was with them, swaggering in his fancy outfit as he showed off how much better his lot had become now that he worked for Ramón Salazar.

Not bothering to conceal her resentment at the inconvenience, Isabel invited the unexpected visitors to eat, then went into the kitchen to supervise the cooking of another dinner.

Watching Ramón, Consuelo tried to see in his easy arrogance what it was that drew her father's affection. Was it because Ramón had replaced Felipe in Papá's muddled mind? Ramón was handsome in his own way, charming when he meant to be, and an accomplished flirt. She was certain there were many young women along the coast who would be glad to marry him. He was generous with his wealth, and he'd brought a fine wool coat for Papá, as well as a string of silver beads for the disconcerted Isabel.

Ramón solicitously helped Papá dress and come to the table to eat for the first time in many days. The old man beamed on this surrogate son, and exclaimed with pleasure over the gift of a new coat.

"Consuelo," Ramón announced loudly as they were seated at the table. He looked around to make sure everyone was listening. "I've brought a present for you from San Francisco."

Reluctantly, she took the package he thrust into her hand. "Open it," he demanded, smiling, his dark eyes possessive.

Consuelo saw that Isabel had returned. Her gaze, gleaming with disdain, was fixed on Ramón.

Inside the package was a white lace mantilla, the edges embroidered with wildly colorful flowers. "For your wedding," Ramón said with a meaningful smirk.

"Thank you," Consuelo managed to mumble. She laid the mantilla carelessly aside on a chair.

Ramón frowned. Isabel distracted him, setting a steaming bowl of chili con carne in front of him.

He began to tell about his trip to San Francisco. Sensing an opportunity to learn things she might need to know about selling cattle at the San Francisco market, Consuelo sat down again. Flattering Ramón with leading questions, she learned the route he had taken on his cattle drive, the location of the cattle yards south of San Francisco and the prices he had bargained from the buyers.

Her father beamed at her, obviously pleased with her attentiveness to Ramón. Isabel's watchful face had a sardonic cast, as though she guessed Consuelo's ulterior motive.

"I stopped in Cambria on the way," Ramón broke in suddenly. His glance slid over Consuelo, but he spoke directly to Don Augustino. "Your Anglo guest, Señor Morgan. They say he's abandoned his wharf project. Even Vicente, who invested in it, doesn't know where he's gone."

"No!" Consuelo gasped. Pain stabbed through her and she tried desperately to conceal her anguish. "I don't believe it."

Ramón frowned darkly. Don Augustino gave her a strange look, then said in a hard voice, "He was a wandering seaman. Perhaps he found the work too hard."

"Not Lucas Morgan," Consuelo protested, unable to stop her indiscreet words. "He would never give up his dream." But her heart sank.

Ramón's dark eyes were on her with a knowing expression. "You like blue eyes, eh?" he asked sarcastically. "Well, Blue Eyes has sailed away across the blue sea."

She couldn't bear to look at his triumphant face. And even if he didn't speak, she could almost hear her father's, "I told you so." Struggling to keep her face calm, Consuelo stood up, nodding to the men at the table and went out through the kitchen.

The black mare's sides were heaving by the time they reached Coyote Creek. Consuelo pulled her to a halt in front of the warehouse, staring in disbelief at the lock on the door already rusting in the salt air.

High tide washed to the edge of the stacked pilings and receded, long-legged shore birds following to feed on the sand crabs left behind. The Indian camp was only a pile of debris, with blackened rocks where they had made their fires.

So it was true. As Ramón had said, the wanderer from the sea had gone back to the sea. For the first time in the long and agonizing week, Consuelo admitted that hope had never really died in her heart. Not until this moment had she truly believed in Lucas Morgan's defection.

Hot tears poured down her cold face as she rode the mare along the banks of Coyote Creek. Lucas's shack stood empty and deserted, a puddle of water in the center where the roof had leaked. Trampled grass and the remains of his camp fire were the only confirmation that he had ever lived here.

Utter despair settled over her, and she felt icy cold to the depths of her being. It couldn't be true, her heart protested. How could he have been so loving, so full of plans for the two of them, and then have disappeared into thin air? Even Vicente didn't know, Ramón had said. And he'd said as well that Vicente had invested in the wharf. Then perhaps the Lucas Morgan who had stolen Pacific Steamship's gold had robbed Vicente, too. He'd taken the money and gone to another place, to convince other people of his grand intentions, to woo and break the heart of another girl.

Turning away, her chest heaving with inner pain, Consuelo's blurred eyes fell on the flattened grass beneath the willows. She wanted to scream aloud at the agony that poured through her. There she had given herself in love, reveling in his mastery of her body, believing all his promises.

"Damn you, Lucas Morgan," she cried into the stillness. "I'll make you pay for this. Someday...somehow."

Chapter Twelve

Through pouring rain, Consuelo rode Mirlo wildly homeward from Estero Bay. She had brought no serape and was soon drenched to the skin. Tears of despair mingled with the rain on her face. For the first time in all the lonely years, she had trusted someone, loved him enough to give of herself. Remembering her initial resentment of Lucas Morgan, she berated herself for having weakened, for having been seduced by his gentleness and warmth. She had come to care for him reluctantly, then with her whole heart. In return he had abandoned her, and betrayed her trust.

Why had she let herself believe she could trust him or anyone else except herself?

Isabel cried out in dismay when Consuelo stumbled into the house. With little resistance, she allowed her aunt to guide her to the bedroom, to peel off the wet clothes, help her into a warm flannel nightgown and tuck her into bed. Isabel also brought heated rocks wrapped in flannel from the kitchen to warm Consuelo.

Then Isabel rushed to the storeroom for a glass of the don's brandy to dose Consuelo. With a frown, she noted the level of the brandy keg. Ramón and his men had not drunk it all, and she understood why her brother had taken to his bed again. Thank God, Ramón had left. He and his vaqueros had been anxious to spend their money at the gambling rooms behind Cambria's taverns.

All through the dark hours of the night, Isabel sat beside Consuelo's bed, watching with fear as the girl's temperature climbed, and her lovely face grew flushed. In her fevered sleep, Consuelo cried out, and Isabel stared, startled at the name and the longing in the young voice.

"Lucas, Lucas, *querido mío.*" Tears ran down the girl's flushed cheeks. Understanding dawned as Isabel listened to the pleas, and her own aging face grew wet with tears.

The fever broke the next morning, but Consuelo still lay in a kind of stupor. She spoke to them, yet seemed far away. Neither Isabel's gentle care nor Rosa's tempting dishes brought a response. Staring at her niece with her own heart aching, Isabel knew from bitter experience that the sickness was more than the dreaded pneumonia. Consuelo's heart was broken.

Don Augustino came into the bedroom, looking down at her with concern on his haggard face. Consuelo managed to smile weakly at him as he stooped and gently stroked her damp hair. He went out again without speaking, and she drifted in a half doze. Suddenly, she was startled into wakefulness by the sound of quarreling voices on the veranda nearby.

"We must send for Father Amateo," her father declared.

"She's not dying," Isabel snapped. Despite the harsh tone, her voice quavered.

"No, no." The don's voice broke on the words. "It is I who shall never again be well. And I must see that my daughter is cared for. Father Amateo will post the banns for Consuelo's betrothal to Ramón. I promised."

"You can't do that!" Isabel cried. "She's ill and unable to speak for herself. Can't you see that Ramón Salazar isn't fit to marry your daughter?"

Consuelo turned restlessly on her pillow, disturbed by the words but only vaguely aware of their meaning.

"I owe Ramón everything I own," Don Augustino said in a hoarse voice. "Everything. He'll cancel all the debts on the wedding day."

Isabel's reply was filled with contempt. "You wouldn't sell one of your Indians as a slave, Augustino. Yet you sell your own daughter?"

"Hold your tongue, woman!" Don Augustino shouted and broke into a fit of coughing that effectively ended the quarrel.

After a bit, he came into Consuelo's room again, sitting beside the bed to take her hand in his. His dark sunken eyes looked into hers, begging her understanding. Papá wanted her to marry Ramón, she thought hazily. What did it matter when the one man she had truly loved was gone from her life forever? Still, she couldn't bear to look at her father, and turned her face away.

"I've sent for Father Amateo," he told her. "He'll post the banns for your betrothal to Ramón."

"No, Papá," she protested faintly, tears welling in her eyes as the little strength she had gained seemed to ebb away.

Don Augustino patted her hand. "He's one of us, my girl, a Californio, and he is my friend." When she would not look at him or answer, he pleaded, "I have no choice, Consuelo. Please understand that."

Father Amateo came and he stroked her hand as he told her in a low, convincing tone that she owed her ailing father obedience to his wishes. Drifting in a kind of stupor, Consuelo listened without comment. Nothing seemed real; nothing mattered. Her heart lay in shreds because of the man who had loved and abandoned her.

"Consuelo, don't let them force you into this," Isabel cried when Don Augustino announced he would hold a fiesta to celebrate his daughter's betrothal to Ramón Salazar.

Consuelo merely shook her head dazedly, almost beyond caring what happened to her. In some distant part of her mind, she wondered why Isabel protested so vehemently, even to Father Amateo. She had kept aloof for so many years.

Isabel struggled with her own private pain. Consuelo was unable to assert herself, and Isabel had no choice and no power to change anything. She must prepare a fiesta, for

Don Augustino had already sent out invitations. If only Lucas Morgan would come back, Isabel thought in despair, for she could only believe the gossip that he had fled from his debts here on the coast.

The *Electra* disappeared over the horizon. There was only the ocean, rolling blue and glistening in the autumn sunlight. Lucas's eyes turned inland to the golden hills just beginning to show green after the first winter rains. A few cottony clouds drifted above the hills and the air smelled clean and salty.

He drew a deep breath, amazed at the feeling of homecoming, as though he had lived here always.

"From now on. For always," he said to himself as he unlocked the warehouse. The weeks in Santa Barbara, waiting for the *Electra* to come back up the coast from San Pedro, had been difficult. Then there was the long, slow tow to Estero Bay.

Consuelo had filled his mind, his dreams, until the waiting grew unbearable. But now he was home again with the pile driver and its owner-operator, Pat Murphy.

"You can sleep here in the warehouse, where I've set up my own living quarters," Lucas said, turning to Murphy, who had followed him after making sure the pile driver was anchored and tied fast. "I'll have to walk to Bain's Settlement to get my horse and my workers."

"I'll have plenty to do while you're gone." Murphy eyed the vast dark warehouse, piled with lumber and kegs of nails and bolts. "Like I said, I want to finish this job in a hurry and get home to my wife and kids in San Francisco."

After helping Murphy carry his belongings to the warehouse, Lucas pointed out the canned food he'd stored, inviting the man to help himself. Then Lucas set off on the two-hour walk to Bain's Settlement.

It was easier to walk along the beach at first. Waves broke on the sand, the glistening water streaming back into the ocean. Sandpipers scurried before him, following the receding waves. Gulls took flight at his approach, crying raucously.

So much to be done, he thought, and more than anything, he needed to go to Consuelo. In his pocket was a gold wedding ring purchased from the jeweler in Santa Barbara. She would have had his message, and she would be waiting. The thought lifted his heart even as his body warmed with longing for her. Tomorrow she would be in his arms once more.

By the next afternoon, Lucas had organized his workers. The pile driver was in place, pounding **away** on the first piling.

Desperate to see Consuelo, he left Soledad in charge of the workmen. Dressed in a new suit he'd bought in Santa Barbara, Lucas rode first to Cambria. Vicente was neither at his office nor at his home. Time enough to see him on the way back, Lucas thought, and pressed his horse hard toward Rancho Estrada.

The rains had left the roads and hills muddy so that his progress was slowed and it was sundown when he rode into the rancho. The vivacious strains of a Spanish dance tune drifted from the courtyard along with the sounds of talk and laughter. Delicious odors of barbecued beef, chili and beans reminded Lucas of Consuelo's birthday fiesta.

He frowned. Why would Don Augustino, whose pockets were empty, be holding another fiesta?

The yard was crowded with carriages, the pasture filled with the horses of guests. Lucas gave his horse's reins to a small boy and walked past the Indian women busy at the ovens, to the courtyard.

"Lucas!" Vicente hailed him as he rounded the corner of the veranda. "*Dios!* I'm glad to see you." Breaking away from a group of people, he pumped Lucas's hand enthusiastically. "You wouldn't believe the rumors being spread about your abandoning your wharf."

Lucas stared in surprise at the words. When he'd sent the message to Consuelo, he'd asked her to tell Vicente his whereabouts. It seemed incredible that she had failed to do so.

"I went to Santa Barbara," he replied, frowning, "to hire a pile driver. I returned just yesterday."

"Ahh..." Vicente nodded understanding, adding, "I wish I'd known."

"But didn't Consuelo..." Lucas began, the words trailing off at the odd expression on Vicente's dark face.

"Consuelo's been very ill," he said. "I haven't spoken to her until today."

"Is she all right?" Lucas began, alarmed by the words.

He was interrupted when Angela came up and took Vicente's arm.

She smiled at Lucas, and said, "We were all so surprised when the invitation came."

"To this fiesta?" Lucas looked around at the torches flaring along the edges of the courtyard, the light flickering on the shadowy couples moving to the rhythms of the dance, and on the crowd of chattering guests grouped along the veranda.

"Yes." Vicente studied him for a moment before he added, "A betrothal fiesta."

A sense of disaster fell over Lucas. Something painful grew inside his chest until he could barely speak. "Whose betrothal?"

"Consuelo's," Vicente replied and his lip curled as he added, "to Ramón Salazar."

Lucas shoved a hand into his pocket, his fingers clutching the gold wedding band so tightly it bit into his flesh. His mind flooded with the memory of Consuelo lying in his arms, surrendering her body to him with sweet abandon. *Querido mío,* she had whispered. My love. How could she? He wanted to cry out the words. How could she offer him her love and now wed Ramón? She had promised herself to him, if not with words, then with her passionate body.

Without replying to some question of Vicente's, Lucas pushed through the crowd to where the dancers whirled and swayed around the courtyard. Pain surged through him at the sight of Consuelo, dressed in an old-fashioned gold silk gown, a high comb in her dark hair draped with a white lace mantilla embroidered with garish flowers.

How beautiful she was, even with that empty expression on her face. Ramón held her close, his dark eyes gleaming in triumph as he seemed to flaunt her before everyone. Impotent rage poured through Lucas, hot and ugly. What could he do? Had she promised herself to this ruffian freely? Remembering the sweetness of the love they'd shared, he couldn't believe it was true. Yet there she was, dancing with Ramón, letting him hold her possessively, a fixed smile on her lovely mouth.

The dance ended, and once more Lucas pushed through the crowd until he stood at Consuelo's side. "Perhaps you will honor me with a dance, *señorita,*" he said.

She turned, her eyes wide with shock as she stared at him in speechless amazement. The music began. Lucas took her waist and whirled her away before Ramón could object.

The music of the waltz was familiar, pulling them with it, echoing the last time they held each other in the dance.

Consuelo looked up into the accusing blue eyes. Lucas's strong hand was on her waist, holding her close. He was here. He hadn't run away, he wasn't lost, and yet he was. For a moment, she feared she would faint from the pain lancing through her heart.

"Why?" he asked in a rough, angry voice, his eyes like ice. "Why would you betray me like this?"

Her mouth trembled and her eyes filled with sudden tears. She struggled to speak without weeping. "I thought you'd gone away forever. They made me believe it."

"And you couldn't wait to find another man to lie with, even a beast like Ramón?" His tone was insulting, and his words cut like a knife.

"You don't understand," she cried out. Then, aware of the curious glances of the other dancers, she lowered her voice to a painful whisper. "Papá is very ill. I did it to please him."

"And did it please you?" he asked harshly, his expression cold.

"You went away," she repeated.

"I sent a message to you that I had to leave for Santa Barbara and would return as soon as I could."

"I received no message," she whispered, frantic to convince him. "They said you had gone. Taken your money and gone away. Now it's too late."

"You would marry a lowlife like Ramón?" he asked bitterly, wondering why Soledad had not delivered the note.

"Papá was desperate." She needed to make him understand and not hate her for what she had done. "Ramón could take everything from Papá, but now he'll cancel the debts on our wedding day. I cannot dishonor my father." The last words came in a soft cry of despair.

"He dishonors you," Lucas answered in a hard voice. "Selling you to the highest bidder like a brood mare."

Of all the hurt and pain she had borne in the past month, Lucas's rejection cut deepest. Tears spilled down her face, and her arm tightened on his shoulders, bringing their bodies close. "Please understand and forgive me, Lucas. I *do* love you."

"You belong to Ramón now." He spit out the words. "Love him." His face set in anger and pain, Lucas released her and walked away. Consuelo stood in the midst of the curious dancers, staring after him.

"Wait, Señor Morgan." A woman's voice called through the gathering darkness. The sounds of music and laughter followed from the courtyard, sounds that only intensified Lucas's pain.

Ignoring the plea, he mounted his horse. He could think only of getting away from this graveyard of his dreams. Perhaps to a tavern in Cambria to drown his misery in liquor.

Isabel grasped his stirrup, looking up with pleading eyes. "Please, *señor*," she implored. "Consuelo loves you. Believe it."

Lucas glared at her accusingly. "Then why is she marrying Ramón?"

"They made her believe you had gone away for good and abandoned Estero Bay. Augustino preyed on her sympathy for his illness, and she was ill, too." Isabel began to weep, great choking sobs. "They've trapped her, and it's so easy for a woman to be trapped, as I know too well. Please, Lucas, only you can help her now.''

"Then she will have to ask me," he said flatly, and reined the horse abruptly away before he, too, began weeping.

Chapter Thirteen

"I won't allow you to marry him," Isabel said, tight-lipped as the two of them sat beside the whale-oil lamp in the great room. A foggy winter afternoon pressed against the windows. "I'll kill him first."

Shocked at the violence in her aunt's voice, Consuelo stared at her. "You'll do nothing of the sort, *tía,*" she said, surprised by the intensity of Isabel's new interest in her welfare. She shook her head in unhappy disbelief. "Even Father Amateo has turned against me, because Ramón gives so generously to his church. Maybe by December Papá will be well and see the awful mistake he's made."

"At least I won that from Augustino," Isabel muttered, turning the shirt she was mending, "delaying the wedding until Christmas."

Consuelo drew a shaky breath, trying not to contemplate the possibility that the wedding day might really take place. With returning strength after her bout with pneumonia she'd pleaded with Papá, then with Father Amateo to cancel the betrothal.

"It was done against my will," she'd told the old priest. Distressed at such a blasphemous thought, he refused to believe her father would go against her best interests. Ramón would be a worthy husband, he said sternly. Sighing to herself now, Consuelo knew it was not so much what Ramón was that she objected to, but that she couldn't face marrying him when she loved another man. And she did love Lucas Morgan, try as she might to tear him from her mind and heart.

"I know it's a daughter's duty to obey her father in all things," Consuelo said now, half to herself. "But Papá doesn't understand and he's not responsible."

Her voice trailed off as she once more studied the letter in her hand. It was the tax bill for Rancho Estrada. An old fear grew cold in her chest. There was no money to pay the taxes. Ramón would pay if she asked, further enmeshing her in the trap he had set with his money. Or perhaps Vicente would advance a loan. Despair hovered near the surface as her mind darted frantically about, searching for solutions to her dilemma.

Men have the power, Isabel had once told her, and it was true. But Consuelo was determined not to be passive like Isabel. She would have her own power. Somehow, she'd find the money to keep the rancho safe, some way other than a loveless marriage to Ramón Salazar. And she knew it was a fight she'd have to make alone. Lucas Morgan had not even fought to win her away from Ramón.

"You could go to Lucas Morgan." Her aunt's voice was tentative, her dark eyes searching Consuelo's face.

Startled by the sound of his name, and the amazing suggestion, Consuelo looked away. A scrap of pitch in the fireplace blazed up suddenly, burning furiously. She watched it intently, ignoring Isabel.

"He loves you. He wanted to marry you." Isabel's words were low and hurried as though she half feared to say them. "I'm sure he'd marry you still, if only you'd go to Estero Bay and talk to him."

The pain Lucas's name always brought tore at Consuelo's heart. "Never!" The word burst from her, as much from hurt as from resentment at Isabel's unwelcome words. "He said things to me that I can never forgive."

"But you can forgive your father and Ramón?"

Her aunt's hard question went unanswered, as Rafael knocked and entered the room. He had been much absent from the rancho, taking the vaqueros with him on the rodeo of Estrada cattle.

"*Señorita, por favor,*" the old man said, a grin creasing his weathered face. "How is the don today?"

"He's sleeping," Isabel snapped, annoyed by the interruption. "He sleeps a great deal. We pray it's the Holy Father's way of healing him."

"I meant to speak to the *señorita,*" Rafael said, abashed by her tone. He turned the brim of his battered sombrero nervously in his hands, bright eyes fixed on Consuelo.

"What is it, Rafael?" Consuelo asked, looking at him affectionately. Isabel had no need to be so sharp with him.

He straightened his stooped shoulders, a self-satisfied look on his lined face. "With your permission, I've been rounding up the cattle. We've gathered a big herd, and the vaqueros are holding them in the cactus corral in the hills near Villa Creek."

Consuelo stared at him in amazement. Rafael had been a head vaquero in the old days, when there were many cattle to rodeo and brand. The awful drought and the death of the great herds, along with Rafael's advancing age, had made him into little more than a house servant. Now pride glowed in his swarthy face as he reasserted his former position of authority.

"You told me before about gathering cattle," she said. "But I hadn't guessed there'd be more than a few head. How many cattle?"

The old man beamed at her. "Come with me. I'll show you."

Consuelo rode along the willow-choked banks of Villa Creek with Rafael, her mind in turmoil as she tried to sort out what she must do. Her father was confined to his bed, and his weakened heart seemed little better. Her brother was dead. Only she could save what was left of Rancho Estrada and the mine.

Without the quick sale she'd hoped for, she'd put aside expectations for a profit from the quicksilver claim Vicente had filed for her. It occurred to her suddenly that if there were enough cattle . . . if they could be driven to sell in San Francisco . . . if Henry Rios would run the mine . . . Possibilities burgeoned in her imagination, both exciting and terrifying. A cattle sale would pay the taxes and provide a living for the people of the rancho, but the money wouldn't last forever. If she invested it in the mine, giving Henry Rios a share for managing it, there would be income for years ahead. And she could endow Father Amateo's church with enough money to win his consent to cancel her betrothal.

The early rains had brought new grass, shining green through the golden stalks of wild oats brushing her stirrups. Fog thinned as she and Rafael rode, and a watery sun shone on the foothills and the dark green oaks. The Santa Lucia Mountains were a hazy blue in the distance.

She could hear cattle bawling and vaqueros shouting long before they rounded a bend in the creek and saw the corral. It had been there as long as she remembered: a circular palisade fence, the posts interlaced and almost invisible beneath the impenetrable hedge of spiny cactus planted years ago to discourage cattle breaking out, or bears breaking in.

They came out on a rise, looking down on the corral beside a spring that fed the creek. A cloud of dust rose where vaqueros and their horses worked nimbly inside the enclosure, riatas flying as they jerked down the unbranded cattle. A vaquero on foot grabbed a red-hot branding iron from the fire just outside the corral and quickly traced the giant *E* that was Rancho Estrada's brand on one animal after another.

Amazed, Consuelo told Rafael, "I never guessed there would be so many." Her heart lifted in relief, for surely so many cattle would bring enough money in San Francisco to do the things she'd begun to plan. Inside her head, she reviewed all she had learned from Ramón about cattle selling.

"More coming," Rafael called, and pointed to a plume of dust hanging over a herd of cattle being chased at breakneck speed toward the corral.

Consuelo stilled the nervous mare beneath her and turned decisively to Rafael. "You said you'd gone with the cattle drive to San Francisco many times, Rafael. But that was long ago. Could you lead this herd to the stockyards?"

"Of course." He looked a bit insulted that she should even question his ability. "We'll have at least two hundred head," he added proudly.

"All Estrada cattle?" she asked doubtfully.

Rafael gave an expressive shrug. "They were unbranded."

Undoubtedly it was best if she asked no more questions, especially about the origin of cattle whose sale would save Rancho Estrada and set her free of Ramón Salazar.

"When can we leave for San Francisco?" she asked, already thinking about what they would need for a cattle drive. Supplies. Someone to cook for the men. And she would have to see Vicente before they left.

"If it doesn't rain..." Rafael began, and then stared at her in sudden comprehension. "What do you mean 'we'?"

"I'm going with you," she told him.

"No, no," he protested, and began enumerating all the hardships of the long drive.

"You can't read or write, Rafael," she said calmly but firmly. "Who would deal with the cattle buyers?"

He fell silent, intimidated by her sternness. Excitement poured through her as she watched the cattle milling in the corral, the new arrivals bunched nearby, held in check by shouting vaqueros. She was taking charge of Rancho Estrada, and of her life. She needed no one, not Lucas Morgan, not Ramón Salazar, not even Papá.

"It's madness, Consuelo," Vicente declared, frowning at her across his cluttered desk. "No woman can make that drive. You'll have to hire a drover."

"And how will I know he won't cheat me?" she demanded, leveling her gaze at him from where she sat in a heavy oak chair. Vicente had the office windows open to the fresh autumn day, and the cries of sea gulls blended with the rumble of wagons on the street below. "I've made my decision, Vicente. I'm going to San Francisco to sell my cattle. Then I can pay the taxes on Rancho Estrada and give enough to the church to end my betrothal."

"Ah, Consuelo—" he shook his head in dismay "—Father Amateo will cancel it if you ask."

"I have asked," she snapped, "and been refused. After all, Ramón has just donated a new altar to the church." She gave him a hard look. "I see I'm alone. I thought you'd help me."

"I can't ride to San Francisco with you," Vicente said patiently, as to a child. "And I cannot allow you to go." He leaned back in his swivel chair, stroking his mustache and looking very stern.

Why argue with him? Consuelo asked herself. They had been childhood playmates, and his expression did not daunt her. She would go, and he would not even know of her departure until too late.

"There's something else." She quickly dismissed the argument. "I know the offers on the cinnabar claim have been too low. If you and Henry would become my partners, I think we could develop the mine ourselves. I'll have money from the cattle sale, and..."

Vicente smiled, obviously certain he had won his point about the cattle drive. "Henry spoke to me just yesterday about it. He knows where he can buy a retort furnace fairly cheap. The ore is so rich that it's all that's required to process it."

Consuelo was suddenly overwhelmed by possibilities. She smiled, flooded with relief. "Make up the papers, Vicente. We'll have ourselves a quicksilver mine. Henry will be manager and buy the supplies."

Picking up his pen, Vicente grinned at her. "And what shall we call this mining company?"

"España," she said evenly. "Anything but Anglo." When she was rich she would get even with all Anglos, especially Lucas Morgan. In what way, she had no idea. For a moment she closed her eyes tightly, trying to still the pain in her heart.

Vicente made some notes on a sheet of paper, then stood, looking down at her as she sat before him. "I'll find a drover for you," he told her confidently. "Now you must come home to dinner with Angela. She's not leaving the house nowadays, with her time so near."

Morgan's Landing. An itinerant sign painter had lettered those words above the warehouse doors, and the settlement beside the ocean had its name.

From the open warehouse door Lucas watched the long, flat cart he had bought, drawn by a donkey and guided by an old Indian, move slowly down to the beach. It was loaded with cheeses and egg crates from the warehouse.

Soledad was in charge of loading the boat. He had proved himself a good seaman already, but Lucas would go with the first boat to make the business arrangements and bring the bills of lading to the captain of the *West Wind*. When the boat was ready to leave, Soledad would come for Lucas.

Today was steamer day, and the packet *West Wind* was lying off the bay, waiting to take on accumulated freight. Teams and wagons thronged in front of the warehouse, ready to load with lumber and merchandise, or off-loading cheese and butter. A herd of hogs, roped together, set up a racket near the beach as they were readied for shipment.

All day, the warehouse had been crowded with merchants and farmers. Most had gone to the beach now, where the lighter boat was being loaded to row goods out to the *West Wind*.

Business had boomed so quickly, Lucas could scarcely believe it. Every day was busy with goods being brought in for shipment, and steamer day was busiest of all. It was the nights alone, when Lucas had time to think, that took the shine off this sudden success. Consuelo wasn't here to share it as he had dreamed. Now, she would never be beside him.

Soledad was unshakable in his insistence that he'd given Lucas's message to Don Augustino. The old man had destroyed it for his own purposes, Lucas had decided.

Yet there was a gnawing sense inside Lucas that he had failed Consuelo in the same way he'd failed his mother and he'd sworn never to fail anyone he loved again. Even after all these years, the memory still had the power to conjure up all the old guilt and sorrow.

Rose Morgan lay in her cold barren room, coughing the last of life from her wasted body. "Take the money, Lucas boy," she had whispered hoarsely. "Go to the chemist for my powders. Hurry sweetheart."

Pity and fear warred in the heart of the twelve-year-old boy looking down at his mother. "Yes, Mama." He would do her bidding, even though he knew nothing in the powders would make her well again. They only killed her pain so that for a few hours she slept in comfort.

The last of their coins, tied in a dirty kerchief, lay in his pocket as he made his way along the crowded, dirty alleys of the waterfront. "Hurry!" she had called after him, and Lucas began to run.

"Bastard Morgan!" The familiar taunt stung as always, and fear sliced through the boy as he faced the gang of wharf rats who made his days a misery. All of them were homeless and as hungry as he, ready to do anything for a coin.

Mama was waiting, struggling with pain. He had to get to the chemist's. Desperate, Lucas turned and ran. As if that were a signal, the boys set upon him, four of them, their fists and their boots pounding at him until he fell into the alley filth and lay unmoving. Quickly, they went through his pockets and fled, laughing.

Dazed and bleeding, the boy staggered home. The ugly room was strangely silent, for Rose Morgan's painful breathing had stopped forever. For a long time, he stared down at her face, contorted in her last agony. Then he wept, knowing he had failed her in that last hour when she trusted him to bring her surcease from pain.

Why was he thinking of that now? Lucas asked himself angrily, as Mr. Ward, manager of Keystone Mining Company walked into the warehouse. He had tried, with all the frail strength of a starved twelve-year-old, to bring help to his mother, just as he had tried to send word to Consuelo that he would return to her. Suddenly, it seemed to him that Rose Morgan had betrayed him by her death, and Consuelo Estrada had betrayed him by her lack of trust.

He wouldn't think of her, he promised himself.

That promise was easy enough to keep in the daytime when he was consumed with business. He had already ordered lumber to add on a store to the warehouse. It was simply good business to have merchandise for sale to the farmers and miners who came here with their goods. He would have to go to San Francisco soon to contact suppliers and order goods to stock his new store.

The monotonous rhythm of the pile driver formed a background to the instructions of Mr. Ward. It was the first shipment for the Keystone Mining Company from Lucas's wharf. The manager was pompously assuring Lucas that if it were handled satisfactorily, he would have all their business.

The two men walked into the warehouse, where it was dim and cool and quieter. On the wide shelves along the walls had been stored the cheese and butter and eggs that were being loaded on the lighter. The odor of cheese still lingered, pervading the building.

The heavy Keystone crates, each carefully packed with seventy-six-pound flasks of quicksilver, stood on the warehouse dock, waiting to be loaded. They had to be handled carefully. At a $1.50 per pound, every drop was money.

"I'll be glad when the wharf is finished and steamers can tie up here," Ward said. "You'll have all our business when we don't have to run the risk of loading from lighter boat to steamer."

"The last of the pilings will be in this week," Lucas assured him. "The *Electra* will be back to tow the pile driver barge to San Francisco, and I'll accompany your quicksilver north myself."

Ward lit his cigar and smiled tightly. "Ever seen quicksilver, Morgan?"

Lucas nodded. Of course he had. Almost every business in Cambria had a tiny flask of the gleaming liquid on display. It was Cambria's most important product, although the agricultural products would become equally important once there was a cheap, safe way to get them to the markets in the city.

Ward offered Lucas a light for his cigar. Then he drew a small vial of quicksilver from his pocket and set it on the wide receiving counter in the center of the warehouse.

Lucas blew smoke into the air, savoring the expensive tobacco. Idly, he studied the small flask, its contents gleaming in the dim warehouse. This quicksilver was important in his new life, but his only real interest in mining lay in the products to be shipped over his wharf.

"I'm selling our old retort furnace to Henry Rios," Ward said, making conversation. "With the new Scot furnace we can process the ore twice as fast, with three times the recovery."

Lucas had met Henry Rios at one of the dinners he frequently shared with Vicente and Angela. Afterward Angela had confided their cousin's story. Rios had been dismissed from New Idria for purchasing outside the company store, and he was blacklisted in California. Though he longed to get back to mining, his prospecting in the Cambria area had come to nothing.

"So Henry's found a mine," Lucas said, reaching out to touch the gleaming flask.

"So he says," Ward replied. "You know how it is. Every two-bit operator with a claim hopes to get rich."

"Did he say where his mine is located?"

"Pretty secretive about it." Ward flicked cigar ashes on the plank floor of the warehouse. "I did find out his cousin Vicente is in on it. It's somewhere on Rancho Estrada."

A chill shot through Lucas, and the tiny flask slipped from his cold hand, shattering on the wooden floor. Quicksilver rolled across the dirty planks, a hundred separate drops glittering there in the gray light.

Rancho Estrada. Consuelo. He scarcely heard Ward's sharp exclamation of annoyance. Was this why Ramón Salazar was rushing her into marriage? So that he could own a quicksilver mine?

All the pain of losing Consuelo descended upon him as he stooped and tried to gather up the quicksilver into a small bottle he took from beneath the counter. She had been his so briefly, but so completely and perfectly that he had been certain it was forever.

The quicksilver eluded his fingers, rolling away as he touched it. Like Consuelo, he thought, his throat tight with pain. The memory of loving her gleamed as brightly as the quicksilver, but she eluded him just as the quicksilver drops eluded his fingertips now.

Chapter Fourteen

"I heard Rafael and his old men were rodeoing cattle." Ramón drew his bay stallion to a halt beside Consuelo. She sat on Mirlo, watching as the vaqueros branded the last of the cattle they had gathered.

Consuelo gave him an uneasy glance. Her cold hands clasped the saddle horn tightly as she summoned all her inner defenses. She'd seen Ramón and his men riding down from the foothills, watched in apprehension as they circled the herd of cattle being held on the meadow adjacent to the corral. If only she could have been gone to San Francisco before Ramón even knew about the rodeo.

Nonchalantly lighting a cigarillo, he grinned at her. "If Rafael made a mistake and branded some of my cattle, it won't matter, my girl. They'll all be mine very soon." Even though she refused to look at him, she could feel the warmth of his eyes on her as he added softly, "When we're married."

Rafael left the branding fire and started toward them. Consuelo waved him away. The old man was so intensely protective of her, and they were still arguing over her decision to ride with the cattle to San Francisco. She feared he might give away that plan to Ramón.

"I'm going to sell the cattle, Ramón." With an effort, Consuelo kept her voice cool and even. She had only her own foolish weakness to blame for being betrothed to this man. Until the right time came, she had no intention of letting him know she didn't intend to marry him.

"You can sell them to me, *querida,*" he said, unexpectedly reaching across to cover her hand with his. She couldn't look at him as he drew her hand up to his lips and kissed it lingeringly. Despite his reputation, Ramón had always behaved like a gentleman with her, and she felt a twinge of guilt that she had never been able to care for him.

"I have made arrangements," she said in a decisive tone, not wanting an argument.

"If it's the expense of the wedding..." he began, his voice low and solicitous.

"Yes." She spoke eagerly, glad he'd provided her with an excuse. "I will pay my own expenses." For the rest of my life, she added silently.

"Ah, the Estrada pride." Through lowered eyes, she saw his possessive smile, and knew she had effectively sidetracked him. But the way he said the words sent a chill of apprehension through her. Ramón had come from nothing, and now she saw his pride that he would wed the daughter of the Estradas, one of the oldest Californio families on the coast—aristocrats.

"Nevertheless, Consuelo," he continued, and his voice hardened almost imperceptibly, "you must keep this herd together for now. When I finish my business in San Luis and return next week, your father and I will decide what must be done with the cattle."

Had she really heard a veiled threat in those words? Consuelo wondered. She stared at his bland face. "So you're on your way to San Luis?" By asking the question, she avoided responding to his command.

"*Sí.*" Once more he lifted her hand to his lips, this time turning it to kiss the palm intimately. A shudder of revulsion ran through her, and she could scarcely restrain herself from jerking her hand from his grasp.

The hard-faced vaqueros who accompanied Ramón everywhere rode up then, laughing and joking about the ancient ones still trying to be vaqueros. Resentment flared in Consuelo, even as she ignored the men, for Rafael and his helpers had worked long and hard at the roundup with never a complaint.

"Adios, querida," Ramón said, and the men spurred their horses away. He looked back to lift a hand in farewell. "I'll see you in a week."

In a week, I'll be on my way to San Francisco, Consuelo thought as she waved in reply. And you won't be able to stop me.

Ramón's voice floated back to her. "Take care of my cattle."

A chill ran down Consuelo's spine at the words, for she knew Ramón could stop her if he wished. He had an entourage of tough *bandidos*. She had Rafael and his five old men, and the Chinese cook he'd hired. If they were to reach San Francisco without Ramón's interference, they must leave immediately.

The cattle herd started at daybreak, moving slowly along a narrow creek bed winding through the foothills. Rafael and Consuelo rode at the head of the long train of cattle strung out along the creek.

"The hardest traveling is here at the beginning," Rafael said, "on the rough trails through the Santa Lucias. Once we cross the mountains we'll travel the wide sandy bed of the Salinas River north to the bay."

Suddenly breaking off, Rafael turned his horse and shouted instructions at one of the men. Several cattle had broken from the herd, clambering up a side hill through thick stands of chaparral.

Exhilaration poured through Consuelo as she watched the vaquero turn back the strays toward the herd. In spite of her determination to make this drive, she'd been apprehensive. Now it seemed everything had fallen into place, and her confidence grew.

Rafael sat straight in his saddle, pride radiating from his worn face. As the majordomo, he was stronger in command and more knowledgeable than she had hoped. The fact that he had gone to San Francisco with cattle herds before, and had taken charge boldly, impressed the men.

Now, Rafael looped one knee over his saddle horn to rest himself. He gave her a gloomy look. "It's hard work, *señorita,* all the way to San Francisco. Very hard for a woman. There's still time for you to go home. It's only a day's ride back.''

Clad in some old clothes of Felipe's—pants, a worn and sweaty black sombrero, heavy shirt and underwear, his thickest serape tied to her saddle along with a blanket— Consuelo rode Mirlo at an easy pace. It was fortunate her brother had been a small man, so that his clothes fit her. No, not fortunate, she thought, and was struck by old sorrow. Felipe had always had to prove himself as small men often do. That, among other things, had probably led to his death.

She shook her head in answer to Rafael's questioning look. Everything depended on the sale of these cattle—the mine, the rancho, her entire future. Rafael was loyal and honest, but she couldn't trust him with that future. And she certainly couldn't trust the unlettered old vaqueros.

''I may not be as much help as a real vaquero,'' she said, with an affectionate smile at the earnest old fellow. ''But I won't be a hindrance either. You might as well give up, I'm going to San Francisco.''

The mountains looked bare and cold in the lowering sun. It was late in the year to be trailing cattle. If they were lucky, the rains would not come. Once they had passed through the Coast Range, the weather would be drier with no cold ocean fogs. And they would be that much nearer their goal, and that much farther from any possible interference from Ramón.

The thought of Ramón sent a sudden chill running down Consuelo's spine. Even though she was not yet his wife, she was certain Ramón wouldn't take her defiance of his orders calmly. But they were traveling fast, and light. Surely they could reach San Francisco before Ramón even learned of her whereabouts.

''We'll camp just ahead,'' Rafael said. ''There's a small valley with a creek and feed for the cattle.'' He spurred his horse ahead to show the men where to bed the cattle down for the night.

The Chinese cook whipped his mules past her, anxious to get supper started. A wagon would slow them down, Rafael had said, so all the supplies were carried on two pack mules led by the cook on his own mule. Later on, they would surely have to buy supplies, and Isabel had furnished the last of the money Lucas paid for his horse. The coins were safely tucked away in Consuelo's boot.

When Mirlo had been hobbled and set to graze with the horse herd, Consuelo approached the cook's camp beside the creek. Already Lee Sing had a fire going and food warming in his heavy iron pans. His thin, pale face seemed to be set in a permanent frown. She watched him moving about his work; his loose dark blue pajamas and the thin braided queue hanging down his back seemed exotic here beside a cattle-drive camp fire.

With sundown, the air grew cool and wisps of fog spilled over the mountaintops. Consuelo donned her serape and sat near the fire, watching the cook at his work, waiting for the vaqueros.

There were five of them besides Rafael, all older men. All the young men had left Rancho Estrada to seek more secure wages elsewhere. Vaguely, she wondered when those who had stayed had last been paid.

Two men were left to watch the cattle. The four who spread their bedrolls just beyond the firelight nodded shyly at her. Gray-bearded Juan, Luis, Tomás and José took their tin plates filled with food from the cook and sat by the fire. They ate quickly and in silence. Consuelo sensed their uneasiness and knew she was the cause.

"How is your son doing in San Luis?" she asked Juan, anxious to ease the tension. He grinned with pride and launched into a long description of his son's success with a café he and his wife ran in San Luis Obispo.

As the story grew repetitive, Consuelo's mind wandered. The parting with her father had been difficult. Although he was weak and ill, Don Augustino had still reacted as though he were in charge.

"You can't ride with a cattle drive," he had objected hoarsely. "It's not seemly for my daughter." Consuelo had shut her lips tight against the recriminations in her heart.

Tears had rolled down Augustino's sunken cheeks. "If only Felipe were here, if only I had a son..."

"You have a daughter," she'd said briskly, and had stood to leave. He would never stop mourning Felipe. Even though Felipe had been wild and improvident, he was still a *son*.

"When you marry Ramón I will have a son," Augustino had protested weakly. "Then the cattle can be sold."

She had refused to hear his pleas or even to meet his eyes as she kissed him goodbye. To her surprise, Isabel had embraced her fiercely and whispered, "I am so proud of you." Even now, Consuelo's eyes stung at the memory of such unexpected affection from her aunt.

Rafael had promised the going would be easier on the eastern side of the mountains, but it was a dry, wild and uninhabited country. The trail was hot and dusty, for no rain fell. The horses shied from rattlesnakes, and at night wolves could be heard howling in the distance. Fortunately the lean range-bred cattle had lost some of their wildness, and every morning strung out in a long line, keeping a slow and steady pace through the day.

Each day brought them closer to San Francisco and farther from any possible interference by Ramón, Consuelo told herself as she rode beside Rafael, a kerchief tied around her face against the dust. It was foolish to fuss with her hair, so she had braided it and let the long thick braid hang loose down her back.

"We'll rest at San Juan Bautista," Rafael told her one evening as they ate beside the camp fire. He openly studied her dusty clothes and her sunburned face.

"Not just for me," she snapped, glowering at him. She had never complained, and now she quickly took offense. Going for days without a bath didn't seem to bother the vaqueros, but she was used to being clean; as a woman among all those men she could not even bathe in the river. Sometimes it was difficult to find a stand of willows thick enough to relieve herself. But she would not accept any concessions made for her.

"It is usual," Rafael hastily informed her. "The cattle fatten a bit before we reach the stockyards, and the vaqueros have a chance to visit a tavern."

"Why must they visit a tavern?" she muttered, thinking of Felipe. Lee Sing had made a stew of dried beef and frijoles from the diminishing supplies. Too bad he had thrown out the chili peppers in one of his daily fits of temper, she thought, and set aside the tin plate with a grimace.

The camp fire gleamed softly in the blue, starry night. Two of the vaqueros were playing monte, and the others had already gone to their bedrolls, except for those riding night guard on the bedded cattle herd.

"Because they are men," Rafael replied. The set look on his strong, old face effectively closed the discussion.

Consuelo shrugged and stretched out her aching legs, leaning back against a fallen oak stump. The awful soreness from long days in the saddle had diminished, but she still fell gratefully into her blankets each night. San Juan would be a welcome respite. She had heard there was a hotel on the plaza. There she could take a room and at last have a bath.

"Vicente will not be pleased." Rafael had said the words almost every night as they sat before the camp fire.

As always, Consuelo shrugged. It was too late to worry about Vicente's opinion. She only hoped Ramón would not learn their whereabouts.

"Vicente will be pleased with the money," she told Rafael. Glancing toward the men concentrating on their card game, she added in a low voice, "The vaqueros know I can't give them any money until we sell the cattle, don't they?"

He reached to stir up the fire. "Surely you could spare enough for a drink at the tavern in San Juan?"

Mentally, she counted the coins in her boot, and calculated the supplies they would have to buy in San Juan. They could butcher one of the calves, she thought. The men had been faithful and worked hard. At Rafael's questioning glance, she nodded. "I'll try."

They fell silent as they watched the fire leap and dance against the darkness. Coyotes howled in the distance, and the cattle lowed softly. The sound of a galloping horse sent a frisson of tension down Consuelo's spine. Juan rode into the circle of firelight and dismounted. Consuelo let out her breath, suddenly realizing how often she felt this unreasoning certainty that one night Ramón and his roughnecks would appear and take the cattle from her and her old vaqueros.

"You will go home on the packet boat, *señorita?*" There was a pleading note in Rafael's voice.

Meeting his worried eyes, Consuelo laughed softly and patted his rough hand. The old man worried about her, and she knew he unobtrusively tried to arrange things for her comfort. She hadn't actually thought that far ahead, but the idea of riding Mirlo back all this long way was not enticing.

"Yes," she agreed, squeezing his hand before she stood up. "We can sell the horses in San Francisco, and you and the vaqueros can sail back, too."

"No, no," Rafael objected hastily. "We can't sell Mirlo, or my own horse. Some we can sell . . . the rest I'll take back to Rancho Estrada."

Of course she couldn't sell Mirlo. "You're right as always, Rafael." She patted his shoulder affectionately. Pleasure flooded the old man's face as she added, "I don't know what I'd do without you."

"*Buenas noches, Señorita Vaquera,*" he said with a faint chuckle. Their eyes met and they both laughed, affection flowing warm between them.

Wrapped in her blankets, on the opposite side of the camp fire from the men, Consuelo quickly slipped into a half slumber. Water rippled softly in the nearby river, and the sharp scent of willows filled her nostrils. Unexpectedly, tears slipped from her eyes and down her sunburned face. Her mind flooded with memories of another time. A hot autumn day, swaying willows, the sound of rippling water and Lucas Morgan's arms, his lips, his body joined with hers in utter joy.

It had been a dream, she told herself, turning over and trying to forget the picture that was filling her mind and reviving longings she had convinced herself were dead. It was a foolish dream to love an Anglo, perhaps even to love anyone. With the money from the cattle, and then from the mine, she could make her life at Rancho Estrada with Isabel, caring for her ill father. She would not need that kind of love again.

San Juan Bautista stood among rolling hills above the Salinas River valley. They made camp in the river bottom where there was plenty of feed for the cattle. Rafael divided the men into two groups, each to have its turn in the town while the other watched over the cattle.

Riding with the first group, Consuelo had her first glimpse of the somnolent little town basking in the late-afternoon sunlight. One side of the plaza ran along the edge of a hill, overlooking a wide, rolling valley. The mission church filled the western side of the square, its long veranda supported by graceful adobe arches. Gnarled pepper trees grew in front of the church and the fine house of General Castro. On the corner and across from the livery stable was the Plaza Hotel.

In the lobby, which was well-furnished with carved old California-style furniture, a stout Spanish woman welcomed Consuelo when she asked for a room. The vaqueros did not bother with rooms or baths. They crowded immediately into the hotel barroom, anxious to spend the coins Consuelo had given them.

The room Señora Garza showed Consuelo looked out over the sleepy little adobe town. There were curtains at the window, and the bed with its bright woven coverlet looked soft and inviting.

"You would like a bath?" the stout, gray-haired woman asked, eyeing Consuelo's dusty clothes.

"Ah yes, thank you," Consuelo said, with a rueful look at her scarcely recognizable image in the mirror above the bureau.

* * *

Luxuriating in the hot bath Señora Garza had sent up to her, Consuelo relaxed for the first time since the foggy morning she had left Rancho Estrada. In a few days she would be in San Francisco, money in her pocket, taking the packet boat back to San Simeon. Or would the boat put in at Morgan's Landing? At once, the image of Lucas Morgan filled her mind and heart. Sitting there in the long tin tub, she unthinkingly ran her hands over her soapy breasts. An ache grew between her thighs. Deny it as she might, she still longed for Lucas's touch.

Angry with herself for even thinking of him, she stood and quickly dried off with the towel the *señora* had brought. Fool, fool, fool, she berated herself. She must cleanse her heart and mind of him for all time.

She dressed in a clean shirt of Felipe's, and a black cotton skirt she had carried in her saddlebag. Then she brushed her hair and arranged it in the familiar manner instead of the braid she had worn on the trail. She smiled wryly at the oddly unfamiliar image in the mirror. At least she was clean and presentable enough to eat dinner in the hotel dining room. Something other than Lee Sing's odd cooking would be welcome.

Halfway down the narrow stairway, she met Rafael. He had come from the barroom, for she could smell whiskey on him. But whiskey would not explain the unhappy expression on his face.

"Ramón's here," he burst out, his dark eyes dilated with apprehension.

Stunned, she stared at him. The secret fear she'd carried these past days had become reality. She gasped the unwelcome name. "Ramón! Why is he in San Juan?"

"He heard about your cattle drive, and rode over the mountains to meet us here." Rafael's expression was at once frightened and angry. "He and his vaqueros have been here two days. Drinking, and . . ."

Rafael looked down unhappily, at his scuffed dirty boots. "He demands to see you, but he's been drinking and I tried to tell him—"

"I won't let him stop me," she cried. "Those are Estrada cattle. He has no right to them." Or to me, the words echoed in her mind.

"I can send for the sheriff—" Rafael began.

"No," she interrupted firmly. "If he's drinking, I'd better face him now, before he gets any drunker."

A clatter of dishes and the odor of barbecued beef came from the café beyond the hotel lobby. Raucous voices sounded from the barroom at the other side near the corner of the plaza.

After a furtive glance in the direction of the barroom, Rafael muttered uneasily, "If you'll stay in your room, the vaqueros and I will handle Ramón."

She looked around the small lobby, deserted now that Señora Garza was supervising the café. There were people nearby she could call on if need be. Besides, she wanted to speak to Ramón alone, to finish off everything between them.

"No," she said tersely to Rafael. "I'll settle this with Ramón myself. Tell him I'll speak to him here."

The old man left reluctantly. Consuelo deliberately seated herself in an ornate horsehair chair in one corner of the deserted lobby, facing the doors into the barroom.

After a moment Ramón appeared through the swinging doors. He walked toward her in the careful, deliberate way of a man denying he has had too much liquor. She rose at his approach, standing very stiff and under control, determined he would not guess how desperately afraid she felt. At once, he seized her hand and pressed it to his lips, his fiery eyes boring into hers.

"Consuelo," he said, attempting to draw her closer.

She placed a hand firmly on his chest and held him away. "What are you doing here, Ramón?" she demanded.

He frowned at the harsh tone of her voice. "I've come to send you home, *querida mía,* where a woman belongs. I'll take the cattle on to San Francisco."

"They are my cattle, Ramón," she snapped. "I'll take them to San Francisco myself." She had no doubt he could take them from her by force, and she trembled inwardly.

"It's not seemly for a woman. A woman should wait at home for her man."

The lustful gleam in his eyes made her turn away in disgust. All the gossip about Ramón was given credence by that one look. Consuelo drew a deep breath to steady herself.

"Anyway," he added carelessly, "in a few weeks they will be my cattle."

Consuelo stepped back from him, stumbling against the chair. Anger poured cold along her veins, until she felt strung tight in every limb. Glaring at Ramón's smug face, she spoke with icy certainty. "I shall never marry you, Ramón. Never!"

Eyes blazing, he grabbed her wrists painfully, dragging her toward him. "You little bitch," he snarled. "It's too late to back out. You will be mine... and Rancho Estrada will be mine. Father Amateo has cried the banns." He bent toward her as though to kiss her, and Consuelo turned her face from the foul odor of stale whiskey. "I anticipate our wedding, *querida*."

"Stop!" Until he spoke she hadn't noticed Rafael watching apprehensively from the doorway into the barroom. "Stop!" he cried again. In a surprisingly swift movement, he reached into his boot and drew his knife.

"Let go of her!" he shouted, rushing toward them. "I'll call my vaqueros and they'll beat you bloody."

Ramón stepped back, and spit contemptuously on the wooden floor. "Those old men, what can they do?" Glaring at Rafael, he seized the old man's wrist and easily took the knife from him. Rafael cursed in furious impotence.

"Don't try to take the cattle, Ramón." Consuelo clenched her fists to steady herself, determined to face him off, even though her heart was pounding in wild fear. "I'll have you arrested for rustling."

"Bitch!" He threw Rafael's knife at a nearby door, where it hung quivering, then grabbed Consuelo's shoulders and shook her so violently she feared she would faint. He flung her away from him and stomped back into the barroom, shoving Rafael aside as he passed.

* * *

Señora Garza brought Consuelo's dinner to her room, where she ate behind locked doors. Rafael promised he and the vaqueros would be nearby if Ramón should try to see her again. Yet even with that assurance, and the locked door, Consuelo could not eat, for her stomach roiled with dread of what Ramón might do. It was quite possible for him to harass the vaqueros until they would leave her, or to follow the herd and scatter the cattle.

Now she understood why she'd never been able to accept his rough, easy charm. Something in her had always been aware that beneath the surface, Ramón was a cruel and violent man. But he was convinced she was his, along with everything that belonged to her. He would not give up easily, and she had no idea how she would deal with him.

Even the soft warmth of the feather bed could not bring sleep to her troubled mind. Noise from the barroom drifted through the window: a tinkling piano, loud laughter, glasses and bottles clinking, rough voices. Finally, she closed the window, cutting out only a small part of the clamor below.

Screams penetrated her fitful slumber. Trembling and disoriented, Consuelo sat up in bed. She heard wood furniture splinter, glasses crash, and vile oaths fill the air. A woman was screaming as though she would never stop. Then an uneasy silence fell.

Consuelo opened the window and peered out. Nothing could be seen but lamplit windows on the first floor and an occasional light in the village beyond.

What if Ramón, drunk and angry, had attacked Rafael for trying to protect her? Terror gripped her. She began to dress hurriedly when a knock sounded on the door.

"It's Señora Garza," came the voice, and Consuelo quickly unlocked the door.

The *señora* looked upset, but she attempted a reassuring smile. "I was afraid you'd be frightened, *señorita*. There was a fight in the barroom, but it's over now and I've closed up for the night. You can sleep undisturbed."

"Someone was hurt?" Consuelo asked. Fear turned her knees to water. What if it was Rafael? He had dared to defy

Ramón, and the drunken Ramón would not have let that pass lightly.

The *señora* shrugged. "It happens."

Consuelo stared, amazed at the *señora*'s easy acceptance of violence. She had to know for herself. Pushing past the woman, she ran down the narrow stairway. A shudder of relief went through her when she saw Rafael standing at the foot of the stairs, his face grim.

Consuelo grabbed his arm, so glad to see him unhurt she would have hugged him if he hadn't backed away.

"Who was hurt?" she demanded. "Was it one of ours?"

"Ramón," the old man said and indicated the limp body being carried across the lobby in a bloodstained blanket.

"Take him to the convent," a tall, hard-faced man was saying in an authoritative voice. "The nuns will look after him."

"Not dead?" Consuelo asked Rafael, staring at the bloody blanket.

Rafael shook his head. "A knife wound," he replied. With an eloquent shrug, he added, "A drunken quarrel."

"That was all?" Consuelo asked as Señora Garza began shouting at someone to clean up the mess. "Just a drunken quarrel?"

Rafael looked embarrassed, as though reluctant to answer. His dislike for Ramón won over discretion. Eyes averted, he said in a low fast voice, "A woman. Her man found her with Ramón and there was a fight."

"Was he hurt badly?" she asked.

She was ashamed of the sense of relief she felt when Rafael replied, "Yes, he won't be bothering you again for a while."

Chapter Fifteen

They bedded the cattle among the grassy hills south of the San Francisco stockyards. The last part of the journey had been more complicated, with more and more farms, homesteads and fences to be avoided. Despite all the difficulties, they were here at last, Consuelo thought proudly. And they had brought all the cattle safely through.

Standing beside the camp fire in the gathering dusk, Consuelo studied the vast corrals of the stockyards and the ramshackle frame offices beyond. In spite of the information she'd managed to get from Ramón, she didn't really know how to begin to sell the cattle tomorrow or whom to contact in that rabbit warren of offices. Within sight, there were two other herds waiting for room in the cattle pens where buyers would look them over and make their bids.

"Everything's changed," Rafael said with a frown as he dismounted and stood beside her, taking the mug of coffee Lee Sing offered. "It's so much bigger than I remember."

Consuelo studied the distant camp fires among the other cattle herds. Her pride faded and she was simply scared. She mustn't let Rafael or the men know she was afraid. Far from home now, in an unfamiliar setting with no information to guide her, she wondered why she had thought herself so brave, setting out to sell her cattle. She hoped her venture into quicksilver mining wouldn't prove as frightening; at least there she'd be on home ground.

It occurred to her suddenly that if she didn't have the information she needed, the men at those other camp fires knew where they were going and what to do.

"Rafael," she said, trying to keep the urgency from her voice, "why don't you ride over and talk with the other cattle drovers? Find out whom we must see to get corrals for our cattle, and how to contact the buyers?"

The wise old eyes gleamed with understanding. She hadn't fooled him at all. "I'll go now," he said. "Before it's too dark."

Rafael was gone for a long time. The vaqueros had eaten frijoles without any meat and no seasoning except salt, growling their complaints in an undertone. Lee Sing was quick to take offense at any criticism of his cooking, and swore loud and long in his own language at any vaquero who dared complain. When approached with a request, he pretended he didn't understand either English or Spanish. Then how did he know the vaqueros were complaining? Consuelo wondered.

The men who weren't working the cattle had already gone to their bedrolls, and still Rafael had not returned. Consuelo sat by the fire, watching Lee Sing pack away his gear. In the distance, cattle lowed. Even farther away, she caught the faint whistle of a passing train. Gray wisps of fog drifted over the mountaintops to the west.

She sighed with relief when at last she heard Rafael call softly to his hobbled horse and walk out of the darkness toward her. He took off his sombrero and beat the dust from it against his thigh, then hunkered down beside her.

"I ate," he said in response to Lee Sing's questioning frown. The Chinese cook shrugged and turned back to his packing. At least Rafael always seemed able to communicate with the aloof cook, Consuelo noted.

"And drank, too," she reproved mildly, catching the smell of whiskey on Rafael's breath.

He shrugged, giving her a guilty grin. "I found out what we need to know. In the morning we'll see Mr. Owens or Mr. Thomas. The two outfits use different buyers."

"We'll see who offers the best price," she said eagerly and he nodded.

"They said wild stuff like our cattle doesn't bring as good a price as their fat cattle," he warned.

"Californio cattle, that's what we have," she muttered, knowing full well her resentment of realities would do her no good.

Rafael poured himself another mug of coffee and sat down. "They're from the Central Valley," he went on, eager to share all he'd learned. "Americanos. They even call their vaqueros cowboys." He laughed aloud at the ridiculous name.

"Yes," she replied absently, busy trying to figure in her head how much her Californio cattle might be worth. After a moment, she gave it up. They had come to the end of the cattle drive. "What about our vaqueros?" she asked Rafael. "What will they do now?"

"Tomás and José have a mind to see San Francisco after they're paid." Rafael shrugged expressively, as though he thought them foolish. "The others will ride home with me."

"What about him?" Inclining her head, she indicated the cook, who was making up his bed.

Rafael chuckled. "Lee Sing only took the job because he had no money and no other way to get home to San Francisco. He'll stay here."

"How do you know all that?" she asked in amazement. "He only speaks Chinese."

Rafael laughed heartily. "He speaks Spanish well enough, but if he let everyone know that, he couldn't ignore their orders and do as he pleases."

"The devil!" she said, glaring at the cook, who had pointedly ignored her existence for the whole trip.

Silence fell between them. Consuelo stared into the fire, which had fallen into glowing coals. She could scarcely believe it was over, that all the discomfort and fear and anxiety were at an end. Tomorrow would be difficult, but once the cattle were sold and delivered she would sail back home with the money to improve her mine. All those who had thought she could never do this would be proved wrong. She would be free of Ramón and would be able to pay her father's debts. Free?

Lucas Morgan's face seemed to look back at her from the gleaming coals. Something in her heart caught and hurt so that she gave a little gasp of pain.

At Rafael's expression of concern, she smiled. "I think I'll be glad to see Mirlo go back to the rancho without me."

Outside the window of the cattle buyer's office the sounds of bawling cattle and shouting vaqueros filled the air. A faint odor of ammonia drifted through the open window from the cattle pens.

Mr. Owens, the buyer whose name was lettered on the frosted glass of the door, did not rise to greet her as she entered the small, crowded office. His desk was piled with dusty papers. The only decoration on the walls was a fly-speckled calendar with a lithograph of a prize bull.

"Well, well," Mr. Owens said, his pale blue eyes moving slowly up and down her figure. "You're the first female cowboy I've seen. Or shall I call you a cowgirl?"

His condescending tone brought a rush of heat to Consuelo's face. He was a tall, bearded man, and now he leaned back in his swivel chair behind the wide desk, and surveyed her with unconcealed amusement.

"I'm a cattle owner, Mr. Owens," she said evenly. "And I have cattle to sell, if you're interested."

"Oh, I'm very interested," he chortled. Standing, he moved around the desk, looking down at her with a suggestive smile, his pale eyes fixed on her breasts beneath the soiled blue shirt she wore. She had washed herself and cleaned up as well as she could before leaving camp this morning.

Consuelo was instantly aware how vulnerable she was, alone with this strange man in his office. Rafael had stayed with the cattle as they were being tallied and turned into a corral. She hadn't dared let herself think how afraid she was this morning as she made inquiries and found her way to this office. Whatever she had feared, this man's behavior was not at all what she had anticipated.

"I'm sure we can work out a satisfactory deal." He smiled again as he rested one cool hand on her shoulder and the fingers tightened slowly.

With a quick step back out of his grasp, Consuelo fixed him with a withering stare. "I'm only interested in selling cattle, Mr. Owens. They're in corral 5, if you'd care to look them over and make an offer."

"Perhaps I can make a better offer, my dear." Unexpectedly, he reached out and placed a hand on her breast.

Consuelo drew in her breath in outrage, and once more stepped out of his reach. Desperation clogged her throat. She had to sell the cattle. This man had the power to say no and dash all her hopes ... or to say yes. And he was making it clear what she must do to win that yes.

Dirty Anglo, she thought, hating him, hating being in his power. Yet in the back of her mind, she was well aware how she must appear to him. A young woman wearing soiled men's clothes, her black hair hanging in a braid, her face sunburned, her hands scarred and calloused. Surely he thought her some hoyden from the back country, willing to tumble with any man for a price.

Drawing herself up, she stared at him haughtily. "You mistake me, *señor*. I am Consuelo Amparo Maria Estrada of Rancho Estrada. I have—"

Before she could finish, the door to the adjoining office opened and a stout, balding man entered. "Good morning," he said, staring at her in amazement.

"This is Señorita Estrada," Owens said in a spiteful tone.

"I'm Asa Thomas," the balding man said, nodding and smiling kindly at her. "Owens's competitor in the cattle-buying business."

Owens gave her a glare and turned away. "Perhaps you'd be interested in the *señorita*'s cattle," he told Mr. Thomas. Maliciously, he added, "She seems to have some preference where she sells."

"The Spanish cattle?" Thomas said, ignoring the obvious hostility between Consuelo and Owens. "Well, if Owens isn't interested in them, I am. Come into my office."

Relieved to have escaped Owens, Consuelo took the chair Mr. Thomas offered beside his desk. Without further ado, he proceeded in a very businesslike manner to make an offer for her cattle. It was less than Rafael had said the Central Valley cattle would bring, but having been forewarned, she decided it was eminently fair.

When she agreed, Thomas began making out a bill of sale, asking about her trip as he wrote in a fine Spencerian hand. She told him she meant to take the packet boat back to Rancho Estrada and would need a place to stay in the city until the boat sailed.

Leaning back, he studied her with kindly eyes behind steel-rimmed glasses. Quickly, he wrote down an address. "This is a respectable boardinghouse, young lady. The best kind of place for you to stay until you're safely on your way home."

Relieved of that decision, Consuelo took the address and tucked it into the pocket of her black cotton skirt, which she had worn over Felipe's trousers. "Could you please order a cab to take me there?" she asked hesitantly. When he smiled and nodded, she felt almost overjoyed to have found someone as good and kind as Mr. Thomas, especially after that vile Mr. Owens.

Thomas went to the outer door and asked his clerk to order a cab. Then they set about the business of payment. With Rafael's help she had figured how much she owed the vaqueros and Lee Sing. She asked for the amount of the wages, and enough to pay her board and room in the city and passage home in gold coin. The rest would be in a bank draft.

Her hands trembled as she took the draft from Mr. Thomas and studied the amount. It seemed a fortune, but she knew it was not, and guessed how quickly it would go for mine equipment and wages. None of it for gambling, though, she told herself firmly. Don Augustino would get his hands on none of it. He had failed her too many times, used her to escape the consequences of his compulsive gambling. From now on, she would be the don at Rancho Estrada.

Thanking Mr. Thomas for more than he could have guessed, Consuelo made her way back through the labyrinth of unpainted wooden buildings to the corrals. The Estrada horses stood lined at a hitching rack, along with the loaded mules. A stranger in a broad-brimmed hat was inspecting the horses. Consuelo smiled. So Rafael had already found a buyer.

Rafael shouted when he saw her, and the vaqueros, who had been lounging nearby in the thin morning sunlight, gathered around. They all talked at once, eyes gleaming at the sight of the gold pieces she was dispensing. She knew they'd started the drive with grave doubts about her. Now, seeing the acceptance and affection in their weathered faces, she knew she'd proved herself to them.

As each man took his wages, she shook his hand and told him, "Thank you, my friend, thank you." One by one, they took off their dusty sombreros and bowed to her. Old Juan even had tears in his eyes, and Consuelo wished she dared to hug him.

Rafael was dickering with the horse buyer, and she called to him to come pay Lee Sing. The cook took his wages with an impassive face. He bowed once to her, his long queue bobbing, once to Rafael. Immediately, he set off at a brisk pace, north toward San Francisco.

The horse buyer beckoned to Rafael. Knowing he must be ready to make an offer, Consuelo joined them. When he named a price, she at once asked for more. The man stared questioningly at Rafael, who shrugged and said, "She's the owner."

The hard-faced Anglo laughed, and agreed to her price. There were bills of sale to be made out while Rafael and the vaqueros led their own horses away. The pack mules would return with those riding to Rancho Estrada.

The gold coins the horse buyer counted into Consuelo's hand were an unexpected bonus. Placing them carefully in the leather bag attached to her belt, she thought of buying gifts for Isabel, for her father and for Angela and Vicente's baby.

"You'll need an escort into the city, *señorita*," Rafael said. "Perhaps José and Tomás?" He glanced at the two men mounted on their horses, waiting to say a last goodbye.

Consuelo laughed. If Rafael only knew what she had been through this morning! José and Tomás had plans of their own, she was certain. And she knew how anxious Rafael was to be headed south, back to Rosa.

"You are not my dueño, Rafael," she said sternly. "I've ordered a cab, and Mr. Thomas has recommended a boardinghouse. Haven't I proved I can take care of myself?"

"But this is San Francisco," Rafael protested. "A big, wicked city."

No matter that she'd made the cattle drive without complaint or mishap, or that she'd sold the cattle for a good price. Now that was in the past, and suddenly Rafael was again seeing her as Señorita Consuelo, to be protected and watched over by everyone connected with Rancho Estrada. It was a part of their tradition. Amused, she studied the old man's earnest face. If he doubted she could look after herself, she had no such doubts. She'd proved herself capable and independent. Even though she felt a few twinges of apprehension about San Francisco, she wouldn't acknowledge that to him, or even to herself.

She laughed aloud, and impulsively flung her arms about Rafael. He stiffened and stepped away, looking shocked.

"You've been a good majordomo, Rafael," she said kindly, seeing that she'd embarrassed him. "Now get a good night's rest and head for home and Rosa. I'll see you very soon at Rancho Estrada."

He stared at her with a doubtful frown, and she smiled confidently at him, certain that he was still unwilling to let her go alone into the great, wicked city. Then, as he looked past her, his eyes lit up, and a grin split his weathered features. "Now, you will be safe," he said with certainty.

Consuelo turned to follow his gaze, and looked into the anxious face of Lucas Morgan.

Chapter Sixteen

Morning fog melted from the hills of San Francisco as the hansom cab swayed over the cobblestone streets, driving north from the stockyards. The air was chill, and Consuelo huddled beneath her heavy serape in one corner of the cab's leather seat. She had pinned up her hair, but knew she still looked like an orphan Indian. Her saddlebags lay at her feet.

On the opposite side of the hansom, Lucas Morgan studied her with questioning eyes that she could not quite bear to meet.

Everything had happened too quickly. Obviously relieved to find someone to take on his self-imposed role of guardian, Rafael begged Lucas to see Consuelo into the city and settled in the recommended boardinghouse, and to be sure she was aboard the first packet boat available.

"I'll see she has a safe place to stay and passage on a steamer," Lucas had assured Rafael.

"I can take care of myself," Consuelo had protested resentfully. She'd come this far without his help, and she had no doubt she could find her way through San Francisco, too.

Despite her protests, Lucas carried her saddlebags to his waiting hansom. There'd been nothing she could do but follow, with Rafael urging her along.

Seated beside him now in the closed hansom, Consuelo tried desperately to sort out her thoughts. The very sight of him had thrown her into a turmoil of longing, anger, hurt, resentment, until she scarcely knew what she was feeling. The things he had said that night at the betrothal fiesta, the way he had walked away from her in the midst of the dancers... Yet all the pain of that night did not quite banish the memory of what they had been to each other for one brief golden afternoon.

Lucas was acutely aware of the way she slid away from him, almost crouching now in the corner of the black leather seat. Her glorious hair was braided and wound around her head in an unfamiliar way, perhaps one that was easier for the long, hard journey she'd just completed. A thick wool serape covered her slender body so that only the black cotton skirt showed. Beneath the sunburn her face was pale, and her dark eyes watched him warily.

Fingers of pain clutched his heart at what seemed her utter rejection of him. She was betrothed to another man, he reminded himself. It was none of his business if the man was a fool and a ruffian, if he was Consuelo's choice. But he couldn't make himself believe Ramón was her choice. Not after what she and Lucas had shared.

Clearing his throat, he spoke in deliberately unemotional tones. "Vicente was frantic when he learned you'd gone with a cattle herd. He said he'd told you he'd find a man to handle the drive."

"Did he send you to find me?" Her eyes flashed with indignation.

"I was coming to San Francisco to buy supplies for my store," he replied in a reasonable tone, knowing he must be careful of her pride. "He asked me to go to the stockyards and make sure you were safe."

When she turned her face away from him, staring out the window of the swaying cab, he added in a chiding tone, "He was concerned for you, Consuelo." After a pause, he said softly, "So was I."

Her dark eyes flashed an enigmatic glance at him, then looked resolutely away. An uncomfortable silence stretched between them.

The hansom turned onto the long diagonal of Market Street, moving toward the center of the city. Lucas could not take his eyes from her exquisite profile, turned toward the San Francisco hills, which were bright now in the clear sunshine, the light-colored buildings gleaming. How lovely she was, how innocent. The memory of how passionately she had given herself to him nearly stunned him. He'd thought he'd lost her forever, and the possibility stabbed through him with such agony that he groaned aloud.

Her dark eyes turned questioningly toward him. Hoping he detected at least a glimmer of sympathy there, Lucas spoke quickly. He was determined to reach her, to somehow win her back. "I sent you a note when I left for Santa Barbara, Consuelo. Soledad gave it to your father."

Her eyes widened and he watched her struggle to accept the implication of his words. "My father would have given it to me," she denied stoutly.

"Soledad never lies," he answered quietly, filled with pity for her. He remembered how angry he'd been when Soledad told him. Don Augustino spoke of honor and pride, and then behaved dishonorably.

Consuelo bit her lip and looked away, the inner struggle reflected on her face. Eyes moist, she turned back toward him. "Papá was ill," she murmured defensively. "Perhaps he forgot."

"Perhaps," Lucas replied, leaving her some pride in her father, although he didn't believe it. Don Augustino was too anxious for her to marry Don Ramón. He wouldn't hesitate to destroy a note from the Anglo who loved her.

Consuelo looked down at her hands, clasped tightly in her lap. Her pink mouth trembled. Lucas longed to still her pain with his lips but his own hurt held him back. She had been ill-used by her father, but she should have believed her lover's pledge. How could she have questioned his honor, and accepted her father's? But he also knew how her wounded pride must sting.

Gently laying his hand over hers, he said softly, "I always meant to come back for you, my love. Every day in Santa Barbara I longed to be with you. See, I bought this for you while I was there." He dug into his waistcoat pocket and brought out the gold wedding ring and held it in his palm for her to see.

Taking a handkerchief from his pocket, he carefully wiped the tears that had spilled down her tanned face. Then he cupped her face in his two hands, forcing her to meet his eyes. "You cannot marry Ramón," he said.

Consuelo drew in a sharp breath. Dark eyes swimming with tears at last met his own. "I know," she whispered brokenly. "I've told him so." Then, in choked, halting words, the story of the ugly scene at San Juan Bautista spilled out. Lucas listened, clenching his fists in fury that Ramón had shamed her so. Consuelo's face crumpled with weeping as she finished her story.

"I could kill him," Lucas growled, and he drew her into his embrace. Dear God, he thought, how right she felt in his arms. He pressed his cheek against her hair, smiling at the faint dusty odor. With a gentle hand, he cupped her cheek and lifted her face for his kiss.

Their lips met, hers faintly salty from her tears, and a familiar flame leaped inside Lucas. His arms tightened around her and the kiss deepened; Consuelo gave herself, warm and willing to his caresses.

The sense of loss that had filled his life these past weeks was drowned in the sweet magic of her kiss. Consuelo was his, had been from the first moment he'd looked into her eyes at Rancho Estrada. Happiness swelled in Lucas's heart. Now he would make all his dreams come true.

Kissing her damp eyes tenderly, Lucas murmured against her ear, "You'll marry me, dear love . . . just as we planned at the beginning . . . just as we both promised."

"Yes, Lucas." She clasped his face in her rough little hands and looked into his eyes. "Yes, *querido mío,* yes." And she kissed him fiercely, not even hearing the clanging trolley and their shouting cabdriver.

Happiness poured through Lucas, more perfect and complete than anything he'd ever experienced. He laughed, holding her close.

"Before we go to the hotel," he said lightly, "I'd like to take you shopping at the City of Paris department store, and buy a fancy dress for you."

"I have my own money," she retorted, sitting straight and moving a little away from him.

"With your own money, then," he conceded, amused by her stiff-necked pride.

"Yes," she agreed looking down thoughtfully at her shabby clothes. She smiled with a brilliance that burned his eyes. "I would like a new gown for San Francisco. As long as it doesn't cost too much."

Geary Street was a raucous clamor of carriages thundering over cobblestone paving, trolleys clanging, dray wagons lumbering about their deliveries and street vendors shouting their wares. The sidewalks were crowded with rough-looking workers, well-dressed dandies and stout businessmen. Elegantly gowned ladies accompanied by Chinese or black servants vied for space with flashily dressed painted women, and house servants intent on their errands.

Consuelo stared in amazement as Lucas paid the cab-driver. The buildings were so tall they shut out the sunlight. When he led her into the City of Paris, she gasped in admiration at the wrought-iron balconies on each floor, all lit by a huge glass cupola.

After inquiring of a nattily dressed floorwalker, Lucas led her up the stairs to the ladies' gowns salon. Consuelo sat in the chair Lucas held for her, which was upholstered in pink velvet, and looked in awed appreciation at the soft gray carpeting and the pink velvet draperies that shut off the dressing rooms.

A haughty-looking lady in a black silk gown approached them. She compressed her lips in shock as she stared at the strangely dressed young woman before her. For one awful, humiliating moment, Consuelo wanted to flee.

Lucas's hand rested casually on her shoulder, and she covered it with her own, looking up at him for reassurance. His blue eyes were dancing with amusement, but he kept a straight face as he asked that the young lady be shown some proper daytime outfits. At least *he* was well dressed and elegant, she thought ruefully, admiring the way he looked in his gray suit with the black-and-white-checked waistcoat.

"No bustles," Lucas said when the tall, imperious saleslady returned with several gowns.

How ironic, Consuelo thought, reaching out to touch the elegant material of the gowns. She had thought Angela foolish to dress in Anglo style, and here she sat, longing with all her heart to possess one of these beautiful dresses. Every cent of the money she carried with her should go back to Rancho Estrada, and yet... She wished she dared ask the price.

The saleslady's eyebrows rose. "Anything else is quite out of fashion," she said with a sniff.

"Nevertheless," Lucas stated firmly without consulting Consuelo, "bustles are a monstrosity. Besides, we live in the country and fashion isn't important." He smiled at Consuelo for confirmation.

When she could only sit, terrified at spending money on such luxuries, Lucas chose for her a burgundy skirt and jacket in a silky wool twill trimmed with black braid. To wear beneath the jacket there was a shirtwaist of fine white linen.

"I can't afford that, Lucas," she whispered in desperation when the saleslady was out of earshot.

He patted her hand and stood up, smiling. "I'll see you get a special price," he assured her.

She didn't understand how he could do that, but now she wanted the gown with all her heart. As she watched, Lucas conferred with the saleslady, who brought out a blouse of soft pink silk, its low neckline trimmed with layers of silk ruffles. It was lovely, but Consuelo tried to persuade Lucas that it was a wild extravagance, when the saleslady was again out of earshot.

"A gift from me," he insisted, and once more conferred with the woman, whose haughty attitude was quickly thawing. She produced a pair of black kid shoes in Consuelo's size, then disappeared, only to return with a shiny box. Consuelo was embarrassed to find it contained the necessary underwear and stockings, as well as a nightdress and robe of pale pink silk. She was certain it was quite improper for Lucas to buy such things for her, and she felt the color rise in her face.

Wishing she could have bathed first, Consuelo left the elegant City of Paris department store clad in the new suit. She waited for Lucas to hail a passing cab, aware that the glances coming her way now were not of amusement but of admiration.

"I can't believe all this cost so little money," she said when they were once more ensconced in the privacy of a hansom cab. The little sack of gold coins she had taken to pay her way home was nearly intact, but she was still assailed by guilt. She should have saved it all to spend on the mine. She wouldn't need such a fine gown when she was home again at Rancho Estrada. But she would someday, when she was Lucas Morgan's wife. At the thought, a warm flush of happiness flowed through her.

"I'd have bought everything in the store for you if you'd have allowed it." Lucas leaned toward her, his blue eyes warm. "You deserve it. Rafael couldn't stop bragging about his *'señorita vaquera.'* You're a dazzling woman, my love," he added. Taking her face in both his hands, he covered her mouth with his.

Desire shot through Consuelo like a flame, and she leaned into his kiss, opening her lips to him. His hand slipped beneath her jacket, cupping her breast through the fine linen of her blouse. She moaned deep in her throat, suddenly bereft as Lucas moved away from her, his breath coming painfully fast.

He took her hand on the seat between them, holding it tight as the carriage rolled into the great Garden Court of the Palace Hotel.

Arched colonnades on the ground floor rose to the balconies on the three sides of the upper floors. In the courtyard, men in silk hats and dark broadcloth suits and ladies in silks and furs alighted from fine carriages. A network of steel girders arched over the courtyard. Cobblestones paved it, and a busy man with scoop and broom cleaned up after the horses.

It was madness to think of booking a separate room for her, Lucas told himself, as they entered the hotel. He noticed the way men's eyes turned to the lovely woman beside him. Tomorrow they would be married. Tonight... He felt a stirring in his loins and bent to pick up her saddlebags and the City of Paris box, forcing himself under control.

"I should have bought a hat." She spoke unexpectedly, frowning at the elegantly gowned women in the spacious lobby, all wearing hats.

"Tomorrow we'll buy you a hat," he assured her with an indulgent smile. "Just now, I thought you wanted a bath most of all."

Consuelo gasped as Lucas unlocked and pushed open the door to his room. In all her life, in the trips with her father and Isabel to Monterey and San Luis Obispo, she had never seen anything so lush, so elegant. Thick wine-colored carpeting covered the floor and rose damask drapes hung at the window overlooking Market Street. A matching rose spread covered the bed. Tapestry-upholstered chairs stood beside a carved mahogany table, and a huge mahogany wardrobe filled one wall.

Lucas watched in loving amusement as she wandered around the room, touching everything, her dark eyes filled with pleasure. Dear God, Lucas thought, drawing her into his arms, he wanted to give her such joy always, to fill her life with beautiful things.

"I love you," he said as her arms slid around his neck, and her slender body molded itself against his.

Her mouth was sweet beneath his, and giving. He could feel her heart leap and pound beneath his hand covering her breast. Go slowly, he warned himself, remembering how wildly he had taken her the first time.

"*Querido mío,*" she whispered hoarsely.

Once more, Lucas forced himself under control. Smiling, he held her away. "I'll run your bath now, *señorita.*"

In the bathroom she watched in amazement as he turned water into the huge white porcelain tub, adding the fragrant bath salts the hotel provided. When she took off her jacket and handed it to him, he went out and closed the door. A man could only bear so much.

Consuelo sighed with pleasure as she slid into the luxurious warmth of the huge bathtub. All the happenings of the past few hours ran again through her mind, and her heartbeat quickened when she remembered Lucas's kisses and his words of love. Now she could let herself admit how terribly she'd longed for him these past weeks, even while she blamed him for deserting her. Of course he had sent a note; she was certain of that now. But her father had been ill, and in any case, he could not read English. He might have thought the note unimportant because it was delivered by some Indian's hand, or he might have been so ill he'd forgotten and misplaced it. When she was home again, she'd ask him.

The scent of lavender filled the steamy room as she soaped her hair and rinsed it. Smiling as she dried herself with thick white towels, she replayed every kiss in the cab, every touch. Lucas hadn't offered to obtain a separate room for her. He meant to make love to her. The thought sent a sharp stab of longing through her. Her heart beat furiously as the ache between her thighs intensified, and she hurriedly slipped on the silk nightdress. The price tag was still attached, and she gasped at the amount. Lucas had deceived her again. He'd salved her pride by letting her pay a minimal amount for clothes that were actually a gift from him. She didn't know whether to laugh or cry. But the feel of silk against her bare skin, the knowledge that her lover waited in the next room, made the flash of resentment vanish in an instant.

Lucas had taken off his waistcoat. Through the half-open door of the wardrobe, she could see it hanging beside her new gown. His white shirt was partly unbuttoned, revealing a glimpse of dark brown chest hair. Crushing out his cigarillo, he rose from the tapestry chair and came toward her, his blue eyes blazing with longing.

Clasping her wet head in one hand, he drew her into his arms and kissed her so that her bones seemed to melt away.

"I must brush my hair," she said with a teasing smile, slipping out of his embrace to dig into her saddlebag for her brush.

"Let me." His voice was rough, but his big hands were gentle as he brushed out her long black hair. She sat on the bed, eyes closed, reveling in his touch. She drew in a sharp breath as he pushed her hair aside and kissed the back of her neck.

Breathless, she watched as he laid the brush on the marble-topped table. His gaze burning into hers, he pushed off her robe, kissing each shoulder as it was exposed. Slowly, carefully, he eased her back on the bed and lay beside her, his mouth hot on her throat, then her breasts. His hands moved to her waist, her hips, her thighs, spreading fire along her skin with every touch.

"Lucas," she whispered, taking his face in her hands, wanting his kiss with all her being.

His mouth devoured hers, his tongue probing, spreading sweet fire. Through the thin nightdress she could feel his hardness burning against her, and a shudder of desire shook her.

"Lucas..." She spoke again, urgently this time, wanting him with a madness that spun out of control. *"Querido mío."*

Lucas groaned, standing to pull off his clothes. The sight of his tall muscular body, completely naked, only added fuel to her longing. As she watched, he turned back the covers of the bed and lifted her in his strong arms. Holding her there for a moment, he looked into her eyes with such passion her whole body took fire.

He laid her on the cool, starched sheets, and tugged off the thin gown so that she lay naked in the faint glimmer of the gaslight. A gaze of desire shimmered between them.

Consuelo held out her arms, calling his beloved name once more. "Lucas, *corazón,* love me, please."

He was beside her, cradling her against him as his hands spread sweet fire along the curve of her stomach, between her thighs. His hot mouth covered her breasts, his tongue teasing at the nipples until they were erect and aching.

Need pounded through her with every beat of her heart, an ache that only he could soothe. Instinctively, her hand slid down his strong muscled back, over his hips, to caress the hot, throbbing center of him. He groaned with pleasure and moved to cover her. Lifting her hips with urgent passion, Consuelo took him home to the very center of her longing.

A wild rush of joy poured through her as she met his thrusts, giving her mouth to his, their hearts pounding wildly against each other.

They seemed one being, melded together, moving in perfect unison. The sweet frenzy grew, pitched higher and higher, until it exploded through her body. A soaring ecstasy whirled her out of time and place. With a hoarse cry of fulfillment, Consuelo took him deep into her. Lucas gasped her name, and they were lost in a blind and perfect rapture.

Chapter Seventeen

Church bells awakened Lucas, the mellow chimes echoing from St. Mary's on nearby California Street. A soft sigh came from his companion, and he turned, lifting himself on one elbow to look into Consuelo's face while she slept.

Something caught painfully at his throat. God, how lovely she was. His eyes drank her in...her black hair spread across the white pillow, her hand tucked beneath her tanned cheek, her dark eyelashes lying against her smooth skin, her soft, white shoulders. He felt himself hardening with desire, his heartbeat quickening as he thought of the love she had given him all through the night. A passionate, abandoned lover beyond his wildest dreams.

"Dear, beautiful Consuelo," he whispered. "I'll take care of you now and for all our lives."

The last echo of church bells died away and something clicked in Lucas's brain. Damn, he'd forgotten it was Sunday. The courthouse would be closed. They couldn't be married today. Well, Monday then. The *Electra* was sailing on Tuesday. Today, he'd show her the city—the Cliff House, Nob Hill and Golden Gate Park. They'd ride the cable cars past the great mansions on Nob Hill, and have dinner at Delmonico's.

Consuelo sighed and turned in her sleep, pushing away the coverlet so that her firm, white breasts were exposed. Desire poured through Lucas. With one hand he reached out to caress the silky softness of her bosom. Consuelo awakened. Lucas's heart stopped, tears stung his eyes, at the sudden joy that flooded her lovely face when she beheld him.

"Are you hungry?" Lucas called through the open bathroom door. She had slept again after they made love, while he bathed and dressed. Now she was stretched out luxuriously in the warm, scented bathtub.

She laughed. In all her life she had never been so happy, would never have believed it possible to feel this way. "We did forget to eat last night, didn't we?" she answered. "I'm starving."

When she came out of the bathroom, tying her thin robe around her, not half so shy as she had been the night before, Consuelo saw that Lucas had ordered breakfast brought to their room. The round table was draped with a white linen cloth, a crystal vase with one red rose in the center. Perfectly folded omelets steamed on the two plates, with a server of toast and butter and jellies alongside.

"You're spoiling me with all this luxury," she said with teasing affection as she sat in the chair he held for her. Lucas bent to kiss the curve of her neck, his hands moving down to caress her breasts beneath the silk robe.

Sitting opposite her, he shook out his linen napkin and grinned conspiratorially. "I have to confess, my love. This is my first venture into luxury, too. I think I could learn to like it." Smiling into her warm eyes, he continued, "I've been meeting with wholesalers and merchants to set up credit lines for my new store. My friend, Captain Roberts, suggested I stay at the Palace, and he was right. It tends to impress businessmen."

Consuelo forked into her omelet hungrily. "But how did you know to do all this, to order breakfast to your room and find hansom cabs?"

He laughed, buttering a slice of sourdough toast. "I listened to the passengers on my ships, and learned from them."

Lucas watched her eating breakfast with as much gusto as a hungry vaquero. Surely she had no inkling how utterly enchanting she looked, her dark hair lying loose about her shoulders, the silk robe fallen open to reveal the delectable cleft between her breasts.

"It's Sunday," he said, deliberately turning the direction of his thoughts. "Would you like to go to Mass?"

He found the faint flush that stained her face unbelievably endearing. After a moment, she answered thoughtfully, "I suppose I wouldn't have to go to confession." The flush deepened as she lowered her eyes. "I haven't heard Mass for such a long time." The dark eyes returned to his. "Yes, could we?"

It was a lovely morning. The early fog had melted away and winter sunlight glittered off the white buildings marching up the endless hillsides. They walked past nearly deserted Montgomery Street, through the financial district to California Street and took the cable car to Grant Avenue and St. Mary's. A salty breeze was blowing off the ocean, crisp and invigorating.

According to the notice posted in front of the small red brick cathedral, Mass would not begin for a half hour. Arms linked, Lucas and Consuelo strolled down the narrow sidewalks of Grant Avenue. He watched with amusement her delight in the goods displayed in the windows of the Chinatown stores: carved teakwood chests, brass bowls, porcelain vases painted with blue chrysanthemums, embroidered silk kimonos. She recoiled, then laughed at herself, when they paused before a grocer's window hung with burnished brown roast ducks and staring dried flatfish.

Some of the stores were open in spite of the Sabbath, and Lucas bought a silk scarf printed with pink peonies for Consuelo to cover her head for Mass. He watched her go into St. Mary's, then took a trolley to the waterfront where he paid for their passage and made sure he booked a private stateroom.

"We sail with the tide Tuesday morning," the purser told him. "It'd be best you come aboard tomorrow night."

Lucas left the shipping office, hurrying to catch the trolley back to St. Mary's. Even on Sunday, the waterfront was a bustling place. Ships were being loaded or unloaded, stout horses pulled heavy drays along the cobbled streets, sailors on leave strolled between the busy taverns.

When he heard someone call his name, Lucas started hoping it was not someone from the central coast. Not today.

"I'll be damned." Lucas chuckled as a burly man strode toward him, holding out a hand. It was a shipmate he'd sailed with on the clippers years before.

"Just back from China," the man said. "What have you been doin', old salt?"

"I'm getting married," Lucas told him, and the words filled him with joy. "To a beautiful lady. And I'm building my own wharf on the central coast."

"Gettin' married, are ye?" The man squinted at him and reached inside his jacket. "Wanta buy your lady a weddin' gift?"

"A little contraband?" Lucas asked wryly, for there was scarcely a sailor on the seas who didn't supplement his income with small-scale smuggling.

The string of pearls gleamed incongruously against the rough brown hand of the sailor. At once, Lucas could imagine the pearls lying against Consuelo's lovely throat and knew she had to have them. No matter that he'd already spent far more than he could afford on this trip.

"How much?" he inquired.

"How much for a friend?"

Chuckling, Lucas reached for his pocketbook.

"You are the most beautiful woman in all the world." Lucas's voice was hoarse with suppressed emotion, his blue eyes darkly adoring.

Consuelo smiled, and turned flirtatiously before him once more. The pink blouse he'd insisted on buying blended perfectly with the burgundy wool skirt, making a dressy ensemble. The low neckline revealed a part of her shoulders and a smooth expanse of throat nearly to her breasts where the wide ruffles began. Those ruffles were the only sleeves, showing her bare arms. Suddenly she wished for the beautiful rebozo he had given her for her birthday. It would have matched exactly. She twirled again, scarcely recognizing the image looking back at her from the mirror in the hotel room.

They were going to dinner at Delmonico's, Lucas said, the finest restaurant in all of San Francisco. Consuelo sighed as Lucas tipped her chin to kiss her gently. The whole day had had a dreamlike quality, from the strange shops in Chinatown to the lovely Mass in St. Mary's. After Mass, bothered by a faintly nagging conscience, she had confessed to a bored priest, who gave her a penance of ten Hail Marys for lying with a man not yet her husband. Then she had met Lucas and they had taken a hansom ride out to Ocean Beach, where they had sipped tea in the Cliff House and watched the waves beat against the rocky shore. Coming back, they had ridden the cable car down California Street. Consuelo stared in astonishment at the enormous mansions of the railroad kings on Nob Hill.

"What do they do with so many rooms?" she had asked in disbelief.

Lucas had laughed and drawn her close to him on the bench inside the rattling cable car. "Not being rich, my dear, I couldn't tell you. But it does impress the neighbors."

It had been a totally enchanted day, something outside ordinary life. And now, dressed like a princess, she was going to dinner at Delmonico's with the man she loved. He looked wonderful, she thought with pride, in a dark suit and starched white shirt.

"I have a present for you," he said, looking down at her with loving eyes. "A wedding present."

She scarcely heard the words as she stared at the pearls he held in his hand, lustrous, gleaming richly in the flickering gaslight. "Lucas..." she breathed softly, stunned, as he fastened them around her neck. Then he bent to kiss her throat where the pearls lay glowing against her smooth olive skin.

"They are beautiful, *querido*," she managed to say, her throat tight. "But they must have been so very expensive. You mustn't spend so much money on me."

Cupping her face in his hands, Lucas looked deep into her eyes. "I want to give you everything," he said, then smiled a bit arrogantly. "Besides, I intend to be a rich man."

At Delmonico's they sat in a curtained booth and drank the champagne Lucas recklessly ordered. Like everything else about the day, the restaurant seemed something from a lovely dream. Red flocked wallpaper covered the walls. Crystal chandeliers gleamed off the silver pitchers and serving platters. Black-coated waiters moved with obsequious efficiency. Even the clatter of china was muted as befitted so grand a place. They ate veal medallions, crab salad and a flaming dessert called fried cream. After the meal their waiter discreetly closed the booth's curtain when he found them kissing each other.

In the hansom cab taking them back to the Palace Hotel, Consuelo leaned against Lucas's shoulder, her head still whirling from the champagne.

"*Querido,*" she whispered, reaching to stroke his cheek. "I never dreamed of anything so lovely. I'll never forget these days with you."

"And the nights?" he prompted with a smile, one hand cupped over her breast. His mouth covered hers, sweetly familiar now, and she returned the kiss with increasing passion.

Breathless, they broke apart, and she teased, "Do you suppose it's possible to make love when one is drunk on champagne?"

Laughing, Lucas held her close. "We'll find the answer to that together," he promised.

Lucas awakened to the sound of fog bells clanging on the bay. Pale watery light filled the room. He turned, reaching for Consuelo, thinking how quickly he'd become accustomed to her lying beside him. Last night, both of them a bit flown with champagne, they had made languorous love, so sweet that when the final explosion came it had rocked him to his depths.

Drifting on the edge of sleep, he remembered holding her, telling her lovingly, "Tomorrow we shall be married."

Sitting up, he saw her at the window, her robe clutched about her as she stared out into the morning fog obscuring the hills beyond Market Street.

His heart constricted as he contemplated for a moment her slender loveliness. "Come here, sweetheart," he called softly, and when she turned, added teasingly, "I want to make love to you once more before you're my wife."

Dark eyes suddenly swam with tears, and Consuelo turned away from him. "I can't marry you, Lucas." Her voice broke on the words. "Not today."

Shock turned him cold. Staring in disbelief, Lucas rose from the bed and crossed the room. He gathered her into his arms and turned her to face him.

"Consuelo." He saw the tears spilling from her eyes, and felt his heart constrict in sudden fear. "I thought it was understood," he protested. "Today we'll go to the courthouse and be married by a justice of the peace. We'll go back to Morgan's Landing as husband and wife."

He cupped her chin in his fingers and bent to kiss her, wanting to heal whatever hurt her.

Consuelo pushed him away. "Please listen, Lucas. I've been up for hours, thinking what I should do." A sob choked in her throat, and Lucas drew her back into his arms.

She yielded to his embrace, her face pressed against his bare shoulder. The words were muffled, broken by some emotion he could not yet fathom.

"I love you, Lucas, and . . . and you have been so good, so generous, and made me so happy."

"All good reasons to marry me," he said tenderly, wondering how to comfort her. He felt the slender body pressed against his tense as she struggled for control.

With gentle fingers he wiped the tears from her cheeks, looking into the unhappy dark eyes lifted to his.

"I went to confession yesterday at St. Mary's," she began.

Lucas swore under his breath, his arms tightened around her as though to hold her safe against whatever might part them.

"The priest said—" she took a deep breath "—he said I had sinned and gave me a penance. But…" She looked away as though she couldn't bear to meet his probing gaze. "He reminded me that I must never marry out of my church."

"I'll be a Catholic," Lucas exploded. "Take me to the man. He can baptize me today and marry us after."

When his words brought a new burst of weeping, he added contritely, "I had always intended to convert, dear one. Does it matter when?"

She came to him then, her arms tight around his waist, holding him fiercely against her. Her dark eyes looked into his unhappy face, begging understanding. "I must go home. I can't get married without my family. And certainly not without Father Amateo's blessing. I have to go home and set things right with my father. I must ask Father Amateo to cancel my betrothal to Ramón."

Anger ripped through Lucas. Damn Don Augustino and the old priest! Why should they have such power over her life? How could she care about the father who had treated her like a chattel? And the priest who had sold her to that bastard Ramón for a new altar?

"You told me what happened in San Juan Bautista," he said in a flat voice, trying to control his anger. "Ramón lay with a woman and her man found them and stabbed him. Good God! Why should you be concerned with formally ending a betrothal to such a swine?"

"It's not just that, Lucas. Please hear me." She stepped back from him, as though his touch could weaken her resolve. "I can't come to you with nothing but my family's debts. I won't be a burden." Her dark head lifted proudly. "I've proved I can stand on my own. I drove the cattle to San Francisco and sold them. Now I'll go home, and when all the debts are paid—" she laid her palm against his morning-stubbled cheek "—I can wed you, my love."

"That doesn't make sense," he growled as panic swept him. The possibility of losing her again was more than he could bear. "Why must we wait? You can pay the debts yourself even if you're married to me." Her mouth tightened stubbornly, and his voice rose. She had to hear him and understand. "What if you're carrying my child already?" he demanded. "What then?"

At the words, her face softened, the stubbornness fading. Dark eyes gleaming, she came to him, slipping her arms around his neck and looking up into his angry face.

"Our child?" she murmured, her lips warm against his ear. "I would be so happy, Lucas." She yielded to his demanding kiss, but when they broke apart, the stubborn pride was back in the set of her face.

"There will be time, *querido*. Only a week or so. A month at most. My father will be free of his debts, and I will be free to come to you. Please, Lucas, please understand."

"Do I have a choice?" he asked unhappily. He'd wanted to go home with her, safely married, so that nothing her father or the priest or Ramón could do would change it.

Consuelo's arms tightened around his neck, her warm body close to his. The silk robe had fallen open, and her naked breasts were like firebrands pressing into his chest. With a groan of defeat, Lucas embraced her, running his hands down the rounded softness of her body to mold her against his burgeoning desire.

"Could we make love before we order breakfast?" she whispered, her lips a breath from his.

She had won the battle, Lucas thought, as he laid her on the bed and covered her body with his, but he would win the war.

Chapter Eighteen

The *Electra* plowed southward through choppy seas, beneath a bright blue winter sky. Clad in her heavy serape, Consuelo paced the deck, exhilarated by the sharp wind. Her hair was bound by the silk scarf from Chinatown, and Lucas's arm steadied her. She'd quickly found that the stale air in her tiny stateroom was more conducive to seasickness than the shifting deck beneath her feet. Because she was the only woman aboard, the room was hers alone. Lucas slept on a bunk in a cabin with five other men.

Tension vibrated between them as they walked, arms entwined, his hand clasping hers. It was more than the constraint imposed by the necessary discretion aboard ship, with the presence of other passengers and the crew. She was certain he still didn't understand why she had refused to marry him in San Francisco. At times she saw him watching her with an expression of hurt and puzzlement. And when desire leaped inside her in response to heated kisses stolen in secluded corners of the ship, she found herself wishing she had agreed, so that they could lie together in love as man and wife. Perhaps she shouldn't have let her pride overrule all the promptings of her heart.

"We'll be stopping over at Monterey," Lucas was saying, bending toward her to speak over the racket of the steam engine. "Do you want to go ashore?"

Looking up into his longing eyes, Consuelo felt her body tighten with desire. It wasn't possible. Monterey was still a small town. There was no place they could be together without the gossips knowing. It wasn't like San Francisco, where they could hide in a hotel so grand that no one from the central coast was likely to appear. Besides, her monthly flux had started. They would have to be satisfied with kisses until they were married.

She smiled at him, wishing she hadn't been the cause of the pain she saw in those eyes. "No, I think not. I have a great-aunt there, but she's very old and wouldn't remember me. I hardly know my cousins."

Lucas's hand tightened on hers, and his blue eyes blazed with desire. He chuckled softly. "I didn't mean to visit relatives. I thought perhaps since the *Electra* will be tied up overnight..." His voice fell away, the unasked question trailing off.

Biting her lip, Consuelo looked away. She could feel a flush climbing her face. "My monthly flux started today, Lucas."

"Ahh." There was relief in his voice, mingled with disappointment. "I have to go ashore on some business, but I won't stay."

They were on the lee side of the ship now, alone, out of sight of the crew. All the other passengers had taken shelter inside out of the wind. Lucas drew her back against his chest, his arms around her as he leaned against the bulkhead. Bending his head, he pressed his cold cheek lovingly against hers and slid his hands beneath the serape to cup her breasts.

Consuelo drew in a sharp breath, amazed at the intensity of her reaction. Being lovers hadn't assuaged her desire for him, but had only increased the need. She leaned back into his embrace, turned her face to him and surrendered her lips to his passionate kiss.

Two sailors came along the deck, heads bent against the wind. With a sigh, Lucas leaned back, but his hands beneath her serape still moved gently on her breasts.

"How long must I wait, Consuelo?" His breath was hot against her ear.

She covered his hands with hers, holding them hard against her pulsing breasts. "Soon," she murmured raggedly as need flowed through her. "Oh, very soon."

There was a hint of triumph in his soft laugh. Another sailor came along the deck, and Lucas reluctantly released her from his embrace. Taking her arm, he led her to a wooden bench, washed in sunshine and out of the wind.

Consuelo sat close to him, the need his caresses had aroused still throbbing in the depths of her body. Watching him cup his hands to guard his flint from the wind and light his cigarillo, she admired every movement, every turn of his big body.

He leaned back against the bench, blowing smoke into the air. With an amused glance, he said, "I know your father doesn't think me suitable. I'm not sure about your aunt."

Consuelo gave him an arch look and smiled. "I think Tía Isabel is quite taken with you, Lucas."

His eyebrows rose in surprise, but he looked pleased. Then his face sobered and he leaned forward, staring down at the cigarillo in his hands.

"There's something I have to tell you, Consuelo. It wouldn't be fair to marry you without your knowing my past, my beginnings."

"Oh, Lucas—" she started to protest, laying one hand on his shoulder. She didn't want to hear what he had to say. The days and nights of loving had swept away all her doubts. He mustn't tell her anything to bring them back to life.

"Listen," he commanded and sat back, staring straight ahead as he talked. "I told you once that my mother died when I was twelve, and that was when I first went to sea. I think I said then that I never knew my father, but not that I was . . . I am . . . a bastard."

His face was set with old pain. Sorrow for what must have been a miserable and unhappy childhood caught at Consuelo's heart. It must have cost him dear to tell her this, she thought as she covered his free hand with hers. Her fingers tightened on his and she lifted the hand to press her lips against his palm.

Lucas's eyes sought hers, uncertain and questioning. Smiling at him, she held his palm lovingly to her cheek. "You are Lucas Morgan," she told him, "the man I will marry. The past is of no consequence, *querido mío.*"

Such love blazed in his blue eyes, Consuelo felt herself stirred to her depths. She leaned toward him, wanting his kiss. At the sound of approaching voices, they hastily drew apart.

The four rough-looking men had come aboard at San Francisco. They did not mingle with the other passengers, but kept to themselves.

"Prospectors," Lucas said as they passed. "Probably heading for the hills around Cambria to search for quicksilver."

The mention of quicksilver brought back all her dreams and hopes for her own mine. Consuelo realized she still hadn't confided those plans to Lucas. Stung by the thought that perhaps something in her still did not entirely trust this man she meant to marry, Consuelo stared at the men, who had gathered to smoke and talk at the forward rail. "I hope Henry has plenty of men at España Mine to protect it from ruffians like that." She gave Lucas a sideways glance, hoping her lack of confidence would not hurt him. "You knew about the quicksilver mine, didn't you?" she added lightly.

"Vicente told me." He frowned, studying her. "He didn't say you were involved, except that the property was on Rancho Estrada." He puffed thoughtfully on the cigarillo. "Will you invest your cattle money in the mine?" When she nodded enthusiastically, he smiled. "There's lots of money to be made in quicksilver while the price is so high."

Relieved by his reaction, Consuelo laid her cheek against his shoulder, remembering how he had told her he would be rich. With the mine, she would be, if not rich, at least solvent. They would be equals. Her pride wouldn't allow her to wed Lucas Morgan until she was free of the burden of her father's debts. The cattle money would develop the mine, and the mine would set her free.

* * *

Lucas's heart swelled with pride as the steamer rounded the point and moved into Estero Bay.

"Morgan's Landing," Captain Roberts said as he paused beside Lucas at the rail. "By spring it'll be the busiest port on the central coast." He grinned and added, "And I've invested in it."

Lucas chuckled. Cupping his hands to light his cigarillo, he blew smoke toward the gray afternoon sky. The pilings for his wharf stretched out into the bay. He was delighted to see how much Soledad had accomplished during the two weeks he'd been gone. He'd have to check the bracing and fenders on the newly laid planking to make certain the workers had used enough to withstand the winter storms.

Word had spread after the steamer's brief stop at San Simeon. Wagons and carryalls and buggies were parked near the warehouse, and a number of horses stood at the hitching rack. He could faintly hear the Indians calling out their singsong greeting from the crowd along the shore.

The lighter boat put out into the calm gray sea, and Lucas could see Soledad's tall, muscular form at the helm, rowing strongly. The sense of homecoming was so intense, Lucas's eyes stung.

"I'll tell Señorita Estrada we're ready to go ashore," he said and turned away. The captain gave him a knowing look.

As he made his way down to Consuelo's stateroom, Lucas wondered briefly how soon gossip of their close relationship on the voyage would be spread around the countryside. Mr. Perkins, who owned the dry goods store in Cambria had been on board, and even though he'd been seasick the whole voyage, he must have noticed the two of them together.

If only he'd been able to persuade her to marry him in San Francisco. None of her arguments made sense to him. She was stubborn and full of foolish pride. It scared him to think that, back here, the priest and her father could bring all their influence to bear on her. Could she hold out against them as strongly as she had against him?

All doubts vanished when she opened the door to his knock. A light flared in her lovely dark eyes when she saw him. "Lucas." She breathed his name in a glad voice, and love for her filled him like the warmth of a summer day.

He stepped inside and closed the door. Consuelo yielded to his embrace, her mouth seeking his with an answering hunger. Dear God, he thought, how could he live through the weeks ahead before she would be his wife, before he could hold her and know her completely again?

"The lighter boat's coming for us," he told her, wondering again how long it might be before he could hold her like this. Lucas's hands clasped her hips to press her fiercely against his body, as he kissed her ear, and her throat.

Consuelo's breath was fast and hot against his cheek, her arms clinging and her mouth moist against his face.

"Marry me," he whispered. "Sweet love, marry me now—today."

"Ah, Lucas, *corazón*." Her breath came out in a long sigh. "You are persuasive. But," she said as she drew away, smiling at him, "we have decided. I know what I must do before I can come to you, free and clear." She laid her palm softly against his cheek. "Trust me, *querido mío*."

"*You* have decided," he corrected wryly. "It seems I have no choice." His arms tightened as he covered her mouth once more, his tongue probing until he could draw the sweetness of her into himself. The stirrings of desire shook him, and Lucas moved away, struggling for control.

"Come on," he said gruffly. "I'll carry your things up on deck."

Lucas carried Consuelo ashore, wading through the surf. As soon as he set her down on the dry sandy beach, he was surrounded by workers welcoming him back, and merchants from Cambria who'd come to pick up expected shipments.

Smiling, she watched him, taller than most of the men, laughing, answering questions with authority. How far he'd come from the half-drowned Anglo sailor her father had dragged from the sea, and certainly from the outcast little child he must once have been.

And how far she'd come from the girl who had protested even bringing this hurt sailor into her father's house. Now he was her lover. She'd given herself to him, body and soul, with no feelings of remorse. She had confessed to a priest at St. Mary's, a priest who didn't know her and would never hear of her again. Now she wouldn't need to confess to Father Amateo. She had only to tell him he must cancel her betrothal to Ramón.

The lighter boat had been pushed off once more, this time loaded with goods and mail bound for Santa Barbara and San Pedro. Lucas was talking to Mr. Perkins, who looked overcome with relief to have the steady earth beneath his feet. Nodding at Perkins, he walked over to Consuelo, laying one big hand discreetly on her arm.

"Perkins's son came to meet him in a buggy. They'll give you a ride into Cambria." He grimaced. "I'll be tied up here the rest of the day with the goods going out and those coming ashore."

His hand moved down her arm and a shudder of longing shook her. Blue eyes, grown dark with desire, looked into hers. "Could you stay with Vicente and Angela tonight?" he asked. "I'll come into town as soon as I can get away."

The fire that dark look ignited blazed inside her. How long it would be before they were together again, she couldn't guess. There was so much to be done. One more night, even in the presence of Vicente and his wife, seemed a precious boon.

"Yes." She smiled up at him, love suffusing her face. "I'll stay in Cambria tonight."

Perkins and his son left Consuelo at the Coast Bank building. She was anxious to see Vicente, but other business had to be taken care of first. Carrying the City of Paris box containing the blouse Lucas bought for her, and her saddlebags where there was a new shawl for Isabel and a soft wool shirt for her father, she went into the bank.

At the teller's window, Consuelo deposited the bank draft from the cattle buyer to a new account she opened in her name only. When the teller showed the draft to Bert Lathrop, the manager crossed the lobby, a smile on his porcine face, his plump hand extended in greeting.

"Quite a thing you did, Miss Estrada," he said, too heartily as though he didn't really approve. "Everyone's talking about your cattle drive."

She gave him a satisfied smile, indicating the draft. "Yes, it was quite successful."

She had never really liked Bert Lathrop. He was too smooth, like a china doll with nothing behind the facade. The rotund banker stood too close to her, and she tried to move away unobtrusively. Why didn't he just go back to his desk? But he stood there, smiling unctuously, obviously bent on continuing their conversation.

To her surprise, he seized her hand and squeezed it familiarly. "I'm anxious to hear about your business enterprises." He gave her an encouraging smile. "You're quite a remarkable young woman."

"Gracias," she replied cautiously. The banker had never deigned to speak to her before she made this sizable deposit in his bank, and now she could only doubt his motives.

"It's said you're part owner of a quicksilver mine, in addition to your cattle enterprise." He waited expectantly for a reply.

Consuelo frowned. The fact that the banker knew about the mine must mean that Henry and Vicente had begun setting up the operation. Why was this unpleasant man so interested?

"I'm sorry," she said, suddenly aware that Lathrop had asked her a question.

"I was saying," he continued smoothly, seeming unoffended by her lack of interest in their conversation, "that the España Mine seems to have extraordinarily rich ore, or so the rumors go around town."

"Yes," she replied, wondering if he was interested in investing in the mine. Was that the reason for his questioning her? Surely he could have learned all this from Vicente. "Henry Rios tells me it assays at eighty-two percent."

"A good man, Henry, knows the quicksilver mining business," he agreed. Leaning toward her, he asked, "How is his retort furnace working out? I've heard they aren't as efficient as the new types of furnace."

Consuelo didn't answer immediately, for she was still wondering at his interest.

"Has Henry spoken about the furnace?" Lathrop persisted.

"Well, yes." She was suddenly reluctant to give him any more information. "Henry says as long as the ore assays so high, a retort is satisfactory."

"Ummm." Lathrop pursed his moist, pink lips, the eyes behind his steel-rimmed glasses gleaming with satisfaction. Consuelo frowned, annoyed by his odd reaction.

"Then you'll be shipping quicksilver soon?" Lathrop asked.

"In about a month," she answered. "I must go," she added, uneasy and anxious to escape his interrogation. "Vicente is expecting me."

"Ah, yes. The lawyer Rios," Lathrop said and laughed.

At the sound of that mirthless laugh, the uneasiness inside Consuelo grew into a chill of apprehension. With a quick nod of farewell, she picked up her bags and hurried toward the exit. The heavy glass doors swung shut behind her. Still uneasy, Consuelo glanced back into the lighted bank. Bert Lathrop stood watching her, a gloating smile on his round face.

Chapter Nineteen

Fog was rolling in from the sea when Consuelo came out of the bank, threading long fingers among the dark pines and eucalyptus trees on the hillsides. She hoped the *Electra* had off-loaded and was on her way, and that Lucas was on his way to her.

"Consuelo!" Vicente cried when she entered his office. He rushed from behind his desk to hug her with such impulsive enthusiasm she dropped her bundles to the floor.

"We've all been so worried about you, going off on that crazy cattle drive in spite of everything I said." He held her away and his eyes warmed with admiration. "Well, look at you—a fashion plate straight from San Francisco."

"Did Rafael get home?" she asked anxiously.

"The old devil." Vicente laughed. "He rushed back, and now everyone's making much over him so that he thinks he's quite a hero." He sobered. "He told me about Ramón's accident in San Juan Bautista."

"It was no accident," Consuelo interrupted in a harsh voice. "Ramón was in bed with the man's wife and the man knifed him. He deserved it," she added.

Vicente shrugged, and she knew he'd say no more about it when he saw the subject upset her.

"Rafael said your father and Isabel are fine, but anxious about you." He paused, the grin widening on his swarthy face. "Angela is very cross with you."

Startled, Consuelo stared at him. "Why?"

"Because you weren't here to greet your godson when he was born."

"Oh, Vicente!" she cried and hugged him joyfully. "Are they both all right?"

"Of course." He beamed with pride. "You must come home with me to see them."

"I thought I'd stay the night, if it's all right," she began tentatively. When he grinned and nodded, she continued, searching for excuses as she spoke. "There must be papers to sign for the mine, and arrangements to be made. And now that I have money I can pay the bills," she stated proudly.

To her surprise, Vicente turned away, walked over to the window and stared out at the fog pouring over the hilltops like whipped cream over the edge of a bowl.

The apprehension she'd felt downstairs at the bank returned, sending cold fingers of fear running down her spine. "What's wrong, Vicente?"

Straightening his narrow shoulders, he turned toward her, his smile obviously forced. "The title papers came in from San Luis Obispo today. I'm waiting for the mine franchise, but Henry already has men at work and the retort furnace ready to start."

"Then why do you look like something terrible has happened?" she demanded, facing him.

"Not really terrible," he insisted, as though trying to convince himself. "I'm sure we can work out some kind of compromise."

"What?" she cried, wanting to shake him.

"The Estero Bay property that your father sold to Lucas," he began reluctantly, "extends back into the foothills, according to the title records."

Foreboding enveloped her as she waited for him to explain.

Vicente spread his hands in a gesture of frustration. "The land the mine is located on belongs to Lucas Morgan, but the mineral rights belong to Bert Lathrop."

Stunned, Consuelo stared at him. It was a moment before she could even speak. "How can that be?" she cried, utterly confused. "If it's on Estero Bay land, it must belong to Lucas."

"No." Vicente shook his head gravely. "It's a separate title entirely. And it's Lathrop's."

Bewildered still, Consuelo felt a growing sense of despair. After all the struggles to drive the cattle to San Francisco for money to open the mine and all the money Vicente had cosigned for at the bank, to pay for the furnace, to pay Henry and the miners he'd hired—after all that, would she lose everything?

Anger grew hot inside her when she recalled the smug look on Lathrop's face just moments ago. "So that's why Lathrop was questioning me about the mine just now in the bank." How could this have happened with no one knowing? she wondered. An awful urge to cry out at the cruelty of fate possessed her and she bit her lip. All the dreams and plans of the past weeks had come to nothing.

"I knew there was something...something underhanded. The way he acted bothered me." She tried, but couldn't still the tremor in her voice.

"I haven't talked with Lathrop yet," Vicente admitted reluctantly. "But I'm sure we can arrange a lease with him, or—" he frowned "—some kind of partnership."

"With a crook like Lathrop!" she cried.

"He has the most to gain by being reasonable," Vicente told her, but she could sense his doubt in the words.

"Did Lucas know about this all the time?" she demanded, struggling to control her voice.

Vicente looked uncomfortable. He paced the room, stroking his mustache, not answering.

There was more, she thought unhappily, watching him delay his answer. She and Vicente had known each other all their lives. When they were children, she had even protected the diminutive Vicente from the rough teasing of her brother Felipe and his swaggering friends. He was her lawyer; he should have checked the titles since he hadn't handled the transfer. How could he have failed her like this? And why hadn't she been more careful instead of forging blindly ahead with excited plans? If she meant to make her own way in the world, she must remember this hard lesson.

"I don't know, Consuelo," he replied. "You must believe that. Lucas is a careful man. He should have checked his land title, but he's not experienced in business."

"He was with Papá when the titles were signed over. He had to know." She cried out the words as though in protest at the ugly truth they conveyed.

Pain scored her heart. All the time they'd been together in San Francisco, all those enchanted days and nights, he'd been deceiving her. Slowly, the hurt gave way to a rising flame of anger. He'd known about this when they were in San Francisco. She had loved him with her whole heart. She'd gone against all the years of her careful upbringing, and betrayed herself for love of him. What a naive and foolish child she had been to trust him.

"My father was a fool," she said, "to deal with an Anglo like Lucas Morgan at all." Half under her breath, she added, "And I have been a bigger fool."

"Lucas is a decent man," Vicente protested. "When he returns from San Francisco, I'm sure he'll help us work this out with Lathrop. A partnership of some kind, perhaps."

"He has returned," she said curtly, walking past him to look down at Cambria's busy Bridge Street. An early dusk gathered beneath the foggy skies. "He came back on the *Electra,* the same ship I was on."

"Oh?" Vicente looked at her curiously. "Then you've talked with him?"

She couldn't take any more, and Consuelo whirled furiously on Vicente. "Do you know where Lucas Morgan got the money to build his wharf, Vicente?"

Vicente stared at her, surprised by the violence of her tone. "He had gold," he answered.

"Pacific Steamship's gold," she cried. "He stole it the night of the shipwreck. He used it to buy my dower lands from my foolish father. He—" She choked on her words, and fought back the tears stinging her eyes.

"He paid it back, Consuelo." Vicente's voice was mildly reproving. "He took it with him on this trip to San Francisco."

Why couldn't he have told me that, too? she thought, staring at Vicente. "The wharf hasn't been in business that long," she said, thinking aloud. "Where would he get that much money?"

"Coast Bank loaned him money with the wharf as collateral." Suddenly, Vicente looked as though he, too, might be dealing with unpleasant possibilities. "Bert Lathrop arranged the loan." His voice dropped and he refused to meet her eyes.

"How generous," she said sarcastically. "A favor for a favor, I presume." An embarrassed flush stained her face when she recalled the naïve way she'd confided her plans for the quicksilver mine to Lucas. He'd known the mine would never be hers, yet he'd let her go on dreaming and planning.

How could he? How could he? The words echoed and reechoed in her mind. Oh yes, Lucas Morgan, raised in poverty and shame, was an ambitious man. He would stop at nothing to gain the wealth he desired, beginning with stealing Pacific Steamship's gold.

"I won't believe that," Vicente replied stoutly. "Don't judge him, Consuelo, until you know all the circumstances."

"It's pretty obvious, Vicente." She gave him a pitying look. "Lucas Morgan has used all of us for his own gain." She cringed inwardly, remembering how she'd confided in him her hopes that the mine would make her family's finances safe for good. Now she had the money in the bank downstairs, but she knew how quickly that would go to pay Papá's debts. And the cattle were all gone, too. There was nothing left to provide for the future.

"Well, I'll reserve judgment until I talk to Lucas," she heard Vicente say calmly. "Can't you do the same?"

She couldn't bear any more, couldn't bear to hear his name and know how he'd deceived her. Without answering his question, she crossed the room and picked up her saddlebags. "I'll go on over to the house to see Angela." She wished that she could flee, that she could escape from Vicente and Angela and their happiness and from any memory of what she'd shared with Lucas Morgan.

"I'll be along as soon as I've finished a few things here," Vicente said. She opened the door and he called, "Wait, you've forgotten your package." He pointed to the City of Paris box.

"That belongs to Lucas Morgan," she said coldly. "You can give it to him when you see him next."

Exiting the office, Consuelo walked briskly to the side street where Vicente lived, trying to hang on to her anger, for only then could she bear the hurt.

On his marriage Vicente had built this small two-story house for his bride. It was white clapboard, with a tiny shaded porch and green shutters at the six-over-six windows. Its patch of green lawn was surrounded by a picket fence, and it was shaded by pine and eucalyptus trees.

The inside of the house was furnished simply, much of the furniture inherited by Angela from the de la Guerra family. As the youngest of the large Rios family, Vicente had inherited only brains and grit to make his future. Knowing her ambitious friend, Consuelo was certain this house would be replaced by a larger one in the years to come, perhaps even by a hacienda.

Greeted by Angela's enthusiastic hugs, Consuelo half forgot her unhappiness in the joy of holding and cuddling the tiny, black-haired creature who was Miguel Vicente de la Guerra Rios.

Left to rock the baby while Angela and her Indian woman made preparations for dinner, Consuelo studied Miguel's chubby face. The baby sighed in his sleep and made a bubble with his tiny mouth. Consuelo's heart constricted as her mind filled with the memory of Lucas's warm voice when he spoke of the children they would have. She fought against the pain, blinking back the tears that stung her eyes. No one must ever know.

"Tell me all about your trip to San Francisco," Angela begged as she nursed Miguel, who had awakened screaming with hunger.

It was difficult for Consuelo to censor all she had to tell. The name of Lucas Morgan must not be mentioned, and yet everything about San Francisco was colored by the memory of sharing it with him.

The gown she wore was suitably admired, although Angela had many finer gowns, and all her exploits as a cattle drover exclaimed over. Angela's dark eyes flashed at the story of the meeting with Ramón in San Juan Bautista.

"You mustn't marry him, Consuelo," Angela warned with a frown.

"I have no intention of marrying him," Consuelo replied in spirited tones.

Men's voices came from the yard, and the sound of boots crunching on the gravel walk. When Lucas followed Vicente in the door, Consuelo wished with all her heart that she had followed her instincts and run for home. She had known he would come here tonight. Perhaps it was best. Later she would confront him and learn the truth, if Lucas Morgan could speak the truth.

She refused to meet his eyes, or to greet him. Lucas watched her with a puzzled frown. Each time he approached her, she made a show of doing something, carrying Miguel into the bedroom to change his diaper or helping Angela set dinner on the table.

The usually ebullient Vicente was a bit subdued tonight, too. His eyes went warily from Consuelo to Lucas and back again as they sat at the supper table. Almost as though he were traversing dangerous ground, he carefully directed the conversation with talk of the subdivision he and Lucas would build at Morgan's Landing. "A whole new town," he said. "And we'll name the next town we build after me."

A flash of dismay crossed Angela's face. Consuelo wondered if Angela was worried that Vicente had overextended himself. He had borrowed money to help develop the mine they no longer owned, and he must have borrowed money to go in with Lucas on the subdivision. She saw Vicente glance at his wife with subtle warning, and there was a brief stiff silence.

Consuelo rose to fill the coffee cups as Angela served apple cobbler with whipped cream. She was all too aware of Lucas's eyes following her movements and her hand trembled.

When she sat at the table again, he turned fully toward her. "On the way over, Vicente told me that the mineral rights on my property belong to Bert Lathrop." Frowning, he watched her face.

Hurt roiled inside her as she glanced at him and away. "A great surprise to you, I'm sure," she said sarcastically.

Lucas's blue eyes darkened. In a searing flash she remembered those eyes, hot with desire, looking into hers. Oh God, she must not remember.

"I *didn't* know, Consuelo," he said evenly, still staring at her with a puzzled expression. "Your father must have sold the rights to Lathrop and never told me."

"My father?" she cried, unbelieving that he would blame this on Papá. "He had no money from Lathrop, only your stolen gold. Besides, he would have told me."

Lucas's face flushed at the words *stolen gold,* and he said evenly, "I've repaid the salvaged gold, Consuelo."

"Yes—" she glared at him "—with the loan Bert Lathrop gave you so gladly, without a question. Was it on a handshake, Lucas, or just a deal between partners in crime?" She stood up so abruptly her chair tipped backward. Lucas reached out to grab it before it fell to the floor.

"Damn you, Lucas Morgan!" She spit out the words, glaring at him. "I thought you were different. I believed in you. I trusted you." She choked on the next words. "I loved you." Forcing herself under control, she went on doggedly. "All the time you were conspiring with that rotten Lathrop to cheat my family of their last hope."

Shock flooded Lucas's features and he stood, too, staring down at her in amazement. "I would never cheat you, Consuelo."

Vicente and Angela sat at the table, staring in stunned silence.

"Damn your Anglo heart, Lucas Morgan." Consuelo's voice shook and she was terrified she might burst into tears.

"Listen to me!" Lucas's voice rose and he reached out for her.

She drew back, eluding his grasp. "I've listened to you once, fool that I am. I shall never listen to you again."

With that she turned and fled upstairs to the attic bedroom Angela had prepared for her. Flinging herself across the narrow bed, she muffled her tears in the pillow. The traitorous Anglo would not know she wept for him.

Chapter Twenty

Morning fog lingered above the familiar hills as Consuelo pushed the mangy, livery-stable horse toward Rancho Estrada. It was not quite the homecoming she had planned. There was money from the cattle, of course, safe in the bank now. But she'd counted so much on the mine for the future of her family. The sense of loss grew more acute the more she thought about it, for it was not just financial security she had lost. Her one and only love had proved false, and she had lost him.

This morning at breakfast, Vicente had argued with her, still convinced that Lucas hadn't conspired with Bert Lathrop. How easily it must have fallen into place for him, she insisted. The mineral rights in exchange for the money to finance Morgan's Landing, the wharf and the subdivision.

"I'll see Lathrop today," Vicente had told her as they walked toward the livery stable.

She had changed into the clothes she'd worn on the cattle drive, her new gown folded in a muslin sack provided by Angela. Several people looked at her strangely as they passed.

"I'm sure he'll be willing to work this out without going to court," Vicente continued earnestly. "Some kind of compromise would be best for all concerned."

Consuelo frowned, thinking of Bert Lathrop's mean eyes, his triumphant laugh. "Perhaps. You're the lawyer, Vicente. Do what you think best."

It occurred to her that perhaps Vicente was in a financial bind. He had advanced the money to develop the mine. Well, she must pay her share of that from the cattle money, after she'd paid the taxes on the rancho. There was likely to be little left.

"I think you're wrong about Lucas, Consuelo," Vicente said, watching her strap on her saddlebags. "You accuse him without proof."

"Logic is proof enough for me, Vicente." She mounted the horse, and looked down at him grimly. "Everything he's done speaks against him . . . the money he borrowed so easily . . . his presence with my father and Lathrop when the land transfer was made. You know as well as I that Papá cannot read English."

"Consuelo—"

"Don't speak to me of Lucas Morgan again, Vicente." Her voice had been flat and final, and she had reined the horse away before he could reply,.

A cry of welcome went up as Consuelo rode into the rancho yard. The women came running from the kitchen, calling her name, laughing and crying. Children danced around her, shouting with glee, as she dismounted. The old vaqueros sauntered up from the corrals, grinning and waving at her.

Tears swam in Consuelo's eyes as she felt the warmth of their love and their welcome. She was home again, safe at home.

Tía Isabel moved sedately through the clamoring throng. To Consuelo's surprise, she found herself clasped in her aunt's fierce embrace. "Beloved daughter," Isabel murmured. "I've been so afraid for you, even when Rafael returned to tell us you were safe in San Francisco."

Safe in San Francisco, Consuelo thought, choking back a sob. How ironic, when it was there she'd given her heart to an unworthy man. She must not think of him, must not remember she had loved him.

"How is Papá?" she asked her aunt anxiously as they moved toward the house. People were drifting away now,

adults returning to their work, children to their games.
Sancho took the reins of the livery horse, looking over the
animal with a wary eye.

"Augustino is much improved," Isabel told her, "although he finds it hard to admit it." She smiled indulgently. "Knowing you're safe at home will mean so much to
him."

Consuelo paused before the kitchen doorway. The warm
familiar scent of baking tortillas came from the clay ovens.
Rosa was grinding fresh coffee. She grinned at Consuelo.

"*Tía?*" Consuelo said to her aunt. "I'll never marry Ramón now. You must help me convince Papá to accept that."

Isabel made an odd sound, deep in her throat. Her lips
twitched as she moved on into the kitchen. "Rafael's
working at the mine now, but he's such a gossip. He's told
everyone about the trouble Ramón had at San Juan Bautista." Laughter spilled from her as though she could no
longer hold it back. "Too bad that husband didn't cut Ramón a bit lower."

Shocked by her aunt's unusual frankness, Consuelo burst
into laughter, too. "*Sí—*" she sobered "—but there was
blood enough, Isabel."

In the great room they found Don Augustino at the table
playing solitaire. A fire, warm and inviting, crackled in the
adobe fireplace, its light dancing on the plastered walls. The
room seemed strange and shabby after the luxury of San
Francisco, but sweetly familiar.

She bent to hug her father, who did not rise. He was less
haggard and gray-faced, she thought, and he had gained a
little weight.

"My daughter is a madwoman...everyone says it," he
told her, frowning. Then he chuckled and squeezed her
hand. "But here you are, my Consuelo, back from your
cattle drive and none the worse."

None the worse, Papá? she wanted to say as she kissed his
cheek. I am far the worse, for my heart is in shreds for love
of the Anglo, who betrayed my trust. I won't think of him,
she chided herself once more, and opened the saddlebags to
produce the gifts she'd brought.

While Don Augustino appreciatively admired his new shirt, Isabel stroked the soft folds of her silk shawl, her face working with emotion. Seeing the tears glistening in her aunt's eyes, Consuelo felt a pang of sympathy. So few presents in Isabel's life, she thought, so little love.

Leaning back in his cowhide chair, Augustino lit a cigar. He inhaled deeply, savoring the taste. His dark eyes glowed as he studied his daughter. "Now we can plan for the wedding," he said, smiling benignly at her.

Isabel's face froze. Consuelo stared at her father in utter astonishment. "What wedding?" she demanded.

"How could you forget, my dear? The banns were posted. You're to marry Ramón at Christmastime. Surely you brought enough money from the cattle drive for a fiesta such as this coast has never seen."

"Papá!" She cried out in disbelief. "You're mad. You heard from Rafael what Ramón did at San Juan. Do you think I'd marry such a man?"

"A young man's foolishness," Augustino said with a shrug, puffing on his cigar. "When Ramón is married, he'll have no more need to..." He searched for a word.

"Whore." Isabel supplied the word in a flat, angry voice. Augustino frowned.

"There will be no wedding, Papá," Consuelo told him harshly.

As though he hadn't heard, Augustino looked at her with a familiar glittering, acquisitive look. "How much money did you get for the cattle? Where is it?"

"It's in a safe place, Papá," she snapped, reading his intentions, his lust for gambling already at work. "You'll never see any of it."

"They were my cattle," he protested. Glaring at her, he rose and leaned weakly against the table.

"Have me taken in for rustling if you wish," she said, unable to keep the anger from her voice. "The money is mine." She turned away, ashamed of the rage she felt toward her father. "And I will never marry Ramón."

Fighting back tears at the shambles of what had begun as a happy homecoming, Consuelo walked down the veranda toward her own room. Behind her, she heard her father command Isabel, "Send Sancho to me at once. Father Amateo will deal with such a defiant daughter."

The pearls. Consuelo stared at them in consternation where they had slipped from her saddlebags onto the coverlet of her bed. She should have left them with the blouse at Vicente's office. Returning every gift from Lucas, including the silk rebozo given on her birthday, should make it clear she meant what she'd said in that miserable quarrel at Vicente's house.

The pearls lay on the blue woven cotton coverlet, cradled within the pink scarf, glowing in the dim light and reminding her of the joy they'd brought when Lucas clasped them around her neck. Those enchanted days in San Francisco seemed a lifetime ago now. She felt as though she'd dreamed it all. Emotion clogged her throat.

At the sound of Isabel's footsteps entering the room, she struggled to arrange her features into calm. Quickly, she tied the pearls in the scarf and shoved them beneath her pillow. When she went in to Cambria to see Vicente, to pay the bills and the taxes, she would ask him to return the pearls and rebozo to Lucas.

Isabel's strong, capable hand clasped her shoulder affectionately. She pressed her cheek against Consuelo's hair. "You've been so strong and brave, my girl." Isabel straightened and looked into Consuelo's eyes. "I know you're tired, but you seem so sad." She smiled. "You've done everything you said you would. I thought you would be happy."

"Not everything." Consuelo looked away, busying herself with unpacking and shaking out her new gown. Isabel stroked the fabric admiringly. "Vicente just learned that the mine belongs to Bert Lathrop."

Isabel drew in a sharp breath, her eyes widening. "How can that be?"

"It's on property Papá sold to Lucas Morgan. Lathrop claims to have bought the mineral rights that same day." She didn't even try to keep the bitterness from her voice.

"You must tell Augustino," Isabel said in dismay.

"I know. I have to ask him about what happened, but not just now." Consuelo turned away to hide her pain, wishing her aunt would go away. She wanted to be alone, to weep, to cry out at the injustice of it. It occurred to her that she would move into Felipe's room now, where she wouldn't have to always guard her emotions.

"But surely Vicente can..." Isabel began. She paused, studying Consuelo's stiff face. "Have you spoken to Lucas Morgan? He must know the truth."

The concern in Isabel's eyes touched Consuelo. Only recently had Isabel shown her this kind of caring affection. But there were too many secrets between them now, too much pain to be hidden away, and anger was the only cover she could dredge up. "I've spoken to him," she said harshly. "He pretended he didn't know the mineral rights were sold." *You* didn't know, an accusing voice echoed inside her head. *You* didn't even check the deed. How typically Californio! You are just like Papá, trusting that all will be as you desire.

"Perhaps he didn't know," Isabel interjected softly. Her dark eyes were studying Consuelo with a speculative expression.

Consuelo refused to meet her eyes. "Well," she said flatly, "we have the cattle money. Perhaps after I pay the taxes and the bills there'll be enough to live on for another year or so." She drew a deep, shaky breath, fearful she might burst into tears. Isabel mustn't know how scared she was of the future. For a few brief days that future had seemed secure, Lucas Morgan by her side, the mine making money to keep her family from poverty. But that was all a dream, a dream that had been swept away, as dreams so often are. Reality was settling with her father's debts, paying the money she owed for developing the mine, paying the taxes. And after that, she must find some way to make a living, short of selling the rancho to George Hearst.

Sighing, she turned to Isabel. "After that, I don't know what we'll do."

* * *

"Do you wish to confess, my daughter?" Father Amateo asked solicitously.

He had arrived this morning, in quick response to Don
Augustino's summons two days ago. Consuelo glanced at
him, then away at the Indian women clearing the dinner table, afraid he might read the resentment in her eyes. She
wanted to shrink and disappear, escape her father's baleful
glare and the knowing looks of the priest.

Papá had been sulky and sharp with her ever since her
return. Yesterday, knowing she must settle the rancho finances, she'd confronted her father, choosing the hour after siesta when he would be rested and easier to deal with.

All morning she and Isabel had been taking inventory of
the household stores, making lists of what was needed.
There were fewer mouths to feed now, although she was
surprised that the vaqueros had gone to the mine with
Rafael. After all, those men had thought any work not done
on horseback was beneath them. Several of the Indian men
had gone, too. To what end? she asked herself unhappily,
hoping she would hear from Vicente soon.

When she told Papá that she must know how much he
owed and to whom, he'd proved difficult and unconfiding.
It was not a woman's business, he said gruffly. He sat up on
the long settee where he had napped.

"I wouldn't make it my business," she told him, "if
Felipe were alive to run the rancho."

"I am alive!" He glared at her. "It's still my rancho."

"Papá, you're ill." Frustrated, she watched him light the
forbidden cigar with trembling hands. His pride had been
wounded by her success, of that she was certain. Placating
that pride would serve no purpose; she must simply do what
must be done.

"I have to pay our bills," she began in a reasonable tone.
"There are the taxes, but I must know how much more you
owe and to whom. I'd hoped one day we'd have income
from the quicksilver mine, but now we may not have a mine
at all."

Don Augustino frowned at her through the cigar smoke. "Why not?"

Consuelo sat down beside him. "Papá, do you remember the day you sold Estero Bay to Lucas Morgan?" When he shrugged and nodded, she continued urgently. "What papers did you sign that day in the bank? How many? Can you remember?"

He was silent for a long time, staring at the glowing end of his cigar. Oh God, she thought, he's drifting again. Maybe he'd been like this that fateful day, his mind filled with fog. He could easily have signed something, unaware of its significance. But Lucas Morgan couldn't have failed to know. That thought sent such pain lancing through her, Consuelo clenched her fists and closed her eyes tightly for a moment.

"I signed a deed over to Morgan," Don Augustino finally said. He was frowning, his face troubled as he tried to dredge up the memory.

"Is that all, Papá?" she persisted.

His face crumpled. "I—I can't remember. There were copies, I think." Suddenly he drew himself up straight and stared at her. "Are you questioning my actions?"

"I'm only trying to find out why Bert Lathrop suddenly owns the mineral rights to Estero Bay. Did you discuss selling them with him?"

"Lathrop?" The flash of defiance melted away, and Don Augustino seemed to shrivel and age before her eyes. "He made up the papers and I signed. Morgan gave me the gold. That's all."

"Papá..."

"Leave me alone, now." He made an impatient gesture as though shooing away a bothersome insect. "Leave me alone."

Sighing, Consuelo stood and looked sadly down at her father. She would get no more from him just now, she knew. And she had wanted to ask about the note Lucas claimed to have sent her. But that would have to be another time; just now, her father's words confirmed her suspicions that

Lathrop and Lucas Morgan had cheated her naive and unsuspecting father of the mineral rights.

"Consuelo?" Father Amateo persisted now, and she looked away from Papá, wondering how he could seem so confident today.

"I'll confess later, Father," she demurred. "First you must cancel my betrothal. I will not marry a libertine like Ramón Salazar."

Father Amateo's thin, ascetic face tightened with disapproval. "I've been to Rancho Santa Lucia where Ramón is recuperating. He's confessed his sins and made absolution. If God can forgive him, it's wrong of you to withhold forgiveness."

Taking her elbow in his hand, he led her out onto the veranda. A thin winter fog hung in the sky, and a chill wind blew off the ocean. Consuelo shivered and hugged herself for warmth, for the priest hadn't given her time to pick up her rebozo.

"Ramón wishes to set a date for the wedding," Father Amateo said blandly, as though he hadn't heard her objections.

A shudder went through Consuelo. She felt oppressed from all sides, by Father Amateo, who was obviously under the thumb of Ramón Salazar; by her father's refusal to discuss business; and by Lucas Morgan's deception and denial. Desperation seized her, and for a moment she wished to run away from all the problems. Then the anger returned and brought the strength she needed.

Facing the priest squarely, she said in a low, intense voice, "You can damn me to eternal hell, Father, but I will never marry Ramón Salazar. Whoever marries him will live her hell on this earth, and you must answer for that."

The priest's face drained of color, and his faded eyes grew wide with shock, for she had always been compliant to the authority of the church. "God forgive you, Consuelo." He managed to gasp out the words and quickly made the sign of the cross.

Desperate to end this interview, Consuelo spoke in determined tones. "You may tell Ramón, Father. There will be no wedding. Not at Christmas, not ever. That's my final word."

Before he could begin calling down the damnation of all heaven upon her for such blasphemous treatment of a priest, she fled into the kitchen.

Later, working in the kitchen, she could hear her father and the priest talking in the great room. Don Augustino's voice was loud and angry, the priest's low and unintelligible. After a while, their voices flattened out into the normal tones of conversation.

"Father Amateo is leaving now." Her father stood in the kitchen doorway, his expression unreadable.

The priest came toward her, holding out a hand, his face a bland, benevolent mask. "There's a rosary tonight for Señor Martinez," he said. "I must be on my way."

"Well," she said coolly, "your business here is finished."

He frowned, eyes flashing at her impertinence. "I brought a message for you, Consuelo. Vicente and Angela have asked that you be godmother to their son. The christening will take place next Sunday at my church."

She smiled, pleased that her friends had honored her in this way. "I'll be there, Father."

He did not return her smile. His face darkened, eyes boring into hers. "Come early, Consuelo." His voice was cold. "You're in dire need of absolution before you can take part in a christening."

From the veranda, Consuelo watched her father walk slowly to meet Sancho, who was bringing up the priest's saddled horse. Grief struck her at how bent and old Papá looked. When Father Amateo rode away without a gesture toward her, remorse filled her heart. She had defied a priest, something unthinkable in her upbringing. Concern for Don Augustino banished the thought, for his face looked gray and ill when he walked back into the house.

"Papá," she said, taking his arm and leading him to the large armchair where he rested. "Are you all right?"

He leaned back in the chair, closing his eyes for a moment, breathing heavily. Suddenly the dark eyes flew open, glaring at her with such fury, Consuelo instinctively shrank from him.

"How can I be all right when my daughter has defied my wishes, and spoken to the priest like a blasphemer? Ah, *Dios!*" His voice rose, his breath coming in gasps, his face scarlet. "That I should live to see this day!"

"Papá," she cried out, hurt to the very core of her. "I'm not a bad daughter simply because I won't marry Ramón. I'll stay here and take care of you always." Tears spilled down her face. "Don't speak to me this way, please, Papá."

He turned his face away, fighting for breath. Slowly the flush faded, and his skin turned mottled and gray.

"Everything will be all right, Papá," she promised, wiping her tears and patting his shoulder.

"No." His voice was a hoarse croak. "No, everything is lost now. All thrown away by a disobedient daughter. Everything is lost. Rancho Estrada. Everything."

Chapter Twenty-one

When Vicente arrived the next afternoon, Consuelo greeted him with relief, certain he brought news about the quicksilver claim. He was his usual ebullient self, which she thought a good sign. But she had to wait impatiently while he greeted her father before they could talk.

Don Augustino had taken to his bed once more. For all their efforts at waiting on him and coddling him, the old man rewarded them only with monosyllables. He greeted Vicente with disinterest. Obviously disconcerted by the don's behavior, Vicente followed Consuelo into the great room, where they sat before a fire blazing against the cold winter day. Isabel went into the kitchen to make tea for them.

"Shall I send Dr. Frame out to see him?" Vicente asked, his dark eyes filled with concern. "He seems worse than when I last saw him."

"Yesterday he was better," Consuelo replied, suppressing a twinge of guilt for her impatience with her father. "That was when he thought he was getting his way, that I would marry Ramón and hand over the cattle money."

"Ah, thank you, Doña Isabel." Vicente's eyes gleamed with pleasure as Isabel set a tray with pottery teapot and cups on the low table in front of the fireplace. She sat down in an armchair to pour the tea. The rich scent of spices rose from the plate of hot sopaipillas and Vicente reached for one immediately. "My favorite!" he exclaimed.

"Vicente!" Consuelo cried impatiently. "What about the mine? Tell me."

With a self-satisfied smile, he swallowed the bite of sopaipilla, washing it down with steaming tea. "I've talked to Lathrop," he said. "He's anxious to negotiate a lease. And he insists we keep the mine operating. He's being very reasonable."

"A dishonest man who's won can afford to be reasonable," Consuelo said, staring in surprise at Vicente. She hadn't expected him to handle this so calmly. "Just how reasonable a share is he asking?"

From the way Vicente's face changed, she knew that his meeting with Lathrop had not gone as easily as he pretended. "That's what we're negotiating," he replied, taking another sopaipilla, deliberately not meeting her eyes. With a wry smile, he added, "Ninety percent is not reasonable, but I think he knows that. It will work out. If we close the mine, he loses, too."

Ninety percent was insanity, she thought, staring at the apparently calm Vicente. She would simply have to trust in his strength and good sense.

"Henry says he expects to start producing refined quicksilver very soon." Vicente's tone was businesslike, as though everything were settled. "Consuelo, I'd appreciate it if you'd take care of the payroll and keep track of bills. You have a good head for it, and since I'm involved in several subdivisions as well as my law practice, I can't take on any more—"

"Vicente!" she interrupted sharply. "This lease isn't signed yet. What if Lathrop refuses? Can he take over the mine with all the improvements?"

Vicente held out his cup for a refill, nodding his thanks to Isabel before he paused to frown at Consuelo. "He can't take our equipment. Understand, Consuelo, he has nothing to gain and everything to lose by throwing us out. Trust me."

"Very well, Vicente," she conceded, knowing she had no other choice. "I trust the lease will be binding enough to keep Lathrop in line."

"Of course." Vicente frowned, annoyed that she should question his expertise.

Consuelo watched him finish off another sopaipilla. He'd promised everything would work out; perhaps he was right. She allowed hope to fill her heart once more.

"If the lease will be ready, I'll come to Cambria the day before the christening so we can take care of our business," Consuelo said, relaxing now that everything seemed settled.

"Why don't you ride over to the mine before then?" Vicente smiled at her. "Henry wants to show you what he's done. I'm sure you'd be interested, and you can bring the payroll to me."

"Yes." She set down her teacup and smiled back at him. Suddenly, her spirits were soaring with possibilities. Excitement filled her at the prospect of seeing the mine. "I'll do that."

He started to speak, then glanced at Isabel and fell silent. Spooning more sugar into his tea, he stirred it with studied concentration.

"Will you stay for supper, Vicente?" Isabel asked.

"No, thank you." He smiled. "I must be home to say good night to Miguel."

Isabel gave him a fond look and laughed softly. "You're so fortunate to have your son, Vicente. I'm anxious to see him. We'll be at the christening on Sunday." She stood up. "Will you excuse me, then?" she asked. "I must see to things in the kitchen."

"I'll come in to say goodbye," he answered, and watched Isabel leave the room.

He'd made it obvious he wished to speak to Consuelo alone, and she felt herself growing tense. If he meant to try again to convince her Lucas Morgan was innocent of any deceit or wrongdoing, he was wasting his time.

The silence stretched between them. Vicente concentrated on finishing his tea and another sopaipilla. Consuelo turned away to stare into the leaping fire. Some pieces of pitch at the edge burned with a hot blue flame, and she was transported back to Delmonico's, to laughter and love, the waiter making fried cream beside their table, the brandy burning with a blue flame in the dim light of the restaurant. Pain tore through her. It's ended, she cried inwardly, an enchanted dream ended forever. When Vicente cleared his throat and began to speak, she fought to compose herself.

"I've spoken to Lucas," he said. The sound of Lucas's name only increased the ache that brief flash of memory had brought.

"I suppose you've invited him to Miguel's christening." She could scarcely believe the sound of her own voice, filled with anger and hurt.

Vicente's dark eyes probed hers. "He's my friend, Consuelo. Why wouldn't I invite him to my son's christening? Besides," he added in a curiously offhand way, "Lucas has spoken with Father Amateo about taking instruction for conversion."

She looked away into the fire, unable to answer, fearing what was in her heart.

Vicente studied her dubiously, then cleared his throat. "Lucas told me he's asked you to marry him."

"I should be flattered, shouldn't I?" she flashed at him. "Everyone wants to wed Consuelo Estrada. Of course it has nothing to do with the acres of Rancho Estrada waiting to be turned into dairy farms, or the hills of Rancho Estrada filled with quicksilver, does it?"

Vicente bit his lip and looked away. For a lawyer, she thought, he was not good at confrontations. "I think, Consuelo," he replied in a low voice, "that Lucas truly loves you."

"Loves me!" she cried out as pain seized her heart. Her whole body seemed filled with the agony of loss, of the dream gone awry. She had to take defense in anger or she couldn't bear it.

"He's no better than Ramón! He has no conscience, no decency. At least Ramón—" She bit off the words, her face suddenly scarlet. She had almost said, at least Ramón didn't seduce me.

She knew Ramón would have, if the opportunity had come to him. But she had gone willingly to Lucas's arms there on the bank of Coyote Creek, as willingly as she had gone to his bed in San Francisco, wanting him as passionately as he wanted her. And all the time he had concealed how he'd deceived and cheated her. A double deceit.

What did it matter now? Consuelo asked herself that evening. She sat near the whale-oil lamp mending one of her father's shirts. From the kitchen she could hear the low voices of Isabel and Rosa planning tomorrow's meals. Across the firelight flickering on the adobe hearth she studied her father's face. He sat in his armchair, alternately dozing and staring into the fire. He lived so much in the past now. She wondered if that was what caused the occasional smile on his lips, always followed by a frown.

What did it matter? She repeated the words to herself, and knew that everything about Lucas Morgan would never cease to matter to her. It seemed ages now since that unhappy time when Lucas had gone away, and her father and Ramón had convinced her he'd gone forever. She stirred uneasily, staring blindly at the shirt in her hands.

"I sent a message for you," Lucas had told her. Angry and hurt, she had refused to believe him, and it seemed to her now that that had been the beginning of the end for them.

"Papá."

He started at her voice, as though his mind had been far away, and turned a questioning look on her.

Determinedly speaking over the hurt clogging her throat, Consuelo asked, "Do you remember, Papá, when everyone said Lucas Morgan had abandoned his wharf and gone away?"

He nodded and shrugged disinterestedly.

"He had only gone to Santa Barbara to find a pile driver. Do you remember?" Again, no answer, but a shrug. Consuelo continued, watching him closely. "He came back the night of the fiesta for my betrothal to Ramón. I had told you then, Papá, that Lucas wished to marry me, and you convinced me he'd gone away and betrayed me."

A shutter seemed to close behind Don Augustino's dark eyes, and he watched her through half-closed lids, his face suddenly impassive.

"Lucas claims he sent a note to tell me where he'd gone, that he'd return soon. Soledad, his Indian foreman, gave it to you because I was away from the house. Do you remember?"

"I was very ill then," he muttered in a low voice. "I don't remember."

Consuelo leaned toward him, something in her urgently needing to know the truth. If Lucas had been honest with her, she had to know.

"The Indian might have lost it," Papá was saying defensively. "He would lie to escape punishment."

She could tell nothing from his face or his shadowed eyes, although she studied him a long time in silence. "Did you get the note, Papá?"

He stirred in his chair, frowning, his eyes still not meeting hers. "I don't remember any note from anyone, or any Indian coming here. I was sick, Consuelo." His voice fell on the last words, filled with self-pity. When she said nothing, he added once more, "I don't remember."

He wouldn't have destroyed the note because it was from Lucas, would he? Besides, how could he have known when he couldn't read English? Already, Lucas Morgan had proved untrustworthy. She had to trust her father, old and ill though he was.

Lucas had selfishly gone away to Santa Barbara, never thinking of what he left behind. If he had guessed how that might hurt her, he could not have cared. Did it matter now, when she was determined to bury whatever feelings she had for him?

Be done with it! she told herself. Throwing down the shirt, she walked out into the cold winter night where the wind smelled of salt and eucalyptus.

Lucas ... The name seemed to whisper from the blowing eucalyptus trees and in the distant roar of the ocean. She stood there in the darkness until she began to shiver uncontrollably, knowing she could never be done with the love she once shared with Lucas Morgan.

Chapter Twenty-two

A trail of smoke drifted above the golden hills, dissipating into a sky just turning blue as the morning fog melted away. That smoke must mean they'd fired up the retort furnace! Excitement gripped Consuelo, and she kicked Mirlo into a faster gait. At the crest of a hill looking down into the rocky ravine at the España Mine, she paused to survey the scene below.

Black smoke rose from the tall cast-iron chimney of a low rectangular brick building she knew was the retort furnace. So Henry did have it operating, she thought, pleased that he'd arranged everything so quickly. She was almost certain he hadn't expected to be in operation so soon.

As Mirlo picked a careful path down the hill, Consuelo saw that a long rough lumber table was set up near the retort. Several Chinese men in their dark pajamas were hand-sorting the ore to be refined; their queues bounced against their backs as they worked.

The mouth of the mine tunnel showed where it led back into the mountain. She could see the shaft already timbered in, with more timber stacked to one side. Primitive lumber shacks had been thrown up for the workers to live in, and a larger shack for cooking. A Chinese man was at work beside an open fire, and the faint odor of stew cooking mingled with the smoke of the furnace. Three men chopped steadily at a huge pile of pine and juniper, cutting it into lengths to fuel the furnace.

A pair of creaking carts drawn by burros made the short trip from mine entrance to sorting table. The carts were being filled by a constant file of Mexican miners dumping their skin ore buckets into the wagons. Rumor had it that the Chinese refused to go underground after another mine had caved in and killed twenty of their countrymen; the bodies were never recovered. As she watched, Consuelo recognized among the miners several men from Rancho Estrada.

Then Rafael came out of the mine, squinting against the sunlight. *"Señorita!"* He ran toward her, a grin splitting his worn and dirty face. For a moment, she thought he intended to embrace her. Then he stepped deferentially back, hauled off his soiled sombrero and bowed.

"Henry's over at the furnace," he told her, his old eyes bright with affection as he took Mirlo's reins and helped her dismount. "He'll be glad to see you. He said Vicente promised you'd keep the records, something Henry hates to do. I'm the one who keeps the record on the miners," he added proudly.

"Good for you, Rafael," she said, surprised, for she knew he was illiterate.

"The miners are paid by the bucket, and I keep track of them," he explained, beaming. "The Chinese are paid by the day." He tied the black mare to a post. "Will you eat with us?" He laughed. "This cook is better than Lee Sing."

"Perhaps I will," she answered, amused by the old man's enthusiasm.

Henry came from the furnace to greet her, wiping his hand clean on his dirty overalls before he shook hers. Rafael went back to his work as though fearful someone might take his job if he were away too long.

"I've never worked with ore so rich," Henry said when they were seated in the cookshack. The rough wooden bench was splintery and the table badly soiled with food and tobacco juice.

"If all continues to go well," Henry went on, "we should have enough flasks to ship soon after the first of the year." He gave her a confident grin. "Everything went better than I expected."

Consuelo let out her breath in a long sigh of relief. All the difficulties over ownership would be ironed out by Vicente. They had the money to start mining and refining cinnabar ore. Perhaps there would be a profit in this venture, after all, as long as Lathrop was reasonable.

That Lucas Morgan had been a part of her difficulties made them harder to bear. Determinedly, she told herself she would not think about him and the callous way he had deceived her. Embarrassment and anger rose in her whenever she thought about how trusting she had been. Well, she had learned a hard lesson. She would never trust her heart again; with that resolved, she thrust the thought of Lucas Morgan firmly away, and spread out the payroll sheets Vicente had given her so that Henry could help her fill in the names.

The men would collect their wages at Vicente's office in Cambria. There had been robberies of payrolls en route to the mines, and Vicente thought that method safer. The day before, Consuelo had agreed to ride to the mine weekly, collect the records Rafael and Henry kept, figure the wages and bring the list to Vicente. Payments for wages and goods would be made from the account Vicente had set up for España Mine at the Coast Bank.

"I'll take these to Cambria tomorrow," she told Henry, "when I go for Miguel's christening."

A wide grin creased his dark face, eyes dancing. "Vicente's mighty proud of that boy, ain't he? It's funny," he ruminated, turning serious, "Vicente was the runt of the family. We all used to tease him. And now he's rich and educated, and likely to be richer. Just goes to show—"

Consuelo never learned what it went to show, for just then the cook began banging an iron kettle with a long spoon to announce dinner.

The miners and the Chinese workers came a few at a time to the cookshack, so that work never really ceased. Rafael appeared, pride glowing in his face, and showed the smooth board where he tallied the miners' production.

"Where did you learn to count, Rafael?" Consuelo asked.

"I've always counted cattle, *señorita*," he replied, a bit defensively. While he ate his plate of stew, he asked about San Francisco. Did she have any trouble finding the boat? A place to stay? Was she afraid? And finally, "Did Señor Morgan look after you?"

She caught the sudden gleam in Henry's eye at that question. Until that moment he had been only half listening to the conversation. Was there gossip about her and Lucas? she wondered.

Carefully, she answered, "Señor Morgan was most helpful and kind."

"I knew he would be," Rafael assured her. Finishing off his bread, he stood and reached for the new tally board Henry held out to him. "Tell Rosa I'll be home on Sunday." He bowed and scurried away.

"That old fellow outworks most of the men here," Henry said with a laugh.

Rafael was happy and excited about his life, Consuelo thought, watching as the old man took his place beside the empty cart with an air of importance. The years he had been a yard servant must have hurt the pride of the former head vaquero. Now he once more held a position of authority.

As Henry helped her mount Mirlo and said goodbye, he reached into his pocket. "Thought you might like a souvenir of the España's first refining," he said with a grin. He held up a small glass vial of silver liquid. It gleamed in the pale sunlight as she held it, flowing with every motion of the vial. This was her quicksilver. This was the product she had dreamed would set her free of poverty and debt.

Carefully placing it in her pocket, she smiled down at Henry. "*Gracias,* Henry. Now I feel as though it will all really happen." Surely by tomorrow Vicente would have a signed lease. Even though she begrudged Lathrop a share of the profits, she was certain now that there would be enough for everyone.

Riding homeward beneath a cold blue sky with fog still lingering along the coast, Consuelo took the vial from her pocket again. It was incredible that this silver liquid could be wrung from the red cinnabar earth. She couldn't puzzle out how it happened. But it was there, a gift from heaven, it seemed.

Tomorrow she would dress in her new gown and drive into Cambria to see her godson christened. Something tightened inside her when she remembered Lucas would be there. Vicente had said he was taking instruction from Father Amateo. He must be sincere in his conversion, for after the things she had said to him he couldn't have any hope she would marry him.

A part of her cringed, remembering the cruel words she'd flung at him. Yet he deserved them for his deceit. He was a thief and a liar, she told herself, wondering how she could avoid being near him tomorrow.

The night before, she had moved into Felipe's old bedroom. Her father was disapproving, for by the old Californio custom, unmarried daughters must be guarded carefully. Isabel had seemed puzzled, but not unwilling to help with the move.

In the darkness of the night Consuelo had awakened suddenly, roused by the wind in the eucalyptus trees. Their spicy scent filled the room. The fragrance always brought Lucas Morgan to her mind.

He had used this bed while he was at Rancho Estrada. In her half-dreaming state, he seemed to lie there still. A ghost of him, with his arms around her, his mouth hot against the pulse beating in her throat, his hardness burning her flesh, arousing a need beyond her power to deny.

Pain lanced through her. With a soft cry, Consuelo sat up in the bed. Hugging her knees with both arms, she bent her head and wept for a longing that refused to die.

Consuelo's heart sank when she saw Ramón's horse tied at the rancho hitching racks. Well, she told herself, she'd known she would have to face him eventually. Such an egotistical creature would never simply accept without argument her decision to end their betrothal, and Father Amateo was in his pocket. Even Ramón's despicable behavior at San Juan Bautista wouldn't seem sufficient reason, to a man like him, for her to break the engagement.

She knew she would have to stand against him by herself. Even if Papá were well, he would be on Ramón's side. Isabel disliked Ramón intensely, but as a woman she had no power, no say. Lately, Isabel seemed so supportive of her niece, even affectionate toward her. Through the years, in her own distant way, she'd been both mother and sister to Consuelo. If there was money from the mine, Consuelo vowed Isabel would share in it and have her own to spend.

The boy, Sancho, was sitting in Ramón's saddle, something he would be soundly cuffed for if Ramón knew. He quickly slid down and came to take Mirlo's reins to lead the mare to the shed where he would unsaddle her.

"Stay off Ramón's horses," Consuelo warned him sternly. With a guilty flush on his face, the boy hurried away.

The sound of men's voices came from the great room—Papá and Ramón, of course. Consuelo went to her bedroom first to shed her heavy serape. Isabel would be in the kitchen just now, after siesta. In any case, Consuelo told herself, she had to face Ramón and her father alone; for the decision had been hers alone.

Steeling herself, she walked slowly down the veranda. In the distance, the gray ocean foamed against the cliffs. An icy breeze blew off the water, adding to the coldness chilling Consuelo from within.

They were at the brandy already, she saw, and sighed, knowing this confrontation might be the most difficult of her life.

"There you are, my little quicksilver miner." Ramón smirked at her, not rising from his chair beside the fire. He looked thinner, but hard as ever. His wound must not have been as deep as she had thought, or he wouldn't have recovered so quickly.

Consuelo's lips tightened, and she gave him a cool look. If she spoke, she feared all the ugly words in her mind would come tumbling out—words no lady should use.

"Papá." She looked at her father. The brandy had brought color to his haggard face, and he smiled at her in a conciliatory way, as though he were certain that now everything would go as he wished. "You must be feeling better to be up," she said, certain that his illness of the past week had been brought on by her defiance of Father Amateo.

"Ramón always cheers me," Don Augustino said, with a sly wink in Ramón's direction. He leaned back in his big cowhide-covered armchair and held out his glass to her. "A little more brandy, please, my girl."

Consuelo looked dubiously at the brandy bottle, already half-empty, and she filled the glass only a quarter-full. Ramón rose slowly to take the bottle from her hand and fill his own glass to the rim. She noted that his wound must still bother him, for he lowered himself very carefully into the chair.

His glittering gaze fixed on her, his mouth curved in an arrogant grin. How could she ever have thought he had a rough charm and even have chastised herself for not warming to him?

"I've come to set our wedding date, *muchacha mía*." He laughed, but she caught an edge of uncertainty in that laugh and felt her courage rise.

"There will be no wedding, Ramón," she said steadily. "I can't believe you dare to even face me after what happened in San Juan Bautista." She glared at him, his face revealing his surprise. "Is there no shame in you?"

The surprise faded as Ramón's expression grew livid. "You're a child, Consuelo." His voice cracked across the room like a whip. "You know nothing of the needs of a man. You arouse the hot blood, but you are a virgin. A man must fill his needs elsewhere."

"And get himself stabbed by the woman's husband," she replied icily. "How is your wound, Ramón?" Her voice was falsely solicitous. "Too bad it wasn't lower," she added.

"Bitch!" he shouted. He rose, lifting his hand as though to strike her. She stood her ground and the hand fell to his side. "You little bitch." He gritted out the words, his eyes flashing with anger. "You still want that Anglo, don't you? One of your own isn't good enough now."

Damn him, she thought, how had he guessed to strike at her where she was most vulnerable? The very mention of Lucas Morgan brought a pain to her throat. Forcing herself under control, she stared at the furious Ramón. "Remember this, Ramón, for it will never change. I would rather die than marry you. Do not come again to ask for me."

All the color drained from Don Augustino's horrified face as he watched the confrontation. "I'll talk to her, Ramón..." he began in a shaky voice.

"Enough, Papá!" Consuelo turned on him, shouting in her anger. "You've ruined us, and I'll never marry Ramón to please you. This is final, Papá. Accept it."

Ramón downed his brandy in a gulp. Under control now, he stood staring at Consuelo. Very deliberately, he reached inside his shirt and drew out a parchment packet.

"These are the chits your father signed for me, Consuelo." His voice was silky now, his eyes sly. "Would you care to add them up?"

Stunned, Consuelo took the papers with suddenly icy hands. Riffling through them quickly, she could see the amount was considerable.

"They will be canceled on the day of our wedding," Ramón told her, eyes gleaming triumphantly.

"At least you weren't selling me cheaply, Papá," she said dryly. When he shrank from her piercing gaze, she could feel no compassion for him. He loved her, she knew that, but gambling was an overpowering passion. Everything else, even his daughter, lost meaning in the grip of that addiction.

She drew a deep, shaky breath. "I have money from the cattle sale, Ramón. Tomorrow when I'm in Cambria, I'll get a bank draft and pay you what my father owes." It was all too possible there wouldn't be that much money, that she couldn't possibly raise the amount, but she intended to bluff it out with Ramón.

The arrogant grin faded. Surprise and anger warred in Ramón's face. "I heard you'd spent all that money on the mine," he protested.

"Never listen to gossip, Ramón," she told him crisply. "My father's debts will be paid. It's a matter of his honor."

She heard a muffled groan from Don Augustino and refused to look at him. Let her father weep, let Ramón do what he would. They had pushed her into a corner where she must fight for herself. When she could speak again, her voice shook with anger. "I'll send the bank draft to you, Ramón. Never come to Rancho Estrada again, do you understand me? Never!"

With shaking hands she surrendered the gambling notes into Ramón's outstretched hand. Don Augustino was weeping into his hands, shrunken in the great armchair.

Ramón seemed stunned by her outburst. As she turned to leave the room, he roused himself. "You won't get away with making a fool of me, Consuelo!" he shouted.

When she did not reply, walking quickly away from him, Ramón's voice fell, low and threatening. "You'll pay for this, you little bitch! I'll have it all, you'll see—you and Rancho Estrada and your precious mine."

In her bedroom, Consuelo's knees gave way. She was trembling, and hot tears poured down her face. Taking her rosary from beneath the pillow, she knelt beside the bed, telling the beads over and over, until peace came into her heart.

Chapter Twenty-three

The small cast-iron stove at one end of Santa Rosa Catholic Church made little impression against the chill winter morning. Hard wooden benches filled the small rectangular room, the prayer rails polished by a succession of pious knees. Foggy light drifted through the paned windows, three on each side, and through the fanlight over the front door. Candles flickered softly before a statue of the Virgin, their light only seeming to add warmth to the church.

The new altar Ramón Salazar had donated was of ornately carved wood, its altar cloth crocheted by an ancient Irish lady far from her native Cork. A carved wooden crucifix hung on the wall behind the altar, the agonized Christ sagging upon it.

The Mass ended. Consuelo leaned back on the hard oak bench, alert for her part in the coming ceremony. Beside her, Isabel still knelt in prolonged prayer.

Father Amateo stepped down from the altar. He was followed by an altar boy carrying a white china basin of holy water, a linen towel over his arm. Imperiously, the priest lifted a hand to summon Vicente and Angela forward. Consuelo rose and walked down the aisle with Vicente's law partner, Domingo Pujol, who would stand as godfather. He and his wife had traveled all the way from the county seat at San Luis Obispo for the occasion.

Angela laid the placid Miguel in Consuelo's arms, so she could fulfill her duty as godmother. He was dressed in a long christening gown of white lawn edged with lace and embroidered with white fleurs-de-lis.

Father Amateo smiled benignly on the group. Dipping his fingers in the holy water, he made the sign of the cross on Miguel's small forehead. The baby screwed up his face in protest, as though he might cry.

"I baptize thee Miguel Vicente Sebastian de la Guerra Rios," Father Amateo said in portentous tones. "In the name of the Father and the Son and the Holy Ghost. Amen."

Miguel wriggled uncomfortably. Consuelo cuddled him against her.

After wiping his fingers on the cloth the altar boy handed him, the priest withdrew to the altar rail to offer communion. The baptismal party took communion first. Consuelo inexpertly handed Miguel to his mother. He wailed once, then snuggled against Angela's breast as she cooed softly to him.

Consuelo refused to meet Father Amateo's eyes as he placed the wafer on her tongue, fearing he would see there her struggle to suppress twinges of conscience over taking communion without confession. She had confessed to the priest in San Francisco, she reminded herself. She would not let herself remember the sins that came after.

Turning to walk back down the aisle to her seat, she found herself looking into the questioning blue eyes of Lucas Morgan.

She'd known he would be here, and had steeled herself against this first meeting. But she hadn't guessed what powerful emotions the sight of this man who had been her lover would arouse. She wanted him still, she knew with searing pain, and he wanted her. It was there in his steady gaze. Trembling, she slipped into her seat. After the church service there would be a reception at Vicente's house; relatives and friends from miles around had come for the occasion. Lucas Morgan would be there and Consuelo wondered how she could possibly get through this day.

* * *

Outside the white clapboard church overlooking the town of Cambria, Lucas watched Consuelo take the reins of the *carreta* where her father and her aunt sat beside her. He loved her so much that he knew he watched her with his heart in his eyes. Brilliants in the tortoiseshell comb holding her black lace mantilla winked in the sun just breaking through the fog. Like quicksilver, he thought, shining and elusive.

Her unreasonable conclusion that he'd been involved in Lathrop's acquisition of the Estero Bay mineral rights had hurt him deeply. Why wouldn't she believe he'd been honest with her? Because he was an Anglo, was his every mistake to be seen as deliberate fraud? Over and over he'd rehearsed the scene in the bank that day, and still he couldn't puzzle out how Lathrop had come by the deed to the mineral rights. However he'd managed it, he'd been less than honest.

As Lucas watched, a slight breeze lifted the black lace so that it fell against Consuelo's smooth cheek. Remembering the feel of her skin beneath his fingers, determination poured through Lucas. This was a love he couldn't bear to lose. He would win her back. Somehow, some way, he'd get at the truth of what Lathrop had done and prove his own innocence.

"Señor Morgan." Soledad's voice interrupted Lucas's thoughts. The young Indian stood diffidently beside him; the crowd leaving the church swirled about them.

"Ah, Soledad." Lucas managed to tear his eyes from Consuelo's averted face and turned to his foreman. "I thought you were working on your house today?"

The indefatigable Soledad had begun building a house for his family on a plot of ground Lucas had given him, using scrap lumber from the wharf and from the new store being added on to Lucas's warehouse. Lucas took a paternal pride in his protégé, who obviously intended to better his lot in life.

"I'm out of nails, *señor*." The young man looked embarrassed. "I should have mentioned it to you yesterday. I hate to waste a whole day. If you could—"

"Here." Lucas took his keys from his pocket and extracted one. "Take the key to the warehouse. Use whatever nails you need."

"Gracias," the young man said seriously. "I'll keep track and pay you for them."

Lucas laughed and shrugged as Soledad hurried away. Turning to walk down the hill to Vicente's house, he nodded to acquaintances, trying to think of some way he could arrange to talk to Consuelo privately.

Consuelo sat very stiff, waiting for her father to finish a conversation with an old friend who had come up to the *carreta* to greet him. Without looking directly at him, she managed to watch Lucas moving through the crowd shaking hands, talking to acquaintances. Regret burned in her heart, for she might have been beside him, his arm on hers, their eyes meeting. It was over, she told herself angrily. But she couldn't stop watching him as a tall young Indian man came to speak to Lucas.

A sharp gasp beside Consuelo startled her. Frowning with concern, she turned to look at Isabel. Beneath a black mantilla, her aunt's face was pale, her dark eyes wide and staring.

Consuelo's eyes followed Isabel's intent gaze. She thought she was staring at Lucas. No. Soledad walked away from Lucas to catch up his horse at the hitching rack, and Isabel's head turned to follow him.

Puzzled, Consuelo watched her aunt, aware now of her quick, labored breathing. *"Tía,"* she said, covering the tightly clasped and icy hands with her own. "Are you all right?"

Isabel started, as though she'd been far away. Her face flushed and her mouth tightened. "We'll be late," she said sharply.

With a shrug, Consuelo snapped the reins on the horse's back, and the *carreta* began to move. She could feel tension emanating from Isabel's stiff figure, and she frowned, wondering what it was about the young Indian that had affected her aunt so deeply.

* * *

"My God, Consuelo" Vicente exclaimed when she told him about the gambling chits. "I don't know what to say." She had asked to speak to him alone, and they stood in the downstairs bedroom with the door closed. Vicente stared in dismay at the figures she had written down. "How could Don Augustino have lost this much?"

Desperately afraid that her father had finally managed to ruin them completely, she shook her head. "Ramón told Papá he'd cancel the debts on the day of our wedding," she said in a shaky voice.

"How can you pay this?" Vicente asked. "According to your instructions, I transferred all but five hundred dollars from your account into the España Mine account." He stared once more at the figures. "Do you want me to take the money out of España?"

Consuelo's heart plunged in sudden anguish. The mine was her last resort; even if Lathrop reaped more than his right from the profits, she mustn't lose her share. "No, no." Her voice was hoarse and she cleared her throat before she continued. "I put Ramón off with a promise to pay. Maybe you could talk to him and work something out. Perhaps offer him land from the rancho." Tears choked her. "I don't want to lose the mine. It's all I have for the future." Again she cleared her aching throat. "Have you settled on the lease with Lathrop?"

Vicente took her hand in his and patted it consolingly. "Lathrop's being very greedy, but we'll have an agreement soon. Don't worry about that. We have to settle with Ramón now."

"Will you talk to him for me?" She couldn't bear to face the man again.

"Of course," he reassured her. "Although he's not a man who usually listens to reason." He studied her for a moment. "I heard he was drinking heavily at the tavern last night, boasting how he refused to marry you after you behaved so wildly, taking a herd of cattle to San Francisco yourself."

Consuelo shook her head despairingly. "I don't care what he says of me. I simply want him out of my life."

Voices from the front room indicated the arrival of guests. Vicente patted her shoulder, shoving the paper in his inside pocket. "I'll do what I can, Consuelo. Now I must greet my guests."

The sun had come out and the day turned pleasant enough so that the overflow of people from Vicente's small house could gather in the yard to visit. In the dining room, the table was loaded with food brought by relatives and friends: roast beef and potatoes, tamales, chili colorado, baked beans, spaghetti. Lucas smiled as he filled his plate, thinking the meal reflected the different origins of the people living in this county. That diversity was one reason he liked the central coast.

People spoke to him respectfully. He was a man of property now, a man with a wharf and a new town named for him: Morgan's Landing. Pride grew in him as he thought of the bitter years of his childhood. If only his mother could know. The old dream of wealth and power would be reality. Yet that dream had lost both urgency and satisfaction, dimmed by the fading of another dream that had bloomed the first night at Rancho Estrada when he looked into Consuelo's lovely face.

Turning away from the table, he saw Consuelo and Vicente come from the bedroom. Two spots of color bloomed in her pale, set face. More bad news? he wondered. Later, he would insist on speaking to her. Somehow he had to convince her she could trust him, that he had never betrayed her in any way.

Struggling to hide the misery her interview with Vicente had brought, Consuelo smiled and moved among the crowd, speaking to friends, joining in the admiration of Miguel, who had fallen into an exhausted sleep.

She glanced across the room, satisfied when she saw that Isabel had found a chair for Papá. He leaned back, looking tired but satisfied as people came up to speak deferentially to him. Isabel was standing to one side, talking earnestly to

Lucas Morgan. Consuelo frowned, wondering what her aunt was saying. At least Isabel seemed to have recovered from whatever had upset her when she saw Soledad.

Isabel then responded to Don Augustino's summons to greet an old friend from San Luis, and Lucas turned away from her. His eyes met Consuelo's across the room. A flash of longing unexpectedly tore through her, so intense that her fists tightened against the pain of it.

"Consuelo." Father Amateo spoke in a low voice.

Struggling to maintain a calm facade, Consuelo tore her eyes from Lucas's piercing gaze. "Yes, Father?" Inside, she felt all her defenses begin to gather against the priest who would have her marry Ramón. But to her surprise, he looked at her with sympathy, maybe even a bit of contrition.

"Ramón came to see me yesterday. He was very angry, and I think he was drunk." His voice was so low she had to lean toward him to hear, and he glanced around as though not wanting to be overheard. "If you still wish it, I'll announce the cancellation of your betrothal next Sunday."

"Thank you, Father." Impulsively, she took his hand and kissed it. For so many years he had been her kind and loving spiritual adviser, and it had hurt terribly when he turned against her for Ramón. She was certain he would never admit he had been wrong, but she was equally certain he saw the situation clearly now.

He smiled benignly. "Señor Morgan has come to me seeking to convert to your faith. I hope you, and all the congregation, will welcome him." Someone tapped his shoulder then, and he turned away.

"Your faith," he had said, Consuelo thought, staring at the priest as he moved away from her. The implication was too obvious. Did Father Amateo and everyone else in the county know about Lucas Morgan and Consuelo Estrada?

"I must speak to you privately."

In the depths of hell, she would have recognized the voice that had just spoken close beside her. Consuelo stood still, fighting for control. It was agony to stand there beside him and remember how it felt to lie in his arms. Worse, to know that he was deceitful and greedy, and that it was insanity to continue to want him.

"That would appear impossible," she replied in a tight voice, one hand indicating the small house packed with people, the sound of conversations rising as the brandy and wine bottles emptied.

"Outside, perhaps," he said. The touch of his hand on her arm nearly undid her. That hand was clasped firmly about her arm, and she knew they would attract unwanted attention if she refused him. Carrying herself stiffly, she walked beside him, through the kitchen and down the steps to the garden behind the house.

A salt-laden breeze blew off the ocean beyond the hills, stirring the fronds of a eucalyptus tree shading the backyard. The pungent odor that always made her think of Lucas filled Consuelo's nostrils. With one hand, she took hold of a frond, stilling its movement, studying the long green leaves to avoid looking at him.

"You've misjudged me, Consuelo," he began.

"Oh?" Her voice was harsh. "You're sitting pretty, aren't you, Señor Morgan, with your loan from the bank so conveniently arranged by Mr. Lathrop."

"It was a legitimate loan," he interrupted.

But she would not listen. Her voice was low and accusing. "Lathrop will never reveal you, Lucas, because that would incriminate him. You've won, whatever it is you wanted."

He drew in a sharp breath, as though she'd struck him. For a moment he stared at her in pained silence. Then he asked in a low voice, "Did you ask your father about the note I sent before I went to Santa Barbara?"

Consuelo ripped the leaves from the eucalyptus branch, crushing them in her hand. She could not look at Lucas. Her head bowed, she stared at his boots, newly polished. He wore the suit he'd worn in San Francisco, but she determinedly fought down that memory. She drew a deep ragged breath, and answered, "He said he couldn't remember."

Lucas made an odd noise. A glance showed her that he doubted her father's words. Defensively, she mumbled, "Papá has been quite ill."

"If he can't remember, then why can't you believe me?"

She couldn't answer, for she did believe him now. She hated it that her father had lied and destroyed the note, yet now that she had seen the gambling chits, she knew just how desperate Papá had been for her to marry Ramón.

A painful silence stretched between them as he waited for her answer.

When she thought she had control of herself, she said in an unsteady voice, "I have something for you." With a trembling hand, she reached into her skirt pocket and drew out the pink peony silk scarf tied tightly about the string of pearls. She had meant to leave it with Vicente, but now she held it out to Lucas, meeting his eyes for the first time defiantly.

"It was a gift for you," he said, and she was stung by the pain in his deep voice. Nevertheless, she forced the scarf into his big hand. When he felt the pearls inside, Lucas drew in his breath painfully.

"Vicente gave me the blouse you left with him," he finally said in a low voice. Looking into her face, he managed a wry smile. "I'm afraid it isn't of much use to me." His voice fell. "And it was so beautiful on you, my love."

"Don't!" Abruptly she turned away from him. "Don't call me your love or speak of love, when you've cheated and deceived me."

"That isn't true, Consuelo," he answered steadily. "In your heart you must know that. Just as you know that I love you."

Lucas held out his arms, wanting her to take the first step. All her being cried out to feel those strong arms around her. Deliberately she clenched her fists, fighting against the overwhelming need his gesture called up in her.

"Ah, there you are!" To her astonishment, the portly figure of Bert Lathrop appeared on the kitchen stoop. He came down the steps and moved toward them confidently.

"I've been looking for you, Lucas," he said. "We have some business that must be taken care of today."

He gave Consuelo a dismissive look, seeming amused by the scene he'd interrupted.

"Liar." She spoke the word between clenched teeth, flinging it into Lucas's imploring face. Ignoring the grinning Lathrop, she fled into the house.

Chapter Twenty-four

"Lathrop's stalling." Consuelo frowned at Vicente. She had delivered the mine payroll this morning, and stayed for lunch with her friends. "In the meantime, we're working the mine on our money," she added unhappily.

"He's greedy," Vicente agreed. He had rewritten the lease a dozen times, never to Lathrop's satisfaction, although he'd signed an interim agreement allowing work at the mine to continue for a percentage to be negotiated. "Still he has nothing to gain by not signing a lease, when we can agree on a percentage. Unfortunately, he's in San Francisco on bank business just now. I'm sure we'll have a final agreement when he returns."

Consuelo gave him a dubious look. Angela had left them to go into the bedroom and change Miguel. It upset her when Consuelo and Vicente disagreed, and they were both anxious to finish this discussion in her absence. Vicente was too trusting, Consuelo thought darkly as he told her the new terms he was working out. But she sighed and shrugged. If she could trust no one else, she had to trust Vicente.

"Have you heard from Ramón?" she asked, wanting to clear up that subject before Angela's return. Ramón had apparently retreated to his mountain rancho. Yet she lived in constant dread of the day he demanded payment for Papá's gambling debts.

"No one's seen him since Christmas," Vicente replied, playing idly with his fork. He gave her a confident smile. "Don't worry about him. After all, España Mine will make the first shipment of quicksilver tomorrow, and then you can pay Ramón."

"If Lathrop leaves anything for us when the lease is final," she replied morosely. Vicente frowned. If he was worried about the lease, she guessed he had no intention of letting her know it. She shrugged away the thought, relying on Vicente to represent her best interests.

She quickly changed the subject. "I told Henry I wanted to ride with the ore wagon tomorrow."

Vicente laughed. "You don't want to miss anything on the great occasion of our first shipment." His voice was teasing, and she laughed, too.

Sobering, Vicente asked, "How is Don Augustino?"

"I asked him to come with me this morning," she replied, unhappily recalling her father's reaction.

Don Augustino had been in his usual seat before the fireplace of the great room. How his world had shrunken, she'd thought sadly. Sometimes he played solitaire; sometimes he commanded Sancho to join him, and they played checkers or he taught the boy monte.

"No." He shook his graying head. "I have no interest in going to town today."

She had kissed him goodbye, thinking he had little interest in anything these days. At Christmas he had inexplicably decided he was still the rich don. He'd bought gifts in Cambria for all the rancho workers, and fine embroidered blouses for Isabel and Consuelo, charging everything to the rancho account at Lull's store. The blouses were returned for credit, and Consuelo still had to pay a bill that sadly depleted her bank account. When she chastised him for such extravagance, he'd simply retreated into sullen silence.

The thought of Christmas brought Lucas Morgan into her mind. A familiar tightening caught at her heart. Tomorrow at Morgan's Landing, she'd see him for the first time since Miguel's christening. Not one day in all that time, had she not thought of him and wished things were different, that he had proved worthy of her trust.

At Christmastime, Lucas's majordomo, Soledad, came to the adobe ranch house. Consuelo had wanted to cry out when he handed her the City of Paris box. Inside were the pink silk blouse, the peony scarf and the pearls…and a note from Lucas.

> These things were meant as gifts for you, Consuelo. Please take them back, and know that they were given out of my love for you. That has not changed, and never will. But you must learn to trust me. As much as I long for you, I can never come to you. It must be you who takes the first step and trusts.
>
> > My love always,
> > Lucas Morgan

She had wept on reading the note and flung it into the fire, immediately wishing she had it back to keep. Closing the box, she placed it in the China trunk.

When she had controlled her weeping and came out of her room, Soledad was riding away. It seemed Lucas hadn't asked him to wait for a reply. Rosa had fed Soledad, and said to Consuelo, "He used to live here before his parents died. A fine boy, as I remember."

Isabel had behaved strangely, Consuelo thought. She had stood on the veranda and watched until Soledad was out of sight, despite the cold and damp of the day.

The golden day beckoned Consuelo as she rode out of Cambria toward the coast road. All through December and January, cold winter rains had fallen endlessly, keeping the coast dwellers close to home. Those winter storms had left the hills clothed in the soft green velvet of new grass. Now February had arrived and the weather had warmed, bringing forth a carpet of wildflowers on the hills: blue lupine, orange poppies and brilliant yellow fields of mustard.

No wonder George Hearst wanted to own this beautiful country. His agent had come to the rancho again to see her father. The Estradas would never sell, she promised herself now. As long as she didn't have to pay Ramón right away, the rancho could run on the cattle money until there was income from the mine.

Her mind elsewhere, Consuelo slowed Mirlo at the intersection of Bridge Street and the coast road. She turned the mare southward without a thought for her destination.

A faint, overgrown trail joined the coast road at the foot of a small hill. The tops of the eucalyptus trees sheltering the ruined stone house at China Point were just visible above the rise. Consuelo drew Mirlo to a halt, staring bemused at the trees, which were scarcely moving in the slight breeze. From China Point she could see Morgan's Landing. Before she realized what she was doing she had turned Mirlo off the road, urging the mare up the hill.

Years ago, a solitary Chinese man had lived here, gathering sea lettuce and drying it for shipment to China, where it was in great demand. One day he was gone, perhaps back to his native China. No one else claimed the property and the house had fallen into ruins.

Reining up the horse beneath the trees, Consuelo dismounted. She walked slowly past the roofless house to the cliffs at the ocean's edge. High tide foamed over the dark rocks of the tide pools, thundering in, then receding. Across the curve of the bay lay Morgan's Landing.

From this distance, the workmen on the wharf looked like dolls as they moved about their work. She found herself straining to pick out Lucas. Perhaps he wasn't there.

Vicente said he had gone to San Francisco and back since Christmas. That news had left Consuelo struggling again with poignant memories, memories that would not die no matter how determined she might be to forget.

The wharf extended far out into the water now, with only a few more pilings left unfloored. Vicente said it would be in full operation by spring. So Lucas Morgan had what he wanted. He would be rich, with a wharf and a store and a town, and with a bank loan he'd acquired far too easily for honesty.

Tears stung her eyes. Why had she come here? Why should she still care? Quickly mounting, Consuelo spurred Mirlo back to the coast road, fleeing her memories.

* * *

The heavy ore wagon with its high board sides was filled with straw to cushion the six crates of seventy-six-pound quicksilver flasks. Even through all the packing, Consuelo caught the gleam of metal in the morning sunlight.

She had left the rancho early and ridden to the mine, anxious to be there for the momentous day of España Mine's first shipment.

Henry couldn't stop grinning as he took his seat on the wagon, and picked up the mules' reins. There was a holiday attitude among the miners, who stopped work to see the wagon off. Even the Chinese workers crowded around to shout good wishes as the wagon lumbered slowly down the rough, winding road. Rafael was left in charge. Consuelo rode ahead of the wagon to make sure no other vehicle coming up the narrow road would block Henry's way.

Alongside the track, blue lupine gave back the color of the brilliant sky. A slight breeze brought salt odors from the distant ocean. Mirlo ambled contentedly along, keeping a few yards in front of the wagon.

Consuelo found herself growing tense with anticipation. It was nearly two months since she'd seen Lucas. Memories of the love they'd shared stubbornly resisted all her efforts to banish them. She mustn't think of that now. She had to remember her resentment of his deceit. If only... No, she'd simply be cool and businesslike, as though they had never been lovers.

Vicente was waiting for them in front of the warehouse at Morgan's Landing, his elfin face alight with excitement. He helped her dismount and hugged her enthusiastically. "Our first shipment," he crowed, looking around at the interested faces of the crowd.

It was steamer day, and the area in front of the warehouse and the wharf was jammed with teams and wagons waiting to disgorge their goods, or to pick up whatever the steamer was to off-load for them. The southbound *West Wind* had departed this morning and the northbound *Electra* was expected this afternoon.

Through the open double doors of the warehouse, Consuelo could see Lucas working behind the counter, logging in all the shipments and collecting the wharfage fee from the shippers. A familiar pain clutched at her throat as she watched him, her fingers aching with the memory of touching him. She hurriedly wheeled Mirlo away to the hitching rack, grateful he hadn't yet noticed her. She had promised herself she would be cool and businesslike; she mustn't let her mind stray like that.

España Mine had the only shipment of quicksilver today. Henry and Vicente hovered about the wagon like nervous hens, proudly accepting the congratulations of the crowd.

Just as Consuelo tied Mirlo to the hitching rack, she heard someone shout, "The ship! The ship!" A confusion of people hurried to the beach to watch the *Electra* ease in toward shore. The wharf did not yet extend far enough into the bay for the ship to come alongside. Soledad and his crew put out from the shore in the lighter boat.

A shiny black buggy drawn by a handsome bay horse drew up in the midst of the crowd. With a casual glance, Consuelo saw that it was Bert Lathrop, the banker. He must have returned from San Francisco on the *West Wind*. Frowning, she wondered whether he'd come to sign the lease for the mine. She turned away, straining with everyone else to see the ship maneuvering closer and closer.

Angry shouts from in front of the warehouse drew the crowd's attention. Consuelo turned to see Vicente facing Lathrop, his dark eyes wide with fury, his face livid. Henry sat on the wagon seat, staring down at the two men, his brown face drained of color.

Beside the wagon, Ramón sat on his tall bay stallion, watching the scene with an arrogant grin on his swarthy face. Shock poured through Consuelo at the sight of him.

A sense of disaster fell over her, like a heavy, smothering blanket. She ran toward the wagon, her heart pounding with apprehension. When she saw Sheriff Haines standing beside Lathrop, fear nearly smothered her.

"What is it, Vicente?" she gasped, out of breath from her dash and from the fear growing in her heart.

Ramón dismounted and sauntered into the midst of the tense group.

Vicente's eyes did not flicker from Lathrop's smug porcine face. "This bastard—pardon—Lathrop says that since he owns the mineral rights to the land where España Mine is located, he also owns the quicksilver we've mined there."

Lathrop's smile widened and he gently waved the papers he held in his fat hand. "A good thing I returned from San Francisco in time to stop this thievery."

"What do you mean?" Vicente cried. "We had an interim agreement about the mine."

Lathrop shrugged. "A worthless piece of paper. My partner and I—" he gave Ramón a conspiratorial smile "—are claiming our quicksilver."

"No!" Consuelo protested, with a furious glare at the grinning Ramón. "You agreed to a lease and asked our company to continue mining."

"Do you have the lease?" Ramón asked, and laughed.

"Sorry, Miss Estrada," the sheriff broke in, his face grim. She thought there was distaste in his eyes for the task Lathrop had set him. "Mr. Lathrop and Mr. Salazar here have the papers to prove they own the mineral rights. It's all been registered at the courthouse in San Luis."

"The quicksilver in that wagon is ours," Ramón interrupted, his eyes gleaming with triumph. "You've mined it illegally, and we have a court order demanding its surrender."

"Damned if we'll surrender anything," Henry shouted. He jumped down from the wagon and started for Lathrop, his eyes blazing.

Ramón stepped forward, clenched fists raised toward Henry. Two of his hard-faced vaqueros appeared at his side. A good reason to take Ramón as a partner, she thought. Those men could enforce anything Lathrop asked.

Lathrop edged behind the sheriff, who held out a hand to stop Henry's advance. "Now cool off, Henry. This is all legal, and you can't do anything about it."

"We'll see about that," Vicente announced furiously, his face scarlet with anger. "This shipment is ours. You have no right to it."

"The court order says he does, Vicente," the sheriff said, shaking his head. His sympathies were obviously not with Lathrop and Ramón.

Lathrop drew himself up so that he stared down at Vicente, who was a head shorter. "When old man Estrada sold the property to Morgan, I bought the mineral rights separately. Ramón bought in with me after the mine was discovered." He paused, then added with a smirk, "And you have no lease, only a so-called agreement I can prove invalid."

Ramón had vowed to get even with her, Consuelo remembered, stunned by this unbelievable turn of events.

"You're a liar!" Vicente shouted. "Everyone in the county knows you're a crooked bastard and I'll prove it." In his fury he failed to apologize to Consuelo for his language.

Ramón's eyes glittered with triumph as they scanned Consuelo's pale face. His lip curled as he sneered at Vicente. "I've always wanted to get even with you, Vicente, you and your damned aristocratic ancestors."

With a cry of rage, Vicente flew at him. The two men tumbled together in the dust, Vicente raining blows on the surprised Ramón. The two vaqueros grabbed Henry, one on each arm. Before the much larger Ramón could begin to retaliate, Sheriff Haines pulled Vicente off, holding his arms behind him. The sheriff led Vicente aside, talking in low, placating tones as Ramón watched with clenched fists.

The vaqueros had released Henry, and he came to Consuelo's side, asking hoarsely, "What shall we do now?"

Lathrop had been knocked down when Vicente attacked Ramón. Now he was dusting himself off, smiling again in triumph at the crowd that had gathered to watch the fight.

"The richest quicksilver mine in the Cambria district," he announced. "And it's mine."

"We want to look at those papers," Consuelo said quickly. Shaking off the sheriff, Vicente held out a demanding hand.

Obviously pleased with himself, Lathrop produced the papers, keeping them in his own hands as Consuelo and Vicente read them.

Indeed, there was her father's name as she had taught him to sign it, granting all mineral rights on the Estero Bay tract to Bertram Lathrop. Another legal paper outlined the partnership between Lathrop and Ramón. In addition, there was a court order signed by Judge Murray of San Luis Obispo, giving the partners authority to confiscate all minerals mined on that property.

Sick despair rose in Consuelo. It was true. Her foolish father had sold the rights to this dirty Anglo banker. Because he was an honest man himself, Vicente had believed this villain. But it had been poor business on Vicente's part to let Lathrop get away with his promises and his delaying tactics. He'd been too trusting.

Like a wolf in hiding waiting to pounce on his prey, Lathrop, with Ramón as his ally, had waited for the day the quicksilver was delivered to the ship and the mine proved profitable.

"We will, of course, make arrangements to pay España Mining Company for the improvements," Lathrop was saying blandly. "Even though you were trespassing."

Lucas had been there when her father signed the deeds, Consuelo thought, and he'd claimed no knowledge of such a transfer. Her eyes sought him in the press of people. Then she saw that the lighter boat had put out once more to the *Electra,* and he was on it.

Old doubts rose in her heart. "Was Lucas Morgan present when my father signed the mineral rights over to you?" The question was like acid on her tongue, but she had to know.

"Certainly," Lathrop replied with a smug smile. Refolding the papers, he carefully placed them in his inside coat pocket. "He made no objection to the transaction, and I assumed he'd settled it with Mr. Estrada."

"Don Augustino," Consuelo corrected him bitterly. Damn the Anglos who hadn't the courtesy to use her father's title.

Lathrop shrugged. "Whoever. He was happy to make the sale." His eyebrows rose as he and Ramón exchanged a meaningful look. Their expressions conveyed something of significance she could not quite fathom. "Lucas Morgan was happy about the deal, too," Lathrop added.

The words were freighted with a meaning that confirmed all her suspicions and justified all the accusations she'd flung at Lucas.

Ramón summoned his men to unload the quicksilver crates from the wagon, and Henry watched in furious impotence. Turning to Consuelo, he growled, "We can't let that bastard Ramón and his dirty Anglo partner steal our quicksilver."

"Don't touch those crates," Consuelo shouted at Ramón's men. "Sheriff!" she called and the sheriff walked toward her with Vicente, much calmer now, beside him.

Before Consuelo could speak, Sheriff Haines said, "Lathrop has a court order, Miss Estrada, and I have to enforce it."

Glaring at him, she whirled about and went toward the warehouse, empty of people now. Behind her she could hear Vicente and Henry arguing with the sheriff. Across the calm blue ocean, the outgoing goods had been unloaded from the lighter boat, which was now taking on freight and passengers from the steamer.

Despite all his denials and protestations of innocence, Lucas Morgan had been a party to the sale of mineral rights, and lied to her from the beginning. A sizable bank loan at low interest had been his reward for that betrayal.

Quickly shuffling through the bills of lading on the warehouse counter, she found the one Lucas had made out for six crates of four flasks each of quicksilver. The space at the top for the name of the consignor was blank. So he had been in on it, she thought. She wanted to cry out in anger and despair.

I loved you so, she thought, but no Anglo can ever be trusted, not for a moment. Picking up the pen she deliberately wrote in the name of España Mining Company as consignor of the quicksilver, pleased to see that Lucas had already signed his name at the bottom of the receipt. Tearing off the original copy, she folded it and pushed it into her skirt pocket. It might prove a valuable piece of paper.

As she came out of the building, Vicente hurried toward her, his face pale with frustration. "There's nothing we can do in the face of that court order," he said. "We'll have to let Lathrop ship the quicksilver, but I want the bill of lading to indicate disputed ownership."

Without a word, she showed him the bill of lading she had written out. "Good." He took it from her and placed it in his inside coat pocket.

"Lucas must have known about this," she said, wanting him to deny it.

A flash of pain crossed Vicente's worried face. Lucas was his friend, and he, too, had been betrayed. "I don't want to think so," he replied reluctantly. "I want to talk to him first."

"And I shall talk to him." Consuelo turned, and hurried through the crowd watching the lighter boat come ashore.

Damp sand clung to her skirt and filled her shoes as she ran across the beach. The passengers, a couple with a small boy, had alighted and were walking slowly up the beach. Lucas was helping his workers unload boxes and barrels and trunks onto a small dray wagon drawn by a mule.

She grabbed his arm, causing him to set a box down heavily. Frowning, he turned on her. The frown faded when he saw who it was, replaced by a puzzled smile. Her agitation must have been all too apparent in her expression, for he asked, "Is something wrong?"

Anger made her voice waver as she cried out, "You can't stop lying, can you?"

"What?" he demanded, staring in amazement.

His eyes shifted from her toward the boat, and her heart sank. He couldn't even look her in the eyes.

"What's all this about, Consuelo?" he demanded, still frowning.

"Ramón and Bert Lathrop, as I'm sure you're aware, have a court order to confiscate the quicksilver we were shipping today."

Workers were shouting at him for instructions. Lucas waved them off, staring at her in disbelief. "I don't believe it."

"Believe it, Lucas," she said, the sense of lost innocence aching in her like an old wound. "You were there with Lathrop and my father when the property changed hands. You had to know."

He spread his hands in a gesture of confusion, glancing distractedly at the men awaiting his orders. "What are you accusing me of, Consuelo?"

"Of conspiring with Lathrop to cheat my father and of lying to me and to Vicente so that you could get your money from the bank and Lathrop could steal our mine. Did you know Ramón was in on it? And I thought you despised him!" Her knees were shaking, her ears roaring. She had to get away while she was still at least a little in control.

"It's not true!" he shouted, glaring at her. "For God's sake, Consuelo, can't you ever trust me?"

Her mouth twisted in disdain as she spit out the words. "I was a fool to trust an Anglo and an even bigger fool to love one!" Her voice trembled on the last words and she tightened her lips. "You're a thief, a liar and a cheat. And you're all Anglo. Nothing matters but your greed."

"Consuelo..." He reached out for her but she moved away.

"I knew you were a thief," she flung at him accusingly, "the day I found that you were carrying stolen gold."

Chapter Twenty-five

"We have to appear in court in San Luis Obispo next Wednesday," Vicente told Consuelo when she delivered the final payroll for the mine to his office. "I sent a special messenger to Judge Murray to arrange a hearing as soon as possible."

Henry was closing the mine until ownership was settled. He and Rafael would stay on to guard the equipment and run off any claim jumpers. The other men had left already and would pick up their paychecks in Cambria as usual.

Vicente shuffled papers on his desk, then made an impatient gesture. "Damn it. If your father hadn't been so anxious to get his hands on Lucas's gold, he'd have waited for me to handle the sale of Estero Bay. Then none of this would have happened."

"My father was cheated," she replied grimly. "He says he never signed the mineral rights over to Lathrop. Can we prove in court that Lathrop forged the deed or the signature? Lucas was there. He has to know what really happened."

"Lucas?" Vicente looked annoyed with her. "We've discussed this, Consuelo. He swears he didn't know, and I believe him. I can't understand why you continue to blame him."

"Maybe you're blinded by the fact that you're in business with him," she snapped. Remorse filled her and she wished she could have taken back the words, when she saw the shock and anger in Vicente's eyes.

He shook his head sadly, studying her with an expression of utter disbelief.

Anxious to escape the tension her accusation had created, Consuelo reached for her serape. "Do you want Papá to go to San Luis with us?"

Vicente continued to stare in silence for a moment, then shrugged. "He'll have to be present to testify. We'll go in my carriage on Tuesday and stay with Angela's parents." Hesitantly, he added, "About Lucas—"

Knowing she must get away from Vicente and his persistent defense of Lucas Morgan before she might say something else she would regret, Consuelo interrupted him. "Give my love to Angela. I'll see her and Miguel on Tuesday."

Vicente stood behind his desk, still frowning as she left the office.

Retrieving Mirlo from the hitching rack, Consuelo turned the little horse down Bridge Street toward the coast road. There was a gnawing sensation in her stomach. She could have gone to Angela's for dinner, but she had promised to meet Isabel as soon as her business with Vicente was finished.

A puzzled frown creased Consuelo's forehead. Isabel was behaving in a most uncharacteristic way. Thinking back, Consuelo realized that ever since Christmas Isabel had been distant and vague, as though her thoughts were elsewhere. For a while, she'd feared her aunt was ill, but she went about her work with the same old efficiency. It was just that her mind wasn't on it.

This morning as Sancho was saddling Mirlo, Isabel had appeared in front of the saddle shed clad in an old riding habit. "I'm going with you," she announced. "Have Sancho saddle a horse for me."

Surprised, Consuelo smiled, glad for company on her trip. "Shall we take the *carreta, tía?* It would be more comfortable for you."

"No." Isabel frowned. She seemed preoccupied and restless. "I'll want my own horse."

Puzzled, Consuelo hurried back to the house for a heavy serape for her aunt. Isabel seldom rode and wouldn't know how cold it might be when they returned.

"I don't understand," she said when she came out to the hitching rack in front of the house, where Sancho was holding their horses. "What made you decide to ride into Cambria?"

"Not Cambria," her aunt replied brusquely. "I'm going to Morgan's Landing. I've been thinking about it for a long time."

Consuelo stared in amazement as Sancho helped her aunt mount. "Why?" she demanded. "To see Lucas Morgan?"

With a closed expression on her face, Isabel reined the horse away, not waiting for Consuelo or answering her question.

The ride through the green hills beneath a polished blue winter sky was strangely silent. Isabel seemed withdrawn, and scarcely answered Consuelo's efforts to begin a conversation.

At the intersection of the coast road and Bridge Street, Isabel said, "I'll ride on to Morgan's Landing by myself."

Consuelo frowned. "I don't understand," she protested. "This isn't like you, *tía*. Why must you see Lucas Morgan?"

"It's nothing to do with you and Lucas," Isabel snapped. Her stony face indicated there would be nothing more forthcoming.

Consuelo drew in a sharp breath, realizing for the first time that her aunt was aware of her feelings for Lucas. With a pang of guilt, she wondered if that was all Isabel had guessed.

"Shall I wait for you at Vicente's house?" she asked, not quite certain how to approach this new Isabel.

"No. I don't want to go into town or see anyone." Isabel frowned for a moment, thinking. "Do you remember the old house at China Point?"

When Consuelo nodded, Isabel said, "Meet me there," and reined her horse away, urging it to a fast trot down the coast road. Bewildered by Isabel's strange behavior, Consuelo had stared until the figure was lost among the pines lining the roadway.

Lucas looked up from the shelf he had just finished nailing to the wall of the nearly completed store, and stared in amazement at the woman standing in the doorway.

After laying down his hammer, he walked toward her, rubbing his hands clean on his pants. "Doña Isabel," he greeted her, holding out a hand.

She touched it briefly as he peered past her into the sunlit yard before the warehouse, hoping to see Consuelo waiting there. "Are you alone?" he asked, unable to stop himself.

"Yes," she replied and her eyes narrowed as she studied him. "Consuelo is in Cambria on business."

"Then what can I do for you?" Lucas asked, hoping he'd concealed his disappointment. Consuelo had refused to see him, or even respond to his notes. He'd resolved that she must come to him, but was finding it difficult to hold to that resolution. Vicente had brought the message that she didn't want to see or hear from him. She was utterly unreasonable. Lucas ineffectively tried to convince himself that no man should wish to tie himself to such a stubborn woman.

"There's a young man who works for you," Isabel began. "I saw him at the christening and again at Christmas." She paused and looked away, her dark eyes darting around the room. "I haven't stopped thinking about it." The last words came in a low, halting voice.

"Soledad?" Lucas asked in surprise.

Isabel's graying head came up proudly, and her strong mouth tightened. "I'd like to see him, please."

"He's working on the wharf," Lucas said, trying to comprehend this bizarre exchange. "I'll send someone for him." He stepped to the door and called one of the young boys who were always playing near the warehouse.

"The store, as you can see, isn't quite finished," he apologized, indicating the still-rough room. "Come into the warehouse and I'll fix some coffee or tea, if you wish."

Without a word, Isabel followed him next door. Lucas built up the fire in the cast-iron stove that warmed the front of the vast room. Tiers of shelves were stacked with goods waiting for the next packet steamer. The odor of cheese and salted meat in barrels pervaded the warehouse.

Isabel's tension seemed to ease as she took the chair he brought for her and sipped the tea he poured into a granite-ware mug. "Do you know where Soledad came from?" she asked abruptly.

Something clicked in Lucas's head. "I was told he was raised at Rancho Estrada, but left there when his parents died. He married a girl from Bain's Settlement." He frowned, wondering if Soledad had stolen something from the rancho, or if he was wanted for some crime. "He's a fine worker," he added quickly. "He's even building a house for his family on a plot of ground I gave him."

Isabel smiled and nodded. To Lucas's amazement, tears filled her deep-set eyes, spilling over to trickle down her wrinkled cheeks. He watched her uneasily, not knowing what to do.

Isabel stared at her teacup and wept in silence. At last, she drew a handkerchief from her pocket to wipe her eyes and her wet face.

Lucas watched sympathetically without understanding in the least what had caused such an outburst of emotion in the usually subdued Isabel. He had thought her a spinster like the ones back in New England, repressed and unemotional.

"What shall I say to him?" she spoke suddenly, staring up at Lucas with unhappy eyes.

Lucas moved about uncomfortably, pausing to put wood into the round Charter Oak heater. When he realized she was still watching him questioningly, he shrugged. "I'm afraid I don't understand, Doña Isabel."

To his surprise, she burst out angrily, "I am not the doña. I'm Señorita Isabel, the spinster aunt."

Seeing the pain in her eyes, Lucas quickly asked, "What is it you must tell Soledad?"

Isabel's hands writhed in her lap, but the piercing look she turned on Lucas reduced him to silence.

"*Señor?*" Soledad stood in the doorway, puzzled to have been summoned from his work.

"The doña wishes to speak with you," Lucas said and went out of the warehouse, closing the door behind him. For a long time, he stood gazing out at the ocean rolling restlessly upon the beach. Beyond the cliffs to the north, the hills rose at China Point, where the ruins of an old house stood beneath a grove of tall eucalyptus.

Consuelo, his heart cried as he remembered the first time he'd held her in his arms, in the dark night beneath the blowing eucalyptus trees. Sadness for what might have been filled his heart. A familiar ache spread through his body, and he wondered whether he would ever recover from losing her.

After a few minutes, Isabel and Soledad came out of the warehouse. Soledad looked dazed, and Isabel had been weeping again. With a brief nod, the sober-faced Soledad hurried back to his work. Isabel stood watching him, a bemused expression on her face.

"So?" Lucas asked, still puzzled by her odd behavior.

Isabel turned to him with a grave smile. "I must go now. It's a long ride back to the rancho, and Consuelo is waiting for me at China Point."

Lucas glanced quickly across the bay again at the ruined house and the eucalyptus trees, wondering if she was there now and if that was what had drawn his thoughts to her.

Isabel moved toward her horse, waiting at the hitching rack. Taking up the reins, she turned toward him, a look of sadness mixed with compassion on her face. "If you could see her, talk to her—" her voice choked "—hold her, then perhaps you could mend it."

Something painful clutched at Lucas's throat, and he could not reply. If Isabel knew of his love for Consuelo, then surely she must know how hard he'd tried to prove himself to her stubborn niece. How could he swallow his pride and try again?

He watched Isabel ride away, slow anger growing inside him. All the hard years he had worked and fought for what he wanted. Why was he now simply accepting the decisions of others? Consuelo's accusations had, he knew, created doubt in other people's minds. He must do something to prove to everyone once and for all that he had no part in Lathrop's schemes.

Over and over again, he'd rehearsed the scene that day in the bank. Lathrop had been slick, but how had he done it? There must be a way to prove Don Augustino had signed the deed unknowingly. Vicente had told him Lathrop would be going to San Luis for the court hearing. There was Lucas's opportunity. Perhaps if he went to the bank while Lathrop was away, he could manage to persuade someone there to let him see the files.

With the decision to take action, some of his tension drained away, but he stood for a long time staring out across the water. Sea gulls wheeled above him in the clear blue sky, their melancholy cries echoing above the hammers of his workers and the roar of the sea. The ocean sparkled in the sunlight, breakers foaming against the dark cliffs below China Point where his love waited, but not for him. Never again for him. If there could be no trust between them, there could be nothing.

The first wildflowers gleamed like gold alongside the road, nearly hidden in the deep green grass that spread as far as eye could see.

"The old house at China Point," Isabel had said, and Consuelo reined in Mirlo there beneath the eucalyptus trees. Her aunt's strange behavior still worried her, and she paced the grass before the ruined house, puzzled and anxious. Why had Isabel been so adamant about meeting at this unlikely place? Consuelo could have been comfortably sipping tea with Angela and playing with Miguel, rather than standing here beside this tumbledown house on a cliff above the crashing sea.

She let out her breath in relief when she finally saw Isabel riding over the crest of the hill. But when Isabel drew up her horse, Consuelo saw that her aunt was weeping silently. Shocked, she ran to her, holding up her arms until Isabel allowed Consuelo to help her dismount.

"*Tía!*" Consuelo gathered her aunt into her arms. "What's happened?"

Drawing away, Isabel took a handkerchief from her skirt pocket and wiped her eyes. A tremulous smile played on her lips as she spoke in a shaky voice. "I told him. He knows. And at last I know about him."

Amazed at Isabel's meaningless reply, Consuelo stared at her aunt, and it was a moment before the words sank in. "Lucas Morgan?" she asked, and her own voice trembled with apprehension at what her aunt might have done.

"No, no." Isabel's voice was impatient, but her smile was brilliant. "Soledad. He's my son."

Stunned, Consuelo could only stare as Isabel's tears again overflowed. She wept and smiled at the same time, and what she had said was absolutely incomprehensible. Speechless, Consuelo struggled to assimilate Isabel's words. She had never thought of Isabel as being young, or as having any life outside the convent and her duties at the rancho.

With a long sigh, Isabel laid her hand on Consuelo's arm. "I must tell you all of it now. It was a secret never meant to be told." She led Consuelo to the tumbled stones at the side of the house and they sat beside each other, looking out across the brilliant sea.

After a long silence, Isabel began to speak, her head averted so that Consuelo had to lean toward her to hear the words.

"Only Augustino knows, and he has deliberately forgotten the sin on his conscience." She caught back a sob. "And on mine."

Consuelo clasped Isabel's hand tightly, waiting as the woman once more controlled her weeping.

"I loved Francisco." Isabel choked out the words through her tears. "Even though he was an Indian and not of my class, I gave myself to him gladly, never guessing it would mean his death. I knew my father loved me, and I trusted he would understand."

In stunned silence, Consuelo listened to Isabel's tale of a forbidden love. An Indian... An Anglo... Did it always bring pain and tragedy to love outside one's own kind?

Furious and humiliated, Isabel's father had taken his vengeance despite his daughter's pleas.

"Augustino was there when my father shot Francisco. He killed him like a dog, accusing him of rape. My brother claimed he couldn't stop it, but I know he dared not try. Papá was wild when he learned I carried Francisco's child. The boy was taken from me at birth and given to an Indian family. The next day I was put aboard a ship and sent to the convent at Monterey. There I stayed until Augustino's wife died and I returned to care for you and Felipe."

With a deep ragged sigh, Isabel stood and turned to look imploringly at Consuelo. "When I saw Soledad in Cambria that day, I saw Francisco again, and I knew he was my son. Yet..." Doubt shadowed her eyes. "Was I right to tell him?"

"Only you can decide that," Consuelo told her gently. Sorrow for all the unhappiness Isabel had borne ached in her heart. Deliberately she stood and took Isabel in her arms. It seemed natural that Isabel embraced her in return, although it was something they had seldom done before. She might have followed the same path, Consuelo thought, and her heart squeezed in pain. She might have conceived Lucas Morgan's child, and then...

Isabel stepped away, under control now. "I'm not sure Soledad really believes it yet. He was fond of the Indian couple who raised him, and it must be hard to accept they weren't his real parents."

"Lucas thinks highly of him," Consuelo said, and watched pride flood Isabel's face.

"He said that even if he is my son, he wants nothing from me or from Rancho Estrada."

"Unlike Lucas Morgan," Consuelo heard herself say, and Isabel looked so dismayed she wished she could recall the words.

Shaking her head sadly, Isabel looked into Consuelo's eyes. "You love him, my girl. I've seen it. And he loves you. I would give anything now if only I had had the courage to leave my home and go away with Francisco. Don't lose what you have. He's at Morgan's Landing now. Go to him."

"Never!" Shaken by Isabel's words, Consuelo walked away from her, staring out across the blue bay toward Morgan's Landing. "Don't you understand, *tía?* Lucas conspired with Bert Lathrop to cheat Papá of any payment for the mineral rights to Estero Bay."

"I'll never believe that," Isabel declared stoutly. "Not of Lucas Morgan."

"Why not?" Consuelo demanded, struggling to ignore the old wounds that would not heal. "He's an Anglo like Lathrop. They stick together in their greed. Maybe when they've taken everything from the Californios they'll be satisfied."

"No!" Isabel cried, and clasped both Consuelo's arms, imploring. "Lucas loves you, my heart, believe me. You must trust him."

Gently, Consuelo disengaged her aunt's clinging hands. "I trust no one," she said in a weary voice. "I've learned well how unwise it is to trust."

Chapter Twenty-six

"At least we have a pleasant day for our trip," Henry said. He rode beside Vicente's carriage, where the scarlet banners with the Rios crest fluttered in the breeze. It was the kind of spring day February often brought to the central coast, the sky a brilliant blue after the morning fog melted off. Bishop's Peak loomed ahead of them, shaped like a bishop's cap and seeming to grow out of fields of blooming golden mustard.

They had stopped beside the coast road to eat the lunch Rosa had packed. Miguel was fed and fell asleep again as soon as his parents' carriage was under way.

Consuelo glanced at her father, dozing beside her, unmindful of the bumpy roadway. He was tired, for they had left Cambria early, planning to be in San Luis Obispo by late afternoon.

Angela dozed, too, with Miguel in his cradle at her feet. Vicente sat next to his wife, frowning as he studied a portfolio of legal papers. The Indian driver kept the team at a brisk pace so that Henry's horse had to trot to keep alongside.

"What time is the hearing tomorrow?" Consuelo asked Vicente as he glanced up and saw her watching him.

"Ten o'clock," he replied absently, frowning again at his papers. "I'll want your father to look at the mineral rights deed before then to see if he remembers it."

"Of course he doesn't," Consuelo replied sharply. "He told you he signed no such thing."

Vicente turned a level gaze toward her. "He admits he signed his name several times without reading what he was signing."

"He can't read English, Vicente," she told him impatiently. "You know that. I taught him to sign his name."

"The signatures will be examined tomorrow," Vicente said. "One way or another, I'll prove fraud. Lucas is supposed to be there to testify that there was no discussion of selling mineral rights."

At the mention of Lucas's name, Consuelo turned her face away. Mustard and blue lupine and golden poppies sped by the carriage, the spring grass bowing beneath the wheels. Lucas. Was that name to be forever engraved on her heart?

"Why is he testifying for my father unless it means the mineral rights will return to him?" she asked, her voice sharp with inner rejection of her own longings. "Lathrop's cooperation has been worth a great deal to him. I can't believe he'd jeopardize that."

Vicente's eyes hardened. "Do you think Lucas would be Ramón Salazar's partner, too?" he demanded.

She could think of no answer to that, and she stared down at her cold hands clasped tightly together in her lap.

In a carefully controlled voice, like a parent speaking to a recalcitrant child, Vicente said, "I don't understand you, Consuelo. Lucas loves you. He asked you to marry him. To my knowledge he's never done anything to hurt you or your family. Your father freely sold him the Estero Bay property." Vicente's brilliant dark eyes pinned her. "Why do you treat him as though he were your enemy?"

Desperately trying to keep her lips from trembling, fighting the stinging tears behind her eyes, Consuelo glanced at her father, grateful that he was asleep and did not hear this conversation.

"Everything he's done has helped destroy my family." She forced out the words, saying them carefully so as not to betray her inner turmoil. Deliberately glaring at him, she asked, "How can you continue to trust him?"

Vicente snorted. "You're a foolish and stubborn girl, Consuelo. You could trust Lucas Morgan as you trust me."

"Trust him!" She blurted out the words before she thought, "You know very well he stole the gold from Pacific Steamship."

For a moment, Vicente studied her in silence. He shrugged. "I know what he did was not entirely honest, but in the end it was only a loan. I told you he returned the gold and replaced it with a loan from the Coast Bank."

"Lathrop's bank!" she lashed out at him.

"Ho! Ho!" the driver was shouting, applying the carriage brakes as they descended the last hill into the town of San Luis Obispo.

Angela awakened as Miguel began to cry. Don Augustino stirred and groaned, sitting up straight and staring about, momentarily disoriented.

"We'll talk later," Vicente told Consuelo. She looked away from his piercing gaze, determined that they would not, at least not about Lucas Morgan.

The carriage moved slowly through the center of town, the pace of traffic a bit more sedate than in booming Cambria. There were fine buggies and drays and *carretas* drawn by patient donkeys. On Monterey Street they passed the old mission, set on the leafy banks of San Luis Creek where it wound through the town. The mission looked shabby in spite of its classic lines, and the white cross rising from the roof peak of the main chapel needed painting, for it had been neglected since the coming of the Americans.

Across the street were some handsome commercial buildings: the old Casa Grande, the mercantile store of Beebee and Pollard, and the French Hotel where Henry left them.

"Lucas will be staying there, too," Vicente said with a significant look at Consuelo.

Farther down Monterey Street the carriage turned into the circular driveway of a substantial two-story house, and came to a halt at the steps leading up to a full-length porch.

Don Franco de la Guerra and his wife had turned the management of Rancho Nipomo over to their sons and moved into this fine new house. The don's interests now were in railroads and land development. Unlike the simple adobes of the past, or the New England-style clapboard houses of Cambria, this grand house was sided with redwood from the north coast. The porch was lined with ornamental wooden fretwork, painted white as were the arched front windows and the bay windows at the side. Young palm trees lined the driveway. It seemed quite grand to Consuelo, who hadn't been in San Luis for nearly two years and hadn't seen the house before.

Doña de la Guerra, dressed in a black silk gown and mantilla, greeted her daughter and grandson with glad cries. The don was a stout man of medium height, with an imposing white mustache and a leonine head of white hair. He obviously approved of his successful son-in-law, greeting Vicente and his guests with utmost cordiality.

Consuelo watched her weary father make a valiant attempt at conversation, and insisted he go upstairs to the guest room for a delayed siesta. Never mind that he had slept most of the way from Cambria, she knew anxiety about the hearing tomorrow was preying on his mind as it was on hers.

"Mr. Lathrop is out of town," the young cashier told Lucas. He patted his overpomaded brown hair and assumed the air of a man in charge. "Without his permission, I can't give you access to any of our files."

Lucas leaned across the shiny mahogany desk the young man had usurped during his boss's absence. "How about my own files?" he asked in a level tone.

A flash of consternation crossed the man's face, quickly concealed. He didn't know what the policy was, Lucas thought, annoyed. His face warmed with anger when the cashier assured him in pompous, confident tones that he could not even look at his own files without permission from the bank manager, Mr. Lathrop.

Lucas felt an almost ungovernable urge to pick up this supercilious young man and shake him until he handed over every key to the bank. Both hands on the desktop, he leaned toward the man, his voice carrying a suggestion of threat. "You're quite wrong about the policy, Mr. . . . ."

"Hart," the man said, his eyes looking everywhere except at Lucas.

"Mr. Hart. I'm entitled to see every piece of paper this bank has with my name on it. In addition—" An idea had just popped into Lucas's mind. He stood, smiling confidently. "I'm thinking of purchasing Rancho Estrada. I'll need to see those files, too. I want to make sure there are no liens on the property, or outstanding loans."

"Quite impossible." Hart was enjoying his moment of power. He leaned back in the swivel chair and looked triumphantly at Lucas.

Punching him in the nose would solve nothing, Lucas told himself, slowly unclenching his fists. "Mr. Hart," he continued, not even trying to keep the anger from his voice.

Hart jumped to his feet. "You'll have to come back when Mr. Lathrop's here. Good day." He walked quickly to the back of the bank and disappeared through a heavy oak door.

Arrogant young pipsqueak, Lucas thought, glaring in frustration at the closed door. He desperately wanted to see those files. But he also had to get to San Luis Obispo in time to testify for Vicente and the court hearing tomorrow, and he'd need some cash to take to San Luis.

Still puzzling over how to get past the miserable Mr. Hart, Lucas walked across the polished wood floor to the ornate, wrought-iron teller's cage. Ezra McIntire was on duty today. His rusty black suit hung on his ancient frame. Steel-framed glasses were perched on his bony nose, and his thinning gray hair looked as though he'd used the same pomade bottle as Hart.

"Morning, Ezra," Lucas said.

"Afternoon," Ezra corrected. He counted out the money Lucas asked for, then leaned closer. "What was you and young Mr. High-and-Mighty having a set-to about?" There was an expression of intense dislike on Ezra's wrinkled face, as his pale old eyes went to Mr. Hart, once more seated at Lathrop's desk.

Lucas leaned one elbow on the counter, glanced at Hart and back at the teller. "Don't like him much, do you, Ezra?"

Ezra's eyes glittered. "Snotty little bastard. I been here since the bank opened, and they promote him to cashier over me. How would you like that?" His angry look challenged Lucas.

"Dirty shame," Lucas said, wondering if Ezra might not turn out to be a valuable ally. "I don't think he knows what the hell he's doing, either. Told me I had no right to see my files here in the bank."

Ezra snorted, still staring hatefully at Hart. "Reckon you could see them if you want, Mr. Morgan. No law against it."

"Hart has the keys," Lucas prompted, watching the old man's face carefully.

"So do I." Ezra was studying Hart now, a spiteful smile growing on his lips.

The stout woman who ran the bakery down the street came in carrying a bag with her day's receipts. She stood impatiently behind Lucas at the teller's cage.

"Meet me at the Pine Tree Tavern after closing," Ezra said in a conspiratorial tone. With that, he looked past Lucas. "Good afternoon, Mrs. Borba."

The tavern grew more and more crowded as Lucas sat at a corner table, nursing his glass of whiskey. Workingmen came in for a drink before making their way home—store clerks, livery workers, drovers. Winter darkness gathered beyond the doors, and Lucas began to wonder about Ezra McIntire. The old boy had a lot of bitterness toward Hart. Enough, Lucas hoped, that he would help him search the files for some evidence of Lathrop's duplicity. On the other hand, Ezra might be a bit crazy. He could have entirely forgotten about Lucas.

The tavern owner's wife was serving steaming bowls of stew along with hunks of crusty bread. The tempting odors made Lucas's stomach growl. When she passed his table, he ordered some stew and another whiskey, wondering if Ezra would really show up.

He'd finished the stew when Ezra rushed in and sat beside him, breathing heavily. "Damn janitor. I thought he'd never get out of there."

"You want a drink, Ezra? Or something to eat?"

The old man shook his head vehemently. "My wife'll be mad enough at me being this late. Let's hurry."

Ezra unlocked the back door of the bank and led Lucas through the dark hallway to the tiny room used by safe-deposit box customers. Only then did the old man strike a light.

By the gas lamp on the small desk, Lucas saw that Ezra had already brought the files: one for his loan on the Estero Bay property and the wharf, the other the deed transfer papers from Augustino Estrada to himself.

"Ezra," he said, grinning at the old man, "you're a wonder." When Ezra grinned back, he added, "But I need all the papers on Rancho Estrada, too."

"Hell's bells," Ezra complained. "You could've told me."

"Can you get them now?" Lucas prompted.

Muttering under his breath, Ezra took a candle from the desk drawer, lit it and went out, closing the door behind him.

There had been three copies of the land deed transfer, Lucas remembered. One remained in the file, his own signature and that of Don Augustino Estrada at the bottom. Scanning it quickly, he saw there was no mention of mineral rights. And where the hell was the deed Lathrop claimed had granted those rights to him? Undoubtedly, he'd taken it with him to the court hearing. Lucas swore under his breath. Nothing in these files proved anything.

Ezra returned with more files tucked under his arm. He blew out the candle and cursed when hot wax dripped on his hand. "Rancho Estrada," he said, and dumped the files in front of Lucas.

There were numerous surveyors' reports, lawyers' depositions and heavy parchment papers written in Spanish proclaiming land grants, all that the Estradas had gone through to prove they owned the land. No wonder they held a grudge against the Americans.

He picked up a thin file labeled "Loan—Estrada." To his surprise, the entire agreement was in Spanish, with Don Augustino's uncertain signature at the bottom. With a puzzled frown, he turned to Ezra. "Why is this loan agreement written in Spanish?"

Ezra peered at the file. "Likely old man Estrada can't read English," he said. "It's common enough in this part of California. A lot of the old-timers were educated in Spain and never learned to read English. See." He turned the sheet to expose another beneath, this one in English with no signature. "That's for bank use since not many of the employees read Spanish."

"Good Lord!" Lucas muttered to himself. Don Augustino didn't read English! He'd had no idea what he was signing for Lathrop that day, when Lathrop had so cagily had them take turns sitting at his desk. Lucas hadn't seen exactly what the don signed, he realized now. And Lathrop's name was written on this loan in approval. He'd known damn well Augustino didn't know what he was signing that day. And all the don could see was the gold Lucas was going to pay him.

Ignoring Ezra's impatient muttering Lucas read the translation of the agreement. He groaned low in his throat. Did Consuelo know her father had mortgaged their home, he wondered, and that nothing except the interest had been paid on that mortgage? Lathrop had his eye on Rancho Estrada, too.

"I'm going to take this one," Lucas informed Ezra.

"Oh, no!" the old man protested, obviously fearful now of what he'd done to spite his rival. "You can't do that!"

"It's all right, Ezra," Lucas promised. "No one will know except you and me." He took Ezra's hand then, slipping him some of the gold pieces he'd withdrawn earlier.

Ezra didn't even look at the money, simply tightened his fist around it, a pleased and amazed look on his weathered face.

"You'll have to help me put the files back," he said. Then he added plaintively, "You will return that one to me, won't you?"

The fog had come in and it was dark as the inside of a grave when Lucas and Ezra came out of the bank. Lucas swore under his breath, knowing there wasn't a chance he could make the ride to San Luis on a night like this.

After reassuring Ezra once more, Lucas went to find a hotel room. He'd have to start out at dawn to get this information to Vicente before court opened. Realizing Lathrop must have known Augustino couldn't read English, Lucas swore aloud. But without this loan paper, there was only Lathrop's word against the don's.

Consuelo and her father had been wronged by a greedy and vicious man. In spite of what Isabel said, Lucas was certain Consuelo no longer loved him. Her angry words proved it. So he had lost her and he was alone once more, as he had been for most of his life. But if he could give her nothing else now, neither his love nor a home, he could see that she had justice.

He had to be in San Luis Obispo when court opened tomorrow.

Chapter Twenty-seven

Morning dawned bright and clear, for the coastal fog often did not drift inland as far as San Luis Obispo. Dressed in her gown from San Francisco, Consuelo rode with Vicente and her father up Monterey Street to the courthouse at the corner of Osos Street.

The courthouse was an imposing three stories high, the first story partly sunk into the slight rise where the building stood in its square of green lawn shaded by the fast-growing eucalyptus trees. The main floor was reached by a long rise of stone steps to a columned portico surmounted by a small balcony. Designed for speeches by the mayor? Consuelo wondered.

Inside, everything was dark varnished wood, the wooden floors smelling of the oil used to clean and polish them. Since this was only a hearing it was to be held in the small hearing room off to the side of the main courtroom.

Tension gathered in Consuelo as Vicente led them down the corridor, through the double doors to the hearing room. A railing separated several rows of benches from the tables and chairs where those concerned with the hearing were to sit. The judge would sit behind a desk raised on a low dais above the rest of the room.

Vicente paused to confer with Henry, who was already seated in the first row, then ushered Consuelo and her father to the table. Giving the don an encouraging pat, Vicente sat down and spread out his papers on the table.

A quick glance around the room showed Consuelo that
Lucas Morgan had not arrived. Vicente was depending on
him to testify, and it appeared he would not even show up.

Judge Murray, tall and gray-bearded, made his majestic
way to his desk just as Lathrop and Ramón and their lawyer, David Martin from San Luis, hurried down the aisle.

Apprehension seized Consuelo. What if the judge ruled
against them? Vicente always seemed so confident when he
talked to her, but Lathrop did have a deed signed by Don
Augustino. And what was Ramón's role in this? He wasn't
involved in the original transaction. She was certain he'd
thrown his lot with Lathrop just to get even with her, to finally ruin the Estradas he had envied for so long. Papá's
gambling chits remained unpaid, and could never be paid
without income from the mine. Ramón certainly knew that.
If they had no mine, he could claim the rancho in payment
of those debts.

The hearing began with the judge gaveling the room into
silence. Martin presented the mineral rights deed in evidence first. The judge verified with Vicente, with Augustino and with Consuelo that the signature was indeed Don
Augustino Estrada's.

When Vicente had the don take the stand, Consuelo could
see her father's struggle to present his old arrogant Californio facade.

"Did you sign this deed knowingly?" Vicente asked him.

Don Augustino glared at Lathrop. "I did not. The transaction was to be simply a transfer of property from myself
to Lucas Morgan." He paused, frowning. "I signed a number of papers, but as you know, I do not read English. I
trusted Mr. Lathrop." Again, he sent a fiery glance in the
banker's direction.

Trust, Papá, she thought sadly. You trust too easily, and
I do not trust at all. Neither way has worked for us.

She saw Vicente glance around the room with a puzzled
frown. Ah, Vicente. She shook her head. You trust too easily, as well. Lucas has failed you, just as he failed me. He's
not here, and he's likely not coming.

* * *

Fog melted away as the morning sun rose higher. Tension coiled inside Lucas as he pressed his horse hard through the dissipating mist. At last they topped the hill above San Luis, where sunlight gleamed off the housetops and the faint echo of the mission bells drifted among the trees.

Vicente's carriage was in front of the courthouse. Lucas frowned when he recognized Ramón's bay horse. The clock in the courthouse tower showed five minutes after ten. Court would be in session already, but he had to be in time. He had to be! His heart seemed about to burst in his chest as he ran up the long flight of stairs.

Lucas cursed softly for the minutes lost searching for the right courtroom. At last he pushed through the swinging doors and walked straight down the aisle to Vicente's side. Ignoring the excited buzz his entrance evoked, ignoring the pounding of the judge's gavel, he laid the file in front of Vicente and let out his breath in relief.

Tension eased from Vicente's face. Grinning, he pumped Lucas's hand, then turned to the judge. "Your honor's indulgence, please. My witness has just arrived. May we confer?"

Despite Martin's objection, permission was granted. Lucas leaned near Vicente's ear to explain the meaning of the papers he'd brought. As he talked, Vicente riffled through the file, nodding, a satisfied look growing on his face.

"Sit there," Vicente finally said, indicating the row of seats behind him. "I'll have you sworn in right away."

Lucas nodded. Before he turned away, Vicente seized his hand and gripped it hard. His dark eyes were warm. *"Gracias, amigo,"* he said. *"Gracias."*

Sitting straight and tense in her seat, Consuelo watched the two men. In the brief moments they conferred, Consuelo's eyes took in all the remembered details of the man who had been her lover—the way his brown hair curled at the nape of his neck, the strong line of his chin with the crescent-shaped scar, the wide generous mouth, the nose with a slight bump where he had told her it was once broken and the blue eyes looking up at her. Those eyes changed even as she met them now, as though a curtain came down between them.

Lucas nodded politely, stiffly, as he turned to take a seat beside Henry. She was so aware of him sitting there behind her, he might have been actually touching her.

Vicente called Lucas to the stand. His dark suit was the one he had worn in San Francisco, just as her gown was from that brief and joyful interlude. As she watched him move confidently to the witness chair, her heart contracted painfully.

"Will you please state for the court the nature of your transaction with Don Augustino Estrada on the twelfth day of September last year, at the Coast Bank in Cambria, California." Vicente stepped back, one hand on the table as he watched Lucas. The confident smile on his face did not lessen Consuelo's fears.

Lucas spoke in the deep, vibrant voice that once had expressed his love for her, and the pain in her heart grew until it filled her chest. "On that date in the Coast Bank, I purchased from Don Augustino the property known as Estero Bay. It was a straightforward land sale. No subsidiary sales were discussed or even considered. As a matter of course, the mineral rights on the property should have been transferred to me as the new owner."

"Who prepared the deeds and transfers for the property?" Vicente prompted.

"Mr. Lathrop prepared all the papers," Lucas answered with a grim look at the bland-faced banker. "At the time, I wasn't aware the don didn't read English. He signed his name as Mr. Lathrop presented the papers, without question." He paused and leveled an angry look at Lathrop. "I read only the papers I personally signed."

"Was Mr. Lathrop aware that Don Augustino was unable to read English?"

"He went into a lot of explanation about what the papers contained, for the don's benefit." Lucas frowned. "At the time I thought it was because of Don Augustino's—er—advanced age."

"So Don Augustino could have been unaware of what he was signing?" Vicente continued.

"I'm sure he was," Lucas replied harshly. "He trusted his banker."

Lathrop gave Lucas a furious look. When Vicente called him to the witness stand after Lucas stepped down, he bent to confer quickly with his lawyer and with the frowning Ramón. Reluctantly, he took the stand.

Vicente attacked at once. "You were aware, sir, that Don Augustino was educated in Spain and does not read English?"

Behind the steel-rimmed glasses, Lathrop's eyes gleamed with hostility. "He lives in an English-speaking country. I assume everyone who lives in America and can read, reads English."

With a catlike smile of triumph, Vicente took from the table the papers Lucas had brought and presented them to Judge Murray. "This, Mr. Lathrop," Vicente continued as the judge scanned the papers, "is the paperwork you prepared for a loan the bank made to Don Augustino two years ago. The loan has never been repaid, only the interest. As you will observe, Your Honor, the original loan agreement is written in Spanish, a fairly common occurrence in this part of California where a number of older residents do not read English. A translation copy for the use of bank employees is included in the file, but not signed by Don Augustino."

Lathrop's face blanched as he began to perceive Vicente's line of attack. He glanced imploringly at his attorney, who was glaring at him accusingly.

"It was a legitimate deal," Lathrop sputtered. "The old man sold the mineral rights to me."

"Not true, sir," Vicente replied blandly. "You tricked him into signing a paper he couldn't read. We have witnesses to that effect." He indicated Lucas. "Mr. Morgan, a well-known and reputable businessman, has testified that there was no discussion of selling mineral rights. Indeed, since he was purchasing the property, he should rightly have signed the transfer to you if it were legitimate."

"You won't get away with this," Lathrop growled at Vicente. There were beads of sweat on his porcine face, and he turned in appeal to Judge Murray.

The dignified judge frowned at him. "I'll wish to study these papers, sir." He looked at David Martin. "Do you have anything to say in defense, Mr. Martin?"

Martin's face was contorted with fury. "It seems my client has no defense, Your Honor. The decision is in your hands."

Anger permeated the courtroom as Judge Murray gathered up the files and retired to his chambers. Lathrop, Ramón and Martin were arguing in low, bitter tones. Vicente turned to Consuelo and her father, a grin on his face.

"With Lucas's help," he said, "I think we've done it. I won't need to call Henry or Consuelo to testify."

With Lucas's help. She wanted to turn and look at him, but could not. He hadn't needed to testify, she knew that. He could have thrown in his lot with Lathrop, as she had accused him of doing. He had chosen to help, somehow obtaining information from the bank that had been denied to Vicente. Shame flooded her when she recalled the terrible things she had accused him of doing, the anger she had flung at him when he offered love.

Pain flooded her heart with the realization of just how much she did love him, had always loved him. I've lost him, she thought miserably, because I couldn't trust him.

When Judge Murray returned from his chambers to declare that the mineral rights deed had been obtained by fraud, Lathrop leaped to his feet, shouting his protests. Martin managed to restrain him when the judge suggested an indictment might be issued against Lathrop.

Almost sick with relief, Consuelo stood and turned to see Lucas and Henry already leaving through the courtroom door.

Her father looked bewildered. "Is it over?"

"It's over, Papá." She hugged him. "We won because we have a wonderful lawyer." Impulsively, she hugged Vicente, whose face colored with pleasure at her praise.

"And because you have a friend named Lucas Morgan," he said with a long, level look at her. "Perhaps you should thank him." It didn't sound like a suggestion.

"I will," she announced, even though gratitude and fear of rejection were waging war inside her.

Hurrying down the aisle to catch up with Lucas, Consuelo found her way blocked at the door by Ramón. Steeling herself, she demanded, "Get out of my way, Ramón. I have nothing to say to you."

His dark eyes glittered with anger. "I have something to say to you," he growled in a low harsh voice. "You win this time, you little bitch, but I'll win in the end. I'm out of patience with your promises to pay, and I'm putting a lien on Rancho Estrada for the gambling debts your father owes me." He grabbed her wrist painfully, bruising the flesh so that she cried out. "You think yourself too good for me, but I'll get even with you if it's the last thing I do."

Chapter Twenty-eight

Consuelo stroked Mirlo's neck and pressed her cheek against the mare's warmth. Across the water from China Point she could see Morgan's Landing, busy even now on this gray afternoon with no steamer in the harbor.

Fog was rolling in off the ocean, blue water turning gray as the mist thickened. It was madness to be here, Consuelo told herself, after what had happened between her and Lucas in San Luis Obispo.

Workers swarmed over the lengthening pier. Once in a while, she caught a glimpse of Lucas's figure as he crossed the beach to inspect some work, or when he came out of the warehouse to see off a customer. That was what she had come here for. It was likely to be all she would ever have of him again.

The scene haunted her days, and troubled her dreams. In her mind she saw herself again, breaking away from Ramón, rushing out of the courthouse to see Lucas taking his horse from the hitching rack. For a moment, she had paused at the top of the stairs, watching the easy movements of his tall figure. He hadn't spoken to her; he'd scarcely acknowledged her presence.

"Lucas!" She ran down the stairs, only half-aware of people staring at her. Breathless, she paused beside his horse, for he sat in the saddle, looking down at her in a way that tore her heart. Cold. As though she were a stranger, and he was merely being polite. By her own actions, she had killed all his feelings for her. A sense of loss seared through her painfully.

"Lucas," she managed to gasp. "Thank you for what you did today."

His voice was cool, his face an icy mask. "You're quite welcome, *señorita*. Lathrop betrayed your father's trust, and I happen to believe in trust."

Despair poured through her with the knowledge that her lack of trust had destroyed his love for her. Tears filled her eyes, hot and painful. "I'm sorry, Lucas," she managed to gasp out the words. "So sorry."

"So am I," he replied in a hard voice and reined his horse away, kicking the animal into a gallop as soon as it was in the street.

She had thought he would come to supper at the de la Guerras, but he did not. She dared not ask Vicente about him, for Vicente had already chastised her for treating Lucas badly. Finally Angela asked for him, and Vicente replied that Lucas had gone home.

Since that day Consuelo had shed a million secret tears, played over in her mind every glorious moment they had been together and dreamed of him every night. She had lost him, lost his love, by her stubborn refusal to believe in his honesty and decency. Now all she had were these distant glimpses of the man she loved, and would love for always.

Reluctantly, she mounted Mirlo and turned the horse down the track toward the coast road and home. In Cambria, she had stopped at the bank for money to buy supplies. Lathrop was not to be seen, and the old teller, Ezra McIntire whispered that he had been fired. Tomorrow she would go to the mine and take supplies to Rafael. Ever faithful, he stood guard there with his dog, Bolo. Henry was busy hiring a new crew to reopen the mine on a lease granted to España Mine by Lucas Morgan.

Vicente had told her about the lease, his dark eyes severe as he emphasized Lucas Morgan's generosity. "He could have taken everything, just as Lathrop intended to do," he said.

Consuelo had turned away from his searching gaze, tears stinging her eyes. She had her mine, but she had lost much more.

Squawking chickens scattered now before the galloping Mirlo. Dogs began to bark. Consuelo reined up the mare in front of Rancho Estrada's courtyard. The ever-present Sancho ran out to meet her, a hot tortilla stuffed with frijoles in one hand. Scarcely greeting the boy, Consuelo hurried into the house, hoping she was mistaken as to the owner of the familiar bay horse at the hitching rack.

The breath went out of her as though she had been punched in the stomach when she saw Ramón and her father at the dining table, a game of monte spread between them.

"What are you doing here, Ramón?" she demanded, all her misery and fear reflected in her angry voice.

"Consuelo," her father chided, frowning at such manners.

Ramón leaned back in his chair, grinning lazily as he blew out the smoke from his cigarillo. "Good morning, Consuelo," he drawled. "How nice of you to welcome me."

"I told you never to come here again." Her voice rose, so loud she was suddenly aware that the chattering women in the kitchen had fallen silent. "I meant it. Now, leave at once."

Ramón's eyes hardened. "I've come to collect my debts, *señorita*."

"Ramón says Lathrop deceived him, too," Don Augustino told her hurriedly, glancing uneasily from one to the other. "He thought the title was clear, or he wouldn't have bought in with Lathrop."

"Ramón lies, as always," she interrupted, glaring at Ramón, who was smiling broadly. "Leave now, Ramón."

With a hard disdainful glance, he gathered up the cards on the table. "Not until I've been paid. Your Papá tells me you'll be rich again from the quicksilver mine. If that's so, perhaps you'll pay your father's gambling debts...now."

"I shall pay you, Ramón," she said, assuming a confident air and determined to bluff him, "as soon as the draft for the quicksilver comes from San Francisco."

With a shrug and a sly smile, Ramón began to deal the cards. "George Hearst's agent was here today. Perhaps the Estradas should set aside their pride and listen to what he has to say." He looked up with a sneer. "So they can pay their debts."

"What did he want, Papá?" she asked, fearing what her father might have done in her absence. Ramón's family had been poor peons in the days when the Estradas were royalty. She realized now how much Ramón had resented that, and how that resentment must have festered and twisted him.

"To buy the rancho, of course," Don Augustino replied impatiently. He gathered the playing cards in his hands, studying them intently. "I told him we were rich now and didn't need to sell."

Ramón laughed, and her father chuckled.

For the first time, Consuelo realized that her father had understood little of the meaning of Judge Murray's ruling. With the lease, the mine was theirs to operate, but so far it had only cost money. It would cost even more to start it up again now. They weren't rich, as he had pompously told the agent. They couldn't even pay his gambling debts. And there was the loan at the bank she had only learned about that day in the courtroom. She had sold all the cattle to finance the mine, and now they had nothing until the mine paid off...which might take months. Nothing except the land the rapacious George Hearst desired.

Ramón blew cigarillo smoke in the air, a sly smile on his lips. "Lathrop tells me the mortgage loan Vicente used as evidence is long past due. The bank will be starting foreclosure proceedings."

"Lathrop's been fired," she told him, watching for his reaction.

With a shrug, Ramón told her, "The loan belongs to the bank, not Lathrop."

Consuelo's heart fell into her shoes. "The interest was paid," she protested, glancing at her father, who looked uncomfortable.

Ramón gave her a sardonic look. "Not good enough, my girl." He smiled smugly. "Perhaps it would be best if you paid the don's debts with a land deed, and then I'll pay off the mortgage."

Consuelo gasped. In a flash of insight, she saw Ramón's plan clearly. Rancho Estrada would be his in return for her father's debts, and then sold to Hearst or some other Anglo speculator for a huge profit. She had worked so hard, and Ramón could take it all.

Anger burned like acid in her throat. Leaning across the table, she jerked the cards from her father's hands and scattered the deck on the floor.

Ramón growled an oath and stood, his face dark and furious. For a moment she feared he would strike her. Summoning all her courage, she faced him down. "I've told you you're not welcome here, Ramón. You led my brother into bad company where he was killed. I'll never forgive you for that, even if my father has. Now you want to ruin us because you've always hated and envied us."

Knowing that to lose control would be to lose everything, she tried desperately to calm herself. "The doctor has forbidden Papá gambling or any other excitement. Come, Papá." She grabbed the bewildered don's arms.

The ruddiness brought by the brandy he had drunk with Ramón drained from his face. He looked old and frail as he allowed her to lead him from the room.

At the doorway, Consuelo looked back at Ramón, her eyes hard. "Your debt will be paid, *señor.* The Estradas are honorable. But your presence here is not welcome."

With a contemptuous glance at Don Augustino, Ramón confronted her squarely, a sneer twisting his face. "I'll get even with you, bitch. I told you that in San Luis Obispo." He straightened, an arrogant smile on his mouth. "I was overly generous in offering you one more chance." Picking up his sombrero, he started for the door. "Now you will pay Ramón Salazar all you owe... one way or another."

Don Augustino was gasping by the time she had urged him into bed and spread the old woven coverlet over his limp, wasted frame.

"What is it?" Isabel hurriedly followed them into the room, looking with concern at her brother, lying slack in his bed. His breathing had eased, and he lay with his eyes closed, the color slowly seeping back into his face.

"Ramón demanded payment of Papá's debts. I ordered him to leave," Consuelo replied, her voice trembling now that the confrontation was over.

"Ah, Augustino," Isabel said, shaking her head. "You will never learn."

Don Augustino frowned and turned his face away.

"Rest now, Papá." Consuelo patted his hand. "I'll bring your supper in later." Taking Isabel's arm she led her from the room.

"I heard you yelling at Ramón, and I was afraid," Isabel said in a small, scared voice.

Consuelo followed her aunt back to the great room, relieved to see that Isabel had already cleaned up the cards, the cigarillo ashes and the brandy glasses. A fire blazed in the wide adobe fireplace, comfortable on the cold clear day. But it could never warm the chill within her.

For a long moment, Consuelo stared into the flames, aware that her aunt was waiting for her to speak. In spite of Isabel's domineering manner toward the workers on the rancho, there was a timidity under that strong facade.

Hesitantly at first, then with growing anger and resentment, Consuelo told her aunt what had transpired between herself and Ramón. As she listened, Isabel's dark eyes widened. Abruptly, she sat down on the settee as though her legs would no longer hold her up, and her work-worn hands writhed in her lap.

Drained by the telling, Consuelo fell silent, staring into the fire.

From beside her, she heard Isabel stifle a sob. "So Ramón wants the rancho and your father owes him money. He'll ruin us if he can and sell to Hearst because he knows how you'd hate that." In a low, shamed voice, she continued, "I heard him boast that he would win Rancho Estrada at monte, and its daughter by force if necessary."

Consuelo sighed. "You should have told me before."

"Augustino would have been furious. He still thinks Ramón is his friend. Sometimes I think he lets himself believe that Ramón has replaced his son."

Consuelo patted her aunt's shoulder. "Sometimes my father is a fool," she said sadly.

"It's been a terrible day for you, my girl," Isabel said. She stood. "Wait here. I'll bring some tea for you."

Worn out from troubles that seemed to have no end, Consuelo sat staring into the fire, listening to the dear, familiar sounds of the rancho—the women chattering in the kitchen, the cries of children at play outside, the shouts of vaqueros and the barking of dogs. She had missed the rancho so terribly when she was at school in Monterey, she could scarcely wait for summer and the boat back home.

Would it all be lost now because of her father's gambling? The cattle money was nearly gone, and there was no income yet from the mine. Perhaps the new bank manager would renew Papá's loan. She wondered how much it would cost to start up the mine again. Henry had promised they would begin work this week, but could they even pay workers? Did it matter what Judge Murray had decided if they had no money to operate a mine?

At the thought of the court hearing, the painful moment of Lucas's rejection flooded back into her mind. She had reached out to him at last, and he had turned away. But she had no one to blame except herself. I've lost him, she thought, stabbed through by a pain too deep for tears. I've lost the only man I shall ever love. An awful loneliness, deeper and emptier than any she had ever known, possessed her whole being.

Rafael came to meet Consuelo, a wide grin on his weathered face. His dog, Bolo, followed wagging his tail, his yellow coat stained with cinnabar red. They had been sitting on the stoop of the cookshack, where a rifle leaned against the wall. Since the mine closed Rafael and the dog had been alone there, except for an occasional inspection by Henry, and Consuelo's weekly delivery of food and supplies.

"*Buenos días, Señorita,*" he said, taking Mirlo's reins and leading the little mare to the enclosure where his own horse neighed a welcome. "You have good news?"

"Yes, good news." She lifted one of the sacks of food she had brought, to carry it inside the cookshack. "We're going to reopen the mine. Henry will be bringing workers in a day or two."

"I knew it would happen." The old man nodded vigorously. "It's sure been lonesome here. I'll be glad to see the men back."

Smiling at him, she began unpacking the food Rosa had sent. The day had turned bright, the last wisps of fog melting away, and they ate sitting on the cookshack stoop.

While they shared the stuffed tortillas, Rafael told Consuelo about the occasional prospector who had wandered by; two of them had spent a night with him. He fed a tortilla to Bolo, who wagged his feathery tail in gratitude.

"I thought I saw someone coming earlier," Rafael continued. "A horseman, just beyond that ridge." He pointed to the chaparral-covered ridge north of the arroyo. "Bolo was barking." He patted the dog, who sat beside him. "He's a good watchdog. But whoever it was, he just rode on by."

As he talked, Rafael grew more and more excited about the reopening of the mine. The miners would be back, filling their skin buckets to empty in the donkey-drawn *carretas*. He would be keeping tally once more. The furnace would be pouring out smoke and quicksilver, and the wood choppers would be busy.

Listening to Rafael, Consuelo let herself hope once more that this place would be the answer to the troubles besetting her. Tomorrow she must go to Cambria and talk to Vicente about the awful possibility that Ramón could claim the rancho in payment for her father's debts.

When they finished eating, she helped Rafael store all the food in tight barrels, safe from the depredations of wild animals.

"Would you like to see the mine, *señorita?*" the old man asked. "When we're working again you won't be able to go inside."

"Yes, I would." It was her hope for the future, and she had never seen its inner workings. Soon it would be full of miners again, with no room inside for spectators.

Cautiously, she followed Rafael past the heavily timbered entrance. It was dark inside and smelled damp as a cave. Rafael lit a lantern and preceded her, Bolo close beside him. He turned to point out the stumbling blocks of an uneven dirt floor, and stones that had fallen during timbering. Darkness closed about them, the only light the gleam of the lantern on the dirt walls of the tunnel and the heavy timbers holding up the roof.

It was a frightening place. She couldn't imagine how the miners spent day after day in here. But they were working every minute, not thinking of the dark and danger.

A sharp sound made her jump. "What was that?" she asked Rafael, her eyes wide with sudden fear. The unease she'd felt the moment the tunnel closed about them tightened all her nerves.

Rafael shrugged. "Just a rock falling, I suppose. They do sometimes, in spite of the timbers." He snapped his fingers at Bolo, who was growling uneasily, and walked ahead. She could only follow him.

"Look, see the quicksilver." He pointed to the untouched cinnabar ore at the end of the tunnel. "The ore is so rich, it oozes out without refining. Well, almost, so Henry says."

The silvery gleam in the lantern light brought back the first day she'd come here with Rafael and the rich gleam of quicksilver she'd captured in her kerchief and carried to Vicente to begin a dream. She was not so naive now. Reopening the mine and keeping it running would bring difficulties just as opening it the first time had.

An odd scraping sound echoed down the tunnel from toward the entrance. Frightened now, Consuelo grasped Rafael's arm. "Let's go. This place scares me." She was even more afraid when he lifted the lantern and stared in the direction of the noise, his face puzzled. Bolo, too, turned back toward the entrance of the tunnel, braced his feet and growled low in his throat.

"Please, Rafael, I don't like it in here." She pulled at his arm.

"Yes, yes." His voice was breathy as though he, also, was suddenly afraid. "Let's go."

Consuelo wanted to run, but the old man beside her moved slowly, holding up the lantern to light their way. With a sharp exhalation of relief, she glimpsed faint daylight seeping in from the open end of the tunnel.

A man's figure appeared, silhouetted against the light, moving toward them. Fear ran like ice along Consuelo's veins. If the man meant no harm he would have called out to them. Trembling, she remembered Rafael's rifle, still leaning there on the cookshack stoop. Bolo barked once, staring toward the figure, his growl a low, steady rumble.

The jingle of spurs and the man's gait gave the intruder away. Consuelo knew his identity even before Rafael lifted his lantern and they stared, wide-eyed, into Ramón's face.

"Must be doing pretty well at that wharf of yours," Ezra said, "to be buying up mortgage notes." The old bank teller sat self-consciously at the desk that had once been Bert Lathrop's. Lucas noted that Hart was glaring at them from across the room. The board had placed Ezra in charge until a new bank manager was named, and the young man was obviously not pleased.

Ezra clipped together the papers Vicente had prepared yesterday, giving Lucas his copies. "Well, sir," the garrulous old fellow continued, "you already know you may have trouble collecting on this from Don Augustino."

Lucas folded the papers and tucked them in his inside coat pocket. When the reply Ezra was waiting for was not forthcoming, he gave Lucas a sly, considering look. "Of course, I suppose you're doing this more to help out Miss Consuelo than for Augustino."

Startled by the words, Lucas stared at Ezra. Did everyone on the coast know there had been something between him and Consuelo? "It's a good investment," he replied coolly.

That lingering ache returned every time he thought of her or heard her name. The most beautiful and perfect part of his life had ended because Consuelo could not trust him. Even her feeble apologies at the courthouse had seemed forced from a reluctant throat. And he had been hurting badly that day. Sitting so near her there in the courtroom, watching the myriad expressions on her lovely face and wanting with all his heart to touch and comfort her had nearly undone him. They could never have a polite and casual relationship. Too much had passed between them.

Yet it seemed to him that if she couldn't trust him, she could never really love him. She *had* loved him those magic days in San Francisco. If he couldn't believe that, he couldn't bear it. Bittersweet memories brought familiar pain, and he thrust the thoughts away.

"Ramón Salazar was in this morning." Ezra leaned back in the swivel chair, puffing on his cigar, obviously enjoying his temporary position of authority. "He inquired about this same mortgage. Got real upset when I told him it'd been sold."

A chill of apprehension ran down Lucas's spine. "He wanted to buy it?" He stared at Ezra, forgetting to light his own cigar.

Ezra nodded wisely. "He figured on marrying Rancho Estrada, but Consuelo turned him down. Guess he thought to buy it now that his schemes with Lathrop have fallen through."

"Damn him," Lucas muttered, lighting his cigar and letting the smoke drift from his lips. It was lucky Vicente had told him the mortgage could be purchased. It had shorted his bank balance, but he wanted to see Rancho Estrada safe. He could give that to Consuelo if he could give nothing else.

"He went stomping out of here like a mad bull," Ezra continued. "Said he was going to have it out, once and for all, with the Estradas."

Again a frisson of apprehension went through Lucas. He'd picked up the papers at Vicente's office this morning, and Vicente had been in a hurry. He was riding with Henry and the new work crew to España Mine. He'd added, with a significant look, that Consuelo meant to meet them there and had asked if he could tell her about the mortgage. Lucas had refused in no uncertain terms. But now he thought of Consuelo riding alone to meet Vicente, and Ramón, angry, looking for her.

Henry and Vicente and the men had left only half an hour ago. They had heavily laden carts and men on foot, and wouldn't arrive at the mine for at least two hours. What if Consuelo were there alone and Ramón knew it?

During all the dangerous years at sea, Lucas had learned to trust his gut instinct. Consuelo was in danger. He leaped to his feet. "Thanks, Ezra," he said quickly and almost ran from the bank to his horse waiting at the hitching rack outside.

Chapter Twenty-nine

Silence spun out unbearably in the cold darkness of the mine. Ramón's grin widened as he returned Consuelo's and Rafael's shocked stares. In the flickering lantern light, that grin seemed to grow more menacing as the moments passed.

Straightening her shoulders, Consuelo forced herself to face Ramón defiantly. She had to clench her fists to still their trembling. Her voice sounded hoarse and strange as she demanded, "What are you doing here, Ramón?"

His eyes glittered in the lantern light. "A fine greeting for an old friend, my girl," he said with a smirk.

"We aren't friends, Ramón," she retorted. "What do you want?"

"You, Consuelo." His voice was low, frightening. "I want you and I want Rancho Estrada." He frowned. "That damn Vicente arranged somehow to pay your bank loan." The frown twisted into a triumphant grin. "But the don still owes me, and if you're not there I can collect from him."

The last words were a threat, Consuelo knew, and a chill ran over her skin.

"Leave her alone!" Rafael shouted. "Get out of here!"

She saw that Rafael had picked up a large rock and was advancing threateningly toward Ramón. Didn't he see the gun belt at Ramón's waist? she wondered. She panicked when Ramón's hand slid across the pistol handle.

Then Ramón laughed. At the sound, a cold knot formed in Consuelo's stomach. Undeterred, Rafael moved purposefully toward the much larger man. Still grinning, Ramón raised his arm. A scream tore Consuelo's throat when he struck Rafael across the side of the head. The old man dropped to the ground. His lantern lay on its side a few feet away, flickering feebly.

Bolo leaped at Ramón. The pistol handle cracked against the dog's skull and he, too, lay still.

"Now, little one," Ramón said, holstering the pistol and moving toward her. "Now, I will have you at last."

Lust gleamed in his eyes. Panic gripped Consuelo as she backed away from him, looking around wildly for any chance of escape. She tried to run, but his hand grabbed her shoulder, biting cruelly into her flesh.

He dragged her toward him, his contorted face barely visible by the dying lantern light. His mouth covered hers in a kiss that brought the taste of blood, and she struggled vainly to loosen his grip.

There was a bark, then a growl of rage. Bolo had revived and leaped upon Ramón's back, making him stagger and lose hold of Consuelo. Ramón cursed and drew his pistol, trying to shove the dog away. Blood poured from his shoulder where the dog's teeth had torn his flesh. The reverberation of the pistol shot echoed through the tunnel; dirt rained from the roof. The lantern flame died, and the mine was plunged into utter blackness.

In panicked fear, Consuelo ran deeper into the mine, seeking only to hide from her attacker in the darkness.

"Consuelo!" Ramón's voice was filled with rage.

She cringed against the damp wall of the tunnel, scarcely breathing, knowing instinctively that silence was her only defense.

"Bitch!" he shouted. Another pistol shot shook the mine, and Consuelo covered her mouth to keep from screaming.

"You've made a fool of me for the last time!" Ramón's voice died away. She thought she heard running feet and a low moan that must be Rafael. Silence filled the darkness. Trembling, Consuelo tried to stand on legs weak as water.

The eerie silence of the tunnel was shattered by an explosion that rocked the hillside. Timbers shattered and fell.

Dust burst from the tunnel ceiling, and a rain of rocks tumbled down.

Consuelo felt herself suffocating in utter terror, then unconsciousness claimed her.

Halfway up the narrow mine road, Lucas's tiring horse caught up with Vicente's company. Donkeys strained against their collars as they pulled the heavily loaded carts up the steep incline to España Mine. Chinese men walked, jabbering among themselves. Some of the Mexican miners rode their own horses. Henry and Vicente rode together at the head of the caravan.

Lucas pulled up beside them. "Is Consuelo at the mine alone?" he demanded without a greeting.

"Rafael's there," Vicente replied with a puzzled frown. "Why?"

An old man and a girl, Lucas thought in despair. "Ramón left the bank this morning, vowing to have his revenge on her. I'm afraid he's found her."

Before his shocked companions could reply, a thunderclap of sound rolled down the narrow canyon, reverberating violently across the rocky hillsides. Horses shied and whinnied, fought their riders for control. Plodding donkeys broke stride, tossing their heads, rolling their eyes in fear. The caravan halted abruptly. The men stared at each other in shocked surprise.

"*Dios!*" Henry cried, "The explosives!"

Fear seized Lucas, and he laid his whip to his mount, spurring past his companions as they raced toward the mine.

Consciousness returned, and Consuelo stared into a darkness as black and impenetrable as the inside of a tomb. Ramón. The explosion! The memory sent terror racing through her, so deep and ugly she nearly screamed aloud.

"Rafael!" she cried. The only answer was the sibilant whisper of dirt still drifting down from the ruined ceiling of the mine.

She had to find him! She moved cautiously back toward where she thought they had faced Ramón, and explored

with careful hands. Searching fruitlessly, she had begun to
panic when she found him, facedown in the dirt and debris. She could not manage to turn him, but let out a sigh of
relief when he groaned with pain.

The lower part of his body seemed weighted with fallen
dirt. Dropping to her knees, she began to dig frantically at
the damp earth trapping the old man. Rocks mixed with the
dirt tore at her hands, which were soon cut and bleeding.
She nearly cried out in defeat when she dug down to the
fallen timber across his legs. Pain shot through her, faint
nausea, and then a deeper darkness possessed her.

Consciousness returned slowly. Drifting in and out,
Consuelo could hear Rafael groaning in pain. She must help
him, yet she could not quite hold herself long enough in
awareness.

Would they die here together? she wondered hazily.

"Lucas." She heard herself speak his name aloud, and
tears muddied the fine dirt on her face. *Querido mío,* she
thought. She longed to say the words to him, to feel his
strong arms about her, his mouth against hers.

Too late. It might have been some vengeful spirit whis-
pering the words, but it was only a slide of dirt down the
tunnel wall.

If only she could tell him how she loved him, ask him to
forgive the wrongs she'd done, and to let her make it up to
him by loving him for all their lives.

Too late. The eerie whisper came again from the disinte-
grating tunnel wall. Such an agony of loss possessed her that
Consuelo cried out in protest, then wept bitter tears. Why
had she blamed Lucas for the lessons she had learned from
others? Because she couldn't trust her family, she had refused to trust in him, surely the most trustworthy of men.
In her fear of poverty, of loss, she'd centered all her old ha-
tred on Lucas Morgan, even as she came to love him. She'd
accused him of deceit, betrayal and dishonesty. And all the
time he'd only loved her and wanted to share her life.

"Lucas!" She sobbed out the name, yearning to make her
peace with him and let him know she loved him no matter
how many times she had denied it.

In a sudden burst of determination, she sat up. "We aren't dead yet," she said to the unconscious Rafael. Fumbling in the darkness, she grasped his shoulders and turned his face upward. He screamed in agony and, horrified, she drew back.

With waning strength Consuelo pushed at the timber pinning his legs, but couldn't budge it. Panting from her exertions, she lay back beside Rafael, gently brushing the dirt from his face. At least he was still breathing, his old heart beating faintly against her fingers.

The silence was as profound as the darkness now, the only sound Rafael's harsh breathing. He could do nothing, she told herself. It was up to her to find a way out. Gathering all her strength, Consuelo managed to pull herself into a sitting position again. At once her head reeled dizzily, and pain poured through her battered body.

She cried out one word just before the last vestige of consciousness fled. "Lucas!"

"Holy Mother of God!" Vicente gasped as they rounded a bend in the road and stared in horror at the disaster before them.

The whole hillside was a sliding mass of dirt and rock and uprooted chaparral, slowly coming to rest now. A few dislodged rocks tumbled aimlessly down the hill, then an ominous silence fell over the awful scene. The tunnel entrance had disappeared beneath the slide. Miners' shacks lay shattered by the violent onslaught of dislodged earth. The roof of the cookshack hung crazily halfway off the eaves.

In the corral nearby, two horses raced wildly in terrified circles.

Henry leaped from his horse, running around the compound shouting, "Rafael! Rafael! Where are you? You old fool, where are you?"

Lucas sat staring at the frightened horses, an awful dread that had been growing inside him confirmed. "That's Consuelo's horse," he said to Vicente, his voice filled with horror.

"Dear God!" Vicente muttered. He sucked in a sharp breath. "Surely she wouldn't have gone into the mine with Rafael."

Cold sweat drenched Lucas's body. It would be just like her, ever curious, ever daring. He hurriedly dismounted, his eyes still fixed on the nervous Mirlo.

"We'd better start digging," Henry was saying. "If they're inside the tunnel, they may not have much time. If they're still..." His voice trailed off with possibilities too awful to speak.

Lucas's heart twisted agonizingly. *Consuelo, my love. Consuelo.* Her name filled his mind as he seized the shovel Henry handed him. Without a word, he ran toward the pile of loose dirt and debris where the mine entrance had been.

Even when the miners arrived and joined in the digging, Lucas kept frantically at it, never speaking, his face black with dust, his hands blistered.

The glaring sun moved toward the western horizon. Lucas stopped for a drink brought to him by the Chinese cook, and looked up at that sun, knowing that each hour made Consuelo's death more certain. His mind went blank with pain. Furiously plying the shovel again, he forgot his aching muscles, all physical pain insignificant beside the fact that Consuelo was in danger... or dead. He dared not think of that second possibility. It was unbearable.

"Dios!" came a shout from one of the miners. The rescuers paused in their digging. Lucas's heart stopped beating as he turned toward the shout. The miner signaled for help, and he and another man dragged a body from the debris near the entrance. A man, Rafael perhaps, but not Consuelo. Once more, Lucas plunged his shovel into the dirt clogging the tunnel.

Vicente walked over to stare down at the dead man. His face was grim when he came back toward Lucas, who was still shoveling single-mindedly.

"It's Ramón Salazar," Vicente told him in a shocked tone. "He must have dynamited the mine. Looks like he was trying to get out and didn't make it before the explosion. Henry says the explosives shed was broken into."

Lucas paused briefly to stare at his friend. "If he weren't dead, I'd kill him," he said in a cold voice and returned to his relentless digging.

They were inside the tunnel now, clearing out dirt and rocks that had fallen inside. Some of the heaviest timbers had held so that the tunnel was nearly intact. But the floor was clogged with piles of fallen dirt and rocks and shattered timber. Shoving the miners aside, Lucas fought his way along the tunnel floor, crawling over the dirt piles, pushing aside hindering rocks, peering through the lantern light.

"Consuelo!" he called, his heart's blood in the cry that echoed and reechoed through the ruined tunnel.

A faint sound made his heart leap with a hope that had nearly died in the long fruitless hours. He fought his way through the fallen timber, through dirt still sifting down from above, through fallen rock.

Her slender body lay inert and bleeding beside the unconscious Rafael. "Consuelo!" The name was torn from his throat in longing and fear. He had left his shovel behind in his frantic bolt through the tunnel. Now he clawed at the dirt and rocks piled around her unconscious body, unaware of the blood pouring from his torn hands.

At last, Lucas lifted her carefully into his arms.

"Consuelo." He stared down at the precious burden, her name wrung from his strangled throat.

Her black hair was gray with dirt, her face bruised and streaked with blood, her hands dark with dried blood where she had tried to free herself.

Several miners appeared, lifting a timber to free Rafael, who groaned in pain. Lucas knew only that Consuelo lay limp in his arms, like a broken doll. He touched her lips gently with his own and was flooded with hope at the gentle warmth of her breath against his mouth.

She was his life, his love. If only he'd listened to her apology that day at the courthouse. If only he hadn't been so immersed in his own hurt and anger. How could he have rejected her that way? If he had listened and tried to make it right again, perhaps she wouldn't be lying hurt in his arms this moment. If she died, he couldn't bear to continue living.

Nearby, the miners were dragging the unconscious Rafael free. The old man's leg was twisted crazily beneath him, his head battered and bloody from the rocks that had rained down upon him.

"Oh, God," someone said. "Here's the old man's dog, dead."

Lucas was scarcely aware of their presence. Everything faded from his consciousness except the fact that his beloved still breathed. As he struggled through the debris-clogged tunnel, she stirred slightly in his arms and moaned in pain. He walked out into the sunlight, tears pouring down his blackened face.

Henry wordlessly spread his bedroll in the shade of the furnace, and Lucas carefully laid Consuelo down. Pain clogged his throat as he looked into her still, pale face. Her eyes fluttered open, glazed and unseeing.

"Consuelo..." He took the wet rag Vicente handed him and gently cleaned her battered face. She winced and cried out softly, then was gone from him again.

"Can you tell if anything's broken?" Vicente asked, hovering anxiously over them.

Unable to trust his voice, Lucas nodded. Somewhere behind him, he heard a man call to Henry. "Rafael's got a broken leg. Can you come and splint it before we bring him out?"

Slowly, with infinite gentleness, Lucas moved his hands along Consuelo's arms. Then lifting her torn and dirty skirt, he ran careful fingers along her legs. Memories of touching that flesh in love flooded his mind, and he drew in his breath painfully. Quickly he covered her, thankful nothing was broken there.

Her blouse was loose and torn, smudged with dirt. Probing gently beneath it, Lucas searched for broken ribs.

"Lucas?"

He had nearly forgotten Vicente's presence. Now he looked up into the worried face and smiled grimly. "Nothing broken, but we'd better get her to the doctor just the same.''

"The rancho's closer," Vicente said, taking charge in his usual manner. "I'll send someone for Dr. Frame to meet us there." He turned away. "Let's get a cart unloaded for her."

She was so still, Lucas thought, and cold fear rose again in his chest. He smoothed back her hair with a loving hand and she stirred, moaning softly. "Consuelo," he whispered, his throat aching.

Behind him, he could hear Vicente shouting orders to have the carts unloaded. Watching Consuelo's face, Lucas thought of all the long miles back to the rancho by the roads the cart must travel. If he carried her in his arms on horseback, she would be there hours sooner.

"I'll take care of you, sweet love," he said and brushed her stained cheek with his fingers.

He stood and walked over to the hitching rack, where someone had secured the horses. With his horse's reins in hand, he told Vicente, "I'm taking her with me on horseback. The cart will take too long."

Vicente stared in dismay. "But we'll have to take the old man by cart. His leg's broken."

"Consuelo has no broken bones," Lucas said in a voice that set aside all Vicente's protests. "I want to get her back to Isabel as soon as possible."

After a moment, Vicente shrugged. He knew arguing with Lucas now was impossible. With another man to help, he lifted Consuelo into Lucas's waiting arms. She lay in his arms, across the front of his saddle, a blanket wrapped around her, her head limp against his shoulder.

Settling himself so that she was secure, Lucas looked down into her pale face. Almost from the beginning, he had known he loved her. But until this moment, he hadn't really guessed how deep that love had grown, how much a part of his total being Consuelo Estrada had become.

Sober-faced, Vicente and the other men watched as Lucas bent to gently kiss her forehead. Then he kicked the horse into movement and headed down the arroyo back to Rancho Estrada, his precious burden cradled against him.

Chapter Thirty

An offshore wind was blowing, bringing the scents of spring down from the Santa Lucias, warming the air above a shining blue ocean. As it always did, that rare warm wind made Consuelo restless.

Rafael was restless, too. Two weeks of lying in bed in the little adobe he shared with Rosa had worn on the old man. In all his active years as a vaquero, he had never before had a broken bone, let alone a broken leg. Today, when Consuelo brought his dinner, he was querulous, complaining about his enforced inactivity. Tears filled his eyes as he spoke of his beloved dog, his lost Bolo.

"You're lucky to be alive," she told him, "and so am I."

Almost every day she said those words to him, and almost always he would begin reliving the disaster at the mine. Over and over again, he would say, "If I'd had my rifle, we could have stopped Ramón."

Consuelo listened patiently, reminding him sadly that without Bolo they might both be dead. In spite of the warm day, she shivered. In all her confrontations with Ramón, she had never guessed at the depth of evil in him, wouldn't have believed that his maniacal thirst for revenge would lead to death and destruction. Henry told her it was obvious Ramón had set off the dynamite. But he had apparently known little about explosives, for he hadn't given himself time to get clear of the mine before the blast went off.

For the hundredth time, Rafael added, "Lucky thing Henry and the miners showed up just after the cave-in." His old eyes narrowed slyly. "And Lucas Morgan, too. Henry said he was like a madman until he found you."

Consuelo looked away. "Are you finished eating?" she asked tersely. Rafael nodded, still studying her face. She seized his tray and hurried out, not trusting herself to speak.

More than two weeks had passed since the disaster. The cuts and bruises on her body were nearly healed, but those on her heart still throbbed. Why hadn't Lucas come to see her? All the undeserved anger she'd turned on him, all the ugly accusations, came back to haunt her. She cringed as she remembered the terrible things she'd said. If only she'd followed her heart and trusted him. Now she was certain she had killed all the love he once felt for her.

Her memories of the ride home from the mine were still hazy. She knew Rafael had been brought later in a cart by Henry and Vicente. Vaguely, she recalled being held in Lucas's arms all the way. Dim memories of his kisses and words of love flitted through her mind, but perhaps she only imagined them for wanting him so.

Tears stung her eyes, and she blinked them away. Why hadn't he come to see her? She knew he inquired about her health of Dr. Frame and Vicente, but since the day he carried her into the rancho bedroom and gave her into Isabel's care she had not seen his face. He had saved her life. Surely he couldn't hate her. She closed her eyes tight in sudden pain, knowing how terribly she'd hurt him with her lack of trust.

"Why couldn't I see?" she whispered to herself, pausing outside the open kitchen door to compose herself. That day in San Luis Obispo, she had swallowed her pride and tried to make amends. He had dismissed her coldly. She couldn't bear to chance that kind of rejection again.

The sound of voices came from in front of the house. Hope soared through her. "Oh, Lucas," she whispered and set the tray down on the stoop. Hurrying around the corner of the adobe, she saw Isabel standing beside the hitching rack, looking up at a tall young man mounted on a gray horse.

Soledad! If only he brought a message from Lucas! But when she hurried toward him, Soledad tipped his hat in greeting and quickly reined his horse away, spurring the animal into a gallop.

"What did Soledad want?" she asked breathlessly, rushing up to Isabel.

Her aunt smiled, soft-eyed. "Perhaps he only came to see his mother."

Consuelo stared in disbelief. Catching the expression, Isabel shrugged. "Not yet," she said with a new lilt in her voice, "but we are becoming friends. Someday—"

"Why was he here?" Consuelo interrupted. She wished for Isabel's dream to become reality, but just now her own dream possessed her.

Smiling, Isabel reached across the sun-warmed adobe wall and took Consuelo's hand. The sharp scent of new grape leaves on the veranda vines filled the air, mingling with the fragrance of the blooming eucalyptus trees. A gray cat lying on the wall yawned and stretched.

"Lucas sent him," Isabel said, and Consuelo's hand tightened on her aunt's. "He wanted to know about your health."

"Why didn't he come here himself?" she demanded, a catch in her voice.

"Perhaps he doesn't feel he's welcome." There was a gently chiding note in Isabel's voice that pierced Consuelo's heart. She was to blame, for she had made him feel unwelcome anywhere she might be.

"You're able to ride again," the gentle voice continued. "Why shouldn't you go to him?"

Consuelo moved away, smoothing the cat's fur, seeing the contented little creature through tear-blurred eyes. "I can't," she said and struggled to control her wavering voice. "I told you what happened at the courthouse. How can I ever again ask his forgiveness?"

"Ah, my girl." Isabel drew her close, pressing her cheek against Consuelo's hair. "Pride is a poor exchange for love. It's known in the whole county how he fought to save you. If only you had been conscious when he brought you home, if you could have seen his face. Such love. Go to him, my dear. Go now.''

"Where are you going?" Don Augustino demanded, looking up from his cards spread on the great room table.

"Riding." Consuelo opened the China trunk and took out the pink scarf tied about the pearls. With one hand she stroked the smoothness of the silk rebozo. It was too warm today. One day she would wear it for Lucas. Please God, one day.

The quicksilver vial Henry had given her lay there, too, a comforting sight. The mine was open again, already refining cinnabar ore.

"Be careful. There are thieves everywhere in this country nowadays," her father said darkly.

The biggest thief is dead, she wanted to say, but did not. Once Papá had considered Ramón his friend, and she knew he'd struggled to accept the reality. She could feel no sorrow for Ramón's awful death, only for the scarred childhood that must have bred the evil in him. She knew now how much he had always hated and envied the Estradas because they were rich when he was poor.

But none of that mattered any more. Only winning Lucas's love again mattered. Before her courage failed, Consuelo tucked the pearls into the pocket of her skirt and hurried out to where Sancho waited with the saddled Mirlo.

This warm offshore wind made a man restless. Lucas came out of the warehouse and stood in the shade of the building. It was a quiet day at Morgan's Landing, with only the usual workers about. There would be no steamer for three days now. He lit a cigarillo and watched the workers laying planks at the far end of the pier. Another month and it would be finished, ready for the steamers to tie up and unload. Since the plan first bloomed in his mind, this had been a driving dream. Why was it that its completion brought him no sense of satisfaction?

But he knew the answer to that question only too well. His achievement meant nothing without Consuelo. Would the night ever come when her lovely face didn't haunt his dreams?

Vicente, Dr. Frame and the notes from Isabel all said she had recovered from the accident at the mine. Yet he longed to know for himself, to look into her beautiful face once more and find welcome there.

A chill ran along his veins and he knew its source. Pride, damned pride. She'd rejected him, turned on him with mistrust, accused him of terrible things. He moved restlessly out into the sunlight as though to leave his unhappy thoughts behind. With a deep and painful certainty, Lucas knew he could never stop loving her. But neither could he seek her out.

He must stop thinking about her, he decided as he started toward the pier to inspect the work. A horse was galloping down the well-worn coast road. Lucas saw that it was Soledad returning. Perhaps this time the message would come from Consuelo, not her aunt.

He waited as Soledad drew rein beside him and jumped down from the saddle.

"The *señorita*," Soledad began, a bemused expression on his face, "she followed me." He grinned. "That black mare is fast."

Hope sprang from the ashes of despair in Lucas's heart. "Why?" He couldn't get the words out. "What...?"

"China Point," Soledad said, his dark eyes knowing as he gestured across the bay. "She said to ask you to meet her there."

Lucas turned to look across the blue waters of Estero Bay to a green smudge of eucalyptus trees blurred against the hills, the dark pile of a ruined house just visible beneath them.

He seized the reins of Soledad's horse and mounted it before the surprised young man could speak. "Take charge, Soledad," Lucas commanded. "I'll return...." He let the words trail off, not knowing when he would return.

Madness, Consuelo told herself as she dismounted beside the Chinese man's tumbled house, it was sheer madness to come here. Desperation had driven that headlong ride to catch up with Soledad. Even then, it had required all her courage to frame the words of a message to the man she loved.

Sea gulls wheeled above the tide pools, their melancholy cries echoing the uncertainty in Consuelo's heart. Slowly, she walked to the ruined house and stood in the remains of the doorway, staring out across blue water, searching for the one tall figure imprinted forever in her being. Her fingers caressed the smooth coolness of the pearls around her throat, and her eyes stung with the memory of the love with which Lucas had first placed them there.

At the sound of galloping hooves, Consuelo turned toward the road. Her heart skipped a beat as she recognized the rider.

Joy and apprehension warred within. Surely he wouldn't have come here if he no longer loved her. Her body stilled so that she could feel the blood pumping wildly along her veins, as she waited for him, watched as he dismounted and walked slowly toward her. Panic flooded her, for she couldn't read his face, or the intent blue eyes.

Lucas paused a few feet away, waiting in silence. He had said it once before. Consuelo must take the first step. He would not go to her. She must come to him.

A cry of longing broke from Consuelo's throat, and she flung herself at him. Strong arms caught her and gathered her close as she clung fiercely to him. She lifted her face to blue eyes blazing with love and desire. Lucas's mouth claimed hers, hot and hungry as her own. All the familiar fires leaped inside her, and her body molded itself to his.

"Consuelo," he gasped at last. "My love, my love." His lips were hot against her throat, and her heart soared with joy.

"*Querido mío,*" she murmured, running her fingers through his crisp, black hair. "Forgive me. I love you so."

Lucas cupped her face in both his big hands, blue eyes searching, probing as they looked into her eyes. "And trust me?" he asked.

Tears filled her eyes with the knowledge that her lack of trust had torn them apart. "With all my heart," she whispered, her voice breaking, "for all our lives."

With a triumphant laugh, Lucas swept her off her feet, lifting her into his arms, bending to cover her mouth with his in a kiss that left her limp with joy.

Beyond his broad shoulder, she could see the ocean where the lowering sun laid a silver path across the deep blue water.

"Look, *querido*," she said in an awed tone. He lifted his head from kissing her throat where the pearls he had given with such love lay against her soft skin. "The sun on the ocean," she said. "It's like quicksilver, isn't it?"

Lucas smiled into her eyes. "Like my love's quicksilver heart," he said, "hard to capture and hold."

"But you have captured it, Lucas, *corazón*. Forever." She touched his mouth with loving fingers. "My love." She laid her palm against his cheek, offering her lips to his kiss.

The offshore wind stirred the eucalyptus trees as Lucas laid her on the grass and gathered her fiercely into his embrace.

Waves crashed against the rocks on the shore below. Seabirds cried in the distance, no longer melancholy, but a sweet accompaniment to whispered words of love.

Heated by the wind, the eucalyptus trees gave off their pungent scent, arousing all Consuelo's senses. With perfect certainty, she yielded to her lover, promising once more, "Forever, Lucas, *querido mío*."

* * * * *

HARLEQUIN
Romance

**This September, travel to England
with Harlequin Romance
FIRST CLASS title #3149,
ROSES HAVE THORNS
by Betty Neels**

It was Radolf Nauta's fault that Sarah lost her job at the hospital and was forced to look elsewhere for a living. So she wasn't particulary pleased to meet him again in a totally different environment. Not that he seemed disposed to be gracious to her: arrogant, opinionated and entirely too sure of himself, Radolf was just the sort of man Sarah disliked most. And yet, the more she saw of him, the more she found herself wondering what he really thought about her—which was stupid, because he was the last man on earth she could ever love....

Harlequin Superromance®

Available in Superromance this month
#462—STARLIT PROMISE

STARLIT PROMISE is a deeply moving story of a
woman coming to terms with her grief and gradually
opening her heart to life and love.

Author Petra Holland sets the scene beautifully, never
allowing her heroine to become mired in self-pity. It
is a story that will touch your heart and leave you
celebrating the strength of the human spirit.

Available wherever Harlequin books
are sold.

STARLIT-A